The Big Valley Returned

Stories Old and New

Christine Toal

NEWMAN SPRINGS PUBLISHING
320 Broad Street
Red Bank, NJ 07701

First originally published by Newman Springs Publishing 2020

ISBN 978-1-64531-784-5 (Paperback)
ISBN 978-1-64531-785-2 (Digital)

Printed in the United States of America

To Barbara Stanwyck, Peter Breck, Richard Long, Lee Majors, and Linda Evans, who brought the original Barkleys to life.

Chapter 1

It's between Christmas and New Year's Eve, and the Barkleys are about to hold their annual holiday party to celebrate their neighbors, friends, and best crop harvests they had ever known. They have invited the familiar faces of not only friends, neighbors, but also ranch and office staff. Victoria had been fussing for days with a cleaning crew whom Silas had supervised before Christmas to get the heavy cleaning done and, after the holiday came back in, to tidy, polish, change the flowers, and generally get everything ready for the guests. The caterers would appear the day of the party to set up the food and arrange the china, silver, serving dishes, etc. During the next two days, the guys and Audra would make sure to be gone all day and well into the evening.

Nick alone was not looking forward to the party. He had already invited Mona Scott, whom he had been dating for the past four/five weeks, and now it was too late to back out. That blasted woman, Joan, who wrote the gossip column in the Thursday local paper, *The Stockton Bugle*, had written about it for two weeks straight! Thanks to her, the rumor was out all over town that Nick was going to propose to Mona, but nothing could be further from the truth. In fact, Nick was trying to find a way to break things off without hurting her too much. It wasn't that she had done anything; it was just that, in Nick's head, there was no "magic." He didn't quite fully understand what that was, but when he met the "right one," he was sure he'd know. In the meantime, how to say goodbye to Mona, the daughter of a friend of his mother's, making a break-up much more difficult than it usually was for him! He had planned on talking to her after the party. He knew he'd end up the bad guy, but there were days when he thought he'd never find the girl he'd been searching for, but then there were days like the ones right now when he was talking to some gypsies who were working for him and told Mr. Nick "that he'd meet the right girl very soon."

Whether it was the certainty in the way they said it or his own hunger to believe, this time, he really felt that, just as they said, "She was very close only a matter of days away. That this time next year, when they came back to work for Mr. Nick, he would be married and happier than he would have believed possible. That his whole world would be turned upside down and inside out. That, for the first time in his life, he'd be deeply and completely in love." Nick knew it could just be gypsy talk, but what was the point if it wasn't true? Then they would have risked losing a lucrative job where not only did they earn good money, but it was a place where the whole tribe were treated with respect. Nick thought about all they'd had to say about the other things they had told him in the past, which had been very accurate, and decided to take a step of faith.

He got out the plans that his friend, Adam Cartwright of the Cartwright Family Holdings, otherwise known as the Ponderosa, had drawn up for him. Adam, like Nick's older brother Jarrod, had not just settled for a ranching career, they both went to university—Jarrod for law and Adam for architecture. A year ago, Nick had prevailed upon Adam to draw up plans, making the entire huge upper level of the west wing of the ranch house into a self-contained apartment. The house belonged to Nick, being part of his ranch inheritance, but he knew that it would always be his mother's home to live in and run, Audra's to live in until she married, and the guys for as long as they wanted. Even when his sister and brothers left home, when it was time for holidays or socials, when they all got together, it would be at his house. That's a lot to ask a wife to tolerate. So he came up with the idea of a four-bedroom, three and a half bath, living room, dining area, kitchen, deck, private access to the pool and Jacuzzi, gated entrance apartment. Adam took that idea and ran with it, even adding an area in the living room where twin desks could be placed so Nick and his wife (if she needed to) could work.

Adam turned what was just a dream into a beautiful reality, and that morning in mid-December, without really knowing why,

Nick gave the word to start the renovations. All he told the rest of the family was he wanted a place of his own. His trusted employee and friend, John McIntire, who had been with the family for over twenty-five years, was going to oversee the work. He was the only one, other than Adam and Victoria, privy to Nick's real reason for the renovations. The appliances were to be the absolute top of the line. Nick picked out the wood floors—distressed oak, the walls were pale cream, and feature walls could be done later. The kitchen had warm wood cabinets with granite countertops which Adam had added his input to.

Adam questioned Nick about what sort of woman would give up living in the Barkley mansion for an apartment. "After all," Adam had said, "it's part of being a Barkley, holding functions in the big white house. They would have to work it out between your wife and your mother, who is the chatelaine! But to ask a woman to give up that social position to live in apartment when a huge house should rightfully be hers is asking a whole lot. You really think you'll find a woman like that?" Adam asked.

"I know I will," was Nick's firm response.

"Brother, he has set the bar so high," Adam had said to John. "I hope he's not going to be too disappointed if he doesn't find her. I think he's gonna have to settle for slightly less!"

"Explain to me what exactly the apartment has to look like," John had asked of Adam when the plans were originally shown to the older man. "I have to know if it's being constructed right."

"The apartment entrance is at the top of the grand staircase. There is a door with a phone—pick it up and it connects with one of the three located in the kitchen, bedroom, or deck. You can talk with the visitor and, if necessary, buzz the door to open it for them. Coming down the hallway, there are three doors on your left, bedroom, bathroom, and bedroom, and one to the right, the master bedroom. At almost the end of the hallway, turn left and go down to the linen closets, door to attic steps, cupboards, and another spare bedroom with bath. They face windows looking onto the deck and pool area. At the very end of the hallway, still on the left, is the laundry room, and to the right, the main door to the apartment, which you enter between the kitchen and living room. Beyond kitchen and dining area, a utility room and half bath, then the French doors leading onto a huge deck. At the other end of the living room is the door to the master bed, and bathroom, all the rooms as large as I could make them. It's not like living in the main house but still a luxurious apartment with everything I could think of in it from steam shower and Jacuzzi tub to a kitchen fit for a chef."

"Nick wants his wife to find her own housekeeper who can have a one-bedroom cottage on the ranch if she wants it. He is doing his best to make it all his wife's home. The back entrance is through a large gate with the Barkley brand symbol on it, which opens by a numerical code and slides to the right to allow the vehicles into the parking and garage area. Up a staircase and onto the deck are the French doors which are opened by another coded lock. At the far end of the deck is a second set of steps leading down to the main house's pool, Jacuzzi, and entertainment area," explained Adam.

Nick couldn't wait for it all to be finished but, most of all, for it to be occupied by the woman he had waited most of his life for. He knew to tell anyone he'd get laughed at, but he held onto his belief with both hands, not daring to think of life if it didn't come to pass.

Victoria sat by the fire in the living room, enjoying a glass of sherry from their own vineyards and going over, in her mind, all the arrangements for the family party. As far as she could see, everything was in order, and the caterers would come in early tomorrow morning and take over the kitchen.

At the beginning of the month, the board of Stockton General Hospital, of which Victoria Barkley was a member, couldn't believe its luck when a resume had been faxed to them in response to their ad in a medical journal for a senior attending physician in the emergency department. The doctor who sent the resume was only twenty-five but had spent the last seven years in the British army, mainly stationed on their bases in the Middle East. She was what most people call a child prodigy, graduating high school at twelve and becoming an attending at the exceedingly young age of eighteen. The British army had taken her under its wing, putting the child of a former officer through medical school with her training on its bases. When she turned eighteen, she officially signed up with the army. The Stockton hospital board were amazed that Dr. Caroline Warner, with her kind of expertise, would want a position in a provincial hospital, but as she explained during the interview, she didn't like living in big cities. Even though, with her background, she could earn three, four, even five times the salary in a metropolis, she was adamant about wanting small-city living.

The board, after the interview, asked her if she could come back in one hour as they wanted to hold an emergency meeting. She was agreeable to that. The plans to move the emergency room to a level one trauma center was almost certain to happen. The progress had been slow, but with a trauma specialist of Dr. Warner's caliber, it would tip the scales completely. The trauma unit was badly needed in the area and would save so many lives.

Dr. Warner returned and was offered the job. She accepted on the spot. One of the board members knew Dr. Warner from her time in Germany. His wife's sister is married to the brigadier general whom Caroline had been under the guardianship of when she had been training there. Judge Peterson asked the new doctor to have dinner with him and his wife that evening. They were able to renew their friendship and offered Kate Warner a place to live when she moved to Stockton.

"With your resume, you could work anywhere. Why there? If you wanted to be on the west coast, why not San Francisco? It's not that big a city, but it gets the ballet and the opera. You'd have loved it. I think you've lost your mind, STOCKTON!" her friend Nan said when Kate returned to New York.

Kate flew back to England for a few days mid-December, winding up her personal affairs, transferring bank accounts, etc., and hurriedly packed up the clothes and items she'd left at Audrey's house and was going to take on the plane with her. Then she arranged for the other clothes and her few personal belongs she'd had in storage to be sent to the United States as quickly as possible. Saying goodbye to her step-mum, she was ready to face the new way of life which she had chosen in a town that held some unknown and sort of mysterious attraction for her

She flew back to New York in time to spend Christmas with Nan. The Petersons called and suggested that, as they were going to spend two weeks in Hawaii starting January first, and as Kate wasn't starting her new job until almost the end of that month, she go with them. Kate wasn't about to turn down an offer like that and changed her airline flight plan and arranged to fly red eye on December twenty seventh to the west coast. Judge Andrew Peterson and his wife Esther welcomed Kate to their home and gave her their guest suite as arranged. Their housekeeper, Uma, had broken her leg, so they had employed a temporary one, Jeanne Nolan, who was soon to become a close friend of Kate's.

Esther informed her that, if at all possible, she should accompany them to Victoria Barkley's party. "Victoria is hoping to introduce you to many of the people of Stockton. A good chance to see and be seen."

"Is it a black-tie event?" asked Kate.

"No, the Barkley's invite a cross-section of people, and not everyone has formal wear, so just a nice outfit will be fine."

"My clothes choices are somewhat limited until the rest of my wardrobe arrives, but I have a black skirt, cream silk shirt, and a hip-length kimono in off white, black, and burnt orange. Do you think that will do?"

"It sounds very elegant and will strike just the right note. First impressions do count."

Kate's life in the last two years had undergone a vast change. Her father had died suddenly, her two favorite aunts, Joyce and Chris, had also passed away, and she had reached the monumental decision that, after seven years, she would not re-enlist in the army. The only family she was close to was her step-mum, Audrey, and she has her own life without Kate. So when Kate, who had gone to New York to stay with Nan for the month of December, saw the ads in the medical journals, she thought, *Why not? Why not a complete change? A three-year contract and green card. If I don't like it or they don't like me, then I find something else!* She didn't own a stick of furniture, so living with Andrew and Esther was perfect. She would unpack her few belongings, pick up whatever else she needed, and, voila, "home to go." She couldn't remember what having a "real" home was like, so for years, she had come up with her "home to go" version; although, if she was truthful, that was starting to wear thin. She had moments when thoughts of a home kept drifting in and out of her reality. Nothing she could pin down; just what it would feel like, whom she'd share it with, completely new thoughts of a cozy, warm, airy place were all new to her, and she had started to keep a small "home" journal.

Chapter 2

It was late, and tomorrow was a long day, but Victoria still sat by the fire and poured herself another sherry, remembering a night four years ago when the family were getting ready to officially introduce someone to their friends and employees. A young man named Heath, he had been with them about five months, but that night was somehow the family officially saying, "He is one of us."

It had been a hot afternoon at the end of summer when a young man had arrived at the ranch looking for work. Nick had turned him down, but Jarrod, feeling sorry for him, had intervened on the man's behalf, and Nick relented and hired him but with grave suspicions. So much so that Nick had woken the new hand up later that evening and wanted to know exactly why the young man had traveled so far—over five hundred miles between ranching jobs. Words were heatedly exchanged, and not so surprisingly, it being Nick, a fistfight ensued, with Nick asking, "Who the hell are you?"

The response. "I'm your father's bastard son."

Nick dragged him into the house, bellowing for Jarrod and Eugene. Audra stood on the stairs to listen, and no one noticed Victoria's bedroom door open. When Jarrod and Eugene heard what Heath had to say, that Tom Barkley had met Heath's mother, Leah Thompson, in the mining town of Strawberry twenty-four years ago and he was the result. He had only just found out a week ago when his mother died. He had been sent for and arrived to find her dying. She told him to get her Bible, and in the back was a newspaper cutting about the funeral of Tom Barkley and how a thousand people came to the service and burial. By the time Heath read the cutting, his mother was dead. He was convinced she was telling him Tom was his father. The newspaper item was six years old, telling of the shooting murder of Thomas Barkley.

The Barkley brothers heard him out in an incredulous silence. Then Jarrod spoke, "There is one easy way to find out the truth—a DNA test. We will do it in the morning. In the meantime, you will stay at a motel in Stockton until we find out the result. I know a lab where we can get it in twenty-four hours. I'll pick you up at nine a.m., take you to the lab, and when we get the results, depending on what they are, we'll go from there."

Heath agreed to Jarrod's plan and left to go to a motel for the night. Nick, the steam almost coming out of his ears, was knocking back yet another drink when Victoria and Audra came into the room.

"When were you going to inform me?" their mother asked in icy tones, her eyes blazing.

"When we got the results," said Jarrod, trying to calm everyone down. "There is nothing we can do until we get those lab results."

"Shouldn't we have a plan in case it's true?" asked Eugene.

"How could you?" screamed Audra, always the daddy's girl.

"Stop it now. We will all meet again, Thursday morning at ten, to find out about Heath. Until then, I don't want it spoken about," commanded Victoria. "I will not have our name dragged through the mud. I'll not have this spoken about outside the family until Thursday. Goodnight." And with that, she marched out of the room.

"She's right," said Jarrod, but privately thought he'd better take a more detailed look at how the shares of the Barkley family holdings were held and what would have to happen to accommodate another brother who'd want a percentage of the ranch to be like the others. He needn't mention it unless it was something he was forced to do. Jarrod, like the rest of his family, was hoping the DNA test would be negative, but there was always the chance it wasn't. Could Tom Barkley really have had a brief affair with Leah Thompson? She had been very beautiful woman, judging by the photographs Heath had showed them.

His father had been away from home a lot in those days, building on the groundwork of four generations of Barkleys to increase the family's now vast holdings. Traveling from one place to another, away for sometimes weeks at a time. Could there have been a moment of weakness, not meaning to hurt Victoria, but needing someone, anyone, and Leah being there? Did he know about Heath? How could he not know? Or did Leah choose not to tell him and run the chance of ruining his marriage but not being able to die withholding from Heath the truth of his parentage.

"Whichever way it goes, people are going to get hurt," Jarrod said to himself.

All during Wednesday, everyone tried to act normally, like the issue of Health was not at the forefront of everyone's mind. The day was an eternity, but somehow, Thursday at ten came around, and everyone met in the living room. There was a knock at the front door, and Silas announced, "Mr. Heath."

The DNA results came by special messenger. The tension in the room was palpable. Jarrod opened the envelope, and though he was a well-trained attorney, even he could not keep from visibly reacting to the results as he read them. Heath was indeed a son of Thomas Barkley. Victoria sat there as though turned to stone. Her children knew by the expression on her face not to hug her nor touch her. After a few moments of silence, she turned to Heath and said, "Welcome to your family, Heath."

The others didn't know how to react, the look on Nick's face said it all for them. Tears ran down Audra's face. Her father, whom she had placed on a pedestal, had come crashing down. It would be hard to say who she was the angriest at, Heath or her father.

Eugene, who had only been a youngster when his father was murdered, was visibly shaken. Jarrod, who was the only one who had prepared himself for this outcome, was nevertheless stunned. Even Heath, who had believed it to be true, somehow hearing the legal pronouncement, was shocked in his own way.

"So where do we go from here?" he asked. "I want what I'm entitled to. I won't be bought off." Nick started toward him, and it took both Jarrod and Eugene to keep him from attacking Heath.

"Calm down, Nick," Jarrod kept shouting as his volatile brother gradually regained control of his temper and sat down. "I have been doing the math, and it looks like this," Jarrod told his family

Thomas Barkley had always known who would take over his empire—Nick. He was the one who, since he could scramble up into a saddle, had wanted to be with his father on the ranch. Jarrod's love of the law was apparent from grade school, and Eugene's interest in medicine made the heir to the Barkley Family Enterprises easy, especially as Nick had a photographic memory and an uncanny instinct for business.

The holdings had looked like that, and with some refiguring, they would now be like this. Everyone must give up a few percentages so that Heath would become a stockholder and have some input into the family's vast holdings, Jarrod and Eugene being the only two having careers outside the family businesses from which they earned a salary.

Nick held seventy two per cent, now seventy per cent.

Jarrod held seven per cent and now holds six per cent.

Eugene, Audra, Victoria and now Heath holding the same amount of shares as Jarrod.

The Barkley shipping line is now Jarrod, Audra, Eugene, and now Heath, holding eight percent each, Nick holds twenty percent, and Victoria forty eight percent.

As Nick was to make all the business decisions and steer the family empire, so Tom Berkley knew he deserved the lion's share of the holdings. Having most of the shares, Nick could never be out-voted; such was the trust his father had placed in his second son. Ownership of the ranch and CEO of the family holdings normally went to the oldest son in the past in order to keep the vast ranch and holdings together, very much in the style of British oldest son inheritance, but this time, Tom, seeing the way his firstborn son's interest lay, made his second born son his primary heir. Tom wanted his wife to have a healthy income of her own, which is why he left her the controlling interest in the family shipping line. She had a manager to run the day-to-day details, but she alone made the final major decisions with Nick's input.

Heath was financially a Barkley, but acceptance as a Barkley was a different matter. This made life difficult at times for Nick, who was forced to come along behind his brother and smooth things over with the office staff and the ranch hands. It put Nick in the middle. He didn't want Heath to know the situations he had to straighten out, but he did have his own workload to deal with. He had come to love Heath and understood what a rough upbringing he had and how hard life had been before he came to the big valley. Being the child of an unwed mother in a mining town meant a life of poverty. The jobs he took when he left school were menial. There was so much he had to learn, from correct table manners to everyday etiquette, to become a Barkley.

The amount of business and political entertaining the family did was all new to Heath. The social small talk and business table talk was a learning experience for him. Most of the time, he had listened and tried to learn, just joining in the conversations when spoken to directly. It slowly dawned on him that having a percentage of the company weighed heavy on him, and the cost was very high, much higher than he had ever expected.

He had known that Victoria wouldn't let him stay silent when they were entertaining for very long, and he would be expected to join in like the rest of his family. The cost of being a Barkley was not what he had imagined. Even in the Cattleman's Club, he was treated differently, the girls paying the kind of attention to the Barkleys they never give to a drifter! Oh the Barkley name! It opened doors he had never imagined were even there! He'd accounts in stores without even asking for them. Someone was always trying to sell him something or wanting him to invest in a project. He asked Nick, "How do you handle it?"

"I just ignore it," was the answer which wasn't much help. His brothers had grown up with the downside as well as the upside of being a Barkley, but Heath had jumped in at the deep end and was having to learn to swim on his own.

You'd think that, in this day and age, the fact that Heath was not a full-blooded Barkley wouldn't make a difference to anyone, but there were still families who didn't want their daughters dating him. They saw a difference between him and his half brothers. In their eyes, he was not quite part of the first family of Stockton. Not the social equal of his brothers. His family never referred to him as a half brother; it was always just brother or son.

Chapter 3

The day of the party dawned bright and clear. The catering firm and Silas had thrown so many parties that there was nothing for the family to do except stay out of the way until it was time to get ready. They all came together on time; the musicians had set up.

Victoria, Jarrod, and Audra stood in the foyer to welcome guests. The other members of the family stationed themselves around the living room to help their guests feel at home. All was well underway, groups of their friends and employees were laughing and talking, and the musicians were playing various show selections when a stranger walked in with Judge and Esther Peterson.

"Dr. Warner, how nice to see you again," said Victoria.

She introduced the doctor to Jarrod and Audra, who had not met Caroline before. The look on Jarrod's face said it all. He had heard about the good doctor and, in fact, had been skeptical about hiring someone so young for the position at the hospital. Ex-army, this wasn't what he had expected! Before he had a chance to make a move on her, Victoria, seeing the signs, quickly drew Kate on to another group of guests which included Heath and Eugene. The reaction was much the same! This beautiful red-headed, green-eyed doctor was going to certainly stir things up among the male population of Stockton!

Well, thought Victoria, *I'll introduce her to Nick and get it over with*. "Nick, I'd like you to meet Dr. Caroline Warner."

Nick turned around and started to shake hands but froze midway. He acted like he was tongue-tied. Couldn't get a word out! Finally, he stammered, "How-how do you do!"

What in the world is wrong with him? wondered his mother. *It's not like he's unused to being around beautiful women. He attracts them like bees round a honeypot. He just has a way with women. But tonight, he turned into a stammering schoolboy!*

She wasn't much better. Instead of being the poised charming woman she been with everyone else, she just stared at Nick. It was left to Victoria to hurriedly step in and take charge of the situation! *I'd better move these two apart before anyone notices the reaction they have to each other.* So for the rest of the party, she made sure they were not in each other's company, which wasn't difficult, as neither one of them seemed to want to be near the other.

By midnight, most of her guests had left or were making their way out. The family tradition after a party was to sit down and take a few minutes together to discuss the evening. Of course, the subject of discussion this evening was the new doctor in town! Everyone had something to say about her, from her wonderful skin and clothes (Audra), how young she is to have such an incredible resume (Eugene), how poised and articulate (Jarrod), what legs (Heath), and how easy fundraising was going to be with her in the emergency room (Victoria).

Conspicuous by its absence any comment about the doctor from Nick. Pretty soon everyone drifted off to bed, but Nick stayed where he was just gazing into the fire. Victoria was about to leave and go upstairs when something made her turn and go to her son.

"What is it, Nick? You've not been yourself all evening. Are you feeling unwell?"

No response.

"Nick?"

"What? Sorry, Mother. What were you saying?"

"I was asking you if you are all right?"

"No, no I'm not."

"What's wrong, son? Are you ill?"

"It's nothing like that."

"Then what is it?"

A long pause from Nick. "You aren't going to believe me!"

"What's going on, Nick?"

"Okay, here goes. Tonight, I met the woman I'm going to marry!"

"What!" exclaimed Victoria. "Who is she? What happened?"

Nick looked at his mother. "You introduced us."

"I did? Who is it?"

"Dr. Caroline Warner!"

"What? You only met her for the first time tonight. You couldn't have said more than half a dozen words to her all evening!"

"I know. I didn't need to say anything to her. I knew the instant I saw her!"

"Nick, think about what you're saying!"

"I know," said her son. "Love at first sight! I'd heard about it, and some gypsies said I would know her when I saw her, but I never truly believed it would happen to me. But, Mother, it did! I know now why I had John start on the apartment renovation—it's for her. Don't ask me how I knew, I just did!

Me, Nick Barkley, two-fisted drinker, gambler, brawler, womanizer. Loudmouthed Nick Barkley is in love at first sight, and do you know what song they were playing? 'Some Enchanted Evening.' 'When you see a stranger across a crowded room, then fly to her side and make her your own, or all through your life, you may dream alone.' I saw her mother, and I'm done for! I don't know anything about her except her name, she's English, she's a doctor, and she served in the British army, and I want to spend the rest of my life with her! It's nuts, right? But you know something even crazier? I think she feels the same! There were those few seconds when we looked at each other, and I'm sure she was as stunned as I, but it was real. She knew it in those few seconds—soulmates.

I've heard people talk about that for years. I was beginning to wonder if I'd ever find the right girl far less a soulmate, then suddenly, there she was, standing right in front of me. I didn't know what to say—I was tongue tied! And you know what, so she was! When was the last time I didn't have something to say?! Well, it sure happened tonight! I must be away the next few weeks at those factories we just acquired, and I heard Andrew say that he and Esther are going to Hawaii for two weeks and taking Caroline with them. She doesn't officially start work 'til the end of January, and that's okay, but come the middle of February, the pursuit of Dr. Warner will start!"

And with that, he kissed his mother on the cheek and ran up the stairs to bed! Victoria just stood there! She had never seen or heard Nick like that, but one thing she knew; when Nick made his mind up to something, he usually got it, so look out, Dr. Warner!

"To watch this from the sidelines is going to be very interesting. That young woman has no idea what her future looks like! Let the wooing of Dr. Caroline Warner commence," she said to the dying embers of the fire!

The next morning at breakfast, Jarrod mentioned he intended to ask Dr. Warner out.

"Back off, Jarrod. She's taken," Nick said, his steel grey eyes blazing.

"By whom?" was the response.

"Me," Nick replied.

"Since when?" Jarrod persisted.

"Leave it, Jarrod. I'm warning you," said Nick as he jumped up from the table, knocking over his chair.

"Whoa, Nick! No problem if she means that much."

"Well, she does," responded the fiery Nick as he picked up his chair.

"Let's all cool down and finish breakfast," Victoria instructed them.

Heath, Eugene, and Jarrod were all exchanging looks as if to say, *What just happened?* They all knew Nick had, just like them, met Dr. Warner for the first time the night before and couldn't understand how Nick could have gotten so possessive of her! Audra was going to tease him about it but thought better of it. You teased Nick at your own peril when he was in that kind of mood! She'd wait and ask her Mother about it later because she was eaten up with curiosity.

"When do you leave for San Francisco?" she asked Nick.

"On the second," he replied. "Then I'll be away for three weeks, and what are you going to do with yourself while I'm away, little lady?"

"I'm working on the committee for the hospital Valentine fund-raising dance. You'll be back for that, won't you?"

"Yes, back and then off to New Orleans but home on the twelfth, so you can count me in."

"You'll definitely be going? You passed in previous years."

"Ah, but I have a special reason for going this year."

"Great! I'll put you down for two tickets," said Audra.

The reason is about five-foot-eight inches and has red hair with green eyes, thought Victoria with a smile on her face.

"What are you smiling about, Mother?" asked Audra.

"Just passing thoughts," murmured Victoria, not daring to look Nick's way but with mischief dancing in her eyes! Oh what fun this is shaping up to be!

Unbeknownst to her, a beautiful vase of wildflowers—how did he know they were her favorites?—were on their way to Kate with a card that simply said, 'Welcome to Stockton' and signed Nick Barkley. When they arrived, Jeanne remarked, "That man must have a special insight to you to pick wildflowers instead of the usual florist's bouquet."

"How could he? We only met for a couple of minutes last night," Kate said.

"Well, if that's what he knows about you after just two minutes, lady, you're in trouble," responded Jeanne with a gleam in her eyes. "The man obviously likes you to send such gorgeous flowers, and that's no cheap vase they're in—that's crystal!"

"I'm telling you, all he said was 'How do you do.'"

"Well, that might have been all he actually said, but he meant a whole lot more."

"This is one ridiculous conversation," said Kate. "Anyway, he was with someone."

"You noticed that, did you?"

"It would have been hard not to, the way she was hanging all over him."

"He wouldn't have liked that, and from the gossip this morning, that's all over."

"You mean the gossip mill works that well here?"

"Stockton is a small city, and the Barkleys are the town's number one family. You'd do well to remember that!"

"What do you mean I should remember that?"

"Nick Barkley's dinner dates are tomorrow's lunch fodder, so watch yourself, girl."

"You mean he's a player?"

"Very much so, if gossip is to be believed, but I also think Nick's like everyone else—he's just looking for that right person, except for him, it happens in the gossip columns. I hear basically he's a real nice guy. The whole family has a good reputation. Mr. and Mrs. Barkley raised them right. It was a terrible thing the father, Tom Barkley, getting murdered the way he did. Found the body out in the woods. Still had his watch and ring, etc., so it wasn't robbery. Someone just shot him and left him there. Mrs. Barkley had him buried where he was found. Over one thousand people came for his service. Nick, although he was just about twenty, took over running things, Jarrod was finishing up studying law, Audra and Eugene were just young. Hit them real hard. Poor Mrs. Barkley, she went around in shock for a good two years."

"But isn't there another son?"

"You mean Heath? He showed up about four years ago. It seemed Mr. Barkley strayed some twenty-plus years ago, and Heath was the result!"

"But Mrs. Barkley introduced him to me as her son!"

"That's what she calls him," said Jeanne.

"Wow, she's more forgiving than I would be," replied Kate.

"Well, the way she handled it, it turned out to be mainly a seven-day wonder with most people, but I'm afraid, with some, still a source of gossip."

"She's quite a lady," Kate replied. "How did the rest of the family handle it?"

"They followed her lead and showed a united front. They're that kind of family. They are one of the wealthiest families in northern California, but you'd never know it from the way they interact with the people. They're always around to lend a helping hand or invest in the community—no airs and graces. Victoria Barkley wouldn't put

24

up with that kind of attitude. I think that's why none of the guys are married yet. A woman will have to pass the Victoria Barkley litmus test, and that won't be easy! Whoever these guys marry won't just be taking on a husband, she'll have to fit in with the entire clan."

As the family were leaving the breakfast table, Victoria pulled Nick aside and asked him how it had gone with Mona Scott last night. "I completely forgot to ask you in the midst of your other announcement."

"We won't be seeing each other again," said Nick tersely.

"Is she all right?" persisted his mother.

"Of course, she is," countered Nick. "We had only gone out for a few short weeks," and with that, he walked away, signaling the end to that subject of conversation.

As Jeanne had rightly commented to Kate, it was already the subject of much speculation as to why those two had broken up. For Mona, it had come out of the blue. Nick had only said that he didn't think things were working out and wished her well. She had been taken completely by surprise. She had not seen Nick's eyes wandering, but as he was going to be in and out of town for almost six weeks, perhaps that was the reason. It would be interesting to see if he went to Valentine's hospital fundraiser dance. He passed on it the previous two years when he hadn't a current date. So everyone would be watching to see if he started seeing someone new by then, and if so, who it would be.

Audra and Eugene talked about Nick's behavior at the breakfast table. Neither could understand it, but on the other hand, Nick was known for fiery outbursts, although not normally at Jarrod.

Heath was over at the corporate and ranch offices, which were adjacent to the main house. He was basically his brother's right-hand man, so with Nick planning to be gone for a few weeks, the job of overseeing the ranch would be left up to Heath whilst John McIntire would run things on a day-to-day basis. They could always call Nick if something major were to happen. In fact, if they didn't, they'd catch hell from him, but there were decisions to be constantly made about the cattle and horses, etc. Being January, there were no crops to be harvested, and it was too early for branding. Heath knew they could always ask Victoria for any help they might need. There wasn't much about running the ranch she didn't know. But he really wanted to prove to his big brother that he could be relied upon to take care of Nick's first love—the ranch.

The rest of the family holdings, winery, lumber, factories, mines, and other investments were Nick's to run, with the help of VPs which were over each section. He had gradually introduced Heath to the inner workings of each of the Barkley investments. Finding that Heath had a special talent of understanding the labor point of view, seeing it was not long ago he used to be part of it, now as a member of management, it gave him a unique point of view during conflict resolution negotiations. Nick trusted his brother to be the company eyes and ears at those times, and both sides of the table knew that Heath would report directly back to Nick, which made the sometimes tempestuous meetings or delicate negotiations go more smoothly.

The photographic memory of Nick's came in extremely useful. He carried much of the family's business dealings in his head. His vice-presidents over each division of the family holdings lightened the load, but ultimately the buck stopped at his desk. He made it look so easy, but few, Victoria being one of them, knew how exhausted he sometimes got. Whatever else was going on in his life, Nick still found time to get involved with ranch work, getting his hands dirty alongside the men as often as he could. What he really needed, in his mother's opinion, was someone to share all this with who could get him to stop working and relax. Maybe the good doctor was just what he needed in his life. Time will tell.

Having his older brother Jarrod as the company attorney meant there was a trust that few company presidents have for the head of their legal department. Jarrod oversaw it all but still made time to practice his first love—criminal law.

Eugene commented to his mother that he would really like to talk to Dr. Warner and pick her brain about emergency/trauma medicine. He hadn't decided what to choose as his specialty, and talking with her might help him with that important decision. *Hmm*, thought Victoria, *I wonder what Nick would say to a little help!*

"Leave it with me, son," she said. "Let me see what I can do."
She had a quick conversation with Silas about a small dinner party
on New Year's Eve. Up until then, she hadn't planned anything, but
first, she had to find out what the Petersons and, more importantly,
Dr. Warner were doing. She went into the library and called Esther.

"As it happens, we haven't made plans because we are leaving for
Hawaii on the first. Let me ask Kate and see if she is free to come and
I'll call you right back."

Victoria found herself pacing in the room. *This playing cupid
business is stressful work*, she thought!

The phone rang, and Esther said, "Kate would be delighted to
come."

Victoria grinned from ear to ear! "Wonderful, see you around
eight o'clock." She knew getting a few more people to come to dinner wouldn't be difficult. An invite to the big white mansion wasn't
something people easily turned down! She checked with Audra and
found she would be available, so would Heath and Eugene, Jarrod
already had plans. Now, all that was left was to casually mention it to
Nick. So at dinner that evening, Victoria turned the conversation to
New Year's Eve and asked Nick what he had planned.

"Nothin," he said. "I'm too busy working on the details for the
factory upgrades to think about dinner plans."

"Well, if you haven't anywhere else to go, you could always join
us," said his mother.

"I'm not sure," he responded. "Anyway, who have you invited?"

She reeled off some names and then added "The Petersons and
Dr. Warner."

Nick's expression froze. "The Petersons are coming? I thought
they were going to Hawaii?"

"No, not until January first, so coming here fits right in with
their plans. Besides, Eugene wants to talk with Kate about emergency medicine, so this way, he'll have a chance to spend some time
with her."

"Kate?"

"Yes, she prefers to be called Kate."

27

The look on Nick's face as he gazed at his mother's innocent expression belied by her twinkling eyes was priceless! He had been outmaneuvered by his own mother!

"Well, in that case, you'd better count me in after all. I have to eat dinner somewhere, so it might as well be at this party of yours," said Nick, acknowledging the help she was giving him.

Over at the Petersons, Kate was grateful for the New Year's Eve dinner invitation as she hadn't known how to thank Nick for the flowers. Should she send a thank-you note or call him at his office? The dinner took care of that problem. She'd just thank him in person.

Jeanne grinned when she heard about the plans. "Got his mother helping him," she said.

"Nothing of the kind," responded Kate. "They are having a small dinner party, and Eugene wants to talk with me about emergency medicine."

"Uh-oh, using his brother too!"

"Stop it, Jeanne, you're turning the most innocent occurrence into some Machiavellian plot!"

"If that's the case," shot back Jeanne. "Why are you blushing? What are you going to wear?"

"I don't know. Haven't really thought about it."

"Is that why half your closet is lying on the bed?" responded Jeanne. "Make it classic and simple. That little black dress."

"I don't have one."

"Then get your ass in gear and buy one! I'll put this lot away for you, now go!"

A few hours later, an exhausted Kate returned home.

"Well, did you find one?" asked Jeanne.

"Not a one to be had," said Kate, "but I found this," and held up a perfectly plain strapless sapphire blue dress with matching bolero jacket.

"It's gorgeous with your skin and hair. It will be perfect. Look out, Nick Barkley. Here she comes!"

Chapter 4

New Year's Eve dawned cold with the chance of snow in the air. Over at the Petersons, they all finished packing, looking forward to seeing the sunny skies and feeling the warm temperatures of Hawaii. Kate had already googled the daytime temps and was going to enjoy eighty degrees on her skin. She had packed two bikinis and was intending to buy more when she got there. She shivered as she started to get ready for the party and looked out the window to see light snow starting to fall. *I'd better wear something warmer than that dress I bought*, she thought regretfully. Jeanne knocked on her door and was going to suggest a change of outfit in view of the weather conditions.

"I'm going to wear this wool mid-length wraparound skirt with matching shawl," said Kate, getting it out of her closet. "The large black, brown, and off-white checks go with my cream silk shirt, and I've this beautiful antique copper pin to hold the shawl in place."

"Perfect choice," said Jeanne. "Do you have any high-heeled black boots?"

"Yes, on my boot rack."

"Let me get them for you. A black purse, and the outfit is complete. You look beautiful. You're so blessed to have that naturally curly red hair. Other women spend hundreds trying to get that look! I'll tell the judge you're ready. Where is your coat?"

"I'll just put my coat around my shoulders and then I'll come downstairs. I'll be glad when the rest of my clothes arrive or I'd be running out of things to wear at these kinds of evenings."

As they drove over to the Barkleys, the snow came down faster, and the temps were rapidly dropping. The car dropped them off at the front door, and they hurried inside. Silas had remembered from the last party that Kate didn't drink alcohol and had a special punch for her. She was so appreciative toward him for remembering. *What a well-mannered young woman she is,* thought Victoria. *Knows how to treat staff and volunteers. She'll go far, that one.*

The guests and family mingled, talking and laughing. "Isn't that a beautiful outfit Dr. Warner is wearing?" remarked Liz Thompson, a fellow hospital board member, to Victoria. "That girl sure has a style of her own. She was telling me that, as she has spent most of the last seven years in either camo or scrubs, she's having fun wearing and buying civvies, as she calls them. She follows no particular style and just wears whatever pleases her. Just wish I had the nerve to do that."

Victoria excused herself and checked with Silas about dinner.

"Another twenty minutes and you can sit," he told her.

Out of the corner of her eye, she watched Nick circulate among the guests. He was walking over to the group where Kate was talking to Eugene. She had seated Kate next to Eugene at dinner, with her permission, so he could ask her all the questions he wanted to, but it was clear he wasn't going to wait to be seated. As Nick joined the group, so did Audra, who drew Kate aside, probably to talk about clothes.

Foiled again, Nick, thought Victoria.

Soon, Silas announced, "Dinner is served."

Eugene escorted Dr. Warner in, and they sat down together. Nick was sitting at the other end of the table and covertly glanced several times at the doctor. When coffee was served in the living room, he caught up with his kid brother and asked Kate, if she needed rescuing from all of Eugene's questions. She laughed and said no, it was her pleasure to talk with him and help Gene make a decision as to what his specialty would be.

"I want to thank you for the amazing flowers and vase you sent me. What a lovely welcome to Stockton," she told Nick.

He smiled at her and said he was glad she liked them.

"I don't know how you knew it, but wildflowers are my favorites, much more appealing than the standard florist's bouquet."

"Would you like some coffee, Dr. Warner?" Silas asked.

"I'd love it, thank you so much." But as he turned to get her some, one of the other staff whispered something to him.

"The hospital is on the phone for you, Dr. Warner," Silas told her. "This way."

She followed him to the hallway and picked up the phone. After a few minutes, she rejoined the Judge, Esther, Victoria, and Nick, who were all standing together, talking.

"I have to go to the hospital," she told them. "The ER is at code black."

"What does that mean?" asked Esther.

"Simply they are inundated with patients and don't have enough staff to treat them. They called the house, and Jeanne told them where I was."

"I'll drive you," said Nick.

"Are you sure you don't mind?"

"No problem, and I have a four-wheel drive which we'll need."

Silas was right there with her coat and purse as Nick went to grab his jacket, hat, gloves, and keys.

"Take care, Nick," said Victoria. "Drive carefully."

The storm was almost getting to blizzard proportions when they went outside.

"Stay here," Nick said. "I'll bring my truck around." He was back in a few minutes, and they set off through the swirling snow for the hospital. What Nick called his "truck" turned out to be the most luxurious Land Rover Discovery she had ever seen. It was black on black, with the Barkley brand logo embossed on the door and was equipped with every extra imaginable.

"It normally takes fifteen to twenty minutes to get to the hospital, but tonight who knows?" Nick explained. The visibility was poor, and the wind was howling. In any less a vehicle, they would have been pushed all over, but Nick's four-wheel drive was big and heavy and hugged the road, plus he was used to driving off road in bad conditions around his ranch. She was very grateful he was at the wheel.

"Here are the controls for the heating of your seat. It also will give you a massage if you want one. Just set it however you want to be comfortable."

"Thank you so much. I'm nice and warm. I'm looking at all the controls. This car has everything."

"More than you know. Do you need to give your phone a charge? The charger in here works really fast."

"Thank you, but I just charged it before I left home."

They drove on in a comfortable silence, Nick concentrating on the road and Kate surveying all the extras this Land Rover had!

"There it is," he said, suddenly pointing into the dark night. The lights of the hospital were dimly in view through the snow trying to pile up on his windscreen. "Where should I drop you?" he asked.

"At the main emergency room entrance," she responded. "Thank you so much for bringing me out here."

"'Tweren't nothin', ma'am," Nick said, laughing.

"Be careful as you drive home. Good night." And with that, she was gone into the night. Nick waited until he saw the doors open and close then put the truck into gear and moved into the ER parking lot. Kate went through the brightly lit waiting room, which was packed with what were obviously patients, and into the treatment area, seeing why they had called her—there were people all over. Obviously there had been multiple auto accidents, slips and falls, and who knows what else! She rushed through into an office and changed into scrubs and set to work. A few hours later, when the treatment bays and waiting room were almost empty and the housekeeping and janitorial staff had taken over, she was able to leave. Now, all she needed was a way to get home. Going to the reception desk to find out about taxis, who did Kate see but Nick Barkley, sitting slouched in a chair, with his long legs stretched out, arms folded, and his Stetson tilted onto his face!

"How long has he been here?" she asked one of the intake staff.

"I don't know. Hours, I would guess."

Kate went over to Nick who had, upon hearing her voice, sat up straight and removed his Stetson,

"All through?" he asked.

"Have...have you been here all this time?" she stammered.

"Didn't have any place else I needed to be and figured I might as well wait out the storm. Besides, you'd need a ride home when you were finished. How about some coffee? I know where you can get the best in town. Come on."

"I can't believe you've been here all this time," she told him. "But as you're offering, I'd love a good cup of coffee right about now."

"Your ride awaits."

She must have looked strange, a beautiful imitation fur coat over scrubs and clogs holding a large plastic bag with her evening clothes in it, but if he noticed, he was too well mannered to say anything. They got to the doorway, and he told her to wait there and he'd get his truck. Got the manners of a gentleman, even got out of the Land Rover and opened the door for her. *I could get used to this,* she thought, then gave herself a mental shake. *I bet he does this for every woman.*

They drove in silence to a little back alley donut shop. Just your basic coffee, no cappuccino here, but they had the most wonderful apple fritter she had ever tasted. "Oh that feels better—caffeine and sugar!" She laughed.

"Was it very bad in the ER tonight?" he asked her.

"No, not too bad. Just so many patients, a few car accidents, the usual slip and falls due to the weather, so lots of broken bones, some minor gunshot wounds, and it being New Year's Eve, drunken fights and brawls. It wasn't dull, but in six hours, we'll be taking off and then it'll be the sunny skies of Hawaii!!"

"Have you packed?" asked Nick.

"Oh yes, I did that yesterday, but how many clothes do you need to lie on a beach!"

She blushed as she realized what she had said. But he just laughed.

"You're going away too, aren't you?" she asked him.

"Yes, I leave on the second, and then I'll be in and out of town 'til the middle of February."

"That's a lot of traveling," she responded.

"We're upgrading some factories we acquired in a merger, and I want to oversee as much of it as possible myself."

They continued to chat about Nick's family business. He was surprised at the intelligent questions she asked; she caught on really fast.

"Changing the subject, I know it's none of my business, but if you are going to be roaming around town at all hours of the night, you might consider getting yourself a handgun which, being in the army, I'm sure you know how to use. You would automatically qualify for a concealed carry permit as you must be carrying narcotics in your medical bag."

Kate just laughed. "I'm already ahead of you. My sidearm is in the glove compartment of my mini, which I'm pleased to say I took delivery of yesterday. I applied for a concealed carry permit the day I came for my interview on the judge's advice, and because of his influence, it was expedited."

"Might I ask what kind of gun you carry?"

"I have a Glock seventeen nine mm, and my rifle is a SA eighty A two bullpup style."

Nick's eyebrows rose. "You don't mess around, do you?"

"I'm sure being a rancher, you have a number of weapons. Tell me about your sidearm and rifles."

"Well, my favorite—what you call my sidearm—is a nineteen eleven, forty five ACP Kimber Desert Warrior. The two rifles that I mainly use are a four sixty four, thirty thirty Winchester Lever-Action, the other is a Remington, model seven eighty three scoped."

"You've got some serious firepower yourself!" she remarked."

"When was the last time you went shooting?" he asked her.

"I was still in Afghanistan when I last got a chance to fire my rifle, and in England, at a small arms range before the holidays with my Glock. I must find a range locally or I'm going to get badly out of practice."

"Tell you what, when I get back into town, I'll take you out to our range."

"You have your own range? What kind is it?"

"Outdoor, so we have clay pigeons plus all kinds of stationary targets."

"That sounds wonderful. I would really enjoy time at a range."

"As soon as I get back, I'll get in touch and we'll fix up a day and time."

It was when he mentioned time that Kate looked at her watch. "I must get home. They'll think I'm still at the hospital."

"Okay, let's get moving," he responded. "I'll have you home in fifteen minutes. Why don't you call them when we get in my truck." Again, he opened the door for her. She called the judge and let him know she was on her way. All she needed was a quick shower and she'd be ready. Nick pulled into the Petersons' driveway just as Jeanne opened the door.

"Thank you again, Nick, for the ride, coffee, and doughnut."

"My pleasure, Kate. Enjoy your vacation." And with that, he was gone.

The look Jeanne gave her! "Out all night with Mr. Barkley. I can just see the headlines now. It's a good job you're going out of town!"

"Knock it off! I've worked hard in the ER for hours!"

"And he waited for you?"

"He took me out for a cup of coffee."

"Does this qualify for a first date?"

That was the same question Victoria was asking her son. "I suppose it does," he answered. "That has to be the smartest woman I've ever met."

"She was what they used to call a child prodigy. Now it's gifted child. She graduated high school at twelve and was an attending physician at eighteen," his mother told him.

"Ah, now it makes sense. I couldn't believe how fast she caught on to what I was explaining and the intelligent questions she asked, plus we actually talked about firearms! That was a first for me. Not the usual subject I talk about with a woman, but then she's no ordinary woman as I'm fast finding out."

"Nothing's changed?" his mother asked.

"You mean how I feel about her? No, nothing's changed. In fact, after having a conversation with her, I can see what a wonderful wife she's going to be. To be able to talk business through with her will make life so much easier. I just hope I can be of as much help to her."

"I think you could, Nick. Just reading between the lines of her resume and reference letters, all she has ever known is work, work, work. You don't get to where she's at without it. I don't think she really knows a life that's not work driven. Perhaps what she needs is to have someone show her there is more to life than her driven variety. She seems to be a loner. Only child, left home at twelve, time spent living with guardians, then army life. I don't think she has ever had a real home. Imagine what kind of mother she had who would give up a twelve-year-old child! What you could give her, Nick, would be a home, stability, and being part of a large loving family."

"I never thought of it that way. It makes me think my approach to her must be slightly different. I don't want to overwhelm her and scare her off. Softly, softly. I don't even know how much dating she's done. I can see I have to be very careful. This isn't your average girl—sorry, woman," he said, seeing the look on his mother's face. Yes, he'd think up a whole new strategy of approaching Kate whilst he was away. He smiled to himself as he recalled the way she had blushed when she realized what she had said about not taking many clothes to Hawaii. Yes, a girl—woman—who would blush at all was new to him, and he didn't want to spoil any of her charms. The next few weeks at the factories kept Nick busy, but thoughts of Kate were never far away. He would have liked to have called her. He finally got her number from his mother's hospital list but didn't want to bother her whilst she was on vacation. Then when she came home, she started her new job. *Softly, softly, Nick*, he kept reminding himself.

Plans were forging ahead for the hospital Valentine fundraiser evening. Tickets were selling out fast. Everyone from hospital floor staff to the elite of Stockton society were going. There was something for everyone; that's what made it so popular. There was the dance itself, refreshments kept at a reasonable price, silent auction, raffle, etc. Audra was on the decorating committee and Victoria, on the steering committee. All the doctors were expected to at least show their faces at the event.

Valentine's Day was cloudy and cold, dictating that the outfits the ladies would be wearing had better be warm.

"Are you going?" Jeanne asked Kate the night before.

"Yes, but I'm working 'til seven, so I'll take a dress to work with me and change there."

"Which dress do you mean?" asked Jeanne.

"This red sweater dress that I bought in New York at Christmas time and never got to wear." Jeanne's eyebrows rose. From the looks of it, the dress would hug every single curve of Kate's very cute figure. *Look out, Mr. Nick Barkley*, she thought, because she knew he wouldn't pass up a chance to see Kate again.

"Don't you think it's okay?" asked Kate. "I know it's plain, but with a pin on the shoulder, it looks nice. It's the tomato shade of red that I can wear, that and suntan shade of thigh-highs and my black suede pumps and black purse, it should be all right."

More than all right, thought Jeanne but didn't say it. She didn't want to make Kate self-conscious about what would obviously be a stunning look.

As it happened, Dr. Warner didn't get off work until after nine p.m., and by the time she got changed, put on some makeup, and got over to the town hall ballroom, the dance was in full swing.

Nick had arrived there at seven thirty with the rest of the family and was mingling but keeping one eye on the entrance. When it was past nine, he was beginning to think the object of his affections wasn't coming when the door opened and there she was. She was greeted by her physician's assistant, Ann, and went over to a table occupied by some ER staff. When she removed her jacket, he took a deep breath, because she was wearing a wonderful red dress that, as Jeanne had predicted, showed to perfection her every curve. He wasn't the only male in the room to notice, and within minutes, there was a crowd of men around her table. He didn't know what she said, but obviously, it wasn't what they wanted to hear because they drifted away with less than happy expressions on their faces. Kate didn't get up to dance with anyone, and soon, a waiter brought her a coffee. *She sure does like coffee*, he thought.

"How about dancing with your mother again?" Victoria asked him.

"Of course, lovely lady," he replied. After his mother, he sought out his sister and danced with her. As he was escorting Audra back to

37

her table, an incident broke out involving, of all people, Dr. Warner and the teenage son of one of the other doctors who, although under-age, had gotten hold of some alcohol.

"Come on, it's only a dance," the youth was saying to Kate.

"No, thank you," she was telling him, but he wasn't taking no for an answer. In a flash, Nick assessed the situation and got the kid by the scruff of the neck and his belt and pinned him up against a pillar.

"The lady said no," he told the young man. "Stop annoying her." By that time, the boy's father and mother were on the scene. "You better get him home and sober him up," Nick said to them.

"We're so sorry, Dr. Warner," they apologized.

"No harm done," she said. "Thank you, Nick. I always seem to be thanking you for something."

"Well, now that I'm over here, we can have that dance."

"What dance?" she asked.

"This one," he responded, and before she could say another word, he was steering her onto the dance floor just as the band leader was saying his group were taking a twenty-minute break, but they had put together a tape of songs so the dancing wouldn't be interrupted.

Nick swung Kate into his arms as the music started and what was it but Chris De Burgh's "The Lady In Red." *How very appropriate!* thought Nick. As the rather seductive music came to an end, Nick said, "You're a good dancer."

"As Ginger Rogers once said, I'm just doing what you do except backward and in heels," she responded with a grin.

He threw back his head and laughed. The strains of Sheena Easton's "For Your Eyes Only" started, and Nick swung her around, and they continued to dance as if they'd been dancing together all their lives. When Charlie Rich's "Behind Closed Doors" started up, Kate tried to pull away, but Nick held her firmly but gently. "One last dance," he murmured.

"Okay, one more," she said, not wanting to admit how much she was enjoying herself. *I'm glad Jeanne can't see this,* she thought. *Nuts! There she is with a big grin on her face!* As the last strains of the music ended, Nick escorted Kate back to her table.

"I'm heading home," she said. "I've been on duty since seven this morning, and I'm tired."

"I'll walk you to your car," he offered.

But just then, Audra came over and told him that Jarrod needed his help.

"That's fine, you go."

"How about having dinner with me Saturday night?" he asked her.

"I can't. This is one of my last nights of freedom. I have been called back to active service by Her Majesty. I'm in what you Americans call the reserves, so for the next two weeks, it's back to camo."

"We'll talk when you get back then," he said.

"I'd like that," was her reply. Nick walked away to find Jarrod just as Jeanne came over.

"You leaving?" she asked.

"Yes, why? Do you need a ride?"

"If you don't mind."

"Just don't turn the drive into the Spanish inquisition!" They got into Kate's mini and set off home.

"You two looked very cozy on the dance floor," remarked Jeanne, who had fast become more than just the housekeeper to Kate; she had become a trusted friend who Kate knew wouldn't go gossiping about her.

"He's a marvelous dancer. So easy to follow."

"Has he asked you out yet?"

"Yes, as a matter of fact, he has, but I'm going on those maneuvers, so I had to say no."

"What did he say to that?"

"That we'll talk when I get back."

"Yes. I didn't think he'd give up easily," shot back Jeanne with a smile on her face.

Chapter 5

Kate's time on maneuvers just reminded her how much she disliked sand and being back in camo. The war games had been out in the Mojave Desert—hot during the day, freezing cold at night, the fine sand finding its way into everything 'til you could even taste it in the food! Kate couldn't wait for the two weeks to be over. The maneuvers had been between American and British Special Forces units, the kind of military units her medical expertise had made her very necessary to in the Middle East. Kate never wanted to be back in uniform again, but she had to put in her eight years as an officer to get a small pension and benefits when she turned sixty five.

When she got home, a bouquet of wildflowers were waiting for her with a card that simply said, "Nick."

She was back at work for a few days and almost on the point of leaving one night when a call came in from paramedics that a gunshot-wound patient would reach the hospital in moments. It was already close to ten p.m., and she was almost three hours past her shift ending due to a patient who had been involved in an auto accident and had required her to perform surgery—all this happening just before seven. However, something made her take her jacket off and wait for the incoming ambulance. To her surprise, following right behind the gurney was Nick Barkley; it was one of his men who had been shot. They just nodded at each other.

The night shift attending asked Kate if she could do this surgery, saying the patient could benefit from her special talents. It was bad, and she wasn't sure if she could save the man. Her patient was in his late fifties who had been shot twice at close range. A few hours later, she was cautiously hopeful that he would make it. She changed from her stained scrubs and went to check on her patient one more time before she went home and found Nick sitting by Sam William's bed in ICU. Nick stood up when he saw her. "Did you do the surgery?" he asked.

"Yes," she replied. "It was touch and go, and he's still not completely out of the woods. He's lost a lot of blood, and so the next forty-eight hours will be crucial, but I'm cautiously optimistic he'll make it."

"I don't know how to thank you," he responded.

The PA who had come over to check on Sam said, "I don't think he'd have made it this far if Dr. Warner hadn't been there to perform the surgery way past her duty hours. This man is one very lucky guy she hadn't already gone home."

"How about coffee, Kate?" Nick asked, "I think we both could use some."

"Not a bad idea. I'll follow you." She gave the PA final instructions, and then the two of them left the hospital. She followed him in her mini to the coffee shop.

"Two coffees and an apple fritter," he ordered. They chose a table in the back, even though they were the only customers in the place.

"How did Mr. Williams come to get shot?" she asked.

"We're having trouble with rustlers," he replied. "We have four herds in winter pastures, and it's impossible to watch them all. Tonight, they hit a herd that was under armed guard, but they snuck up on Sam before he saw them. He didn't even have time to get a shot off."

"You still have rustlers in this day and age?" she asked, amazed.

"Oh yes, some things never change," he told her. They went on to talk about the ranching business for a while, but both were almost out on their feet.

"When do you go on duty again?" inquired Nick.

"Not until Monday. My contract says I work seven am to seven pm shift, Monday through Thursday and have Friday, Saturday, and Sunday off. So now I'm going home to sleep."

"How about you have dinner with me Saturday night?" asked Nick, holding his breath, hoping for a positive response!

"That sounds delightful," she said, smiling. "Just one thing. Could we go somewhere low key? I'm not much for trendy "in" type restaurants. I much prefer the mom-and-pop, hole-in-the-wall type places."

"So do I," said Nick, grinning at her. "I'll pick you up at seven thirty."

And with that, she made one more call to the ICU to check on Sam, gave Nick the update, and both headed home, Kate looking forward, more than she was willing to admit even to herself, about the dinner Saturday night!

Victoria was up when Nick got home, eager to have news on Sam, who had worked for them for almost twenty years. Nick updated her, telling his mother what the PA had said about Sam being lucky Kate was still at the hospital when he was brought in.

"You two certainly seen destined to spend time together," she remarked. "So when are you seeing her again?"

"I'm taking her to dinner Saturday," said Nick with a big grin on his face.

"Well, it beats coffee and an apple fritter," responded his mother.

When Jeanne heard about the dinner date, her first question was "Will he take you to a fancy restaurant?"

"No. I already asked him if we could go somewhere low key. I really don't want my name to be the latest gossip item," Kate told her.

"Good thinking," responded Jeanne. "I bet that was different for him. Women normally want their names linked with his!"

His mother was hearing the same thing and, like Jeanne, was commenting to Nick that this must be new to him.

"It is," said Nick. "I was a bit taken aback when she asked, but it fits in with what I've come to know of her. She's certainly different from any other girl—sorry, woman. I'll never get that right, but somehow, I don't think she's the kind that would object! Anyway, I'm taking her to the Mexican family restaurant we go to, Jose's."

"Sounds like a good choice. The food is wonderful, and it's definitely not one of the 'in' places," commented Victoria.

43

Kate slept most of Friday, periodically checking in with ICU to see how Sam Williams was doing. "He's still holding his own," she told Jeanne.

"Good, now we can talk about your outfit for tomorrow night," was the response.

"I'm not wearing anything too dressy. Just comfortable. How about a skirt and sweater?"

"What skirt and what sweater?"

"I have this teal-colored skirt and matching sweater with a cowl neckline."

"The color is perfect for you. Just a nice pendant and you're set. Your high-heeled black suede boots and matching purse will complete the look."

She was dressed and ready to go when Nick rang the doorbell at exactly seven-thirty on Saturday night. Andrew answered as Kate was putting on her suede jacket. "Have a good evening, you two," Andrew said as they left. Again, Nick opened the truck door for her. She updated him on Sam's condition as they drove to the restaurant.

"I went in to check on him today, and he's a little stronger," Kate told him.

"I know," Nick replied. "A nurse said I'd just missed you."

"I ordered a blood transfusion last night," she told him. "It gave him a little boost, but it will be a slow recovery. Does he have family?"

"A daughter. We sent for her, and she arrived last night. I'm sure it'll help him knowing she's here," Nick said to her.

They pulled up at the restaurant as it began to rain. The valet took the keys and greeted Nick with a smile. "Nice to see you again, Senor Barkley." They hurried into the small restaurant and were greeted by its owner, Jose. There was a fireplace over in one corner and the couple were led to a booth close to it.

"Glad to see you, Senor Nick. What can I get you?"

"A light beer and a diet Sprite with lime for the lady."

"'Right away, sir."

"Oh, and bring us some guacamole. They make it fresh at the table," Nick explained to Kate.

"How delightful," she said, looking around.

The owner's wife, Rosa, rolled her cart over to their table and set about making the guacamole. It tasted wonderful and was served with homemade chips.

"She makes her own tortillas," Nick told his date.

"How did you find this place?" asked Kate.

"My family has been coming for years," he answered. "You won't find yourself in the gossip columns coming here!"

Kate blushed at his comment. "I hope you didn't mind my asking to go somewhere low key."

"Not at all," he responded. "It was a refreshing change." He was dressed casually, grey striped pants, a sweater, and leather jacket. "You look beautiful, if I haven't already told you," he said. "My sister envies you your dress sense. At least, that's the gist of what she was saying!"

"I have spent so long in scrubs or camo that it feels good to wear some of the civvies I've collected on my travels."

"Have you traveled a lot?" Nick asked her.

"A fair bit," was her response. "I used to meet my dad and stepmum in Europe and spend my holidays with them. It wasn't very often I went back to England. It's a long flight. If I only had a week or two's pass, I'd just pick a country and go lay on a beach somewhere. If I had a longer time off, I'd either stay with my folks, go back to the brigadier general's family in Germany, or spend my time traveling. I haven't had what you'd call a real home in years. Just lived in other people's houses like I do with the Petersons. It works out. This way, I don't have to worry about furniture, etc. Just a few personal possessions, my clothes, and that's it."

"Do you ever miss not having a real home?" asked Nick, thinking of the one he was preparing for her.

"How can you miss what you've never had?" said Kate. "I suppose, at some point in my life, it would be nice to settle down, but for now, being at the Petersons works out just fine for me."

At least she's open to the idea of a home of her own thought Nick. They looked at the menu, and Kate decided on *chile relleno* with beans and rice. Nick ordered some steak dish. They chattered away as they ate dinner. Neither felt the "first date" nerves. In fact, it was very

45

comfortable for both. After dinner, the restaurant owner told Nick that the heat lamps were lit on the semi-enclosed patio if he wanted to go out there and smoke a cigar with his coffee.

Nick looked at Kate, who said, of course, they would go, and picked up her purse.

"Are you sure you don't mind?" asked Nick.

"I like the smell of tobacco," Kate told him. "My dad mainly smoked a pipe but occasionally had a cigar."

It was warm on the patio, and Kate remarked how she loved rainstorms even better when they were accompanied by thunder and lightning.

"Well, you're getting your wish tonight," said Nick as the sky suddenly lit up with forks of lightning. Thunderclaps seemed to be right overhead, and the torrential rain started. Kate just laughed.

"What a wonderful storm," she said. "If there's one thing coming from England that I know about is rain and a good storm!"

"I had it made to order," responded Nick.

"I believe you did," Kate retorted. They sat there in silence until the thunder and lightning abated.

"How about some dessert?" the waiter asked.

"The flan here is great," said Nick.

"Okay, I'll try it," replied Kate.

"One flan and more coffee," ordered Nick.

It was after eleven when Nick and Kate left the restaurant and he drove her home. The rain was still pouring down as he started to get out of the truck.

Kate said, "Nick, please don't get out. There's no point in you getting wet. I can manage." And as she said that, Jeanne opened the front door.

"Well, if you're sure."

"Thank you for such a wonderful evening and for ordering up the storm," she said with a big grin.

"How about dinner on Friday?"

"Thank you, Nick. That sounds good, but you don't have to conjure up another storm," she told him, laughing. And with that, she let herself out of his truck and went in the open front door. What she didn't hear was the loud "Yahoo!" from him as he pulled out of the driveway.

As soon as Kate went in, Jeanne wanted to know about the date.

"How about I make you a cup of tea while you get changed for bed, and then you can give me the low down?"

"Jeanne, there's nothing to tell."

"Wait 'til I get your tea."

By the time the housekeeper had brewed the tea, Kate was in her PJs.

"Now give me the skinny. What's it really like being on a date with the infamous Nick Barkley?"

"Honestly, I don't know what to tell you. We had dinner at this family Mexican restaurant, sat and talked, then went out onto the patio and watched a wonderful storm, and then he brought me home. End of story."

"That's not what I meant. I mean what's it like being out with Nick Barkley, the man?"

"Well, he's very attentive, easy to talk to, a good listener, and... err...um."

"And err um what?"

"Well, being close to him, you sort of feel how incredibly masculine he is, plus he's so tall. I mean, I'm not short, but even so, it feels like he towers over me, and you can tell he takes care of himself."

"You mean he's got a good bod?"

"Jeanne!"

"Well, you brought it up! Anything else?"

"He smelled good. I don't know what kind of aftershave he uses, but it's really nice. There, have you gotten enough details?"

"I suppose so. Oh, one more thing. Did he hold your hand or kiss you good night?"

"No, he did not."

"Hmm, that's not like the Nick Barkley I've heard about. Wonder what his game is?"

"It was only our first real date!"

"From what I've heard, first dates with him can end up in bed!"

"Jeanne!!!"

"Well, I'm only telling you. That's why his behavior seems so strange. This hands-off treatment is really unlike him. Wonder what he's up to."

"Well, I, for one, appreciate him acting like a gentleman, and if he'd been anything less, it would have been our last date."

"Hmm, maybe he's figured that out and that's why he's holding back!"

"Jeanne, this conversation is over, and I'm going to bed."

The next morning at breakfast, as he was leaving the table and the others were not around, Victoria asked him how things had gone on the previous evening.

"It couldn't have been better," he responded. "Even down to the storm, which she loves!"

"I'm so glad, Nick, that things are going well. What's next?"

"We are having dinner Friday, but I'll call her mid-week."

"Anytime you want to ask her over here, feel free."

"Thanks, Mother. I'll bear that in mind, but for right now, I don't want to share her with others."

"I completely understand."

The next morning, Jeanne said, "Is there another evening planned? I forgot to ask you last night."

"Friday is our next date, and it's St Patrick's, so I'd better wear something green!"

Esther talked with Kate later that day and said she just realized that this coming Friday was St. Patrick's and she'd invited twenty people, including the Barkleys to dinner. Her sister in Germany had told her that Kate made a mean corned beef and cabbage and if she would be free to help Jeanne and herself fix dinner. She would have staff to serve and clear, but the actual cooking she was hoping they could do by themselves.

"Of course, I'll help," said Kate. "We just have to borrow as many crock pots as possible."

"If you could make the corned beef, gravy, and soda bread, if that's not too much trouble," asked Esther. "Jeanne will make dessert, and I'll take care of the potatoes, cabbage, and carrots."

"No problem," Kate replied, "just make sure we have plenty of Bisto."

"Now I have to make a quick phone call," Kate said. She ran upstairs to her room and called the Barkley ranch as she didn't have Nick's cellphone number. Silas answered the phone. "May I speak to Nick please?" she asked.

"One moment, please," he told her.

"Is everything all right?"

"Well, yes and no," she said. "I can't go to dinner with you Friday night because you and your family have been invited over here for corned beef and cabbage to celebrate St. Patrick's Day, and I'm one of the cooks!"

"I'll still see you there Friday night, and we'll have dinner together Saturday. How's that?" he said.

"Um...err...sounds okay," she stammered.

"Here's my number. five, five, five, nine, three, four, six. That way, you can reach me directly."

"I'd better give you mine," she said.

"I already have it," he answered, laughing. "I'll talk to you later," and rang off.

"He already has my number and assumes I'm free for dinner with him Saturday. He just takes charge."

"Well, you don't mind that, do you?" said Jeanne. "Better that than some wimp that expects you to plan everything! I'll think a take-charge guy is great."

It was a busy week at the hospital with people getting in practice for the big day! Mostly fights and falls due to excess drinking! Kate finished work on Thursday and rushed home to start work on the soda bread. She made eight small loaves. *I hope that will be enough,* she thought. When she had gone over the guest list, out of the twenty, twelve were men, and she knew how much they could eat!

The guests started arriving at seven fifteen and the serving staff took care of drinks. At seven forty five, dinner was served. Heaping platefuls of steaming corned beef surrounded by cabbage, platterfuls of carrots and boiled potatoes, jugs of gravy plus soda bread and pats of butter—a real old country meal. The gravy which Kate made was amazing. The conversation soon ceased, and all that could be heard was the sound of knives and forks scraping on the plates. They decimated the platters. Comments of "This is so wonderful" and "This meat is incredible" went around the table. All the women wanted to know how Kate had cooked the meat and her secret to the gravy. Nick had a grin on his face as they all walked into the living room. He pulled Kate aside and said her cooking was amazing. Irish coffees were being served along with Baileys Irish Cream.

"All I want is a plain cup of coffee with cream," said Kate to a server, but it was Nick that brought it to her.

Jeanne, thinking Nick should have all the help he could get understanding Kate's sometimes volatile Irish ancestry, had bought him the films *The Quiet Man* and *McClintock!* starring John Wayne and Maureen O'Hara. That evening, she gave Nick the heads up that, if he really wanted an insight into Kate, he should watch them. She slipped the DVDs to him as he was leaving, telling him that under no circumstances was he ever to let Kate know what she'd done or that he'd watched them or there would be hell to pay from Kate for both of them! Nick decided that now was as good a time as ever, so when he got home, he settled down to view the movies. *So that's what you're really like,* he thought, *and that seems to be the best way to deal with you! This gets more and more interesting!*

As she was getting dressed for her dinner date with him on Saturday, Kate was wondering where they would go tonight. He knew the real Stockton, all the great mom-and-pop, hole-in-the-wall places. The trendy restaurants and clubs just didn't seem to be his style at all, and she wondered why he went to them. This time, she wore a slim-fitting silk wraparound dress in olive green, red, and gold with a very small paisley design which, with her skin coloring and red hair, made her a real knockout in Jeanne's opinion. High-heeled olive-green suede shoes and matching purse completed her ensemble.

She was putting on her sheepskin jacket as Nick rang the doorbell.

"You never keep a guy waiting," he said as he started up his truck.

"That's army training for you," was her response.

This evening, they drove to a small Italian restaurant, again family owned, where Mama did all the cooking. Nick's eyes opened wide as Kate took off her jacket and he got a good look at her.

"Something wrong?" she asked, unable to read the expression on his face.

"No, nothing," he said, trying to cover up his feelings. She was breathtaking in that dress, but it was too soon, he told himself, too soon to tell her how incredible she is. *I run the risk of scaring her off if I even give her a hint of how I feel,* he told himself.

"The food is all homemade and delicious," he said, trying to bring his thoughts back to the here and now.

"What can I get you to drink?" asked their waiter.

"Do you want your usual, Kate?"

"Yes, please," she answered.

"One diet Sprite with lime and a lite beer," he said. "How about some fried mozzarella sticks?"

"That sounds great."

"Where did you learn to cook the way you did last night?" Nick asked.

"Well, I learnt to cook and bake watching my grandmother, and then, when I lived with my guardians, the kitchen was always my favorite place to hang out, a change from all the studying I had to do."

"Beautiful and can cook," said Nick. Kate just laughed. Their appetizers arrived, and as they ate, they looked at the menu.

"Eggplant parmesan," said Kate.

"Are you sure?" Nick asked, somewhat astonished at her choice.

"I like to order something that I don't normally get at home or is complicated to make, and that fits the bill."

Nick choose the meatballs. The helpings were enormous. They each ate only half of their servings and had the rest put in to-go containers.

They sat and talked about growing up in the valley and how running the family enterprises was all Nick ever wanted to do. When they discovered that he had a photographic memory and she had an eidetic memory, and they couldn't believe it.

Kate could understand why college was not for Nick, and he had insight into her rather lonely life growing up.

"Would you want to be friends with the twelve-year-old know-it-all who was graduating in your high school class?" she asked him, laughing. After that, she was put under the guardianship of a general and his wife in London as she entered medical school—a twelve-year-old medical student! When she was fifteen, she transferred to a British army base teaching hospital in Germany and was under the guardianship of a brigadier general whose wife was Esther's sister. She finished her training and was a fully qualified attending physician at eighteen, which was when she joined the army as a captain, resigning seven years later as a major.

Nick noticed that apart from one mention of watching her grandmother cook, she didn't talk about her family life, so he didn't push it. *When she's ready*, he thought, *she'll open up. But it must have been pretty bad. She doesn't mention her dad when she was a child, only when she's an adult, so obviously, something happened that caused him not to be in the picture then. A lot of hurt in her early life. I'm so blessed to have been raised in a large loving family, and I want to introduce her to that lifestyle. But I realize how slowly I must go. I don't think I have ever met anyone who basically has no one*, he thought to himself.

On Wednesday night, when Kate walked to her car, who should be parked next to it and leaning up against her mini but the man himself! *He really is very ruggedly handsome*, she admitted to herself as she took in his appearance, which included an expensive leather jacket, Stetson, and leather gloves—all items he most always wore. She couldn't help but notice his black hair, which he let grow long in the back in true cowboy style, and twinkling grey eyes. All that plus a killer smile which showed his dimples! *Stop it*, she told herself. *You didn't come here to get involved with a man, no matter how extremely good looking and very charming he is.*

"What are you doing here?" she asked, unable to keep a grin off her face.

"Well, I thought after a tough day at the ER, a plate of fish and chips might make things seem better."

"Fish and chips. Where can you get those?"

"At a little pub I know."

"A British pub? Is there one here in Stockton?"

"Sure is. Are you up for it?"

"Am I! Lead the way."

He led her through a maze of streets until they came to a building with the sign "Kings Head" over the door. They both found parking places and went in together. Kate immediately felt at home. A real British pub. The smell of beer was so familiar. They found a table and sat down. Being mid-week, it wasn't overfull.

"What kind of beer do you recommend I have?" asked Nick.

"Have you ever tried Newcastle Brown Ale? It's a black beer brewed in the city I was born in."

"Okay, I'll try it."

"No, no," said Kate. "I was only joking. It's a heavy black beer, and you normally drink lite beer."

'No, I want to try it."

"Then on your head be it," she said laughing.

He ordered the beer for himself and the usual for her. When the server brought the order, Nick picked up his glass, said, "Cheers," and took a drink. "Wow, that's some beer," he said.

"Please don't feel that you have to drink it on my account," she said, laughing. "May I have a sip?" she asked.

"Of course."

She took a drink. "Just as I remember it."

"Do you want one of your own?"

"No, the reason I don't drink is I never know when I could be called back to the hospital, and you wouldn't want a doctor operating on you or a relative who's been drinking. So it's just easier not to drink at all!"

"When you were in Hawaii?"

"Yes, I had a few drinks, but basically, I'm just as happy with a soda."

Their server came back.

"Fish and chips all round," said Nick.

"My goodness, I feel like I've died and gone to heaven. That was so good," Kate exclaimed as she put down her knife and fork.

"That was good," Nick commented, finishing up his dinner.

"Nick, thank you so much for bringing me here. It was just the lift I needed."

"I'm so glad you enjoyed it, and now you've introduced me to a new beer," he said, finishing up his Newcastle Brown. "It's the perfect beer to go with fish and chips." He settled the bill, and she followed him back to the main road, knowing she'd see him Saturday. Only thing she wondered about, he hadn't made any attempt to kiss her. They had been out on three dates besides the coffee times, and he still hadn't kissed her, not even held her hand! He seemed very comfortable with her when they talked and put his arm around the back of their booth, but not on her! *Well, we'll see what happens Saturday,* she thought. *Perhaps I'll talk to Jeanne and see what she thinks.*

Friday, Kate was looking through her closet, trying to decide what to wear Saturday when Jeanne came into her room carrying a beautiful floral arrangement of wildflowers.

"No need to guess who these are from," the housekeeper said.

"What does the card say?" Kate asked.

"Just says 'Nick.' Well, he certainly doesn't stint on his come-ons, does he? Hang on, someone's at the door. It's a box addressed to you. Oh my goodness, it's a box of Godiva Truffles. Wow, he's certainly upping the ante."

"How does he know that they're my favorites? Have you been talking to him?"

"Well he did ask at the St. Patrick's dinner what kind of chocolates you prefer, and I think I might have mentioned Godiva Truffles to him!"

"So you're where he gets his information from?!"

"Well, what do you want, a bar of Hershey's, no insult intended, or a box of truffles? Someone's got to give him a helping hand!"

"And what else have you told him about me?" demanded Kate.

"I hear the judge calling. I have to go."

"Come back here," demanded Kate.

"Later," replied Jeanne.

Damn, now what else has she said to him about me, thought the good doctor as she went back to scrutinizing her closet.

On Saturday, she decided a jade green silk dress was just the thing to wear to dinner. The dress had no frills, it was the color that seemed to bring out her eyes that did it all. She had bought new black pumps with three-inch heels to go with the dress, which had a slit on one side, preventing her from wearing thigh highs, so she had to buy panty hose, which she rarely wore, in a suntan shade. She wore a hip-length black silk kimono over the dress.

"Well Jeanne honest opinion what do you think?"

"I think if he doesn't make move on you in that outfit, then there's something wrong with him is what I think!"

When they were settled in the Land Rover, Nick couldn't help but notice the slit which was on her left side. A glance down gave him a good view of a very shapely thigh!

"How about we go to a little French restaurant I know?" he asked.

"Sounds good," she responded. They chatted about the local news as they drove, and like all the places Nick took her to, she was immediately lost in a maze of unfamiliar streets. They pulled up outside a doorway with a canopy over the door which simply said "Paul's." A valet helped her out of the truck, and they went into a low-lit bar. Again, Nick was greeted by the owner himself, Paul.

"A table for two immediately," Paul told the head waiter, and they were escorted past a piano bar and a small dance floor to a back booth.

She took off the kimono, and their server immediately took it away to be hung up. She missed Nick's expression as he got a good look at the jade dress and her in it!

Kate ordered her usual, and Nick got a glass of the house red, explaining it was from Barkley vineyards. Paul came over to chat and was exceedingly charming, kissing Kate's hand and then sent over a plate of *hors d'oeuvres*.

"What a lovely restaurant this is, Nick," Kate said.

"And not a gossip columnist in sight," he countered. "I'm sure you were warned about being seen with me."

"Well, some things were said, and what's this about pumping our housekeeper for information about me."

"I guess that makes us equal." He laughed.

A piano player sat down at the keyboard. "Gus is the best kept secret in town," Nick told her. "He also plays requests. I sometimes come here to unwind and just sit at the piano bar for an hour. He plays some very good jazz at times."

"Your job is very stressful, isn't it?" Kate asked him.

"That's why they pay me the big bucks," he joked.

"No, I'm serious," she countered.

"Sometimes," he said. "I just need a change of scene."

They sat in silence, enjoying the *hors d'oeuvres* and listening to the music.

"Would you like to dance?" Nick asked her.

"Yes, that would be nice," she answered.

He slid out of the booth and held out his hand as she stood up. She took it, and they walked hand in hand onto the dance floor where two other couples were swaying in time to the music. He held her close, inhaling her wonderful perfume. He'd have to ask Jeanne what it was. She didn't seem to mind being held close and followed his every move. Either she was a natural at dancing, or someone had taught her very well. They danced through two songs, and then he suggested they go order dinner. As they walked back to their booth, Nick kept his hand in the small of her back.

Lord, she thought. *I could get used to this, but am I ready for a serious dating relationship?* They sat down and picked up the menus. One thing Kate had noticed was the beautiful suit Nick was wearing. It screamed a bespoke tailor. Even his shirt looked very expensive, with French cuffs, beautifully etched gold cufflinks, a silk tie, and his watch—a Rolex. *The man sure pulled out all the stops tonight,* she thought. *Wonder why?*

"Oh," Kate said.

"What?" Nick asked.

"Would it be really awful to be out with a cattle rancher and order lamb?" she asked.

He burst out laughing. "Order whatever you want. Just don't ever tell anybody," he countered.

He ordered steak, of course, and she the lamb chops. "Well done!"

He raised his eyebrows.

"I'm English," she said by way of an explanation.

"You're the one eating them," he said.

They were having their entrees when Paul stopped by to see how everything was.

"Wonderful," said Nick.

"Out of this world," said Kate.

"You must be sure to bring the doctor back again, Mr. Nick," Paul said.

"I intend to," he replied.

"How about I send someone over to make *crepe suzette* for dessert?"

"How would you like that, Kate?"

"I'd love it."

"Then send him over, Paul."

"Half the fun of that dessert is watching them make it." Laughed Kate. They slowly ate their delicious dessert and sipped coffee.

"How about another dance?" said Nick when Kate returned from the ladies' room.

"That's a good idea."

As they walked toward the dance floor, Nick stopped at the piano bar and gave Gus a note and bank note. Then he joined Kate and they began dancing. The next song Gus played, Nick hummed very softly.

"That's from *South Pacific* isn't it? Some Enchanted Evening?" she asked.

"Yes," Nick told her. "It's a very special song to me."

It dawned on her that Nick must have requested Gus to play it. *Why does it mean so much to Nick?* she thought. *Does it have something to do with me? It must, otherwise why request it? I'll have to think about that later.* They finished dancing and sat down. Their server brought them fresh coffee. Just then, Gus came over on his break.

"Is there anything the young lady would like me to play?"

"No, just surprise me."

57

"You from England?"

"Yes, I am."

"And out with Mr. Barkley?"

"Yes."

"Then I know just the song for you. It will be the first one I play when I go back. I'll even sing it for Mr. Barkley's benefit."

Nick slipped him a bank note as Gus went back to the piano a few minutes later.

"We'd better dance to this because he doesn't usually sing."

"Okay, it's one way to work off all the calories I've consumed tonight!"

They walked toward the dance floor as Gus played the opening bars of the song. Kate burst into laughter.

"He's got quite a sense of humor has your Gus."

"Why?" said Nick. "What's the song?"

"Listen," she said.

> That certain night
> The night we met
> There was magic abroad in the air
> There were angels dining at the Ritz
> And a nightingale sang in Berkley Square
> I may be right I may be wrong
> But I'm perfectly willing to swear
> That when you turned and smiled at me
> A nightingale sang in Berkley Square
> The moon that lingered over London town
> Poor puzzled moon he wore a frown
> How could he know we two were so in love?
> The whole damned world seemed upside down
> The streets of town were paved with stars
> It was such a romantic affair
> And as we kissed and said goodnight
> A nightingale sang in Berkley Square
> When dawn came streaming up all golden blue
> To interrupt our rendezvous

I still remember how you turned to me and said
Was that a dream or was it true?
Our homeward steps were just as light
As the tap dancing feet of Astaire
And like an echo far away
A nightingale sang in Berkley Square
I know 'cos I was there that night in Berkley
Square

"'A Nightingale Sang in Berkley Square' is a British WWII song, except Barkley is spelt *Ber*. Yes, you are right. Gus is having fun with us!"

"He has a bigger sense of humor than you know," said Nick. They danced to another couple of songs and then finished up their coffee.

"I think it's time I went home, Nick," Kate said, trying to cover up a yawn. She went to the cloakroom to get her kimono, and Nick had a few words with Paul. Their truck was at the door when they stepped into the cold night air.

"You'll be home in fifteen minutes," Nick told her.

"I'm fine. The night air is waking me up." Again, she lost track of the streets they took until they turned onto hers. Nick pulled into the driveway and put the truck in park, jumped out, came around, opened the door, and helped her out. They walked to the front door with his arm around her shoulders. At the door, before she could open it, he took her in his arms, kissed her softly on the lips, whispered goodnight, opened the door, and gently pushed her inside, closed it, and was gone.

Kate was standing in the foyer, not sure of what had just happened. Jeanne came out of the darkened living room. "Well, he finally got around to it," she blurted out.

"Were you watching?"

"Of course I was. Somebody's gotta keep an eye on you!"

"Jeanne, for the last seven years, I was in the army under fire and all kinds of things I'm not at liberty to discuss!"

"Doesn't mean you know diddly about men," countered the housekeeper.

"What am I going to do with you?" said Dr. Warner.

"Well, let's go to your room before you have the judge and Esther in on this conversation." They went upstairs. "Do you want some coffee?" asked Jeanne.

"No, but a cup of tea would be wonderful."

"I'll make it. You get ready for bed."

When Jeanne came back in the room Kate had on her PJs and robe, her dress was hanging up, and her bra and panties were lying on a chair. Jeanne's eyebrows rose. "If that man only knew the kind of lingerie you wear, he'd have you in bed so fast it'd make your head spin!"

"I can't believe the things you say!"

Kate told her about Gus playing "Enchanted Evening" for Nick and "Nightingale" for her. "That piano player knows more than all of us! Think back, Kate. What happened the night you met Nick?"

"'Enchanted Evening' must have been the song they were playing when we met!"

"What happened then?" asked her friend.

"Well, it was kind of strange, Nick had his back to us when Mrs. Barkley started to introduce us. He turned around, we both put out our hands to shake, and we just looked at each other, and it was like we both froze. It was kind of embarrassing. Mrs. Barkley had to step in and cover the situation. She had to hustle me away to meet some other people."

"Are you just now telling me it was love at first sight?" said an exasperated Jeanne.

"I wouldn't say that," countered Kate.

"I would. That makes this whole relationship easier to understand."

"There really isn't much of a relationship," said Kate.

"Darlin', you can't see what's right in front of you. The man is in love with you and doesn't know what to do about it."

"No, you're wrong. This is just a casual dating relationship."

"Okay, have it your way. Time will tell."

Chapter 6

Kate pushed the whole conversation to the back of her mind, convinced Jeanne was reading way too much into it. Meanwhile, Nick was checking on the progress of the apartment conversion. The guest bedrooms were finished, and he had the furniture that had been in them put back. He enlisted Victoria's help in buying new bed linens.

"What's her favorite color?" asked his mother.

"Green," he answered, without even having to think. "And she likes something called a duvet instead of blankets. Jeanne told me."

"It must be handy having a direct line like Jeanne to her," said Victoria. She chose pale green sheets, queen for one bedroom, and four sets of twins for the two bedrooms that shared a bathroom. Medium weight duvets and green silk covers and shams for them all. She picked up new accessories for the two bathrooms, and those rooms were finished. Nick had instructed her that she chose the top of the line appliances washer, dryer, fridge, etc. She had a fun day picking them out for what she hoped would be her daughter-in-law. *Nick*, she thought to herself, *if this doesn't work out, you are going to be devastated. Please, God, let this relationship be right for them both.*

The furniture, their bedding, all the things needed for the kitchen, china, glassware, etc. would be Kate's choice, Nick told his mother.

"Once you are engaged, you can register for all the things you need," Victoria explained to her son.

"Whatever she wants to do," said Nick.

"When are you seeing her again?" his mother asked.

"Well, Saturday, but I'm having dinner with Robert Ito and his wife on Friday, and I'm going to call Kate and ask her if she'd like to go along." When he asked Kate, she was a little hesitant, but Nick explained if he and Robert talked business, it would be nice if Nancy had someone who "You know what I mean," he said. "Could talk girl type talk to."

Kate laughed. "In that case, I'd love to come."

"Okay, I'll pick you up about seven thirty, and I'll have the Itos with me. We can go to Paul's again if that's all right with you."

"Sounds marvelous. One thing, how dressy will this be?"

"Whatever you choose to wear will be great. You always look so beautiful," he told her before ringing off.

The Itos were native Hawaiians of Japanese descent. When they heard she had been in their beloved islands just a few weeks earlier—that really broke the ice. Paul was his charming self, treating the foursome like royalty. Nick and Robert discussed some business, and it was obvious that not only did they do successful business deals together but genuinely liked each other.

Kate and Nancy chattered away about Hawaii and, of course, fashion! After dinner, during a visit to the ladies' room, Nancy asked Kate if she and Nick had been dating long and was surprised to find it was just short time. "Well, he's obviously head over heels about you," remarked Nancy. Kate passed no comment, and when they joined the men, Nick asked her to dance.

"Thank you so much for this evening," he said. "You coming along made all the difference."

"I have enjoyed myself," she said. "They're a delightful couple."

"I do quite a bit of business with Robert," Nick told her. "But I have a feeling after tonight, we'll be doing even more!"

When they pulled up at the judge's house, Nick walked her to the door. "Thank you again Kate for a wonderfully successful evening."

"My pleasure," she said, giving him a big smile. This time, the goodnight kiss lasted longer but was still just a light touch of his lips on hers, nothing more.

"See you tomorrow," he said and kissed her again, this time on the cheek.

When he got back in the truck, Nancy said, "That young woman is a definite keeper."

"Don't I know it," he replied with a grin.

Saturday, they went back to the Mexican restaurant where they'd had their first real date. Kate had counted this was only the sixth date, but it felt so felt so easy and comfortable being with him they might have been seeing each other for months.

This time, the weather was mild enough to sit on the patio. She had chosen a green leather skirt and matching lightweight sweater.

"I know I should try something different," she said. "But the *chile relleno* was so good the last time that I'm going to have it again!" They had just put in their order when Kate's phone started "blowing up." "Uh-oh," she said. "That's not good. Dr. Warner," she said, answering it. She listened for a few minutes and then said, "I'll be there as soon as possible." Disconnecting, she turned to Nick and said, "I'm so sorry, but they are at code black, and I have to go in."

"No problem," he answered. He called Pepe over quickly, explained the situation, and within minutes, they were speeding toward the hospital.

"April fool's day gone nuts," she explained. "It happens every year. People dare each other to do crazy things, mix that with alcohol, and they end up in the ER. Even in the army, it would happen!"

Nick leaned over and took her hand. "Don't worry about it. Let's go to the pub on Wednesday to make up for it. Get a ride to work, and I'll pick you up there at seven."

"Sounds great," she said.

He kissed her hand and let her go, watching as she disappeared into the brightly lit, packed ER. He was disappointed, he had to admit. He had been looking forward to spending the evening with her.

Victoria was curled up in the living room, reading a book, when he got home. "You're in early," she remarked, and he told her about the code black. "That's a tough job she has," his mother said. "Knowing she can be called out at any time, are you sure you can live with that?"

"It's a small price to pay. I have some paperwork that I can do. Good night, Mother."

True to his word, Nick was leaning against his truck when Kate left the hospital Wednesday night. He came toward her and gave her a quick kiss as he walked her to the passenger side.

"Ready for some fish and chips?" he asked.

"Am I ever, we never stopped all day," she told him. "I don't know how many cups of coffee I left lying around. I've been looking forward to this all day," she told him. "I grabbed my things and dashed out as soon as it reached seven before anyone else came in!"

She was surprised when Nick ordered a Newcastle Brown Ale for himself. "Can I have a cup of tea?" she asked the waiter.

"Of course, tea for one," he said.

Nick was happy to tell her that he and Robert Ito were going to do much more business together.

"That's wonderful," said Kate as she poured herself a "cuppa."

"I owe it all to you," said Nick.

"I didn't do anything. Just had a good time chatting with Nancy. I liked her."

"Well, I don't know what you said, but I do know she has a lot to do with her husband's company, and her good opinion goes a long way, so here's to you," he said as he raised his beer glass and clinked with her tea cup. They both laughed and talked about the Itos and what the new contract would mean to the Barkley companies. "With Robert now more involved, it'll mean a lot less work and travel for me, so thank you," he told her.

"I was glad to help, and lightening your workload is good news. I know how hard you really work," she said.

As they left the pub, they walked hand in hand to his truck. Before he opened the door, he gave her repeated short kisses on the lips.

"I have a cattlemen's association meeting on Friday night that I must go to," he told her. "But are we on for dinner Saturday?"

"Yes," she said with a smile.

"By the way, April sixteenth is my mother's birthday, and we'll be throwing a big party. It's a black-tie event," he told her. "It starts at seven thirty, so I'll pick you up about seven fifteen."

"No, don't do that, Nick. You must obviously be one of the hosts, so I'll just drive myself over. What day is that?" she asked suddenly.

"A Wednesday."

"That means I'm working until seven, so I'll take a change of clothes with me and get ready in the office. I'll be there as soon as I can."

She told Jeanne about the party, and as expected, her first question was "What you are going to wear?" Kate reached into the back of her closet and pulled out a garment bag.

"I bought this in New York for a Christmas party," she said. What she showed her almost took Jeanne's breath away. It was a red dress of some silky type material that made it hang beautifully. It had a bare shoulder and was hung in the front with inch-long beads and had sequins all over that shimmered, reflecting the light. The dress was obviously very short, and the three-inch strappy sandals and clutch were a perfect match to it.

"My goodness, it's beautiful," said Jeanne. "You can tell this is not a small-town dress. This is a big city or European number. You'll be the belle of the ball."

"You don't think it's too much?" worried Kate.

"Of course not. It's just what the situation demands."

"What situation?" Kate asked.

"You know, for someone with your IQ, you are really dumb when it comes to some things! Just trust me, Mr. Barkley is going to get his mind blown! Do you want me to come to the hospital to help you get dressed?"

"No, I think I can manage," Kate replied.

I'll be there whether you like it or not, thought her friend.

On Saturday night, Nick and Kate went back to Jose's, and this time no code black interrupted their evening. After they had dinner, they sat on the patio, and Nick enjoyed a brandy with his cigar, loving the fact she didn't mind in the least him relaxing like that. Most

65

women in his past had wrinkled their noses at the odor or given him a lecture on the evils of smoking. Yet here was a doctor who actually enjoyed the smell of tobacco. *Thank goodness her father had smoked a pipe*, he thought.

After he finished his brandy, he leaned over and took her hand. She made no attempt to pull away. Instead, she put her feet up on a chair and also leaned back, as relaxed as he was.

"Hey," he suddenly said. "I completely forgot I promised to take you shooting. Why didn't you remind me?"

"Well, we've both been busy, and I just figured you'd get around to it eventually."

"I'm so sorry. When I get home, I'm going to check my schedule and then call you, and we'll fix up a time. I want to see how good British army training is."

"Not so fast. I wasn't in the infantry, I'm medical doctor. We weren't expected to have the same scores as them."

"I hope you're not trying to chicken out," Nick said teasingly.

"Not on your life, Nick Barkley. Bring it on!"

They chatted a little more but mostly just sat hand in hand, enjoying each other's company. Finally, Jose came out and said, "Mr. Barkley, I'm sorry, but we are closing."

"What time is it?" asked Kate.

"Midnight."

"My goodness, we've been here for hours," she exclaimed.

They walked to the truck—the valet had already gone home—with their arms around each other. When Nick walked Kate to her front door, he said, "Thank you for the most perfect evening."

"It was, wasn't it?" she replied. He pulled her close as she put her arms around his neck. They stayed like that for a minute, neither saying a word, just holding onto each other, both knowing their relationship had undergone a change that evening.

"MOTHER!" yelled Nick when he got home.

"Nick, stop yelling," said his exasperated mother. "You'll wake up the whole house. What's wrong?"

"WRONG? Wrong? Nothing's wrong. I've just spent the most perfect evening of my life, and she felt the same way!!!"

"Really, she told you that?" asked Victoria.

"Yes, she did. She did!!! Oh, Mother, it's all working out."

"Now, Nick, calm down, calm down. You've a ways to go from a perfect evening to the altar."

"Yes, we have, but the path is getting SHORTER EVERY DAY," he countered. He ran up the stairs two at a time.

That young man is going to find it hard to sleep tonight, thought Victoria!

Friday night, Nick had promised Kate that they'd go out for Italian food, but on the way, he got a call that one of his mares had started to foal.

"I need to be there," he explained to Kate.

"That's fine," she assured him. "Our jobs interfere with our social life occasionally, and we both know that," she said as he turned the truck around to take her back home.

"Unless you'd like to come?" he said.

"I wouldn't get in the way?" she asked.

"No. I'll show you where to sit so you can see but be out of the way, and you've got pants on, so you're dressed for it." Kate had chosen to wear a pair of slacks, ankle boots, and a shirt with a matching sleeveless cardigan.

"Well, if you're sure I won't be in the way, I'd love to come. I've seen plenty of human births but never a mare foaling."

They went into the stables, and she sat where he showed her. Nick said to Kate, "You could try talking to her. She's frightened, and anything to help calm her would be great."

Kate moved a little closer and started to talk in a soft gentle voice to the scared mare. After a few minutes, to Nick's surprise, the mare turned her head toward Kate and was listening to her soothing voice.

"That's a good girl. You're doing just fine," Kate said. The mare, Cedarbalm, whined softly, and Kate continued to talk to her in the same vein.

After nearly two hours, a beautiful colt was staggering around on its shaky legs. "You did a wonderful job," Nick told her. "You calmed her right down."

"I just said to her what I'd say to a woman in labor."

"Well, it worked, and for that, you get to name the colt."

"ME?" she said, obviously surprised. "I don't know anything about naming horses."

"You can call him whatever you want," Nick told her.

"Any name?" she asked.

"Sure, what do you have in mind?"

"How about Jack, or is that too ordinary?"

"No, Jack it is."

"Really?"

"Really, you've named your first colt. Now let's give them some peace and quiet and see what we can find to eat up at the house. Ciego will keep an eye on them."

Victoria met them as they went in. "Well, how did it go?" she asked.

"Cedarbalm has a colt which Kate named Jack," Nick told her. "And we are starving. Silas, can you find us something to eat? Sandwiches would be fine, and make us some coffee please?"

"Could I wash up?" asked Kate.

"Here, I'll show you the restroom," said Victoria.

Kate cleaned up and joined the others in the living room. Audra wanted to see the colt, but Nick said, "No, leave it until tomorrow. Let them both rest tonight." She didn't argue with him; his word was the final authority on all ranch matters. Soon, Silas arrived carrying a platter of sandwiches and pieces of cake. A pot of fresh coffee soon followed.

"Is this the first foal you've seen born?" asked Victoria.

"Yes, it was," answered Kate.

"And she was just wonderful," interjected Nick, the pride in his voice obvious. "She said all the right things and kept Cedarbalm calm," he told everyone. Just then, Silas came in with champagne and poured a glass for everyone, including Heath who had just arrived. Silas hesitated when he came to Kate. "A small glass," she said. "I must join in the toast, and coffee just won't cut it!"

When they all had a glass, Nick raised his and said, "To Jack," and everyone joined in.

"To Jack."

Kate finished her glass and had a slice of cake with a fresh cup of coffee.

"Have you had enough to eat?" asked Victoria.

"Yes, I'm fine, thank you," she answered.

They continued to chat, then Nick said, "I'd better get you home." She gathered up her things, and they headed out into the night. They were silent, both lost in their own thoughts as they drove back to her home.

"I could pick you up early and take you to see Jack some night before we go out to dinner," offered Nick.

"Would you?" she answered. "I was wondering when I would see him again."

"You can stop by whenever you want to," Nick told her.

"That's quite an honor to name a foal," said Jeanne, who had lived in small western towns all her life.

"Not just anyone gets to do that!"

"Jeanne, I'm starting to get worried about where this relationship is going. I came here to do a very difficult job—help take the ER to a level one trauma unit. I can't let anything or anyone get in the way of that. It's what I've worked for my whole life."

"And what about you? Don't you deserve some happiness outside of work?"

"I've never thought about it. Work is all I've ever known."

"Well, if you don't stop and look around, you're going to let the best thing that's ever happened to you get away."

"But Nick deserves more than I can give him," said Kate. "I honestly believe that, in a committed relationship, the other person has priority. Their wants, needs, and desires are paramount, and I don't think I'm capable of doing that. For me, work has always come first."

"I wouldn't worry about that. Nick is no fool. He's been around, and he's well aware of what he's getting into with you, and it hasn't deterred him yet, has it?"

"Lord, what have I gotten myself into? I should never have started dating him. But I never would have guessed it could ever get serious."

"Don't decide anything now. Give yourself a chance to really think it through. Leave it 'til after the birthday party, and when you see him Friday, be honest with him. Tell him what you've told me and see what he says!"

"Good advice," said Kate.

It was Sunday and time to get ready for the ride Nick was taking her on that afternoon. She drove over to the ranch and parked by the stables. Nick was waiting for her and laughed softly when she got out of the car.

"What's funny?" she inquired.

"You couldn't look more British if you'd tried," he told her, chuckling.

"What do you mean?"

"You're wearing English-style riding breeches and boots, a polo shirt, and cap. Round here, we're used to seeing jeans, western boots, shirt, a neckerchief, and Stetson!"

"Does that mean you don't want to be seen with me?" she asked him teasingly.

"Not at all, but I put a western saddle on your horse. Can you handle that?"

'Of course," she told him. "When I rode in the Middle East, that's all they had. What are the names of the horses we'll be riding?"

"My horse is Big Duke, who's a cutting horse that I broke myself. The one I used to ride and have had for twenty-two years is CoCo, but I had to put him out to pasture. I still miss the old boy. The one you'll be using is Jingo. He's from some of the best bloodlines we have."

"That is one gorgeous black saddle you have there, Nick. It's so unusual. Where on earth did you get it?"

"Believe it or not, I won it in a poker game from an attorney named Clay Culhane, who was passing through Stockton. Oh, it must have been five years ago now. It's one of my most prized possessions.

70

"I can understand why," Kate replied.

"I have never seen another like it in my life. I keep it locked up in a special area in one of the tack rooms, and god help anyone who touches it. John McIntire is the only one other than myself allowed to handle it. I take care of it myself, and the black leather is in better condition now than when I got it!"

They mounted up and rode off, Nick keeping a watchful eye on her 'til he was sure she was competent in the saddle. As soon as he was comfortable Kate could handle her horse, they broke into a short gallop. After riding for about thirty minutes, they took a break and sat down by a stream and let their horses have a breather. She talked about her riding experience in Afghanistan and how, on her travels, she had ridden a camel, donkey and, even once, an elephant! Making him laugh when she told him how bad-tempered camels can be.

He, on the other hand, explained to Kate about his experiences saddle breaking horses.

"Isn't that dangerous?" she asked him.

"Well, I suppose it is, but if that's all you've ever known, you don't think about any risks. If I'm going to ride a horse, then I'm the one who is going to break and train it. That way, we get to know each other from the beginning. Trust is everything between rider and horse, but I'm sure you know that already."

They went on talking, but two things happened. The first was when Nick was looking at Kate, trying to work out if she really was so oblivious to the way he felt about her as she seemed, and he didn't cover his puzzled expression quite fast enough. She caught sight of the look on his face, and she didn't understand why it was there. The second, she glanced over at him as she was chatting and found him looking at her, showing the deep feelings he felt for her on his face! She was obviously startled, but it was almost as though they were hypnotized by each other and neither could look away. He started to take a step toward her, but his phone rang, breaking the spell they were both under. It was his ranch foreman, John McIntire, and Nick had to take the call. By the time he'd finished talking, Kate had herself well under control. He tried to initiate a serious conversation with her, but she headed him off, saying she couldn't spend any more time with him because she had things to take care at the house and should be getting back. Rather reluctantly, Nick led the way home, both silent until they reached the stables where he told Kate he'd take care of unsaddling her horse. All she said was "Thank you for the ride" and "She'd see him later." She, unfortunately, made it rather obvious that she couldn't leave the ranch fast enough!

Hell, Nick thought to himself. *Why did John have to call at just that time?* It completely spoiled the moment for Kate and himself. He had been going to take her in his arms and kiss her the way he'd wanted to do since the night they'd met. Lots of tongue action, whether she was ready for that or not. At this point, he couldn't have cared less. *I can't go on pretending that this is some kind of friend-only relationship!* All he wanted to do after kissing her was take her to bed and make love to the woman he wanted to spend the rest his life with the way she deserves and the way he was sure, with his considerable experience, he could bring her nothing but pleasure. But now, he was afraid she might not even come to the party! Kate had said that she'd see him later, but when later? Damn and blast, he'd have to wait until Wednesday to find out how much damage, if any, that phone call had made. But he'd made up his mind to send flowers to her tomorrow. *Please, God, let her come to mother's party. Don't let her try to run from me, not now! These days are gonna be the longest three days of my life. But I'd better not try to crowd her just stay out of the way until Wednesday.*

Kate was shaking by the time she got home. Jeanne was in the hallway when Kate walked in the door.

"You're home early, aren't you? What's wrong? You don't look so good? Don't tell me you two had a fight?"

"No, Jeanne it's nothing like that. Make me a cup of tea and I'll tell you all about it. I could use some good advice. I think I'm in more trouble than I thought possible!"

By the time Jeanne walked through Kate's bedroom door, the doctor had changed putting her PJs and robe on.

"Okay, tell me what's been going on?" Jeanne asked.

So Kate told her friend everything that had happened.

"He had his head tilted slightly on one side and was looking at me with this puzzled expression on his face. I just didn't understand it! And then we were just chatting, and I glanced over at him. Jeanne you should have seen the look on his face! I know I wasn't meant to see it, or maybe I was! I'm so mixed up. This is why I stay away from serious relationships. I can't read what's going on right under my nose! I think you were right all along, and he cares for me more than I ever realized! I don't know how to handle this! Oh God, what am I going to do? Well, for sure I'm not going to that party on Wednesday! I've got to stay the hell away from him until I figure out what to do next!"

"Calm down, just calm down! First, I think the puzzled look you saw was him trying to work out if you are really as dense as you seem to be, and the answer is YES! You have an IQ that is out in the stratosphere, you're a world traveler, a medical doctor, and you're dumber than shit when it comes to men and affairs of the heart! How you can be twenty-five, a member of Her Majesty's forces, a major no less, and be as dumb as you are beats the hell out of me! What kind of men did you serve with? I mean, were they a bunch of eunuchs or what? Just how many men have you dated anyway?"

"Er…um…not that many!"

"Well, no shit! That's not exactly a big surprise! I know you're a doctor, but you do know all about the birds and the bees?"

"Jeanne! Of course I do!"

"I'm just asking! With you, it's always good to double check! Now, here's what you're gonna do. First, you are going to Mrs. Barkley's birthday party. And before you object, here's why. You told Nick you would. When he asked you to go, you said yes. In other words, you gave him your word, and it's unacceptable in my book for a real lady not keep her word unless she's at death's door, which you're not! Besides, how often do you get a chance to get all gussied up and wear something as gorgeous as that knockout red dress? Next, you are not going to avoid Nick. You'll see him Wednesday and then you're scheduled to have dinner with him Friday right? So when he picks you up on Friday, tell him that before you guys go eat, you need to talk to him. He'll know of a quiet place where you guys can be alone,

73

and then tell him the truth. That you're dumber than a fencepost and you had no idea what's been going on right under your nose, and now that you do, HELP! Trust me, he'll take it from there!"

"Jeanne, I can't do all that!"

"Why in the hell not?"

"Um…er…I just can't say stuff like to him."

"Kate, suck it up. Put your big girl panties on and start acting like an adult, not some silly teenager!"

"Yes, ma'am! I'll go to the party and then I'll do my best to talk with him on Friday, just like you said. Thank you for your help. I've had sergeant majors and drill sergeants who were easier on me than you!"

Chapter 7

Just my luck, thought Kate, as seven p.m. the night of the sixteenth had come and gone. They were slammed in the ER, and she couldn't walk away. Jeanne had arrived about six thirty to help her get ready. Although she'd said she could manage alone, she was secretly rather glad of the help. *At this rate, I'm not even going to get there*, she thought. But around eight thirty, things slacked off, and she went into the office and started to get changed, praying that, whatever came in, the night shift could cope with. Jeanne zipped her dress up and stood back to admire the finished effect.

"You look awesome," she told Kate as she surveyed the sparkles Kate had sprayed into her hair, to the glittering earrings, the knockout short dress, down to the sparkling high-heeled sandals. "Now hurry up and get out of here." Kate slipped on her black silk evening kimono and hurried out the side door, leaving Jeanne to tidy up the office.

She clutched the small gift-wrapped box containing Victoria Barkley's birthday present in her hand. It was a little after nine fifteen when she reached the ranch house, which was ablaze with lights. One of the ranch hands helped her out of the mini, and hurrying inside, she shed the kimono.

"WOW," said Jarrod, whistling softly.

"What?" said Nick, turning around. What he saw made him inhale deeply. Kate was standing in the foyer and looking more beautiful than he could have imagined possible. She was handing Silas the small package to put with all the other gifts Victoria had received and were piled on the foyer table waiting to be opened. Nick crossed the living room and reached her just as his mother noticed her arrival.

He hugged her and whispered, "You look stunning," before stepping aside to allow his mother to greet her.

"I'm sorry to be so late, Mrs. Barkley, but happy birthday."

"My dear, don't worry about the time. I'm just glad, as I'm sure Nick is, that you could make it. I must tell you how beautiful you look. Now I know Nick will look after you whilst I say hello to some other latecomers." It was, in fact, the governor and his wife who had just arrived.

Later, Audra said to her mother, "Isn't Kate's dress fabulous? It just screams New York, London, or Paris."

"Yes," said her mother. "That frock definitely wasn't purchased in Stockton!"

Silas had made sure Kate had her favorite Sprite with lime, and Nick asked if she wanted something to eat.

"Not right now, I had a late lunch," she told him.

"Then how about we dance?" he asked.

"I'd like to," she said. As they started to dance, what should the band begin to play and sing but "The Lady In Red."

"Did you request that?" Kate asked Nick.

"Indeed I did!" he answered. "That was the song we first danced to at the Valentine benefit." *He puts on a tough front but he's very romantic underneath*, she thought. They danced oh so close for a while, and for the first time, he wrapped her right hand with his left and held it to his chest. He glanced at her, but she showed no signs of objecting to the change in the way he was holding her. He knew that he couldn't go on with the pretense any longer, so he suggested they go outside to get some air.

They walked to a secluded area of the garden, and suddenly she was in his arms, being kissed so passionately yet so tenderly, unlike any way she'd ever been kissed before! Little by little, she melted completely into his arms, wrapping hers around his neck and slowly massaging his neck with the tips of her fingers. His tongue gently and hungrily sought hers as she gradually opened her mouth wider and wider, allowing him to probe until he found what he had been searching for. Then, tentatively, she put her own tongue into his open mouth. She heard Nick give a kind of low moan. This was what he'd hoped and waited for since they'd met in December, and was, in his opinion, well overdue! Once started, it was like a dam broke for both, and they hungrily continued to kiss each other on the mouth, face, neck, and back to their mouths. He couldn't believe what passions had been released in her in just the matter of a couple of moments more than he would have dared imagine possible. They just got lost in each other! He was holding her so tight that they eventually had to move slightly apart as they virtually gasped for air! They just stood there, arms entwined around the body of the other, each with their foreheads resting on the other. Both stunned at the intensity of the embrace. *Oh God, help me*, she thought. *What just happened?!*

"Nick, Nick," they heard Audra calling. "Where are you?"

The spell was broken. "Damn! What do you want?!" Nick asked tersely.

"There you are. I've been looking all over for you. Mother is going to cut her cake and open the gifts, and she wants you to be there."

"Hell and damnation," said Nick under his breath.

Kate gave a sort of nervous laugh. "Don't worry, you're a host, and you should be there."

"Come on, Nick. Mother's waiting," insisted Audra.

Kate started to walk in with Nick, his hand staying on the small of her back. They went back into the living room where Victoria was in the process of cutting her cake. She glanced up. *Oh*, she thought. *Nick doesn't look very happy. Why do I think Audra just interrupted something very important to him.*

After making the initial cut, she left it up to Silas and his staff to serve the cake and went over to the table where the gifts had been set up. Her guests, cake in hand, gathered around as she started to open her beautifully wrapped packages. She saw that Nick had passed on cake—a first for him—to stand with him arms around Kate's waist. *How very cozy*, she thought as she picked up the first present and read aloud the tag. Victoria worked her way through the pile coming to the small package Dr. Warner had brought.

"Happy birthday, best wishes, Kate Warner," she read aloud. When she opened it, she gave a little gasp. It was the most beautiful miniature horse about three inches in length and five inches tall, made of some kind of metal that shimmered in the light with bright dancing colors. Even the legs, which were made from highly polished nails that also reflected colors. "It's exquisite," Victoria said, hugging Kate. "Thank you, thank you so very much, my dear. I have never seen anything quite like it before, and I'll treasure it always! The detail on this piece is amazing."

Nick was very impressed when he got a good look at it.

"She loves anything to do with horses," Nick murmured to Kate. "You couldn't have made a better choice. May I ask where you found it?"

"I saw it in the New York Museum catalog the day after you invited me. So I called them and had it shipped to me overnight."

He continued to stand behind her, occasionally kissing her neck, which she was obviously not objecting to! In between opening the rest of her gifts, Victoria observed them. *Well*, she thought. *Things have certainly advanced. I wonder what has happened to bring about such a change.* After the last gift was opened coffee and more cake was served, this time, Nick got a slice and shared it with Kate by feeding her a small piece off his pastry fork every now and then. *Cozier and cozier*, thought his mother.

"Do you want a fresh drink?" Nick asked Kate.

"Yes, please," she answered.

"Just wait here and I'll get you one." He left her to go into the library where the bar had been set up. It was crowded with people so he was forced to wait his turn.

Meanwhile, the band was about to play another song when a guest came toward Kate. She saw him coming, weaving his way toward her. *Oh no*, she thought. *Just what I don't want to deal with, some inebriated guy!* He stood in front of her and, in a slightly slurred voice, asked her to dance.

"Thank you for the offer," she replied, "but I'm waiting for my date to bring me a drink."

"Your date, Nick Barkley?"

"As a matter of fact, it is. Why do you ask?"

78

"Think you're too good to dance with the rest of us just 'cos Nick Barkley's f—ing you? Everybody in the room knows he's been bedding you for weeks! You must be a real good lay 'cos he's been screwing you for ages! He doesn't usually stay with a woman more than two to three weeks, so you must be really hot stuff in the sack!" The things he continued to yell about her were much more vulgar and explicit.

Whilst he continued to spew his venom at Kate, the rest of the guests were standing around, listening to it in shock and horror! Jarrod and Heath, who weren't even in the room when this all started, were alerted to it by Eugene whilst Nick was told by John McIntire! Nick came running back in time to hear Kate being referred to as "Nick Barkley's whore." He launched himself at the drunken guest, recognizing him as a man he'd known since childhood. Nick was so incensed by what he'd heard Kate being called that he was on top of Mike Richards, punching the living daylights out of him, and it took the combined efforts of Eugene, Jarrod, and Heath to pull him off!! John and Mike's father, plus another guest, dragged the drunken man outside before Nick could break free and attack him again. Between them John, the guest and Mike's parents got him into the family car and drove away. Calming down, Nick looked around for Kate, only to be told by his mother that as he'd started to attack her abuser, she'd run out of the door. Nick dashed outside and was informed by the hands, who were doubling as valets, that she'd grabbed her car keys and asked where her car was. Being one of the last guests to arrive, her car was parked nearby. She'd run off to it, and to quote one of the hands, "Took off like a bat out of hell."

"Hell and damnation!" yelled Nick!

Going back inside, he found that his brothers had talked to their guests and tried to smooth things over, got the band to start and play, and generally tried to pick up the pieces of their mother's party. Nick pulled his foreman aside and asked him exactly what had happened and what had been said.

"I heard all of it, and you're not gonna like it, Nick."

"I want to know every word that was said to Kate."

So John told him all that had happened and exactly what Mike had shouted in front of everyone at Kate. Nick's face was purple with rage, the veins standing out in his neck when John was finished.

"This was all because she refused to dance with him?" he asked John.

"Yep, and she was very polite when she turned him down. I was close enough to hear her. Then he just started spewing this venom at her, and I couldn't get to him fast enough to stop it. I was so shocked to begin with. It was like I was rooted to the spot. I couldn't believe what I was hearing, then I figured the best thing to do was to get you."

When he was through talking with John, Nick went over to Victoria. "I'm so very sorry that happened to Kate. She was so upset when she ran out the door. I was too far away to stop her, but I could see she was crying!"

"I'm going after her," Nick said.

"Do you think that's wise?" his mother responded. "Perhaps now's not the best time."

"Oh God, I don't know what to do! I'm going to call Jeanne and talk with her."

He called Jeanne and told her what had happened and asked her opinion as to whether he should follow Kate.

"Don't come over right now. Let me see what kind of state she's in when she gets here. Oh boy, she's already home! She must have driven eighty miles an hour to get here. Call you back as soon as I can. Bye, Nick." She opened the door for Kate and told her she already knew what had happened. When Kate asked how, Jeanne explained about Nick calling and wanting to know if he should come over.

"I promised I'd call him back and tell him how you're doing. What do you want him to do, come over or not?"

"Oh Lord, not. Definitely not! I couldn't deal with him right now. I don't know if I ever want to see him again!"

"Because of what this guy said to you? You can't blame Nick for that, surely?"

"No, it's got nothing to do with what that drunken fool said to me. It's what happened earlier in the garden with Nick that's the problem! Then what that man said about me, Jeanne! Nick told you everything? Can you believe what he said about me in front of all those people? The entire hospital board and all senior attending physicians were there plus all the leading citizens of Stockton, and can you believe even the governor of California heard it! How am I ever going to show my face at the hospital or around town? He called me Nick Barkley's whore!"

"Let me make you a cup of tea, then we can talk if you're up to it."

Jeanne made Kate her tea, and by the time she took it back to her, Kate had changed into her PJs and was sitting on the bed.

"Up to talking about what happened between you and Nick?"

Kate told her friend the way she had been kissed and how desired by Nick it had made her feel! He had revealed by his behavior tonight that he might indeed be in love with her, that what Jeanne had told her about him could be true! That he'd said when he came back from getting her the drink that they should go somewhere quiet because he wanted to ask her something, he seemed very serious when he'd said that. One thing she knew, she would not agree to having an affair with him. She knew his reputation with women, and his affairs were freely gossiped about! There were even rumors about the number of his one-night stands! She didn't intend to be just another notch on Nick Barkley's bedpost, no matter how he felt about her!

"What's your heart telling you? Are you in love with him?" Jeanne asked her.

"I think I am," was the response. "But it's all happened way too fast, and when he kisses me, I can't think straight!"

"I told you weeks ago he was in love with you, but you wouldn't believe me. Now you've got to face facts and decide what you're going to do."

"After what just happened tonight, I've made up my mind as I was driving home. I won't be seeing Nick Barkley again. I don't know if I'll ever get my good name back, but for sure, it won't happen so long as my name is linked in any way, shape, or form with his. So as of tonight, we are through, finished, done, over with!"

"Do you really think that's going to make much of a difference?"

"I've got to start somewhere! My name, my reputation, is in shreds just because I went out for a few dinners and some dancing with Nick! How could that drunken idiot be so cruel! Didn't he realize what saying what he said would do to me? Or didn't he care? What did I ever do to him?"

"When I called Nick back to tell him not to come over, I asked who this guy was and if he had any idea why he said those things. Nick told me that there has always been rivalry between them on this Mike's part since kindergarten. He was always trying to one-up Nick but could never quite manage it. Wanted to be class president but lost to Nick, wanted to be the quarterback but ended up the substitute to Nick and spent the season sitting on the bench, etc., etc. And Nick hazarded a guess that seeing you, the most beautiful woman in the room with Nick, just got to Mike, and he really started drinking and then noticed Nick wasn't around and thought he'd try to at least get a dance with you, but you turned him down, so that kinda pushed him over the edge, and he lashed out at you to somehow hurt Nick, but you got caught in the middle! I feel bad for Nick. He doesn't know what to say or do to make it up to you!"

"It's not his fault, I'm not blaming him, but being seen with him is just going to keep all this fresh in everyone's mind! And I can't afford for that to be happening. It's going to be tough enough as it is to try and redeem myself in the eyes of those people without being seen with a constant reminder of who it was all about."

"Is that really being fair on Nick? It really seems like you're blaming him for it!"

"No, like I said, I'm not blaming him. I just don't need to be connected with him in any way from now on, that's all. And in any case, I don't need a romance in my life. I'm too busy with work to even think about making room for someone in my life. Work is all that's important to me. I don't have time for anything or anyone else."

"Who do you think you're fooling? Keep telling yourself that nonsense and maybe one day you'll believe it!" Jeanne told her.

"Knock it off. I know what I'm doing! The only way those people are even going to start and forget what happened tonight is if there's a gap the size of the Grand Canyon between Nick Barkley and myself!! Good night, Jeanne!"

But the next morning, it proved to Kate she couldn't have been more wrong! Patients were coming out of the woodwork all asking to be treated by Dr. Kate Warner, and it seemed to the triage nurse that there was nothing wrong with any of them! Staff members from all over the hospital were finding excuses to come down to emergency/trauma and hang around, hoping to get a glimpse of the now infamous doctor! Chaos ensued in the department until Dr. Harry Greene pulled Kate aside and suggested she take the rest of the day off. She would have her normal next three days off, and following that, she was on a week of medical leave, and hopefully, by the time she came back, the furor would have died down. Silent tears ran down Kate's face as she drove home. Phones and social media must have gone into overdrive last night, people telling each other what had occurred at the party. *This is worse, much worse than I had imagined*, she thought. *How am I ever going to recover from this?* When she got home, no one was there. She remembered that Jeanne was going to the local discount warehouse and the judge and Esther were going along to look at barbecues.

Kate changed out of her scrubs, put a pot of coffee on, took her laptop and went to sit on the patio. She became so absorbed in an article she was reading online that she forgot the coffee! When she remembered, she went inside to get herself a mug. Hearing a noise in the hallway, she thought everyone must be back and went to see if they needed help bringing everything in. She saw the front door partially open and a stranger standing on the bottom stair!

She made a run for the open door, but he was too fast for her and caught her around the waist, spinning her around. Trying to defend herself, she lashed out at him, scratching his face. This so incensed him that he threw her head against the solid oak newel post, momentarily stunning her. And whilst she was temporary unable to fight back, he flung her down on the floor. Feeling herself falling, Kate put out her right hand to try and save herself and felt a fiery pain go through her hand as it hit the floor! The thought flashed through her mind. *Shit, it feels like I've done something serious to my hand,* but before she could think about it any further, her assailant had grabbed both of her arms and pinned them behind her back and put what felt to her like handcuffs on her! *Oh God, help me. I'm in real trouble now!* she thought. She was now laying on her back, with the large man on top of her, straddling her. She continued to scream at the top of her voice, but he only laughed and told her to scream away, no one could hear her. He unbuckled his belt and unzipped his pants, completely exposing himself, then he began to pull down Kate's pants. Just then, the front door burst open the rest of the way, and Judge Peterson flung himself at the would-be rapist and knocked him sideways off Kate. They were both struggling on the floor when Jeanne, who had run in behind the judge, picked up the old flat iron that was used as a door stop and hit Kate's assailant on the head with it, knocking him out completely! Esther had rushed to Kate and was helping her stand up and pulled up her pants for her. The judge called nine one one and asked for the sheriff's department and two units of paramedics to be sent. He tried to find the key to the handcuffs on the unconscious man, but it wasn't in any of the pockets he could reach. When the deputies got there, they used one of their keys to free Kate, and by then, her right hand was swelling and starting to change color!

"Damn, I think I've broken a bone in my hand, and my head hurts like hell where he threw me into the newel post," Kate said.

"You need to have to go to the hospital," one of the paramedics told her. "You have to have your hand x-rayed, and you could have a concussion from that blow to the head."

Kate tried to argue that she'd go later but was overruled by the judge and Esther. By the time Fred Madden got there, all she had time to do was give him a quick statement as to what had happened before she was whisked away to the emergency department. Her would-be rapist was taken to the county hospital emergency facility, which had a prison section. The paramedic van was just leaving when

Nick arrived bringing Kate's evening purse and kimono that she'd left behind the previous night. He knew nothing that had happened and was only going to stop in, drop off her things, and find out how the love of his life was doing. When he heard what had happened to her, he just about came unglued!

"It's a good job they've already taken that guy away, or I swear, Nick would have killed him for trying to rape Kate," the judge said to his wife, Esther.

"Where is she now?" Nick wanted to know.

"She's at the hospital. It will take a while for them to run tests to see if she's got a concussion and if she's broken any bones in her hand," Jeanne told him.

"I'm afraid it just gets worse," said Fred, coming back downstairs. "Our would-be attacker has been in Dr. Warner's room, got into her things, namely her bras and panties, got many of them out, threw them on the floor, then...um...urinated on them. Which makes her room also a crime scene. I'm sorry, Judge, you and your wife will have to stay somewhere else for the next couple of days. Your home is a crime scene."

"Not a problem, I'll check us all into a hotel. After you are finished with Kate's room, I'll have that carpet ripped up and a new one laid, so she'll have to stay in the hotel a little longer. I'll book you a room next to hers, Jeanne. She's going to need help if she has broken any bones plus she's having that procedure on Monday and has to stay resting for three days after."

"She's not staying in any hotel. I don't know what medical procedure you're talking about—you can explain that to me later—but I'm taking her to stay at my ranch, and yes, she'll need help, so you, Jeanne, will come too! Fred, is it all right if Jeanne packs some bags for Kate? She's going to need clothes and other things for maybe a week, perhaps even ten days."

"All right, but put these gloves on so you don't leave fingerprints, and be as quick as you can. Yes, Nick, you can help!"

"Pack clothes for about a week, even ten days, including something to wear for that reception we were supposed to attend on Saturday night, in case she still feels like going. She'll need her laptop, phone, and chargers for both. I don't see them in here. They might be on the patio. I'll go and check while you're busy with the packing."

Within a few minutes, Jeanne had gathered all that she thought Kate would need for her for stay at the Barkley ranch, and Nick had found Kate's electronic gadgets and chargers. Jeanne had also packed enough of her own clothes to stay with Kate. Nick helped Jeanne load everything into her car, and she set off, and with Silas's help, unloaded, unpacked, and got everything ready for Kate arriving. Nick went to the hospital to find out how Kate was doing and to transport her to his home as soon as she was released. When he told the intake worker who he was and with whom he came to inquire about, she immediately went into the treatment area and told Ann he was out front. Ann came out and updated him on what was going on.

"They've done an MRI, and she's got a mild concussion for which she's adamant she won't stay in the hospital overnight for observation! She's also broken a bone in her hand, and right now, they are putting a splint on it. She should follow up with an orthopedist in about a week. She'll be out in a few minutes and has a couple of prescriptions that need to be filled."

"Okay, I'll take care of those. Anything else I should know?"

"Just be gentle with her. She's be through a lot between last night—yes, I've heard about it, it's all over the hospital—and then the attack today."

When Kate came out, all Ann had told her was someone was here to give her a ride. She expected it to be Jeanne and was astonished to see Nick.

"What are you doing here?"

"I'm here to take you to the ranch."

"The ranch? Your ranch? I'm not going there. Why can't I go home?"

"Because it's a crime scene, and Jeanne has packed yours and her things, so you are coming with me to the ranch where you'll be safe and well taken care of. You have to have some kind of procedure on Monday, so I'm told, and you'll need help to recover from that. My staff plus Jeanne will take good care of you. You'll have everything you need. So stop arguing, get in the truck, and let's be on our way. Give me your prescriptions and tell me which pharmacy you use and I'll get them filled, then we can get back to the ranch and you can get settled in, eat if you want, and get some rest."

Kate was too tired and in too much pain to argue with Nick, so she climbed into his truck and sat leaning up against the door, her head resting on the window. They stopped at the pharmacy, the same one the Barkleys used, so the prescriptions were filled in record time! As they set off toward the ranch, Nick leaned over to put his hand on Kate's shoulder to try and comfort her, but she jerked away, saying, "Don't," and moved even further away from him in her seat! He was a little startled by her reaction but thought he better just leave her alone. He did ask if she wanted to talk, but all he got was the one word answer, "No."

When they pulled up at the front door, Silas came out to meet them and opened the truck door. Nick put his hand out to help her down, but she pulled away from him, getting out without his help. Victoria was waiting for them to come inside and immediately went to Kate and put her arms around the doctor and gave her a hug, telling her how sorry she was that all this had happened to her.

"You must be exhausted and maybe hungry. It's way past lunch-time. How about a cup of tea and something light to eat before you go and rest?" Victoria asked Kate.

"A cup of tea sounds wonderful, and maybe a little something to eat. I can't take my meds on an empty stomach."

"Come over and sit down, Silas will be right out with a tray for you. Jeanne has already unpacked and gotten your room ready for you. I'm sure you'll be very comfortable. Anything you want, just ask, and Silas will get it for you."

"Oh, this looks wonderful. An afternoon tea! Just the thing!"

Kate drank her tea and ate some of the food Silas had prepared for her then, excusing herself, went up to her room to lie down for a while. A couple of hours later, after she had napped, she went down-stairs to find a book to read, something Jeanne had forgotten to bring for her. Silas pointed her in the direction of the library, and she went in only to find it had another occupant, Nick.

"Oh, I'm sorry for disturbing you. I'll come back later," she told him.

"Not at all. I was just knocking a few balls around on the billiard table, so you're not disturbing me a bit. Help yourself to any book you want. How are you feeling? Still in pain?"

She just shrugged her shoulders in response. Picking out a book, she turned to go, but Nick spoke up.

"Kate, I really don't know what to do or say to apologize for what happened to you under my roof. I know that I'm responsible for what occurred. Mike was trying to get at me and you got caught in the middle. How can I make it up to you?"

"It wasn't your fault, Nick. I'm not blaming you—the guy was drunk. And the damage to my name has been done, so unless you know how to un-ring a bell, there's nothing you can do." She started to leave, but Nick stepped in front of her and attempted to put his arms around her.

"DON'T TOUCH ME!" she yelled at him, pushed him away, and dashed out the library door, leaving behind the book she'd come to fetch. Nick was stunned and followed her to the doorway. On her way down the hallway to the stairs, as she made her way back to the safety of her room, Kate nearly bumped into Jeanne, and without saying a word, hurried past the housekeeper. Jeanne looked at her in astonishment as she'd seen the tears coursing down her friend's cheeks. Looking over at Nick still standing in the library doorway, she marched over to him.

"What in hell did you do or say to her to get her that upset? Don't you think she's been through enough in the last fourteen-fifteen hours?"

"Come in here," he said, as they walked into the room and he shut the door. "All I said was it was all my fault it happened, and I didn't know how to make it up to her. She said I couldn't fix it unless I could un-ring a bell. She just looked so forlorn standing there that I went to put my arms around her, but she freaked out, yelled at me not to touch her, and ran out of here like the hounds of hell were after her! I don't know what happened!"

"I think I do, Nick. You tried to touch her, and she's very sensitive right now. You're a very masculine man, and just a few hours ago, a man attempted to rape her. I think even the touch of a man would be hard for her to take!"

"God, I never thought of that. When we were in the truck, I tried to put my hand on her shoulder, and she pulled away from me and said 'Don't'. Then when she was getting out, she wouldn't let me help her. I never meant to upset her, Jeanne. How could I have been so insensitive!"

"Don't worry about it. You couldn't know. I'll go up and make sure she's okay."

"Here, take this book with you. It's what she came in here for in the first place."

Jeanne went to Kate's room, knocked on the door, and when Kate told her to, she went in. Kate was sitting on her bed, silent tears running down her cheeks.

"I just talked to Nick, and he explained what happened. Don't worry about it. He understands what he did and is sorry for it."

"It wasn't just what he did, Jeanne. It brought back a memory of something that happened whilst I was in the army. An incident that I thought I'd dealt with, but the events of the last few hours showed me it was still there, just below the surface, and the memories came pouring back."

"Do you want to talk about it?" asked Jeanne.

"Maybe it would help." Kate proceeded to tell her friend about the event that had happened to her.

"Gawd, I can't imagine being in that situation. No wonder you reacted the way you did!"

"But I shouldn't have taken it out on Nick."

"He's got broad shoulders. He can take being yelled at once in a while."

"I've got to apologize to him, but right now, I just can't face him!" Kate told her confidant.

"I shouldn't worry about that, right now. I think what you need is some sleep."

It was close to midnight when Kate woke up. Her first thought was, *I've got to find Nick and explain to him why I acted the way I did. I'll check his study and see if he's in there.* When she got to the door, there was a light showing underneath. She tapped softly.

Nick's voice called, "Come in." She opened the door and slowly stepped inside. Nick looked up, surprise showing on his face when he saw who it was.

"Could I talk to you for a few minutes?" she asked, not really looking at him.

"Of course you can. What's on your mind?" he responded, getting up and walking around his desk. "Sit down."

"I don't need to. I just have to tell you something that happened to me whilst I was serving in what you would call a MASH unit. It was a very small unit, only about a half-dozen doctors plus support staff. Anyway, the fighting near us got really bad, and I still don't know how it happened, but we got cut off from our forces! There was a break off-group of radical extremist rebel insurgents surrounding us, and we were taking fire. It was pretty bad, and as the day wore on, it only got worse! We all were armed, trying to defend our position and, of course, our patients. Suddenly, they launched an all-out attack on us, rockets and mortars were flying everywhere, and then they broke through into the compound. We got a message that rescue forces were on their way but were facing stiff resistance. The reality we...er...all had to face was help might not get there in time! I was defending a small ward along with another doctor and orderly. An enemy fighter broke through, and I was...um...shot in the low back. The orderly shot him dead. I made a decision there and then, Nick. I...er...was a woman and a non-Muslim, and I knew what would happen to me if I was captured. It would mean...er...being tortured and probably gang raped for weeks, months, even years, 'til I was either rescued or traded. I knew of a British nurse who...um... had been captured and was held for almost fourteen months before a trade could be arranged."

90

At this point, Kate stopped for a minute, trying to keep her emotions in check. Nick felt his heart breaking as he watched her fight to keep control of herself, and then she continued. "It took three surgeries to repair the damage they had done to her because they didn't just gang rape her they used foreign objects on her. Of course, she was under psychiatric care, but even so...er...she committed suicide just five months after she was freed. I made up my mind that wasn't going to be in my future, so...er...um...I made the decision. If it came right down to it, I was going to save my last bullet for myself!"

As she told her story haltingly, Nick tried not to show the emotions he was feeling. He struggled with his natural impulse to rush over to her and take her in his arms and hold onto her and somehow try to lessen the impact of all these terrible memories. But he knew that was the worst thing he could do, so he just continued to lean up against the desk and listen as she continued with her story.

"The fighting continued to be fierce, and I lost many friends that day. I was down to my last eight bullets, Nick, when the rescue forces broke through. I was seven bullets away from putting a slug in my brain. I came that close! I thought I'd dealt with those memories, but the events of the last few hours just brought them flooding back, and when you tried to hold me, something in me just snapped! I am truly sorry, Nick, I handled the situation badly, and if I offend, insulted or embarrassed you in any way, I do apologize."

"My God, Kate, you don't owe me any kind of apology! I had no idea you had gone through anything like that! Seven bullets away from using the next on yourself. I can't begin to imagine what was going through your mind! I do appreciate you telling me, and I realize how hard it must be for you to talk about it."

"I just felt I had to explain why I acted the way I did, so I'll say good night now." And with that, she turned and left, hurrying back upstairs. Nick remained where he was, trying to come to terms with all that she'd just told him. He was stunned by her revelations, having no idea that being a doctor in the army, she could find herself in such a dangerous situation and shot in the back! How bad had that injury been? He would talk to Jeanne in the morning and see if she knew more about the extent of the gunshot wound. For tonight, he didn't think he'd get much sleep, going over and over all she'd confided in him and trying to work out how he could be of help to the woman he loved so very much.

The next morning, Kate didn't come down for breakfast. Jeanne took a tray up to her with a muffin and a bowl of fruit. When she did come down, Kate took her book and went to sit on a lounger out on the patio. Nick ran into Silas taking her a mid-morning cappuccino.

"I'll take that out to her. Here you go, Kate. Silas sent this for you. How are you feeling this morning? Does your hand hurt a lot?"

"It's okay as long as I take the pain meds. Silas is such a sweetheart. He's spoiling me rotten!"

Nick sat down sideways on the lounger next to her. They sat in an uncomfortable silence for a few minutes. He was wondering what to say and then decided to take the bull by the horns!

"When are we going to talk about the elephant in the room?" he asked, watching her face intently.

Without looking at him, she mumbled, "What elephant? I don't know what you mean?"

"You know what that expression means, don't you?"

"Um, I think so."

"Well, to clarify things, it means the thing that neither of us is talking about and which we have to! In other words, what happened between us in the garden at Mother's party."

"Oh, that!"

"Yes, that, Kate. It moved our relationship to a whole new place, and we have to talk about it."

"No, we don't, Nick. It just happened. It shouldn't, but it did, that's all."

"What are you talking about? 'It just happened?' Babe, it can't have escaped your notice that I'm very much in love with you. It didn't 'just happen,' it was long overdue to happen! I said that to you then, and you didn't argue."

"Nick, it was just the evening and maybe the music, and we both got carried away, that's all. You're reading way too much into it."

"Kate, I've spent a lot of hours in your company, and I think I know you pretty well, and one thing is for sure, a lady like you doesn't kiss a man the way you kissed me because she got carried away! It wasn't just a something that 'happened!' I can still taste your kisses, feel your lips on mine, my face, my neck! I love you, babe. I want us to be married, for you to live on my ranch with me, to take you to bed and, for our first time, make sweet gentle love to you, and one day, when the time is right, put a child inside of you."

"NO! Oh no, no, no, no, no. This can't be happening. It was never supposed to be like this! You're wrong, Nick. You don't love me. Maybe a bit of infatuation, but that's all. It was only meant to be a casual relationship, nothing more. How did it all go so wrong? Oh Lord, now what?"

"Kate, what's wrong? I tell you I'm in love with you and you act like it's the worst thing in the world that could happen to you? I don't understand."

"Nick, I don't get involved in serious relationships for a reason—I'm no good at them! I can't read what's going on right in front of my face! Jeanne says I'm dumber than a fencepost, and she's right! Can't we just forget what happened the other night and go on from there? Please, please, Nick?"

"You've got to be joking. I'm in love with you! How can I forget that? I fell in love with you the moment I met you. I knew right then and there I wanted you to be my wife. Now you're asking me to just wipe out all that I feel for you? It's not gonna happen, Kate. I'm going to fight for you with everything I've got. I can't—I won't—let you go!"

"But I'm all wrong for you. I'd just bring you pain and grief. Really, I would."

"Explain that to me."

"I'm an only child, I've never had to think about anyone else in my whole life. I do as I please, I don't know how to share my life with anyone, I don't play well with others, I like being on my own, I'm a workaholic, and I like my life just the way it is. I came to Stockton to do a job, and that's my only focus. I really believe that, in a committed relationship, the other person's wants, needs, and desires have to come first, and I know I'm just not capable of doing that. You deserve much more than I'm able to give, so forget all about me and find someone who can care about you the way you deserve, 'cos it just isn't me! Why the hell did I come to Stockton in the first place? It's been an unmitigated disaster! I'll never get my good name back after what that guy said about me, and then another tries to rape me in my own home. Just calling it quits and going back to England looks better and better!"

"You can't mean that!"

"I do, Nick. The way I see it, I need to start afresh somewhere where no one knows what's happened to me. Somewhere where my name carries a little respect and people don't stare at me and whisper things about me as I walk by."

"Will you just give me a chance to address some of the concerns you've brought up?"

"Oh okay, not that'll do any good."

"First, you've shared your life since you became a doctor. You work unselfishly, day after day, on behalf of your patients. In other words, babe, you constantly put others before yourself! And don't try and tell me different! Next, being married doesn't mean we have to live in each other's hip pockets—if you need time alone, you'll have it. And by the way, you're not the only one who needs a little solitude. Growing up in a big family, there were times—and still are—when I've got to get away from everything and everybody, and when I feel like that, I normally saddle up and go for a long ride. Sometimes, I even spend the night on the range. I would hope you wouldn't object to my still doing that after we're married! And as for being a workaholic, well, I suffer from the same disease, so maybe we will be able to help each other overcome the need to want to work when we know we have each other to come home to. I know both our jobs are demanding, but we understand that already. Now, as for being able to put your partner first in everything. Nobody knows how to do that, babe. That's something we'll learn how to do together. It's called working on a marriage. And as for you hurting me or bringing me grief, I'm more than willing to bet you'll do neither of those things. As to you getting your good name back, well, you'll have a new name.

How does Kate Barkley sound to you? Now, have I answered all your fears, or is there something else you're scared of?"

"I'm not scared! I'm just being realistic!"

"No, you're scared! Scared of making a commitment to me, but that's okay. When you've had a chance to think things over, you'll come to realize that making vows to each other on our wedding day is the only natural thing for us to do. There's only one problem we haven't dealt with. In all that you've said, there's one thing you haven't mentioned."

"What's that?"

"How you feel about me."

Silence.

"Well, Kate?"

Still silence.

"Can't say it, can you?"

Silence. All this time, Kate was looking at the floor.

"Three little words, and you can't bring yourself to say them, can you?"

Just then, Silas came onto the patio. "Mr. Simms has arrived. Also, Mrs. Simms and Miss. Lily Simms."

"WHAT! I thought he was coming by himself. I had no idea he'd be bringing his wife, far less Lily! I'll be right there, Silas. I have to go, Kate, Joe Simms and his family have just arrived. He's here to see Jarrod and myself about a business deal, and they'll all be here until Tuesday morning. Please excuse me."

Kate continued to sit on the patio, staring into space, lost in thought, thinking over all that Nick had said to her. She was leaning against one of the supporting pillars of the patio roof when Jeanne came out to tell her lunch was being served in the dining room.

"I'm not hungry," was the response.

When Nick asked Jeanne why Kate hadn't come in to lunch, she told him what had been said. He stood in the doorway for a few minutes, watching his love, and then walked over and stood behind her. She was aware of his presence but didn't say anything for a while.

Finally, in a low soft voice, she said, "It's so peaceful here."

"Yes, it is," he responded just as softly.

A few minutes later. "And so quiet."

"Mmm."

Silence for a few more minutes.

"I love you."

"I know you do," he told her. "I just wanted to hear you say it!" And he slipped his arms around her waist as she leaned back against him with a smile on her face.

"I take it this means we're going to get married?"

"Yes, it does," she answered.

"How soon?"

"Just as soon as we can arrange it. I don't want a big wedding. I have so few people to invite."

"We'll talk to mother and see what she can do to help. Do you mind if we don't announce our engagement today? If we wait until tomorrow, you'll have your ring to show everyone, that is, if you like it."

"Ring? What ring?

"The last time I was in San Francisco, I ordered your engagement ring, and it will be here tomorrow morning. But if you don't like it, I can easily return it, and you can pick out another one."

"I'm sure it will be beautiful and I'll love it, but one question? How did you know what size I wear?"

"A little bird told me!"

"Jeanne!"

"Well, a guy's got to have a little help now and again."

She turned around, and they gazed at each other and gently started kissing with short slow kisses, gradually increasing in fervor that seemed to go on and on until Jeanne walked out on the patio carrying a tray with some lunch for Kate.

"Damn it, is there no privacy in my own house!" fumed Nick.

"Well, the patio isn't exactly private," retorted Jeanne. "And I thought Kate should at least eat something!"

"Okay, okay, thank you for bringing her some food, but could you now give us some space?"

"Sure, I will, but you should know Mrs. Simms and that daughter of hers were asking where you were, and as soon as lunch is over, I suspect they are gonna come looking for you!"

"Oh hell, there is something I should explain to you, Kate. A while back, Lily Simms and I had a thing going, but not for long, because before I knew it, she started telling me the kind of diamond she liked, and her mother was talking about places to hold wedding receptions. This was when I was going to San Francisco regularly. I mean, I liked the girl, but talk like that made me run like hell in the opposite direction. Anyway, the last time I met with Joe for dinner, lo and behold, who should be there but his wife and Lily! All evening, that woman contrived to find ways to leave me alone with her daughter, and Lily intimated she wanted us to get back together! I tried as gently as I could to tell her it wasn't going to happen, but obviously, I didn't get through to her because they're both here, and I can guess why! This could get awkward, babe. I don't think Mrs. Simms is gonna take kindly to finding you here, especially after we announce our engagement tomorrow."

"Well, she'll have to get used to the fact that you're taken!!"

"Taken! I like the sound of that. Now do you want to tell me what this procedure you're having on Monday is all about?"

"Oh boy, I knew you were going to ask about that! I severely injured my spine in a crash whilst I was in the Middle East. A troop carrier I was riding in hit a landmine, and in the explosion, I was thrown clear, but I landed awkwardly on a large rock. By the pain, I knew I was in trouble. Fortunately, we were close to the base we had been headed to, and a rescue party were with us fast. I was taken to the local MASH unit, and then the next thing I knew, I was on a hospital transport plane to Germany to one of our hospitals there. I had done some damage to my spine and had surgery, but it's left me with a continuing problem. So every four to six months, to control the pain in my back, I have some nerves burnt by way of radio frequency. It helps a lot, and then I manage the remainder of the pain with medication. My doctor in London who gave me the treatments used to insist that, after I have the procedure, I rest up for three days. She told me most doctors say you can resume your normal life after a day, but she disagreed in view of the spinal injurie I had suffered. So I take her advice, rest for three days, gradually resume life on the fourth, and get back to normal on the fifth. It's always worked for me, and she was such a great doctor I don't see any reason to go against her advice now."

"Shot and blown up! Is there anything else you haven't told me about your time in the service?"

"Er...um...not really."

"Now, about this procedure. They give you a local or a general anesthesia?"

"Well, actually, neither!"

"What do you mean neither? Are you telling me you are going to have this done without any anesthesia? Are you nuts, woman?"

"I can't have anything because when they put the needles in, they have to know they are hitting the right nerves."

"WHAT! This whole thing sounds barbaric! How do you stand the pain?"

"By thinking when it's all over how much better I'll feel. It only lasts for a short while, Nick, and then it is three days of lovely rest!"

"You're one tough cookie, you know that? Now, what time is your appointment on Monday?"

"Ten a.m."

"So what time should we leave?"

"We? Jeanne is taking me."

"Oh no, she's not! From now on, it's my job to take care of you, and that starts with me driving you to this appointment. No arguments, young lady."

"All right, if that's the way you want it."

Silas came out onto the patio and announced that Sheriff Madden was here to see Dr. Warner.

"Show him into my study. She can talk with him there."

"Please come with me, Nick. He must want me to give my full statement, and I'd rather talk about what happened with you there."

All three sat down in Nick's study, and Kate gave Fred a full and detailed statement of what had occurred the day before. When she was finished, he had some news for her.

"The would-be attacker, Alan Simpson, had been at the party working as a server. His cousin worked for the catering service and had got him the job; otherwise, he'd never have been hired as he'd just got out of San Quinten after serving a prison term for attempted rape! Simpson had been witness to the scene and thought Dr. Barkley would be an easy target for his next attack in view of all that was said about her. It was like a woman with her reputation deserved to be raped! He had gone to the hospital and hung around outside, not sure what time she left work, but as luck would have it, she left much earlier than usual, owing to the furor her presence was causing, so he followed her home. Seeing there were no other cars in the driveway, Simpson forced the lock on the front door and went in. Going upstairs, he soon found out which was her room and, in his twisted logic, took out a kind of revenge on her most intimate things! Going back downstairs, he heard a sound coming from the kitchen. Realizing it must be Kate, he was ready to go in there and attack her when she walked out into the hallway. He couldn't believe his luck and grabbed her. This time, there would be no 'attempted' rape. He had taken enough male enhancement drugs to make sure of that! Now he'll be going away for a very long, long time."

Sheriff Madden reassured her. "That's one very sick puppy! But the good news is he's admitted to everything and is pleading guilty, seems to be rather proud of himself, which means you won't have to testify in court. Just make a statement at his sentencing if you would do that?"

"Of course, I will. I want him put away for the longest time possible," Kate replied.

"Well, that's it. I'll have your statement typed up, and a deputy will drop by with it for you to sign. Sorry this had to happen to you, Dr. Warner. Just glad the judge got there when he did! And that was some mighty whack Jeanne gave Simpson when she hit him with the old iron! Fractured his skull for him! Took him a long time to come around!"

After Fred left, Kate breathed a sigh of relief. "It's over, Nick. No testifying in court, thank goodness!"

"Now let's find my mother and see if she can help us with wedding plans."

Chapter 8

"Mother, do you have a few minutes to spare?"

"Certainly, Nick."

"Kate and I are going to be married, and we want you to help us plan the wedding, but we're not announcing the engagement until tomorrow, when she'll have her ring."

Victoria hugged and congratulated them. "If you don't mind, I think we should bring Silas in on this. He's so good at arranging events, and we'll need his expertise."

When Silas joined them and offered his felicitations, Kate said, "Okay, today is Friday. How soon can we put together a wedding? I have no family and only a handful of friends who will be attending, so I really don't want a church wedding. My side would be empty!"

"How about holding it here?" Victoria suggested.

"That would be perfect!" exclaimed Kate. "I know you have certain people that you have to invite, but could you keep it to a small group. Say, about fifty or sixty?"

"That's doable," said Victoria, glancing at Silas, who was nodding in agreement.

"If we make it a morning wedding, say about ten am, then all we would have to serve are light refreshments and the cake," suggested Silas.

"Silas, you're a genius," said Kate. "Could we make the wedding two weeks on Saturday?" she asked hesitantly.

"It's short notice, but I believe we can do it," said Victoria.

"I'll call my friend Nan in New York and ask her if she'll be my maid of honor, and maybe Audra would play the piano for us," said Kate.

"Did I hear my name mentioned?" Audra asked, coming into the room. They updated her on their plans, and she said she'd be happy to help.

"What is the color scheme?" she wanted to know.

"I think peach would work with the furniture," Kate told them.

"Wonderful!" said Victoria. "I'll take care of the arrangements, including the flowers. All you have to do is find the right dress."

"Find the right dress in two weeks. That's a tall order!"

Nick wanted to know if they were finished discussing wedding plans because there was something he wanted to show Kate. They agreed that they would meet the next day for an update and left the couple alone.

"I have something to show you," Nick told her and took Kate's hand, leading her upstairs.

"I had been working on this for a few weeks before we met. Some gypsies told me I'd meet you soon, so I took a leap of faith, and when I met you, I knew I'd done the right thing. I hope you like it. This is the front door to our apartment."

"Our apartment?"

"I had a friend draw up plans to give us a self-contained apartment within the house."

"Are you serious?" she asked.

"These are guest rooms with a bath, down the hallway, another guest room and bath, linen closets, cupboards, door to the attics, this is the laundry room, and in here the living room." And with that, he threw open the door and ushered her into the main part of their new home and held his breath. She walked in, looked around, went into the bedroom, inspected the bathroom, and came back to where he had remained standing with tears running down her face.

"You did all this for us?" she said.

"For you," he told her. "I wanted to give you a home of your own."

"Oh, Nick." She flung herself into his arms and just cried. "I can't believe this, that you'd do all this for me. No, it's not for me," she corrected herself. "It's for us. It's our home, our flat."

"Flat?" he asked.

"That's English for apartment," she told him.

"I like it, 'The Flat' it is."

She took his hand, and together, they inspected the kitchen and what would be the dining area.

"There is a utility room and half bath here, then this huge deck," he told her. He showed her the staircase to the parking/garage area and the steps at the end of the deck leading to the pool.

"Nick, I just can't believe it. I thought we'd just move into your room. I never dreamed we'd have a self-contained flat to live in. We'll actually have some privacy!"

"There is a phone at the entrance at the top of the stairs, and from the flat, you can buzz visitors in. The same goes for the gate. No one can just walk in. Now all we need is some furniture."

"What's wrong with the bedroom set that's in there now?' she asked.

"Well, that was mine, and I didn't know if you'd like it."

"Let's look at it again." They walked hand in hand to the bedroom. "It's beautiful," said Kate. "It's mahogany, isn't it?"

"Sure is, weighs a ton." He laughed.

"What size is the mattress?"

"I think queen, but you'd better check with Mother."

"Are you busy tomorrow?" Kate asked him.

"I'll be able to get away about three."

"How about I meet you here at our flat then and we can go over what we need?"

"Our flat. I like the sound of that. It's a date."

Victoria told the family that she had arranged a brunch for Saturday morning and had invited the judge and Esther.

"I think they would like some home cooking, a family atmosphere, after being at the hotel."

Friday night after dinner, Nick said he and Kate were going into his study to watch a movie, but as soon as he said it, Lily suggested that they all watch a movie in the small cozy media room in the Barkley mansion. There was nothing Nick could do but agree! He knew what Lily was trying to do get him to sit next to her! By the time he and Kate walked in after spending a few minutes alone in the dining room exchanging some very passionate kisses, the only seats left were singles. Very politely, Nick asked Lily if she'd mind moving down one so he could sit next to Kate.

"She needs someone to pass her, her drink, etc., with that splint on her hand," he explained to the now angry young woman. He started off with his arm around the back of Kate's seat, but soon, it was around her shoulders. Then his hand was rubbing her neck. Seeing this, Mrs. Simms made a comment on how Nick couldn't behave himself when he was in public! He glanced at Kate and winked and then whispered to her to cozy up to him, so she moved a little closer, if that were at all possible, and put her head on his shoulder, her left hand on his chest.

"Nick, really!" Mrs. Simms commented.

"Just ignore her," whispered Nick.

When the movie was over, Lily suggested they watch another one, but Victoria intervened and told everyone that Silas was serving coffee, liqueurs, and more cake in the library and that they should all go in there. Kate started to get up, but Nick caught her hand and motioned for her to sit back down. When everyone had left, he sighed and said, "Alone at last," and pulled her into his arms. They were busy kissing, with him leaning over her, when she lost her balance and fell backward with him almost on top of her just as Mrs. Simms walked into the room!

"Oh my goodness, what's going on in here? Nick Barkley, how could you? I've never been so embarrassed in my life, you should be ashamed of yourselves, especially her! That's no way for a lady to behave!" And she marched out of the room slamming the door behind her!

"Lord, will we ever have some time to ourselves? It's my home, and we can't even get some privacy here!"

Just then, there was a knock on the door!

"Hell and damnation, what now! Come in!"

In walked his mother. "I'm sorry to disturb you, but Alice Simms has just come to me in quite a state about something she said she saw in here. According to her, you guys were in the process of making love when she walked in on you! Tell me that isn't so. I mean, you're both consenting adults and what you choose to do is your business, but not to lock the door, Nick. Really!"

"WHAT! She said what? We were doing nothing of the kind! If you must know, Kate and I were making out, and she fell backward, and I kinda fell on top of her, and that's when that blasted woman barged in here without knocking! She knew fine well that Kate and I were in here, she just wanted to interrupt us. She's madder than a wet hen that Kate sat next to me tonight instead of that daughter of hers. She's determined that Lily and I get back together again, and nothing I do or say will convince either of them it's not going to happen.

"Oh, that makes much more sense than the story Alice told me. I'm sorry I disturbed you. I'll see you both at brunch tomorrow. Until then, good night."

"Mother, one thing. For your information, up to now, Kate and I have not been sleeping together. That's what got her so upset about the other night—people thinking we have been."

"Like I said, you're two consenting adults, and what you choose to do is entirely between yourselves, but I do appreciate you telling me, and of course, it goes no further." With that, she left them alone.

"Nick, I should call it a night. My hand is really hurting, and I have to take a pain med."

"Okay, babe, I understand. I'll walk you to your room." As they walked up the stairs, Jeanne caught them up.

"I'll help you get ready for bed," she told Kate. At her bedroom door, the couple kissed goodnight under Jeanne's watchful eye.

"You did that deliberately," Kate said to her friend.

"Well, I'm not sure how things are with you two, and I didn't want him to take advantage of you just because you're staying under his roof!"

"It's okay, Jeanne. We're engaged. We'll make the announcement tomorrow after my ring arrives from San Francisco, which I gather you had a hand in helping him with the size!"

"Oh that! Well, I guess congratulations are in order. See, I told you he was in love with you, and it was love at first sight. I was right, wasn't I?"

"Yes, you were right. Happy now? Now please help so I can get to bed. I need to get a decent night's sleep. It's at the brunch that we're making the big announcement."

When she'd talked to Nan the next morning, who had immediately said yes at the prospect of being Kate's maid of honor, they had discussed styles, and Kate told her of her preference of as little skin showing as possible. "It's a wedding, not a night on the town," she'd told Nan.

"I know what you mean," said her friend. "I'll start looking today for a peach-colored dress and let you know how it goes."

A few minutes later, Silas knocked on the door, and when Kate answered, he handed her a package. The return address was Agent Provocateur in San Francisco, an expensive lingerie shop. When she opened it, nestled in the tissue paper were replacements for the items she had just purchased and had been ruined by her attacker. She had found this store online, and although they were expensive, they had a wonderful sale on, and she'd treated herself to some bras and panties, loving wearing extravagant lingerie. Underneath the items was an envelope. Opening it, she found a gift certificate to the store in the amount of five thousand dollars. Immediately, she knew who had sent the lingerie and certificate—Nick! She found him downstairs just going into the kitchen.

"I'd like a word with you," she told him.

"Sure, what's up?"

"I just receive a package from Agent Provocateur with replacements for some of the lingerie that was destroyed plus a gift certificate for five thousand dollars. Nick, have you lost your mind? five thousand dollars? I mean, that's a ridiculous amount of money to spend on lingerie! Five grand! You must have more money than sense! I can't accept that certificate! And how did you know about Agent Provocateur? Jeanne!"

"Well, yes, she did happen to mention that you'd just got some things from there and hadn't even had a chance to wear them when they were destroyed. So I just called the store and had them duplicate your order and add the gift certificate and then ship the whole thing overnight. Why not? It's not like I can't afford it! And in any case,

I'm sure you'll need to replace the rest of the things that were ruined. Plus, I really like the lingerie they sell!"

"How do you know what kind of things they sell?"

"Well, I...er...have shopped there before."

"Oh, you have, have you? I might have known a man of your reputation would know all about a store like that!"

"Look, you're getting married, don't you women want—I think you call it—a trousseau? Well buy it there and have them ship it overnight to you. And when you use up that certificate, let me know and I'll get you another one. No, in fact, I'll just set up a charge account there for you, then you can buy to your heart's content. After all, I'm the one who'll get the benefit of it all, so it's only right and fitting I should pay for it all!"

"Nick, you're crazy!"

"Crazy in love with you! Now go get on your laptop and do some shopping with your gift certificate and I'll tell you when your ring arrives. It shouldn't be long now."

At ten thirty, Nick asked Kate to come into his study. Laying on his desk was a heart-shaped red velvet ring box.

"It arrived a few minutes ago by special messenger," he explained. "I hope you like it."

He opened the box, took out the ring, and put it on Kate's finger. She looked at it and gave a gasp!

"Oh, Nick, it's the most beautiful ring I've ever seen! Thank you, thank you so much," she said as her eyes filled with tears.

"Babe, don't cry, you're supposed to be happy. You really like it? You're not just saying that to please me? The three stones represent our past, present, and future, but of course, the present one is the largest, and then the tiny ones on, I think they are called the shoulders of the ring, are just to balance things out."

"Nick, I love it! I'll wear it with pride and joy knowing you picked it out for me. I love you so much!"

They spent some time kissing and then, at eleven, walked hand in hand into the dining room, where all his family, plus the judge and Esther and the Simms were assembled.

"We have an announcement to make," Nick said. Everyone turned to look at the sound of his voice. "Kate and I are getting married!" There was a chorus of congratulations followed by hugs and kisses. Mrs. Simms and Lily looked thunderstruck and offered luke warm felicitations! Silas brought in the champagne, and Jarrod offered a toast to Nick and Kate, which Silas and Jeanne joined in.

"Another Mrs. Barkley," said Silas.

"Actually, she'll be Dr. Barkley," Victoria put in.

"I've decided that at the hospital I'll be Dr. Barkley, but here at the ranch, I'll be Mrs. Nick."

The pride shone in Nick's eyes when he heard that, and it brought tears to his mother's eyes. *She's putting aside her title of doctor that she's worked so hard to get in favor of showing everyone she's Nick's wife. What a girl*, thought Victoria. They all sat down for brunch, and Kate informed everyone of the date of the wedding, and the talk was of nothing else. Nick had to sit in on the meeting with Joe Simms and Jarrod for a little while, but told Kate he'd see her in the flat at three.

Kate checked her watch and, seeing it was two fifty, headed for the flat and what was to be her new home. Nick was already there. "Silas is making us some coffee and will bring it upstairs," he told her. Standing in their living room, Nick gave her a passionate embrace that only stopped because Silas knocked on the door. "To be continued," said Nick, kissing her on the nose!

Kate pulled out her notebook and said, "Let's start in the bathroom." Two hours later, pages of notes covering everything from a first aid kit to a sofa and loveseat were listed.

"Can we take a break?" asked Nick. "My head is spinning."

"Of course we can, darlin'. Maybe we can go downstairs and get a soda?"

"Oh, I was thinking of something else we could be doing," said Nick, playfully pulling her into his arms.

"Down, boy, we've got a lifetime for that," she told him. As if on cue, there was a knock on the door, and Victoria's voice asking if she could come in.

"Of course," replied Kate.

"If you can take a break, I'd like to update you with the plans," Victoria told them. "Why don't we go back downstairs and get comfortable?"

"Good idea," they said.

After they settled down in the living room, Victoria with a sherry, Nick with a beer, and Kate with her usual Sprite, Victoria went over all that she'd been able to arrange. "The invitations are ordered, and I'll pick them up tomorrow morning. Audra will help, so they should be addressed by lunch time and in the mail by two p.m. The caterers and wait staff are taken care of courtesy of Silas. I don't know how he pulled it off on such short notice, but he did."

"He's a marvel," said Kate.

"The florist is also arranged. The limo will be coming over to your house to pick you and Nan up. By the way, who is giving you away?"

"No one," said Kate. "I'm giving myself away."

Unusual, thought Victoria, *but then she's a very unusual young woman*. "Pack up your honeymoon clothes and bring your luggage over the day before when you come at two thirty for the rehearsal."

"Andrew and Esther are hosting the rehearsal dinner at seven," Kate told them. "All of you are invited."

"That's lovely," Victoria told her. "Please tell them that all six of us will be attending. I know I can speak for everyone when I say that."

"Great, that means there will just be the ten of us. Nan gets in lunchtime Friday and leaves Sunday afternoon. The Petersons will take care of her after the wedding. I'll pick her up from the airport, take her to lunch, and then we'll come to the rehearsal."

"Then we're all set," said Victoria.

"I can't believe how much you've been able to arrange," Kate exclaimed.

"Do we have much more to add to the list for upstairs?" asked Nick.

"Well, there is the whole kitchen, but I'll not put you through that," said Kate, seeing the look on Nick's face. "How about we just look at what you want for the deck?"

"Why doesn't Nick go with you when you register?" suggested Victoria. "That way, he can look at the barbecues and firepits and see exactly what he wants."

"Great idea, Mother," said Nick hurriedly.

Dinner that evening was a barbecue, with Nick and Jarrod doing the cooking. Afterward the happy couple retreated to Nick's study for a little alone time but before they did Jeanne was looking at Kate's ring and of course had to ask how many carets.

"It's three point eight, and it's not white gold. It's platinum," Nick informed her.

"Jeanne, don't be so nosy," Kate told her.

"Just asking!"

Nick and Kate settled down with some coffee and talked about the furniture they'd need for the flat.

"Nick," she suddenly said. "Where are we going on our honeymoon?"

"That's a surprise," he informed her.

"I don't want a fancy honeymoon," she told him. "Just a cozy inn on the coast would be fine with me."

"What?" he said, looking at her.

"I know you, Nick," she said to him. "You could be planning a fancy European or east coast honeymoon, but honestly, I would prefer a local place. I don't want to share you with lots of traveling and different hotels."

"Really?" Nick said, with his arm around her, looking her full in the face. "You don't want to go to Rome or Venice or Paris?"

"I'd love to go to those places with you sometime," she told him, "but not on our honeymoon. Please, Nick. Don't plan a trip that has a full itinerary. I just want to be with you. There'll be plenty of time for travel and sightseeing, but not on our honeymoon."

"You're a most unusual woman," said Nick. "I thought every woman wanted a fancy honeymoon."

"Nick Barkley, don't you know the only place I want to go with you on our honeymoon is bed!"

He just stared at her and then kissed her in the way she was starting to get used to.

"Okay, I'll plan a honeymoon just the way you want, except a little more upscale than you had imagined," he told her. "Bring all your glad rags, and what you don't have, we'll buy when we get there. Oh, and don't worry about the number of bags or the weight of your luggage. We'll be traveling on a private plane."

"You have access to a private plane?"

"Of course we do. We don't have time for airline schedules! I'll bring Nan out and send her home in one."

"Really!"

"There are a few perks to being a Berkley! Give my secretary Nan's number, and they can make the arrangements together."

He made a mental note to talk with Jeanne about what to have Kate pack. He decided there and then that they'd go to San Francisco—he knew she'd never been—and book the honeymoon suite at the St. Gregory for two weeks. That way they could have the benefits of a city or stay in and order room service. The St. Gregory was the hotel his family had always stayed at in San Francisco since he was a boy. It was a beautiful traditional place with excellent restaurants and incredible service. He knew the staff would look after him and his bride. *Just the right place for us*, he decided. *I'll call their concierge and start making plans with his help.*

He also couldn't forget the comment Kate had passed about where she really wanted to go with him on their honeymoon—bed! He really couldn't get a read on Kate when it came to intimate things. She had seemed perfectly willing just to hang back and let him set the pace of their romance. He hadn't kissed her 'til they were on their fourth date! He didn't feel that she was the kind of girl to rush into an intimate relationship. She never mentioned anyone in her past. Nick knew that she must have heard about him and some of his past relationships. Who and what the Barkleys did was a constant source of gossip in Stockton, and he, more than the rest of his family! *I'm sure Jeanne must have told her something of my past*, he mused. *I must ask that housekeeper exactly how much she knows about Kate's dating history.*

"Can we call it a night?" his fiancée asked him. "I need to get a good night's sleep. I have so much to do tomorrow."

"Sure," he replied, admitting he hadn't gotten much sleep himself last night.

"I'm going to look for my dress in the morning," Kate told him.

They indulged in what could only be described as some passionate making out! Nick was leaning over partway on top of Kate, who was just as ardent as her fiancé, when she shot out his arms liked she'd been fired out of a canon! "Bloody hell, Nick Barkley, take your hand off my breast! How dare you?"

"Easy, easy," he said, surprised at her reaction to what he considered just some mild petting. After all, in his head, they were going to be married in two weeks, so what's the difference when they started getting to "know" each other a little better. Obviously, Kate didn't think so!

"What's wrong, babe?"

"What's wrong?! You had your hand on my breast, that's what's wrong!"

"So? Kate, in two weeks we'll be married and after that when I have my hand on your breast it won't be covered by a dress and bra! When you do give me the privilege of taking you to bed and making love to you I can promise you one thing babe, I'll make sure you get a lot pleasure out of it. I've been around the block a few times and I do know how to please a lady!"

"Nick I'm not going down that rabbit hole with you!"

"Kate, I've heard sex called a lot of things in my time, but never going down a rabbit hole!"

"Now you're making fun of me."

"No, I'm not. It's just, in this day and age, I don't understand your reluctance to our sleeping together. We're engaged, after all."

"I don't care, Nick, we're not married, and I'm not about to become a notch on Nick Barkley's bedpost!"

"A WHAT? Is that what you think you'd become if you slept with me? That's all I see you as is some kind of conquest? Is that where your head is at? Don't you understand how very, very much in love with you I am? I have been head over heels in love with you from the very second I saw you. I'll never think of you as anything but the love of my life. Notch on my bedpost indeed! I don't know where you've gotten that crazy idea from, Kate, but you couldn't be more wrong. The fact is I'm a red-blooded American male with plenty of testosterone, and you're a very beautiful, very desirable woman, and put the two together, and things just start to happen!"

"Well, as far as I'm concerned, we are still waiting until May second. So I'll say good night and I'll see you tomorrow." And she left Nick still wondering why she was so reluctant to go to bed with him.

It was just after nine when Kate started on her hunt for the perfect wedding dress. By eleven, she was feeling very disheartened. *All these dresses look alike*, she thought. *I'll know exactly what I'm after as soon as I see it.* As she walked down the street to a coffee stand to refuel her energy, she passed an antique store. *I wonder*, she thought as she pushed open the door and went in. The overhead doorbell jangled as she stepped inside. *What a charming store, I wish I had more time to look around. I'll come back when I'm not in such a hurry.*

An old lady came from a back room. "Can I help you, dear?" she asked Kate.

"Well, I'm not sure," she replied. "I'm looking for a wedding dress, but the ones in the bridal stores all seem to look alike, almost strapless and glaringly white, the exact opposite of what I'm looking for!"

"What are you looking for?" the lady asked her.

"Cream, lace, and high-necked," said Kate rather ruefully. "I'm getting married in two weeks and am running out of places to look."

"If you can wait a few minutes, I'll see what I have packed away."

"How about I get a cup of coffee and come back?"

"Perfect," the old lady said.

"Can I get you one?" asked Kate.

"That's kind of you. Just black. My name is Pearl," the lady told her, "and I must tell you how beautiful that ring of yours is. Did you pick it out?"

"No. Nick, my fiancé, did," responded Kate.

"That man must love you very much to pick out a ring like that," Pearl told her. Kate just smiled but looked at her ring with new eyes! When she went back into the antique store, she couldn't believe what she saw—there hanging up was the dress she had dreamed of. Her eyes started to fill up with tears. "Now don't cry dear," Pearl said.

"I can't help it, I'm so happy," replied Kate. This is exactly the color and style I had envisioned. "Where did you find it?" she asked Pearl.

"I've had it packed away for months," Pearl told her. "I actually forgot about it. It was when you described what you wanted reminded me I had such a dress. I got it in an estate sale but had no room to display it when I bought it, so I just stored it away," continued Pearl. "What size do you wear?" she asked Kate.

"six or eight, depending on the designer."

"It might be a little on the big size for you, but a good dressmaker can remedy that."

"I know just the person," said Kate. Jeanne had told her last night that, in between housekeeping jobs, she had worked as a dressmaker.

"You did?" Kate had exclaimed.

"Sure did, and a darn good one at that, if I say so myself, so if you find the right dress, providing it's not too small, we can make it fit you."

She told Pearl about her closest friend on the west coast.

"Would you like to try it on?" asked Pearl.

"Would I?" In a few minutes, with some help from Pearl to do up the thirty-plus tiny buttons in the back, she had her dream dress on.

"Oh my goodness, you look so beautiful," exclaimed Pearl. "The fabric and style are perfect for you with your complexion and hair color. You certainly know what looks best on you, if I may say. You must look awful in white."

"I do," said Kate. "I've tried on white garments, a blouse or sweater, and I look terrible, it drains all the color from my face. I knew it would have to be cream or at least off-white. The deep cream is perfect for me."

"What color is your maid of honor going to wear?" asked Pearl.

"Peach," said Kate.

"Perfect."

"Please help me out of this and I'll get it to Jeanne right now so she can start altering it straight away."

Pearl carefully unbuttoned the dress and packed it back into the box it had been living in for the past few months. Kate settled the bill. It was no more than she'd expected to pay for a dress. Perfect. All she needed now was the veil.

Victoria had loaned her the headdress that she'd worn at her wedding. It was the right color, so she had the something borrowed. She had the something old, the dress itself, something new, her shoes, something blue, Jeanne was going to sew a blue thread into the seam of the dress, so that took care of everything in the rhyme.

She was passing a jewelry store on her way back to her car when she glanced in the window. What did they have displayed but a cigar case, lighter, and cutter in a matching set. *That would be perfect for Nick*, she thought and went in.

"That set is kind of expensive," the salesman told her. "It's white gold, not silver."

"Even better," Kate said. "Could you engrave it?"

"Of course," he told her. "Initials?"

"A combination of his ranch brand and initials. Here, I'll show you," and she drew it out for him.

"No problem."

"How soon can you have it ready?"

"Monday be okay?"

"Perfect."

Before she left, she noticed some white gold cufflinks. They would make wonderful gifts for Nick's brothers for being best man and ushers.

"Let me call my fiancé. Nick, where are you?"

"I'm in town," he told her.

"Could you come over to Stapleton's Jewelry Store and look at some gifts for your brothers?"

"Sure, I'll be there in less than five minutes."

"While we are waiting, I want a set of those cufflinks with the same brand and initials as the cigar set," she told the salesman, "but don't let my fiancé know. I'll pick them all up on Monday." Standing

115

there, she spied a small diamond pendant which she just knew Nan would love and would go with her bridesmaid's dress.

When Nick arrived, he agreed the cufflinks would be great for his brothers and that the pendant was a good idea for Nan. "We'll take them all," he said. "Here are the initials to go on each set. Please giftwrap them."

"Sure," said the salesman with a grin on his face. This was a big sale to Kate and the Barkleys.

"I'll take Nan's, and you may as well take your brothers."

"Okay, you go on, and I'll wait for them," he said.

Nick and Kate had arranged to meet at the flat at two to go through the attics and see if there was any furniture in there they could use. After such a successful morning and having her wedding dress fitted by Jeanne, Kate was floating on air. When she saw Nick, she flung her arms around his neck and gave him the kind of kiss he usually initiated. To say he was surprised would be an understatement, but he enjoyed it nevertheless!

"You are full of surprises," he told her.

"You don't know the half of it," she told him with a saucy grin on her face.

"I guess I don't," he agreed. *But I'm going to enjoy finding out,* he thought.

They went up into the flat and looked in at the bedroom where the furniture had all been put in place. "I have a full-length mirror that contains a jewelry case. Also an off-white reclining chair that will fit in just fine," she told him. "While we are away on our honeymoon, Jeanne will take care of my clothes being packed and moved here."

"And I'll have John supervise moving the boxes and furniture," said Nick.

"When we get back, everything will be unpacked, hung up, or put away in drawers. Oh it's wonderful not to have to worry about that," Kate said.

"Now let's look in the attics before I get any ideas about trying out the bed in here," said Nick with a big grin on his face.

116

They climbed the stairs into the extensive Barkley attics and began to look around. They found tables and lamps for their living room. "My flat-screen television can go in the bedroom, and yours, being bigger, will be perfect for the living room."

"John can have those hung while we are away and have the Blu-rays, and DVRs hooked up. The speakers are already in place. My desk will fit in, so all we basically need is a desk for you, desk chairs for both of us, and sofa and loveseat."

"Can we get a sectional instead?" she asked him.

"Of course," he answered, "do you want to go look for them now?"

"Sure, I'm up for it."

They headed for a furniture store that had supplied the family in the past.

"Mr. Barkley, nice to see you. How can I help?" the salesman asked.

Nick explained what they were looking for, and they were led to an area of the store where the sectionals were displayed. After looking around for a while, Nick and Kate settled on a leather one and picked out a dark green color.

"It will match the existing rugs beautifully," said Kate. "Now we need to look at desks." She picked out one similar to Nick's, and they decided on matching desk chairs in dark green leather to match the sectional.

"I think we're done shopping for the day," said Nick.

The reception that evening, held at the Barkley mansion, was in aid of one of the charities Victoria supported. Jeanne had brought Kate an off-the-shoulder, cream, very short evening dress. Nick wore one of his beautifully tailored suits, but of course, the talk of the evening was the engagement of the couple, all the women wanting to see Kate's ring. She danced with a variety of partners, but when the slow dancing started, Nick made it clear he was the only partner she would have from then on! By midnight, the reception was over, and Kate gladly went to her room, knowing she and Nick had a full day tomorrow.

Sunday dawned, and Kate thought over all they had accomplished in the last few days, almost making her head spin! They got engaged, had a place to live, which was almost furnished, the wedding plans were well underway thanks to Mrs. Barkley, she'd found the perfect dress, and today, she and Nick were going to register for household items.

After having brunch, they went to a local store that Victoria had recommended. It took them nearly three hours to pick out all the necessities for a kitchen and the china and glasses. Neither of them wanted fine china or crystal, so the items at the store suited them fine. They took with them a coffee maker and a set of mugs. "We'll need these as soon as we get back from our honeymoon," Kate explained to Nick. Next stop, a store specializing in outdoor furniture to pick out a barbecue and patio items, including a fire pit and double hammock.

"I'll go to Macy's to register for the bed linens and towels, etc.," she told him. "You don't have to come if you rather not."

"I'm not sure how much help I'd be," he replied.

"You're off the hook. I'll take care of that while you're at work."

"I'm going to have a half roof and partial walls put on the patio so we can still sit outside when there's a storm," said Nick, remembering how she loved them. "The sound system can either be set for the patio, living room, or bedroom."

"How wonderful. You've thought of everything," said his love.

By the time they'd got through registering for gifts, they were both tired.

"Let's head back to the ranch, and you can get a rest before dinner this evening," he told her.

Monday at nine, she and Nick set off for the doctor's office, where her procedure was going to be performed. By eleven, it was all over, and Nick was driving her home, treating her like she was made of glass! Getting back to the ranch, Kate went straight up to her room and lay down, with Jeanne and Silas fussing over her! She hadn't been back long when her boss called her. He told her that he'd looked at her x-rays and had seen the break in her hand and that she was going to be incapacitated for a number of weeks, and as she had a wedding coming up, he'd worked out her vacation and sick leave. She was already off this week, and she'd need at least another three weeks of sick leave because of her hand. She wouldn't be of any use at work, being unable to perform surgery or even write a prescription! Then she had three weeks of holiday leave, so he wasn't expecting her back to work for another six weeks after this one!

Kate gasped. "I can't take that much time off!"

"It's what you're entitled to, and by the way, congratulations on your engagement. I hear the happy day is the second."

"Boy, news travels fast in this town! Thank you so much, Dr. Greene."

A few minutes later, Ann, her PA, called. "We've all heard about your engagement, and the staff in the ER are going to throw you a personal shower a week on Wednesday at seven in the clubhouse at my apartment building, and we are not taking no for an answer!"

"Okay, okay," stammered Kate. "I'll be there, and thank you all very much."

When Nick stopped by to check on her, she told him about both phone calls.

"The time off is wonderful, and what is this personal shower?" he asked her.

"It's a shower where they are going to embarrass the hell out of me and give gifts that you'll get all the enjoyment out of! Why they don't make you the guest of honor instead of me, I'll never understand!"

That made Nick laugh, and Kate ended up laughing too, although she wasn't in the least looking forward to going to the shower if all the raunchy stories she'd heard about personal showers were true!

The judge had worked fast and had had the new carpet laid in Kate's room so she was going to move back home Thursday morning. Jeanne had already taken most of her things back over and had moved back herself to see everything was in order for Kate's return. Wednesday night, Kate felt well enough for Nick to take her to dinner at Paul's. Gus didn't work on weeknights, but the music Paul played through the concealed speakers was very romantic. Nick and

Kate danced a couple of times but mainly sat in "their" back both and talked, he with his left arm around her shoulders. As the evening wore on, they began kissing and soon were very involved in that enjoyable pursuit. Kate was wearing the jade green silk dress with the slit up the left side, the one Nick liked so much. He really appreciated her wearing things she knew he admired. Over the sound system came Johnny Mathis singing "The Twelfth Of Never," Kate's special song to him. They became more ardent, and Nick was leaning right over her when, suddenly, she slapped his face hard! Nick let her go, jumping back in surprise!

"What in damnation was that for?" he asked, rubbing his stinging left cheek.

"For putting your frickin' hand up my skirt and on my thigh! What in hell did you think you were doing?"

"Damn, babe, I would have thought that would have been obvious!"

"Gawd, didn't we have this conversation just a few days ago? Bloody hell, what part of 'no' don't you frickin' understand? Take me back to the judge's now. I mean right now!"

"Kate don't you think you're over reacting just a little?"

"Take me home, I'm not going back to the ranch with you after what you just tried to do. Either take me home now or I'll call a bloody taxi myself." She took her cellphone out of her purse.

"Put that away. Waiter, bring me the check." Nick paid the check, and they left in stony silence. Not a word was said on the drive to the judge's home, and Nick had barely stopped his truck when Kate was out of it, slamming its door behind her and then slamming the front door, also. Nick revved the truck up and peeled out the driveway at what seemed to anyone listening like a hundred miles per hour! Hearing all this was Jeanne, and it wasn't hard to work out that the couple had gotten into an argument and both were plenty mad!

"Trouble in paradise?" asked Jeanne when she brought Kate a cup of tea.

"What was your first clue?"

"Oh, you coming back here ahead of time, the doors slamming, and the over-revved engine gave me a pretty good hint!"

120

"I suppose you want to know what happened."

"Only if you want to talk about it. Do you?"

"Well, we had a lovely dinner, then we kinda got romantic."

"You mean you two were necking?"

"Yeah, right, and he was kinda leaning over me, and suddenly, I feel his right hand up my skirt, the left side that has the slit, and it's on my upper thigh.

"So what did you do?"

"I slapped the son of a bitch's face hard. Real hard!"

"You did what?"

"I told you, he's lucky that's all I did! I was so bloody mad at him I could have caused a real nasty scene at the restaurant but behaved myself and just demanded he bring me back here immediately."

"What did he say?"

"That I was overreacting. What a nerve!"

"Well, don't you think you did overreact just a tad?"

"What do you mean? Only a few days ago he had his hand on my breast and I told him then NO! That I wanted to wait until we were married. Then tonight, he's got his hand so far up my skirt, of course with that damn slit, it made it easy for him! A few more inches up my thigh, and he'd have got more than a slap, he might have given up his chances of fathering children!"

"Kate, you wouldn't have?"

"You bet I would! We were in a public place. What was he thinking? Because he wasn't thinking with his brain. His thoughts were coming from way below his belt!"

"You do realize you're going to be sleeping with the guy, as in—to make it crystal clear to you, in case you haven't completely thought this through—having sexual intercourse with him in just a few days? So he wants a preview of the coming attractions! Can you blame him? He's a man, you're a woman. Stuff like tonight is bound to happen sometime!"

"Jeanne of course I know what sleeping with a guy means, I'm a doctor, I know all about intercourse! But that is only going to happen if there is a wedding and as of now that is looking very doubtful."

"What? Did I hear you right? You're thinking of calling off the wedding because of one little spat? You've got to be joking?"

"It's more than a little spat. Tonight was the tip of the iceberg, Jeanne. The real problem is if we discuss something and I have a different opinion from him and the subject is important to Nick, it's like he ignores my opinion. Just steam rolls over it and only his point of view counts, I've noticed it before, but tonight it really brought it home to me. Can I spend the rest of my life with someone who doesn't value my point of view? And the answer I keep coming up with is NO, I can't. That's what I was thinking about as he drove me home probably for the last time. Don't get me wrong, I admit I do love that bloody arrogant, son-of-a bitch, but that's not enough to build a life on if I know going in that he is not going to listen to me unless I agree with him. That thinking belongs in the 1870s that he loves so much, but I live in the twenty-first century and can't give up the way of life I've fought so hard to achieve. So I'm going to call Mrs. Barkley first thing in the morning and ask her to put the plans on hold and let her know I'll make my final decision by afternoon."

"When he hears that, he'll be right over."

"He can't, he's got some business meetings tomorrow in Stockton that will go on until about eleven at night. If he comes over, it won't be until Friday morning, but he's plenty mad at me for slapping him, so I don't think he'll show up here, but if he does, don't let him in. Tell him I don't want to see him. He'll get the message eventually. I won't be answering any calls he might make. But really, I think he's as done with me as I am with him. It was all wrong from start to finish. Maybe last night was a blessing in disguise, a wakeup call for both of us to the terrible mistake we almost made! I'm going to try to doze until it's time to call Mrs. Barkley. I don't think I'll sleep properly. I've too much on my mind. Good night, Jeanne."

"Good morning, Mrs. Barkley."

"Good morning, Kate. How are you?"

"Not too well I'm afraid. Has Nick told you that he and I got into it last night?"

"Well, he was pretty upset when he came in, and when I asked him what was wrong, he said the two of you had a disagreement and you'd parted on less than good terms. I think he was more upset about that than anything else."

"We obviously saw last night from two very different perspectives, and that's why I'm calling. I'd like you to put our wedding plans on hold, and I'll call you by this afternoon to let you know if there will indeed be a wedding at all! Which I may as well tell you doesn't look very likely."

"My dear, you can't mean it! Why don't you talk to Nick first and try to sort out whatever it was you two disagreed about last night before you reach any decision concerning the wedding?"

"Well, that's the trouble, Mrs. Barkley. Nick sees the problem as only last night, but I saw it as only the tip of the iceberg! The problem has been there for a while, I saw it, but Nick is completely unaware there is one, and I can't deal with that. I can't commit to spending the rest of my life with someone who doesn't recognize we have a major problem in our relationship. I really think we'd both be making the biggest mistake of our lives and end up paying a terrible price for it! You know what, I don't have to call you back, Mrs. Barkley, the more I'm talking, the more it becomes clear to me that the only thing to do is to cancel the wedding!

"Kate, think about what you're doing! You and Nick haven't even haven't had a chance to talk. Please, my dear, give him a chance to speak to you, not just because he's my son, but because you two love each other so much. I can see it in your eyes, the way you look at each other. Don't throw away the life you could have together without sitting down and at least hearing what the other has to say."

"No, I've made up my mind please do as I ask Mrs. Barkley and cancel the wedding. I'm sorry."

"Very well, I'll do as you ask. Goodbye, my dear."

"Nick, I've just had Kate on the phone," his mother told him.

"Oh, what did she want?"

"You're not going to like hearing this. She called to tell me to cancel the wedding arrangements. Your wedding is off!"

"IT'S WHAT!?"

"She sounded very calm and in control, said she'd been up most of the night thinking about it, that you and she have two different points of view of what happened last night. That, as far as she's concerned, you guys have a major problem in your relationship but you don't recognize that and she can't commit to spending the rest of her life with you because of that situation. And you'd both be making the biggest mistakes of your lives."

"She said all that to you?"

"Yes, she did. I tried to convince her to talk to you before she cancelled any arrangements, but she was adamant the wedding is off. She didn't say it, but I got the distinct impression she doesn't want to see or talk to you."

"Well, I don't give a damn what she wants. She's gonna talk to me. It's not just her wedding she's just cancelled, it's also mine! Just ignore what she told you. I'll talk to that young woman and set her straight about a few things. Like the fact we had a conversation just a few nights ago about who would make the major decisions in our marriage, and she seems to have forgotten what she said to me that, in her words, I was to be 'the head of the household,' so after we discussed things, she'd leave the final decisions to me. Well, if cancelling our wedding isn't a damn major decision, I don't know what is! I'll call her today, but with all the meetings I have scheduled, I won't have much of a chance to have a real conversation with her. So I'll just tell her I love her and then Friday, I'll go over and see her and we can talk face to face."

"Kate, I'm sure by now, you'll have realized my mother has told me about the phone call you made to her this morning. I don't know what's going on, and I very much want to, but as you know, I have meetings all day and evening, so I won't have a chance to really have a conversation with you today. Besides, this should be discussed face to face. I'll call you in the morning, and we'll go somewhere quiet where we won't be disturbed and talk. But please, at least call me and let me know how you are doing. I'm worried about you, babe. I do love you very much. Gotta go."

"Kate, it's me again. I still haven't heard from you, and it's now lunchtime. I'm really concerned. All I'm asking you to do is let me know how you are doing. I'm going back into a meeting, so I won't be picking up. Just leave me a message. Love you, babe. Please call me."

"Kate, babe, what in the hell is going on? Can't you do me the courtesy of a least responding to my calls? I don't know what has gotten into you! You've been acting squirrely for days now. Ever since I made what was, to you, the unpardonable sin of letting my hands wander, are you sure this is not all just wedding nerves? Dinner is over. By the time I get out of the last meeting, which should be around eleven, I expect a message from you, otherwise, I'm not going to get much sleep worrying about you. Sweetheart, I'm so in love with you, and whatever is bothering you, we can work it out together. Until tomorrow, good night, darling."

"What are you going to do, Kate?" Jeanne asked her friend. "He's determined to see you, and don't forget, you have the hospital fundraiser/reception that you have to go to Saturday night. Nick is going as your escort."

"Shit, I completely forgot about that. Well, obviously I won't be going with him. I can go on my own. I don't have to be on the arm of Nick Barkley!"

"So what happens when he comes over here tomorrow? And you know he's gonna. He won't take 'She doesn't want to see you' very well. It would be just like him to come storming into your room whether you want to see him or not!"

"Well, the best thing to do is for me to take off and only come back in time to get ready for the reception. If he does indeed come by, you can tell him from me that I'll be driving myself Saturday night. Better still, I'll leave him a message on his voicemail telling him just that!"

"That man is not going to like getting a message like that!"

"Tough!"

"Nick, it's me. I just wanted to let you know I'm going to the reception for the hospital Saturday night by myself. That includes driving my own car there. So you don't even have to go if you don't want to, which I think would be best under the circumstances, but that's up to you. Goodbye."

Friday morning, around nine, Nick was ringing the doorbell at Judge Peterson's home. Jeanne opened the door.

"I take it she's not here as her car is gone? Is she running errands?"

"I'm afraid not, Nick. She left yesterday and will only be back in time to get ready for the reception Saturday night.'

"SHE WHAT? Where the hell did she go?"

"I honestly don't know. If I did, I'd tell you because you two really need to talk, and her taking off like that so she doesn't have to face you is just plain ridiculous! And I told her so!"

"Do you have any idea what this is really all about? According to her, I overstepped the mark, but I'm flesh and blood, and she's so damned beautiful, and it's not like she was fighting me off when I, as she puts it, got out of line! That woman was just as into making out as I was. What happened was no big deal. We were in the middle of a damn restaurant! It's not like we were in my truck parked on my ranch somewhere. Then she might have had something to be concerned about what I might have tried to do next! But in Paul's? Give me a break! Jeanne, you really have no idea where she's gone?"

"No idea whatsoever. She just threw some clothes in a bag when she got your message about wanting to talk to her today and took off in that mini of hers like a bat out of hell. Why don't you come in and have a cup of coffee and I'll tell you all I know. She never said what she told me was in confidence, so I have no problem helping you understand what's going on in that head of hers! I know she's considered brilliant, but at times, if you ask me, she's nothing short of just plain screwy!"

"Thanks, Jeanne. Anything you can tell me that would help me understand what has gotten into that blasted redhead's brain would be wonderful! May God give me patience dealing with her!"

"Are you still going to the hospital reception now that's she's insisting on going alone?"

"Of course I am, she wants to play things her way, that's okay, but at the reception, then we'll play by my rules!"

Saturday night, Jarrod, Heath, and Nick were standing together at the hospital reception, dressed in their best suits and all looking extremely handsome. Suddenly, Heath nudged Nick. "Boy howdy, look at that," and nodded toward the entrance of the ballroom in city hall where the fundraiser was taking place. When Nick turned, there was Kate, looking absolutely stunning in a chic black tuxedo-style very short dress, her exceedingly long shapely dancer's legs encased in sheer black tights with seams up the backs, very high-heeled black shoes, and carrying a small black purse.

Nick murmured, "Oh God, help me," which made his brothers grin at him and each other, both well aware when their sibling hadn't escorted his fiancée that evening that all was not well between them! But before Nick could reach Kate, he was beaten by Scott Breckenridge, Jarrod's friend who was staying with the family to do some business with them and had, of course, come along to the reception with the brothers. Scott was a tall, very good looking man who had taken over his father's business and turned what had been a million dollar corporation into a multi-million dollar concern, hence his nickname, the Midas Man. He had been introduced to Kate at the same party where Nick had met her. What Nick was unaware of was Scott had been pursuing her since then, calling, sending flowers, and expensive candy, even taking her out a couple of times. Scott was unaware that she had been engaged to Nick or that she had even been dating him, and tonight, she wasn't wearing Nick's ring, having messengered it back to him on Friday. Scott immediately showered Kate with complements on her incredible appearance and even offered her his arm to squire her around the reception, and much to Nick's annoyance, she accepted.

Just what in the hell is she playing at? he thought. *Is she trying to make me jealous? Well, it damn well won't work!* He walked back to where his family were watching all this play out and escorted his mother, who was on the hospital board, around the reception. About an hour later, when the reception part of the fundraiser was over, the dancing part began. Nick couldn't help but notice that Kate danced the first dance with Scott, then men were lined up for their turn to dance with what was the most beautiful sexy woman in the room. He waited his chance, and when she was surrounded by people, he walked over and said to her, "I believe this is our dance," and held out his hand. Kate couldn't refuse without making a scene, and they both knew it! She just glared at him and walked onto the dance floor without taking his hand. Instead of wrapping her left arm around his neck, she just laid her hand on his upper arm, the way she'd done when they were first dating.

"Did you have a good trip?!" he asked her sarcastically. "And are you now ready to talk with me?"

"We have nothing to talk about, Nick. We're over, through."

"Don't be so ridiculous. You're talking absolute nonsense!"

"Stop talking to me like I was a child!"

"Then stop acting like one! You're a grown woman, act like one! Be an adult and sit down with me and rationally discuss what has happened between us! At least explain to me what I'm supposed to have done that's so terrible in your eyes that you'd cancel our wedding. It's my wedding too, and so far, I've had no say in the matter. I think you owe me that much. Why don't you come outside with me right now? I know this place, and there's a spot we can go to that's private and where we won't be overheard."

"All right, it won't take long to tell you how I see things and then I'm going home. I've done my duty here. I have shown up and socialized. That's all I was asked to do."

They walked outside through the French windows. Nick tried to take her hand, but she pulled away.

"Have we really gotten that far apart in just a few days that I can't even hold your hand?"

"We are over, Nick. No point in making it any more painful than it already is."

She sat down on a bench in a secluded area as far away from Nick as she could get, he standing a few feet away, watching her intently.

"Okay, tell me what the problem is?" he asked her.

She told him that, from her perspective, he just swept her opinions aside when she gave an opposing one to his on a subject he felt very strongly about and that she just couldn't see herself spending the rest of her life being treated like that. He took what she considered valid reasons for having an opposite stance to him and ground them to dust under his boot heel.

He just stared at her in total unbelief at what he'd heard.

"Kate, I've listened to every word you've said, and I don't understand a damn thing! Grinding your opinions under my boot heel?! What utter nonsense! Now, will you tell me the real reason you cancelled the arrangements? I know you're mad because, according to you, I got out of line, but I don't understand your reluctance to go to bed with me! You're a very beautiful woman, and I'm the man who's going to be your husband, and as for those nights that, according to you, my hands wandered, that's when nature was taking its course."

"Even though it's my body you're after and I clearly said no, which I have every right to do! But you didn't like hearing that, so in the usual Nick Barkley fashion, you find some excuse for not hearing what I've said and go on your own merry sweet way, with no thought as to how that makes me feel. Well, I'm here to tell you, Nick, I won't be treated like that for the rest of my life, so therefore, there is going to be no wedding. Now, do you understand what I'm saying to you? I don't think I could say it anymore clearly." She stood up to start and leave.

"Sit down! I haven't had my turn to speak," Nick said in a tone of voice he'd never up to that point used to speak to her.

"Don't you use that tone of voice with me, Nick Barkley, I'm not one of your hired hands!"

"I'm sorry, but you make me so damn mad. Oh God, grant me patience! When have I—except for this sex issue which, in this day and age, I still don't understand your reluctance—have I ever disagreed with what you've had to say? You're the smartest woman I have ever met. I'd be nuts not to listen to you. So the only issue we're arguing about is sex, right? I want to make love now, and you are insisting on waiting until we're married, have I got it right? There's nothing else we're disagreeing about?

"Um…yes."

"You're absolutely sure?"

"Yes, okay. It's the sex issue that I'm so fricking mad about."

"And because of that, you've cancelled our wedding? So what happened to my making the final decision on all important issues?

129

Isn't our wedding an important issue? Yet not once did you call me and ask me what I thought. Now who's disregarding whose opinions?"

"The head of the household only applies if we were married, and as that's not going to happen, it's a moot point," she told him.

"But I say we are going to get married, now what?"

"Nick, it takes two to get married, and right now, only one of us wants that."

"Bet I can change your mind!" Nick countered.

"That would be a sucker's bet."

"No, I don't believe it would be, and I've been a gambler since as far back as I can remember, and I've won way more than I've ever lost, so I'm willing to bet my future happiness that I can get you to change your mind and marry me!"

"And just how do you think you can do that?'

"Come over here and I'll show you!"

"Not on your life, Nick Barkley. You're not going to start your famous sweet-talking on me. I've heard all about it."

"Just what have you heard? Never mind, you can tell me some other time. Sweet-talking wasn't exactly what I had in mind!"

"No, oh no, you don't, Nick, I'm not coming anywhere near you, I know just what you've got in mind, and that won't fix our problem, even if it is only about the sex issue!"

"Yes, it would. We can't be mad at each other or misunderstand each other if we are involved in, let's say, more pleasurable activities."

"Nick, that just doesn't make sense."

"Then come over here and prove me wrong, Kate."

"Not on your life!"

"Then I'm coming over to you."

"Don't you dare!"

"Daring me? Shouldn't have said that, babe." And in a flash, he had reached her, pulled her up onto her feet, and wrapped his arms around her. It was a repeat of the night of Victoria's birthday party where Kate had tried to resist but ended up kissing him just as passionately as he was kissing her.

After many moments had passed, he whispered in her ear, "Well, have I won my bet?"

"No, but I did enjoy you trying," was her response.

"WHAT!"

"You could keep on attempting to win if you want to," Kate said with a sly grin on her face.

"Do you think I have any chance of winning?" he asked with a mischievous grin on his face, his charming dimples showing.

"Maybe if you try hard enough and do what I believe is called upping the ante!"

"If you just want me to continue kissing you, why don't you just say so?'

"Because that wouldn't be ladylike, and my granny taught me to always be a lady!"

"What about nature taking its course? And don't even think about slapping my face again for doing what comes naturally."

"And do you remember what I said about rabbit holes and how I wasn't about to go down one with you until we are married? I'll defend myself anyway I can."

"Jeanne told me about the comment you passed, that if I'd gone any further that night in Paul's what you'd have attempted to do to me!"

"She's got a big mouth."

"You wouldn't really have risked my chances of putting a child inside you, would you?"

"Yes, I would, now maybe you'll understand how serious I am on that subject!"

"Kate, there is a place I can take you that's very quiet, very private, and oh so discreet. We can go there right now, and I will show you how much I really love you, and we can get the first-time love-making issue out of the way for you. I can promise you, you'll find nothing but pleasure in my arms, babe, and we can stay there as long as you want to—all night, if you'd like. No one will ever know."

"But I'll know, Nick, and that's the problem. As wonderful as you make an interlude like that sound, the answer is still no. And don't even try to disregard my opinion or we'd be back to cancelling the wedding!"

He gazed at her for a second, shrugged his broad shoulders, and they went back to making out for quite a while before deciding to go back in, but not before Nick pulled her engagement ring out of his pocket and put it back on her finger.

"And leave it there this time," he told her, kissing her fingers.

They walked back into the ballroom just as the band was playing the last dance. This time, Kate wrapped her arm around Nick's neck and he held her right hand on his chest, exchanging a gentle sweet kiss now and again. Victoria saw them and reasoned the wedding was back on. Nick insisted on following Kate home, which gave them a chance to say goodnight properly. When she went in and Jeanne saw the ring back on Kate's finger, the housekeeper grinned.

"I guess the wedding is back on?"

"Yes, it is."

"And just how did he talk you into it?"

"He didn't talk!"

"He didn't…oh, I get it. Used the famous Barkley charm, did he?"

"It wasn't his charm that did it!"

"What then?"

"Do you remember what I told you happened in the garden at his mother's birthday party? Well, it happened again!"

"Yes, I can see how that would change your mind! He's that good a kisser?"

"Do you really have to ask? I can't think straight when he takes me in his arms and starts kissing me."

"Methinks you're gonna have one hell of a wedding night!"

"Personally, I don't think he'll wait that long. More like wedding afternoon!"

"You lucky lady, a wedding afternoon and night!"

Just then, Nick phoned to tell her that the furniture store had called his cell earlier that day and he'd forgotten to tell her to let him know the furniture would be delivered while they were away on their honeymoon.

"Mother will take care of setting everything up," Nick assured her.

"It's going to look wonderful," Kate said. "But, Nick, you know what we've forgotten—a table, chairs, and buffet."

"You're right," Nick answered. "I'd forgotten too. Tell you what, we'll go Monday morning and look for them."

"That's perfect."

Mrs. Barkley had arranged a reception for them a week after they got back from their honeymoon at two in the afternoon. The invitation list was growing by leaps and bounds and wasn't going to be much short of three hundred fifty people. There was a four-tier wedding cake ordered, that much Kate did know, and she was going to wear her wedding dress. All the other details, Kate really didn't want to know!

Jeanne had finished altering her wedding dress and had made a veil. They had a dress rehearsal. The dress now fit beautifully along with the veil and headdress.

"You're all set. The shoes you found are great and will also match your going-away outfit."

"What did you find for that?" asked Esther.

"A peach dress with a bolero jacket." Kate showed Esther.

"Oh, that's beautiful," she said.

"I'm all set. Just have to pack."

"I'll do that for you," Jeanne said. "I have a good idea what you need."

"How do you know that?" asked Kate.

"A little birdie told me." Jeanne laughed.

"Do you realize in six days we'll be married?" Kate said to Nick as they sat down to dinner at Paul's.

"Can hardly wait," was his response, kissing her hand.

"We had a dress rehearsal this morning, and everything is ready," she told him.

"I'm sure you'll look beautiful," he murmured as he kissed her neck.

"Hey, down boy. Six days to go."

"Don't remind me," he answered her. "Can't I just practice a bit?"

"No, you can't," she told him.

"Spoilsport."

"I'm having the lamb," she said, changing the subject.

"Let's dance," he suggested.

"Okay," she told him, "But keep control of your hands!"

"You really know to wreck the moment!"

She wrapped her arm around his neck as Gus sang "Nightingale In Berkley Square" and then "Some Enchanted Evening."

"Our songs," Nick whispered. They enjoyed their dinner as Paul came by to talk to them. It seemed everyone knew that next Saturday was their "big day." Gus joined them, and they all had a glass of champagne.

"Are you going to let me in on the honeymoon surprise?" she asked Nick as he drove her home.

"Nope, just let Jeanne do your packing and you'll be fine. I hear you bought new luggage."

"Boy, you do have a direct line to me, don't you?"

"Better that you know," he said.

"What else do you think you know?" she asked.

"Oh, that would be telling," he answered her. They spent a few minutes kissing goodnight, and then reluctantly, she went in and he went home. *Last Sunday I'll have to do this*, he thought.

Nick called Kate late Wednesday night to ask how the shower had gone.

"I've never been so embarrassed in all my life," Kate said.

"Why?" asked Nick.

"The things I got as gifts. I don't know why they didn't just ask you to be guest of honor instead of me. After all, everything I got was for your benefit, not mine!"

"Like what?" asked Nick.

"Try crotch-less panties!" said Kate, a disgusted tone to her voice.

There was a long pause on the phone. "Did you just say what I think you said?"

"Sure did, to say nothing of the nightgowns and other stuff which I'm dropping off for you tomorrow and hope your mother is not around when I do!"

"When you come by, I need a four-digit code from you to open the side gate, so you can be thinking of that. What things did you say you are bringing by?"

"Wait and see. You can decide if you want to bring any of it with you on our honeymoon!"

"That's very cryptic!"

"Cryptic is not the word I'd use to describe this stuff," she said.

Thursday morning, she found a box and packed all the "stuff" she had been given as gifts at the shower and put it in her car and drove over to the ranch. Silas opened the door and tried to take the box from her. She hung on to it and said it was "for Mr. Nick." Nick came downstairs and gave her a strange look, took the box from her, and removed the lid. When he saw what was inside, Nick hastily put the lid back on and took the box upstairs to his room. When he came back down, Kate was having coffee with his mother and sister.

"Could I talk to you for a moment?" he asked her.

"Certainly," she answered him.

"You got all that stuff at the shower?"

"Well, you don't think I went out and bought it!" she exclaimed. "I don't frequent adult-only stores, so I've never experimented with the sexual stuff that's in there. But I'm sure you know all about the type of things that men and women use, so I'll leave it up to you if you want to bring any of it with you on our honeymoon!"

"WHAT! Why would you think I know about that kind of stuff? Are you are trying to take the mickey or what?"

"Me?" she said. "Why would you think that?"

"I have a feeling there is something important that you're not telling me," said Nick, giving her a shrewd look!

"Well, as a matter of fact…no, it's okay. Another time! I'm going to finish my coffee with your mother," she told him and hurriedly left before he could ask her any more questions!

There's definitely something she's not saying, thought Nick. *Every time she gets close to telling me, she just shies away from it. What on earth can be so difficult to tell me? Am I so hard to talk to? I've got to try and make it easier for her to confide in me.*

Thursday afternoon, she had an appointment, along with Esther for a manicure and pedicure. She wondered if she should have come clean and told Nick her secret, but she hadn't the courage. When was she going to tell him, or should she just let him find out? There wasn't much time left for her to make up her mind.

When she got home, she sat on her bed and watched as Jeanne packed her suitcases. The housekeeper put in city day clothes, dressy sport clothes, casual outfits, her new lingerie, and sweats. *A bit of everything*, she thought. The bags were packed but not closed until morning. The garment bag was hanging with her evening gowns and black silk kimono in it. *It is nice not to have to worry about the weight or numbers of bags*, she thought. *I could definitely get used to this. So this is how the Barkleys live.*

It was Friday, and at eleven, she picked Nan up at the airport. In fact, it was she and Nick who picked Nan up because she didn't know where to pick up private passengers, and he said it was easier to show her than to tell her!

So he picked up his fiancée, and they headed out to get Nan, who had loved the idea of not having to worry about the weight or total of her luggage pieces. Nick took them to lunch and then to the ranch for the rehearsal. Everything went smoothly. Kate and Nick had already picked out their vows. Everything had been timed out. The limo to pick up Kate and Nan would be there at nine forty. It was all going with military precision. When Nick dropped Kate and Nan off, he picked up all Kate's luggage and didn't bat an eye at how much she had.

"It will stay locked in my truck," he said, and, "Heaven help anyone who messes with it!" Nan told Kate that she, for one, believed the threat! After Nick left, Nan wanted to go and buy the wedding gift, but Kate needed to do her hair, so Jeanne took the maid of honor. When they got back, Nan left a beautifully wrapped gift sitting on the living room table.

"Which reminds me," said Kate, and she dashed upstairs to call Nick. "Don't forget to bring your brother's cufflinks over so we can give the wedding party their gifts tonight."

"Okay, will do," he said. "See you later, sweetheart."

The dinner was the opposite of the rehearsal—laid back and easy. The brothers really liked their gifts, as did Nan. When everyone was getting ready to leave, Nick announced he needed ten minutes with Kate alone.

He went and got a gift-wrapped flat box that he'd left in the hallway. "My wedding gift to you," he said.

When she opened it, she stared at a pearl necklace with matching earrings. "Nick, they're incredible," she stammered. "I have never seen anything so exquisite." Kate thanked him in a very appropriate manner, and he started to leave.

"Where are you going?" she asked. "Don't you want your wedding gift from me?" And she handed him a box. In it were a pair of the same cufflinks they had bought his brothers, except these had his initials and the Barkley brand on them. This time, it was Nick's turn to be surprised.

"These are wonderful, not just my initials, but with the brand incorporated. Thank you so much." He threw the door open and said, "Hey, everybody, look at what my wife-to-be gave me, and it's trademarked just for me!"

"And look what my husband-to-be gave me," said Kate, showing off her pearls.

"And on that note, it's time we all went home before it becomes their wedding day," Victoria said. Everyone hugged and kissed.

"Well, this is it," said Nick. "In a few hours, you'll be my wife."

"I can hardly wait," Kate said. "Now, get out of here so I can get some sleep."

He kissed her long and hard. "I love you," he said.

"I love you too," she told him and locked the door as he got in his truck and drove away.

Chapter 9

It's my wedding day. It's here, she thought as she woke up. *It's my wedding day, and I still haven't told Nick. Well, it'll have to be after the ceremony*, she thought. *There'll be no time to talk with him before. Oh, why did I wait so long? Just scared, I guess.* She heard a knock at her door, and there was Jeanne with breakfast trays followed by Nan carrying her own tray.

"We thought we'd bring breakfast to you," they told her. While she sipped her coffee and ate her fruit and muffin, they chattered and laughed. Soon, it was time to take a quick shower, and then start and get dressed.

"The flowers have arrived," Andrew called from downstairs.

"Oh, your bouquet is really beautiful. All cream-colored wild-flowers. Victoria has thought of everything," Esther told her. Lots of pictures were taken, and then it was time for Andrew and Esther to leave. "We'll see you over there."

Then came the knock at the door which was the limo driver. Between the two women, they got Kate into the car, followed by Nan, and finally Jeanne, who sat up front beside the chauffeur. It took them twenty minutes to drive over to the ranch. Many of the ranch and office employees were waiting outside the front door cameras at the ready to get a shot of the future Mrs. Nick Barkley as she arrived for the ceremony. They got out of the car in reverse order; Jeanne, Nan, and finally the bride herself. There were oohs and aahs from the spectators. The press was also waiting by the door. The official photographer got the shots he needed, and then the signal was given, and Audra started to play the wedding march as she had promised.

This is it, thought Kate as she walked between rows of people and then caught sight of Nick looking at her. *Oh, he looks so handsome in that tux. There's Jarrod standing next to him, and the other two brothers alongside their mother.* She took it all in at a glance but kept her eyes on the man she loved and was about to marry.

When she reached Nick, he leaned over to lift her veil and whispered, "You look amazing, darling."

She smiled at him and whispered back, "So do you," and the service started.

She fought back tears of joy as they gazed at each other while making their vows and exchanging wedding bands. *This really has happened. I'm married,* she thought, as the pastor was introducing them as "Mr. and Mrs. Nicholas Barkley," and everyone was applauding. They walked together to the foot of the staircase where the rest of the photographs would be taken for the next fifteen minutes or so as the photographer did his job. Then they were free to circulate among their guests. They cut the cake, leaving Silas and his staff to actually slice it up, and dutifully fed each other a small piece, drank a toast, and then went upstairs to change into their going-away clothes, Kate in the master bedroom while Nick went in one of the guest rooms.

Suddenly, they were both ready. The bouquet and garter were tossed, and they were in the back seat of the car driven by John, heading for the airport. "Now let me greet my wife properly," said Nick, and it took Kate gasping for air before he let her go! "That's better," he said.

Kate gazed at her new ring. "Nick, it's so beautiful. Where did you find it?" she asked him.

"I got it from San Francisco," he told her. "I didn't think I could find anything like it in Stockton."

"Are you sure your ring is what you wanted?" she asked.

"It's exactly what I wanted. I didn't want anything too fancy, and this braided design was perfect, but I wasn't expecting you'd get me a platinum one," he said to her as he fingered it. "But wearing it is going to take some getting used to!"

The car pulled up next to the plane, and their luggage was loaded on board.

"I've got your list of everything you want done, and I'll take care of it all while you're away," John told his boss.

"You can call me if there is a real problem," Nick said. "Otherwise, use your own judgement and coordinate with Jeanne."

"You got it, sir. Have a wonderful trip."

They climbed aboard and thanked John again for all he'd done. After takeoff, Nick and Kate sat back and relaxed.

"So now are you going to tell me where we are going?" Kate asked.

"We are spending the next two weeks in the honeymoon suite of the St. Gregory in San Francisco," he told her.

"San Francisco," she replied. "I've always wanted to go there, and now I get to see it and spend our honeymoon close by home so we don't have lots of traveling. Thank you so much. You don't mind, do you, Nick?"

"Of course not," said her husband. By lunchtime, they were at the hotel, which drew oohs and aahs from Kate.

"The suite is so gorgeous," she told him. Their luggage was brought up, and a maid and valet arrived to unpack it.

"May I suggest you order lunch, sir?" the maid said. "They could serve you on your private deck while we unpack for you."

"That's a good idea, Nick," said Kate.

He ordered a steak sandwich and she, a fruit salad and a pot of coffee. It was served on their private terrace. Before she started eating, she went into the bedroom and returned with a gift bag. "For you, Nick," she said.

"For me?" He opened it and pulled out the cigar case, lighter, and cutter. "They are wonderful, and all have the Barkley brand and my initials. I can't thank you enough." He opened the case to find it filled with cigars, the kind that were made just for him. They even had a band on them which said "Made Especially For Nick Barkley."

"How did you know where to get these?" he asked.

"I used Silas on that," she told him. "I got fifty. The rest are in a box in the bedroom."

"You are too much," he said as he finished his sandwich and lit a cigar. "Lady, you are spoiling me already!"

Soon, the maid and valet let them know they had finished unpacking. Nick walked them to the door, giving them a generous tip and making sure the "do not disturb" sign was on the door, and it was locked!

He walked back to the terrace and pulled Kate out of her chair, not caring that she hadn't finished the salad, and kissed her. They stayed locked in their passionate embrace and moved toward the bedroom. Nick had already taken off his jacket and vest, undone his tie, taken out his new cufflinks, and rolled up his shirt sleeves. She had taken off her jacket and removed her shoes. It didn't take long for Nick to be shirtless and barefoot and her dress to be lying on the bedroom carpet. She was wearing just a bra and the smallest excuse for panties from her favorite lingerie store, Agent Provocateurin San Francisco—that she was so looking forward to visiting while in the city.

"Oh my god, you're so incredible. More beautiful than I had imagined," he whispered to her as he started to unhook her bra with only one hand!

She stopped him and said, "Nick, there's something I should have told you before now."

"What's that?" he asked and, not being able to stop himself, had started to caress and kiss her neck.

"I've never done this before," she murmured to him. She felt him stop nuzzling her neck and looked at her with a puzzled expression on his face. "Do you mean you're a...?"

"Yes," she said. "I'm still a virgin. Does that make any difference to you?"

His expression changed to one of enlightenment. "So that's what you've been trying to tell me!" He looked down at his bride softly and lovingly and told her, "I always knew you were special, I just never realized how special." And with that, he picked her up and carried her to the already turned downed bed.

"Babe, you know this is going to hurt," Nick told her. "I'm sorry, there's no other way. I can't help having to cause you pain, but that's the way it is for a woman. I'm so sorry. I'll be as gentle as I can."

He hurt her more that she'd anticipated, and she couldn't help, when the pain was at its height, crying out. But after, as she was lying naked in the circle of his arms, she thought, *This is how I want to spend the rest of my life.* He held her tight and softly crooned to her.

"More than the greatest love the world has known,
This is love I give to you alone.
More than the simple words I try to say,
I only live to love you more each day.
More than you'll ever know my arms long to hold you so,
My life will be in your keeping,
Waking, sleeping, laughing, weeping.
Longer than always is a long, long time,
But far beyond forever you'll be mine,
I know I never lived before,
And my heart is very sure no one else could love you more."

Tears of pure joy slowly ran down her face. When he saw them, he gently kissed them away.

"My darling, I don't think you have any idea the depth and breadth of my love for you, but starting now, and over the next two weeks, I hope that I can teach you," he whispered to her.

She nestled even closer to him, if that was at all possible, and dozed off. When she woke, Nick was gone. She got up, put on a robe, and went looking for him. He was on the terrace, smoking his cigar, wearing pants and a shirt, unbuttoned. He turned around as she opened the door. "Are you all right?" he asked her, his voice full of concern.

"I'm waiting to come back to earth," she told him.

He put an arm around her. "Are you sure you're okay?" he persisted.

"I'll be fine, just sore," she told him. "I expected I would be like that, but I'll be all right, really."

"I'm so sorry. I knew that I had hurt you judging by your reaction, but there was no way I could avoid it," Nick said, his voice still full of concern for her.

"Please stop. I knew what to expect, and I'll be fine. The soreness will gradually go away. The more we make love, the easier it will get for me," she explained. "So you've got no excuse to hold back."

"Just how did I get so lucky to have you fall in love with me?" he asked her.

She sat down and finished her salad.

"Do you want some fresh coffee?" he asked her.

"Sounds good," she said.

"I'll call room service and housekeeping at the same time and have them change the sheets."

"Why?" she asked him.

"There was a little blood from you making love for your first time. I'll take the bottom sheet off so the staff won't see the reason we're asking for clean sheets. They'll just think we got kinda rough and tumble!"

"Oh, Nick," said Kate, blushing and looking away from him.

"Don't be embarrassed about it, babe. I think it's amazing, and something I know I'll remember for the rest of my life. Very few men can say the woman they married came to them a virgin like you came to me, and I love you for saving yourself like that. A woman as beautiful as you must have been fighting men off with a stick!"

"Actually, I haven't dated all that much. My guardians were very strict with me. Then, when I got into the service, I knew that was no place for a serious romance. A lot of men were married or had girlfriends back home and were just looking for a bit of fun on the side, and that wasn't for me. And the others, the ones without attachments, wanted a girl only for the length of their posting and I wasn't about to do that either. So I just stayed to myself."

He shook his head and gave her a big hug, still marveling at the woman he'd just married.

"I better make those calls," he told her, and then went into the bedroom and pulled off the sheets. When housekeeping arrived, he just laughed and gave them a large tip and a wink. Soon after, room service arrived with Kate's coffee. They continued to sit outside, each lost in their own thoughts.

"Where are we going tonight?" she asked.

"I thought we could dine right here in the hotel," replied Nick. "They have a wonderful restaurant with an orchestra, so we can dance. How about you wear that red dress you wore to Mother's birthday party."

The evening was magical for them both. They had a wonderful dinner and danced so close. Nick kept whispering to her how beautiful she was and how much he loved her, kissing her repeatedly until both knew it was time to go back upstairs to their suite and make love once more. He hurt her again, and when he did, she made a groaning sound, an almost involuntary reaction to the pain. Nick was full of concern afterward, but she told him it was something that, given time, she'd get used to. He held her tight, and they went to sleep wrapped naked in each other's arms. *I've died and gone to heaven,* Nick thought. *Now I've gotten to make love to the woman of my dreams and she's mine, all mine. I can't believe I'm her first.*

Kate was aware Nick had slept with many other women. She knew he'd been quite a womanizer, always seen with a beautiful woman on his arm, and his affairs with many of those ladies was gossiped about. *But I don't care,* she thought. *What's important to me is I'm the one whom he made vows to, has given his wedding band and now has his name!*

When they woke up, they made love again. *This is the kind of honeymoon I have dreamt of,* thought Kate. *Married to the man I love and adore and who doesn't mind I have no sexual experience.*

Nick was thinking along the same lines. *I know it's not easy for her, but she's not complained at all. The more we have sex, the easier it will get for her. What a wonderful prospect.*

Nick got up, showered, and shaved, getting ready to go downstairs for the famous brunch the hotel offered. Kate had lazed around in bed, and after he was finished in the bathroom, took a quick shower. By this time, the splint on her hand was gone, and her little finger was just taped to the next one, which made things a lot easier for her. As she was getting dressed and putting her makeup on, Nick was sitting on their balcony with his feet up, reading the newspaper and drinking the coffee he'd ordered from room service, her phone rang. She answered it, surprised it was Scott Breckenridge calling her. In a nutshell, he told her he'd just got back into the county after being in Europe and the Far East for the last three weeks and had come straight to Stockton to see her. Imagine his surprise to find that only the day before she had married Nick Barkley!

What in the hell was she thinking? Barkley would only wind up breaking her heart. He might stay faithful to her for a few months, but then he'd revert to his old ways of skirt chasing! He had known Nick for years and years, and she obviously didn't know the extent of his reputation with women. His affairs and one-night stands were notorious in certain circles. Had her husband told her about them? Knowing Nick, probably not!

Scott wanted to know what exotic place Barkley had taken her to for the honeymoon? When she stammered, "San...San Francisco," Scott just laughed.

"Is that the best he could do with all his money? If it were me, I'd have taken you to some romantic South Seas Island and shown you just what romance was all about. I take it the marriage has already been consummated? Of course it has, Barkley wouldn't have waited any longer than he had to, to bed a woman as beautiful as you. Kate, let me get you out of this marriage before he gets a chance to really hurt you. I can be on my plane and with you in just over an hour and get you away from him. I have a whole team of lawyers who work for me. They can get you an annulment in no time flat, then you can marry me! I'll treat you right, Kate. I love you. I'll show you what real love is all about. You'll travel the world with me. I'll give you anything your heart desires. Just say yes and I'll take care of Nick Barkley. He'll never bother you again!"

Kate had listened to Scott speechless. She couldn't believe what she had just heard him say to her. She'd always known he was interested in her, but she hadn't realized he loved her. There was silence for a few seconds before she responded.

"What you haven't taken into consideration is that I'm very much in love with Nick. I wouldn't have married him if I wasn't. He's my husband now. I made vows to him yesterday to love and honor him for the rest of my life, and I fully intend to keep those vows. He gave me his name and wedding band, and I intend to keep both forever. I don't care what he did in his life before he met me—that's all in the past, and that's where it's going to stay. I don't believe for one minute that he'd ever hurt me by being unfaithful. He took the same vows that I did. I saw the look in his eyes as he was saying those words, and he meant them. I appreciate your concern for me, but I know what I'm doing, and because you're so close to the Barkley family, I'm going to forget all about this phone call. Goodbye, and please don't ever call me again."

But what Kate hadn't realized was Nick had walked into the bedroom to bring her a cup of coffee and, standing in the doorway, had heard every word she had said! As she shut off the phone, she glanced up into the mirror and saw her husband's reflection there.

"Mind telling me what that was all about, Kate?" he asked as he handed her the coffee.

"Nothing important," she answered.

"What I just heard was not nothing important," he countered. "I thought there were no secrets between husband and wife, yet here we are, married less than twenty-four hours, and already, you're keeping something that sounded very important from me. Who called you, Kate? I think judging by the way you responded, I have a right to know."

She was silent for a few seconds before answering him. "Nick, I said it wasn't important. Please let it drop. Forget all about it. I'll finish getting dressed, and we'll go get some of that wonderful brunch you've been telling me about."

Nick stood there, looking at her, arms folded, feet planted wide apart, face stern. "We are not going anywhere until you tell me what's going on," he told her. "I repeat, who was that on the phone and what did they say to you that made you respond the way you did? Do you realize you haven't once looked me in the eye since that call ended? Now, what the hell was it all about, Kate? Don't make me ask you again!"

Kate knew when Nick used that tone of voice, which he'd never done with her, coupled with that look on his face, he wasn't kidding around, and the last thing she wanted was to get in an argument after less than twenty-four hours of marriage, but she also knew if she told Nick Scott had been on the phone, there was no knowing what her new husband would do! *Shit, what do I say?* she asked herself.

"Nick, you are gonna have to trust me on this one when I tell you it's better just to leave it alone. In any case, you shouldn't have been eavesdropping—that was a private phone call. You should have made your presence known to me."

"Don't you even try that excuse on me, young woman! You still haven't looked me in the eye! I dare you to do that now and tell me it was an innocent phone call! See, you can't do that! Now, answer me, because we are staying in this room until you do. I don't care how long it takes. I want to know why my wife was defending me by saying, 'I wouldn't hurt her and that I'd stay faithful to her.' Now, goddamn it, what was said and who said it?"

Lord help me, I'd forgotten I'd said that, Kate thought to herself. *Nick has an uncanny knack of knowing me, so if I don't tell him everything, he'll know at once and keep on at me until I do, so I might as well get it over and tell him the whole thing now!*

"You better sit down, Nick, because you are not going to like what you are about to hear. But before I start, you have to promise me one thing. As angry as this is going to make you, you will not take any action against the person who called me. Do I have your word?"

Silence. "Your word, Nick?" Again silence. "Then we'll be sitting here 'til the end of our honeymoon, because I'm not going to be telling you anything about the call." And she folded her arms and looked Nick full in the face and set her jaw. He knew she meant every word she was saying and that she could be just as stubborn as himself.

"Okay, you have my word. I will not take any kind of action against whoever called you. Now, will that satisfy you?"

"Well, here goes!"

And she proceeded to tell him as best as she could, as close to word for word, what Scott had said to her. As she was talking, she could see Nick getting madder and madder, his face turning nearly

148

purple with rage and the veins in his neck starting to stand out. She ended up saying, "You heard for yourself what I said to Scott in response, so I guess I don't have to repeat that."

There was about five seconds of complete silence as they looked at each other, then Nick exploded! "That f—king son of a bitch said all that to you? How f—king dare he? Now I understand why you wanted me to give you my goddamn word I wouldn't retaliate against that son of a bitch, otherwise I'd have damn well broken every bone in that goddamn motherf—ker's body!!! He actually had the f—cken balls to ask you was our marriage consummated? What in the f—king hell did he think I was gonna do for nearly god damn twenty-four f—cking hours, play tiddly-winks with you? Come and get you on his damn f—king plane, indeed! It must be driving him f—king berserk to think I won your hand and he f—king didn't!"

On and on, Nick ranted and raved for the next five minutes or so using every cuss word he could think of. Gradually, the color in his face returned to normal. He continued, but by now his anger was pretty much abated.

"One thing I know about that son of a bitch Breckenridge is he hates to lose! To know you're damn well here with me and I'm the one who is taking you to bed and making love to you must be killing him, especially if that motherf—ker's in love with you himself. Let me ask you something. How long has this 'thing' with Scott being going on? When did you meet him?"

"I met Scott at the same party I met you at."

"Is that all?'

"No, over the months, he's called regularly and sent me flowers and chocolates."

"I repeat—is that goddamn all?'

"He once sent me a gift from a well-known New York jeweler."

"You mean Tiffany's?"

"Yes."

"What was it?"

"I don't know. I sent it back unopened."

"I know you didn't have an affair with him because, as I found out yesterday afternoon, I'm you're first lover! Breckenridge would really go f—king nuts if he knew that! But that aside, did you actually ever date him?"

"I don't know why it's such a bit deal, but yes, I did date him twice."

"Before or after we started seeing each other?"

"Both."

"Did you date anyone else?"

"Yes, a couple of doctors from the hospital."

"And you never thought to mention it to me?"

"At the time, it had nothing to do with you."

"And there I thought we were in an exclusive relationship!"

"Nick, we never once discussed anything like that."

"Where in the hell did you find time to see all these other guys? I was taking you to dinner most Friday and Saturday nights!"

"Well there were five other nights in the week, to say nothing of lunch times Friday, Saturday, and Sunday."

"You were a busy little bee, weren't you?!"

"So what, Nick? And it was all just casual dating! That's all in the past. Now I'm married to you. Remember, I promised to 'forsake all others,' and I meant it, and I'm assuming you meant it too?"

"Has Breckenridge put doubts in your mind already?"

"Of course he hasn't! You started this by asking me all those questions about him."

"Did any of your other dates know about me?"

"No. Why should they? As far as I was concerned, we had a casual dating relationship. It was only the date we had before your mother's birthday party that I began to realize how you felt about me."

"It took you that long to work it out?"

"It's not the first time I've been accused of not seeing what's under my nose in regards to things like that. Jeanne has told me that, for someone with my IQ, I can be pretty dumb!"

"That woman never spoke truer words! I'd been carefully throwing you signals for weeks."

"Nick, it couldn't have been that long. We only dated about a dozen times before you announced we were getting married!"

"I'd have said that to you the night I met you if I didn't think you'd laugh."

"Well, I guess now is as good a time as ever to tell you that the moment we looked at each other, I fell for you! My heart started to pound, and my stomach lurched, but I wasn't going to admit those feelings even to myself, so I told myself it was jet lag and just a trick of the light. But truth be told, I didn't want to stay away from you, and that night in the coffee shop, after I had operated on Sam Williams and you asked me to have dinner with you, I was so delighted. But I was just going to keep our relationship on a causal footing. For me, work has always come first, and I thought there was no room in my life for a serious relationship. But I so enjoyed our dinner dates and was pleasantly surprised, after what I had been told about you, how easy it was to be in your company! I should tell you that the other guys, and that includes Scott, failed miserably compared to you! And you didn't live up to your womanizing reputation with me, you were a perfect gentleman. That is, until we got engaged!"

"You mean to tell me it was love at first sight for you too? And you're just now getting around to telling me? We could have been married the day after the party by a justice of the peace and done away with that merry dance you led me on—and was that some dance!"

"If you had asked me to marry you then, I'd have been on the next plane back to England! No, my love. I really needed those hours we spent together just talking so I could really get to know you. Actually, I almost didn't even get to the party!

The Sunday before, when we went on that ride, twice I caught you looking at me in a way I'd never seen before. Once, you had your head tilted slightly to the side with a kind of puzzled expression on your face. I didn't understand why you looked at me like that because it didn't fit in with what we were discussing. Jeanne suggested when I explained it to her that you were trying to work out if I was really as dumb about the way you felt about me as I seemed, which, of course, I was! But it was the second time I looked over at you and the look on your face really, really perturbed me. I thought it was telling me right then and there that you cared a lot more for me than I'd ever realized. And remember how you'd caught me looking at you, and it was if neither of us could look away? We were—how can I put it—almost mesmerized by the other! You started to take a step toward me, our eyes sort of locked on each other, then you cell phone rang. It was John McIntire, and you had to take the call. After that, I made some excuse about having to get home, and even though I knew you wanted to talk, I insisted I had things to do at the house and needed to get there! We were both so silent all the way back to the stables, and I left with just a quick 'bye.'

"When I got home, I confided in Jeanne what had happened after she was surprised how soon I had gotten back. She, of course, did the 'I told you so' routine, as she'd been telling me all along that you were in love with me, and of course, I had been telling her she was nuts! But that day, the truth was beginning to dawn on me. It was her insisting that I'd promised you I'd go to the party that made me finally go. But after both the episodes at the birthday party and the reaction of people at the hospital the next day, then the attack, all I could think of was getting out of this country fast and back to England. Then you insisted on talking about 'the elephant in the room' and really mixed me up big time! I didn't even want to admit to myself how I felt about you. I honestly didn't think I was capable of putting you first in everything because, for me, work had always come first. But after you had left me alone and I really had the chance to think things through, I realized that YOU had become my everything, and the thought of living my life without you in it was more than I could bare. That was when you walked up behind me, and I couldn't hold it in any longer. I just had to tell you that I loved you! And the rest, as they say, is history!

There. I think I've talked long enough except to say, Nick Barkley, I love you with all my heart and soul and now my body! Now, will you please pass me my dress, zip it up for me, and take me to brunch!"

"Kate Barkley, you are one hell of a woman, and I'm so glad you're my wife! Eat your heart out, Scott Breckenridge, she's mine, all f—king mine! Now, how long will it take for you to get ready so we can go down and eat? I'm starved?"

"Five minutes tops."

She was ready in four, and they went down and enjoyed the food. As they drank their mimosas, it dawned on them, as they sat there kissing, they wanted to do much more than that. In fact, they didn't want to keep their hands off the other!

"Can't this elevator go any faster?" complained Nick. They were shedding their clothes as soon as they got inside the suite and, within less than a minute, were back in bed. Nick was even more ardent than he'd been before, and maybe it was the result of the mimosas, but Kate responded just the way he had hoped.

"Oh Lord, that was incredible," she said as they both lay there, trying to get their breath back, neither one wanting to break the spell. "Nick."

"Mmm."

"My arm is going to sleep, I'll have to move.

"Oh, sorry about that," and he rolled away. He got up and pulled on his pants. "What clothes can I get for you?" he asked her.

"A robe will do. Are we going anywhere this afternoon, or can we stay here and just be together?"

"Your wish is my command, my lady," he answered her with a bow.

They got a drink out of the fridge; a lite beer for him and the usual diet Sprite with lime for her. She curled up on the sofa beside him in the living room, finding a wonderful old movie to watch. Barbara Stanwyck is marvelous, isn't she?" Kate said, "*Double Indemnity* is such a film classic." Nick hadn't seen it before, so he thoroughly enjoyed it. After the movie, they sat on the terrace his arms around her as she snuggled up to him. The famous San Francisco fog rolled in, and they sat there, watching it.

"Are we going out tonight?" Kate asked.

"Yes, but you better eat something now. Dinner will be late."

"How about an afternoon tea?" she suggested.

"That sounds good," Nick answered.

He called room service and ordered tea for two.

"Put on an evening dress," Nick told her. "We are going to a private supper club."

"Sounds very fancy. How about that strapless sapphire blue dress?"

"That's perfect."

They were dressed and ready to go by eight forty-five. A car took them to a very tall building. They went to the top. Kate was thrilled at the view.

"How'd you manage this?' she asked.

After dinner, the lights dimmed, and Tony Bennett was introduced.

"Tony Bennett," said Kate in an awed voice. "Mr. San Francisco himself!"

"Thought you'd enjoy this," murmured Nick.

For the next forty-five minutes, they sat entranced, listening to the wonderful voice of Mr. Bennett. He received a standing ovation when he was finished.

"That was a once-in-a-lifetime experience," murmured Kate.

Nick had his arm around her shoulders and kissed her thoroughly!

"Let's go back to the hotel. That way, you can have your brandy and cigar, and I can have my coffee," she suggested.

"It's a deal," he replied.

They sat on the terrace and enjoyed the memory of the evening, Nick with his cigar and brandy, Kate with a vanilla cappuccino.

"Thank you so much, Nick," she said. "That's an evening I'll never forget. It's getting a little chilly out here. Let me find something warmer to wear," and she went into the bedroom, trading the bolero jacket and her sandals for a bathrobe and slippers.

"That's better," she told him. He had settled down with his feet up on a chair. She leaned against the terrace wall and looked at the fog for a while. "What a wonderful night," she exclaimed.

"And it's not over," said Nick, coming alongside her and putting his arms around her. They started what she knew was going to be another night of lovemaking. As Nick unzipped her dress and let it fall to the ground, he inhaled deeply. All she had on was a strapless bra and a tiny pair of panties, both of which matched her dress. He undressed with her help and they were, once more, back in bed. This time, Kate didn't experience too much pain.

Sex morning, noon, and night, she thought. *I like this.* Although she was still sore, it was a small price to pay for being Mrs. Nicholas Jonathan Barkley.

Nick didn't want her catching cold, so he fetched her a night-gown. *Not that it's going to exactly keep me warm made of such fine silk,* she mused. He held her as she fell asleep. She woke during the night and found they were sleeping front to back, with Nick's arm around her, his hand cupping her breast. *What a way to sleep,* she thought!

She woke first and, this time, initiated the lovemaking, which Nick thoroughly enjoyed. She had learned fast the things that brought her husband real pleasure, which took him completely by surprise!

"Kate, I know you have only been sexually active a couple of days. How come you know so much about doing the things that pleasure me in so little time?"

"I'm a doctor, so I do know a little about male anatomy and where nerve endings are. I just put those long-ago classes to good use. That plus I do have nails!"

"Good lord, Kate, are you telling me that was just a sample of what I can look forward to for the rest of my life?"

"Oh darlin', you ain't seen or felt nothin' yet!"

"May heaven help me!"

After breakfast, they decided to explore the city and, in particular, look for more evening dresses.

"Are you sure you don't mind that kind of shopping?" she asked Nick.

"Not at all," he answered. They checked with the concierge for an area of the city where there were small boutiques, called for their car and driver and set off. After a couple of hours, they had picked out three dresses, with sandals and purses to match. Putting them in the car, Nick and Kate found a bistro to have lunch. Afterward, they wandered around, picking up a few items for the flat. They called for the car and went back to their suite. Kate hung up her new dresses and slipped into a robe. She found Nick on the terrace, enjoying a beer. She sat on his lap, wrapped her arms around his neck, and started nibbling his ear. "Okay, lady, I get the message," he murmured.

Afterward, lying in bed, Kate said, "Can we just stay in tonight and do something simple like order pizza?"

"Of course we can," he told her, marveling at the way that all she wanted to do was just be alone with him as much as she could. And then he remembered how she had told him that the only place she wanted to go with him on their honeymoon was bed. *She sure was making good on that*, he thought.

"Tomorrow, I thought we could go to Chinatown and have dinner there."

"What a wonderful idea," she told him. "And one night, could we go to a baseball game. I've never been to one, and it looks like fun?"

"You really want to go to a game? I think we can take care of that. I'll call the concierge and have him get us some tickets." He grabbed a robe and then put in the call. "Thursday night," he told her. "We have tickets behind home plate."

"Does that mean they're good seats?"

"The best," he assured her. "The concierge here is wonderful."

"This is so much better than going to the east coast or Europe," she told him.

Their visit to Chinatown was fascinating, and he bought her a beautiful jade green silk kimono to use as a robe. Dinner was fabulous.

"Oh, Nick, this is the perfect honeymoon," she whispered as she snuggled up to him in the car on the way home.

The next day was pouring rain. "Just a day to stay in," she suggested. They ordered room service for breakfast and lunch and spent much of their time in bed making good use of the "do not disturb" sign! The rain eased up toward dinner time, so they decided to brave the weather and go to a French restaurant, La Folie, that Nick knew up on Russian Hill.

"That was so wonderful," Kate whispered as they drove back to their hotel in the backseat of their limousine, and she cuddled up to him as he caressed her breasts and kissed her in the way he had normally reserved up to now for when they were completely alone.

"And the evening isn't over yet," he murmured, very glad that they had a driver as he'd had way, way too much more than his usual amount to drink.

In the elevator ride up to their suite and going down the hallway to it, he was, surprisingly for him in public, all over her, almost bruising her mouth with the force with which he was kissing her. Kate was even more stunned by his next move, because before the door to their suite was closed completely, she could feel Nick lifting her skirt and his hands moving swiftly up her thighs and then forcefully removing the small and delicate pair of very expensive lace panties she had been wearing.

"Kate, I've had way, way too much to drink, and I can't wait any longer. I've got to have you right now!" he said with slightly slurred speech as he unzipped his pants! Kate was further surprised as he showed her how rough he could be when inebriated! Nick pushed her up against the wall in the living room and took her there and then! He was standing with his legs apart to brace himself as he picked her up and she wrapped her legs around his hips, his fingers leaving bruises on her upper thighs as he held onto them so tightly, not a further word being spoken. All she could do was hold onto him with her arms around his neck until he was through with her. All the time he was taking her, she could smell the fumes of liquor on his breath.

Nick started to say something when he was finished but seemed to think better of it. Instead, he just put her down and went into the bedroom, grabbing his silk pajama bottoms—which was all he ever wore to bed—and his robe and then disappeared into the bathroom. A few seconds later, she could hear the shower running, followed by the sound of him brushing his teeth. Unsure what to do next, she put on her silk nightgown and slipped into bed. Nick came out of the bathroom, and without saying a word, or even looking in her direction, went into the living room. After waiting for about fifteen minutes and he still hadn't come to bed, she decided to go see what was going on. She found him in the living room, sitting in the dark, slumped in the corner of the sofa, his head in his hands with a cup and pot of what smelled like freshly brewed coffee on the table in front of him. Sitting down next to him, she asked if he was okay.

Nick wouldn't raise his head and look at her as he replied, "I'm extremely sorry, deeply ashamed, and so embarrassed at what I just did to you. I have no excuse except to say I drank so very much more than usual even for me, and you looked so beautiful and desirable. Room service has delivered two pots of coffee, and I took a long cold shower, so I'm doing all that I can to sober up. But if you want me to leave, I understand completely. I'll pack my things and be out of here in just a few minutes."

"Leave? I don't expect you leave. I love you. You're my husband. For better or worse, remember that? Look at me, Nick. Look at me right now. I'm okay. I didn't mind. Really, I didn't. It was just a bit of a surprise, that's all!"

"My God, 'a bit of a surprise,' she says, and 'she didn't mind at all!' Kate, you know you're one in a million, no, make that ten million! Any other classy lady like you would be asking me for an annulment for doing to them what I just did to you!" he said, at long last managing to look at her.

"Nick I'm your wife, all you have to do is tell me what it is you want, but I'm so new to all of this that I'm not saying I can do it immediately, just be patient and I'll do everything for you as soon as I can."

"Dear lord, what did I ever do to deserve a woman like you! Kate my darling if I ever suggest we do something you don't like or are not comfortable with you've got to tell me. This shouldn't be a one-sided relationship."

"Nick, all I want to do is please you. You're the one with the experience, so we'll do whatever you want. I really believe that my body no longer belongs to me, it's yours, just as yours now belongs to me, and that, my darling husband, is straight out of scripture! So you see, I can't object to anything you do to me, just as you can't object to what I do to you. 'The two shall become one flesh' is what the Bible says. That means, from now on, there's no longer a you or a me—only an us."

"I honestly don't think you understand what you've just said! Basically, as I understand it, you're telling me you'll never say the word 'no' to me when I want to make love to you! What about if you don't want to have sex, have the preverbal headache, or just aren't in the mood, what then? You're way too new to lovemaking to even think about making a commitment like that! Of course, from my point of view, that's the most unusual and, quite frankly, liberating idea of what a committed relationship should be about that I've ever heard of, and it would be incredible to live like that. But there is no way I could, in all good conscious, take advantage of you like that! We'll just take new ideas slow and easy from now on. No more sudden surprises like tonight, okay?"

"You really don't have any say in the matter, Nick, the commitment was made this morning when I made my vows to you. You'll soon find out how serious I am! And to answer your questions, I can't imagine not wanting you to make love to me, and I guess it's your job to keep me thinking like that. The headache. Well, being a doctor, I'll take two aspirin and call myself in the morning! And what was the last one? Oh yes, my not being in the mood. Well, again, Nick my love, that's your department. We'll both have to trust that you can get me in the mood. Like they say, sex doesn't start in the bedroom but in the kitchen hours earlier, so if you just remember that, we'll be okay! Any more questions? No? Then can we please go to bed and get some sleep?"

Nick was too surprised by her responses to argue with her!

The next morning, Nick was awoken by his wife making the most definite sexual advances on him!

"What a wonderful way to wake up," he told her as he responded to every kiss and special touch she had for him! "You are just full of surprises, my darling. Anytime you want to do to me what you just did, please feel free! For someone who's so new to the art of and practice of sex, you are proving to be one fast learner!"

They took a trip down to Fisherman's Wharf and a boat around the bay to get a closer look at Alcatraz. When they got back, they put their feet up until it was time to get ready to go to Candlestick Park. She thoroughly enjoyed the baseball game, and when the fans around

159

them realized it was her first game, they were more than willing to join Nick in explaining to her what was going on. Hot dogs, pretzels, and nachos was the dinner fare. "I'm going to put on weight if I go on eating like this," she told him, laughing.

Nick decided the way to initiate sex later that night would be to very slowly seduce his wife, which was something she enjoyed more than she could say! He couldn't believe her response to his touch and kisses. For someone who was so new to lovemaking, Kate was proving to be a fast learner to the art, understanding what he wanted like a partner whom he'd been sleeping with much longer than just a few short days!

"Tomorrow, have something like your afternoon tea, because we won't eat until about eleven. It will be a late supper."

"What have you got planned now?" she asked.

"You'll find out tomorrow," he told her, grinning.

They spent most of Friday just wandering around stores in a different part of town, picking up a few more items for the flat.

"Let's go in here," he said, steering her into a jewelry store. "I noticed that what you need to go with most of your clothes is a diamond pendant, and this is the store the family usually buys its jewelry from, so we'll take care of that now."

"A diamond pendant! Nick, it's too much."

"Nonsense," he replied. He told the jeweler what they were looking for, and he began showing them a variety of styles, one of which caught Kate's eye. It was like a lariat. "Nick, this one—it reminds me of you."

"It does?"

"Yes, this is definitely the one."

"We'll take it. Now, all we need are earrings to match it."

"What size?" the salesman asked.

"Not too big," Kate said.

"How about four tcw?"

"That's perfect," she replied.

"Do you want to wear them all now or have them gift wrapped?" the salesman inquired.

"I'll wear them now," Kate told him as Nick fastened the chain and kissed her neck in the process as she put in her new studs.

"Nick, they're beautiful. Thank you so much," she told him.

"You could wear them tonight," he suggested. They went back to the hotel and ordered afternoon tea.

"We should be ready to go by seven fifteen. It starts at eight," Nick told her.

"Okay by me. What dress should I wear?"

"How about the jade one with the—what did you call the neckline?"

"A halter-neck."

They stepped into the car right on time and pulled up in front of a theatre, and when she saw what was playing, Kate almost cried. "Phantom of the Opera! How on earth did you get tickets for this?" she exclaimed. "They're supposed to be scarcer than hen's teeth!"

"As soon as we had that discussion about honeymoons, I called the concierge, and he started working on it."

When they went inside, they were escorted not to the general seating but to a private box! "I just can't believe this," she kept saying. Champagne was served with their program. Nick enjoyed the expression on Kate's face as much as he did the performance. At the intermission, a server brought more champagne and asked them how they were enjoying the show.

"Oh, it's wonderful," exclaimed Kate.

As they left, their car took them to a small exclusive supper club. They ate and danced until Kate couldn't hide the yawns any longer.

"I think it's time we went back to the hotel," Nick said.

"And bed," said Kate, with a wickedly mischievous grin on her face!

"It's our anniversary," Nick announced when they woke up. "We've been married one whole week."

"And they said it wouldn't last," Kate replied, laughing. "Let's celebrate. Come here, husband, and help me make our first week anniversary memorable!"

After, when they were lying in bed, Nick suggested they take the car and go to Sausalito.

"What a great idea."

They had breakfast and set off, Kate's head on a swivel as they drove across the Golden Gate Bridge. Finding a place to park, they just wandered around. Going into an art gallery, Nick stopped to admire a painting of a roundup in the style of Russell. "I really like that," he told her.

"It would look good on the wall across from the fireplace between the windows," Kate said.

"You wouldn't mind having something so western hanging in our 'cozy' living room?"

"Of course not, silly. It's part of your way of life, so it should be represented in the flat."

The gallery owner told them that crating and having it delivered to the ranch was no problem. While Nick was making the arrangements, she found a beautiful silver frame which would be perfect for a wedding photograph.

"I'll take this," she told the owner.

"Just add it to the bill," said Nick. They found a little cafe and had a light lunch and continued to look around.

"How about we go dancing at the hotel tonight?" Nick suggested.

"Oh, that sounds wonderful," she answered.

They went back to the St. Gregory, and what started as just putting their feet up ended up as a sweet time of lovemaking.

She wore another of her new gowns that evening. A rather sexy red dress with spaghetti straps. Nick really liked to see her in red, and she was perfectly willing to oblige. Over dinner, they discussed the housekeeper situation. "Uma, the Petersons regular housekeeper, has gone back to work," Kate told him. "That's put Jeanne out of a job. Could we hire her to take care of the flat? I know she doesn't have much, and a steady wage would mean a lot to her."

"We can do better than that," replied Nick. "There is a one-bedroom house available on the ranch, and she could have that if she's interested. It would mean no commuting to work, and she would save on rent."

"Oh Nick, that sounds perfect. I'll call her tomorrow morning and ask her. I'm sure she'll say yes."

"If she does, I'll have John make sure the house is ready, then she can move in as soon as possible."

"You know they would make a cute couple!"

"Who?"

"John and Jeanne."

"Now don't start matchmaking."

"A little nudge here and there won't hurt. After all, she did her fair share with us, and look what happened." She leaned over and kissed him. "Now, let me think of a way to thank you for offering to hire her," she whispered in his ear as they rode the elevator back up to their floor.

"I can think of a way," Nick replied, putting his arms around his wife and kissing her hungrily. They couldn't get to their suite fast enough!

Sunday morning, Kate called Jeanne and put the proposition to her. Nick had suggested a very good salary, and that, plus a house, made the offer so great that the housekeeper was in tears as she accepted. Nick then called John and told him of the plans. "I'll get right on it," he assured his boss. "It should be taken care of this week."

Again, they enjoyed the famous brunch at the St. Gregory, and after spending the afternoon in bed, they made plans to drive up the coast on Monday and perhaps find a bed and breakfast and stay the night.

"This coastline is beautiful," Kate said in an awed voice. "Every bit as good as European coastal drives I've taken." They found a cozy B and B and behaved like the honeymooners they were! They drove slowly back and stopped in at an antique store and found another silver frame to use for a wedding photograph. They also found some unusual pins. One for Victoria, Audra, Esther, and Jeanne, for all they had done to give them such a perfect wedding. As they were about to leave, Kate spotted some antique silver cufflinks. "Let's get these for Silas," she said to Nick.

"What a good idea. I know he's a favorite of yours."

163

"Well, he's always treated me so well. I feel like we need to acknowledge all he does."

They returned to the hotel with their packages and decided to just stay in and order the delicious pizza again.

The next day, as they were wandering around in a different section of town just window shopping, who should they run into but Jarrod. "I forgot your office is near here," said Nick.

"How about I buy you lunch?" Jarrod offered. "Then if you have a few minutes to spare, I have that paperwork ready for you to sign."

"That's fine with us," Nick responded as Kate nodded in agreement.

They enjoyed their time together and then walked over to Jarrod's place of business. His secretary brought Kate coffee as the two men pored over some legal documents. Jarred brought in two of his staff to witness Nick's signature.

"There, it's all taken care of."

Nick turned to Kate, "The papers I just signed make it official. You now own everything I have jointly with me."

"What!" She gasped.

"I've also signed my new will, leaving the balance to you."

"Whoa, what do I know about running a ranch and the other businesses? This is crazy!"

"Well, you would have plenty of help, and I wouldn't have done it if I didn't think you were capable of doing the job."

"Nick, I can't believe you've done all this. My head is spinning! Jarrod, you'd better draw up my will while we're doing this. I've got a half-million dollar life insurance policy through the hospital that I made Nick the beneficiary of. In my will, I want to leave ten thousand dollars to the local 'no kill' animal shelter and the rest, of course, to Nick. I have some money my dad left me."

"That's simple enough," said Jarrod. "I'll draw it up and bring it out to the ranch."

They called for their car and went back to their suite, neither of them saying very much.

They sat on the terrace, and Kate again said, "Nick, I can't believe the terms of your will. You sure know how to take a girl's breath away!"

"You are more than just my wife, you're my lifelong partner, and I intend to keep you informed of all that goes on in the businesses. I won't keep anything from you. When the time comes, you won't be blindsided by anything!"

"Nick Barkley, you really are full of surprises," said his wife!

"Let's go to Chinatown tomorrow. It was so much fun, and the food was awesome," said Nick, changing the subject.

They spent a leisurely afternoon looking around the shops and stalls. Nick insisted on buying Kate another silk kimono to wear over her evening dresses. When they got back to their suite, there was a message waiting for them from Jeanne to say she had moved into the house that day and she was so happy.

First thing Friday morning, Nick called the florist he used in Stockton and ordered flowers to be sent to Jeanne. 'Welcome to your new home, Nick and Kate Barkley.'

"You think of everything, darling. That was a really nice gesture. Is there anything planned for today?"

"Tonight we're going to see a show."

"Can I ask what show?"

"You can ask, but I'm not telling you!"

It was a chilly rainy day, so they looked around the stores in the hotel, Nick buying some shirts, sweaters, and a couple of pairs of slacks and jeans. Kate also found some jeans plus day dresses. They went back upstairs and again enjoyed being the honeymooners they still were!

Kate wore the third of her new evening dresses, a rust-colored bias cut little number. Nick was getting used to his new role of zipper upper. "It's a lot more fun unzipping them," he said as he fastened the hook and eye at the top, kissing her neck in the process.

Once more, they got into the car and were driven downtown. "One Night Only, Shirley Bassey in Concert," said the banner outside the theatre.

"Nick, how did you manage this? I didn't even know she was in town!"

"I know how much you like her, so I pulled a few strings, and here we are," he said, grinning.

The show was better than she could have believed possible. The seats were awesome, and Ms. Bassey sang all her hits and more. After the show, they went out for a late supper.

"I can't believe this is our last night in San Francisco," Kate said to Nick. "It's been the most perfect honeymoon."

"You have really enjoyed it?" asked Nick.

"'Are you kidding? Just staying in our suite would have been enough, but all the other things you planned—Tony Bennett, Phantom, the trip up the coast, Chinatown, and tonight—Nick, you couldn't have done anymore, but you want to know the best part? Lying in your arms with or without clothes. I love you so very much, Nick Barkley!" They stayed and danced to a couple more tunes and then, for the last time, went to their hotel. Of course, they made the most passionate love as they did the next morning.

Whilst they had breakfast on the terrace, the maid and valet packed their clothes. The bags were taken down to the car, and soon, they were on their way to the airport, where the plane was waiting for them.

Chapter 10

John was waiting for them at Stockton airport with Nick's Range Rover. Their belongings were loaded, and they drove to the ranch. John told them that a crate with what looked like a painting had arrived. When they got to the door, Silas opened it and announced, "Mr. and Mrs. Nicholas Jonathan Barkley are home." Nick picked his wife up and carried her across the threshold! All the family except Audra were assembled, along with a magnum of champagne. While Silas and John unloaded their bags, Jarrod poured them each a glass of the bubbly from their own vineyard. Silas said Jeanne was already taking care of the unpacking for them. They sat and talked for a while, then Nick told them that he and Kate were eager to see the new furniture. At the door to the flat, he again picked her up and carried her over the threshold of "Our Home." They were both thrilled with the way the sectional, desk, desk chairs, and dining room set looked. Jeanne said she'd come back later and finish the unpacking.

"I thought we'd never be left alone in our new home," Nick murmured as they walked just inside their bedroom, unfortunately for them, leaving the door open. Nick was down to wearing only his jeans, which his wife had just unzipped; she to her panties and about to lose her bra to him, when the living room door opened and Audra came walking in! When they all saw each other, everyone froze. Nick recovered first. "Get the hell out, Audra, just get out!" he yelled.

"I'm sorry!" she stammered.

"Just get the hell out!"

By this time, Kate was hanging onto Nick and giggling!!

When they heard their front door slam, Nick said, "Damn that girl."

"You didn't close it properly. You were so busy carrying your bride." She laughed.

"I'm so very sorry," he told her.

"It's okay, really. Let's just get back to what we were doing."

"I'm making sure that door is locked first," he told her, zipping up his pants.

"I'm glad I checked," Nick said, coming back a few minutes later. "The door to the deck was unlocked."

"Now can we please get back to trying out this bed?" Kate asked.

Much later, Nick asked her what she wanted for lunch and what were they going to do for dinner.

"This weekend, let's just stay in," she suggested. "I told Jeanne to stock the fridge and freezer, and there's always delivery. I just don't want to share you with anyone yet. Am I being selfish?" she asked.

"No, I feel the same way. Maybe Monday or Tuesday we'll have dinner with the family. I'll talk with Mother. She'll understand," Nick assured her. They had both dressed in casual clothes and were checking out the fridge when the phone to the front door buzzed. "I'll get it," he said. "It's Mother. She's asking to come in?"

"Of course," replied Kate.

He buzzed Victoria in. "Audra told me what happened," his mother said. "She's so upset and embarrassed."

"So she should be," retorted Nick. "She was told this flat is off limits unless she's invited in."

"I know she was in the wrong, but she was late getting back from town and just wanted to see you both. I know that's not really an excuse, but rest assured she won't ever do that again," said Victoria, trying to placate Nick, who was still upset with his sister.

"Nick, she made a mistake, which I'm sure she won't ever repeat, and it is our first day home. Let's just forgive and forget," put in Kate.

"Okay, okay. This time," he said with a shrug.

"How do you like your new furniture?" asked his mother.

"It's gorgeous," Kate told her. "Thank you for taking charge and having it arranged. It's perfect." On the dining table and floor, gifts were piled up. "These have been arriving since the wedding plus the ones that were brought to the ceremony."

"I ordered seventy-five thank-you notes, but I can see that's not going to be enough," Kate said.

"What are your plans for the weekend?" her mother-in-law asked.

"We just want to take today and tomorrow to settle in and adjust to living in the flat," Nick told her.

"That's a good idea," Victoria said to them. "I'll tell Audra all is forgiven." And with that, she left them.

Kate's cell phone rang. "It's Jeanne. She says she just pulled a quiche out of the oven and there is a green salad already made in the fridge. She could finish the unpacking while we eat lunch. What do you think?"

"Sounds good to me," Nick replied.

A few minutes later, Jeanne put a beautiful quiche on the table and left them to enjoy their meal. After she had completed the unpacking, she put their luggage in a cupboard in the hallway, thanked them again for her job and house, and was on the point of leaving when Kate asked her to wait for a moment. Going into the bedroom, she got the package with the pin that was their thank-you gift for Jeanne. When they gave it to her, she was almost in tears and gave the couple a hug.

"By the way, where did the plates, flatware, etc. come from?" asked Kate.

"Mrs. Barkley loaned you what we thought you'd need until you get your own. I noticed you had already bought a coffee pot and mugs."

Just then, Nick's phone rang. It was Jarrod to tell him that a large delivery was downstairs for them and if it would be okay to have it brought up?"

"I guess so," said Nick.

What arrived was a huge patio table, patio umbrella, two chairs and two benches. "That's from me," said Jarrod. "The barbecue Nick had picked out—"

"That's from me," Heath chimed in.

"A two person hammock—that's Eugene's contribution, and from the boys in the bunkhouse, a loveseat and two chairs to go

169

around the fire pit, which is from your executive assistant, two benches that are actually storage containers were from some of the office staff. Outdoor plates, glasses, flatware, and serving pieces are from Audra, as well as placemats and hanging plants," Jarrod told them.

Everyone got to work assembling the items with the tools they'd had the foresight to bring with them. John McIntire bought them a huge portable ice cooler with bags of ice and plenty of beer. Soon, everyone was enjoying a cold beer or soda as they worked. In the middle of this, Kate's phone rang, and it was Victoria to tell them the gift she had ordered for the couple had arrived two days ahead of schedule and it was going to be brought upstairs. It was a beautiful drinks cabinet that, once uncrated, Victoria proceeded to stock with every liquor imaginable.

"I noticed that you didn't have anything like that, and your buffet wouldn't be big enough to hold all the drinks. I do hope you like it."

"It's wonderful," said Nick, and Kate was in complete agreement.

"Listen, Nick it's getting on toward dinner time. Why don't we forget our 'alone' plans and just order pizza for everyone. We've got plenty of beer in the utility room."

"You sure you don't mind, Kate?"

"After what these people have done for us today, how could I mind? You call in the pizza and I'll call Jeanne and Audra to join us."

So an improv party was held. The deck looked marvelous. They'd even managed to get the plants hung.

"Nick you've got to say something," urged Kate.

"I really don't know what to say," said Nick. "Except that, every time Kate and I step out on our deck, we will think of our wonderful family and friends." He raised his beer. "To family and friends."

They cleared up the boxes and cartons the items had come in and even found some wind chimes that had been overlooked and hung them up. After everyone had gone, Kate and Nick looked around, hardly believing their good fortune. The half patio roof had indeed been put up whilst they had been away, and tiny white lights were around the supports and the roof edge. They tried out the hammock as Nick smoked his cigar. "Oh, babe, this is the life," he said. "Being out on our deck like this with you in my arms, a little slice of heaven."

Later, they went inside and had a chance to examine the drinks cabinet. "The workmanship on it is amazing. If we get any decanters, they can sit on top on silver trays. Tomorrow, we should make a start on opening the gifts," Kate told him. "You can do that, and I'll write down what it is and who gave it. Then I'll write the thank-you notes. Now, let's go make sure that bed was really as good as we thought it was this afternoon! But first, make sure the doors are locked."

"We are actually waking up in our own home," Kate whispered to Nick.

"And in our own bed," Nick murmured back. "How can we celebrate?"

"I know a way," she murmured in his ear!"

Later, Kate made coffee while Nick showered. They had a leisurely breakfast and then set about opening their wedding gifts. Kate had bought a notebook to write down the details. Almost two hours later, they had opened the last one!

"I can't believe how generous people have been," Nick exclaimed.

"These things are exactly what we put on our list," Kate said as she loaded the dishwasher with the first round of their new china, glasses, and flatware. "I'll put your mother's stuff on the counter to give back to her." She continued to run the dishwasher for the rest of the day until everything was clean and put away.

"I'll take all these boxes and trash downstairs, and then maybe we can relax for a while," Nick said with a grin. "Don't forget, we're still on our honeymoon!"

"How long does it last?" she asked.

"Just as long as we want it to!"

When he came back upstairs, John was with him. "He offered to help with the cleaning up and then hang our painting," Nick told her. Between the two men, they got the trash out and the crate opened. There was a knock on the deck door, and here came Jeanne, who wanted to help tidy up the mess in the flat.

"The best laid plans!" Nick murmured to Kate with a grin. The painting hung, the crate and packing material removed, at last, they were alone!

"I hate to admit it," Nick said, "but I'm hungry."

"How about some roast beef sandwiches and potato salad."

"Sounds good."

They sat on the deck and ate lunch.

"I have to keep pinching myself to make sure this is real and not a dream," Kate told him.

"It's real, my love, and I'm gone show you how real." And with that, he took her by the hand and led her inside, making sure to lock the door behind them!

"How much food did you order, Nick?" Kate asked him as she unpacked the bag of Chinese food.

"I couldn't decide what to have, so I ordered a little of this and a little of that! Anyway, I plan to come home for lunch tomorrow and we can have leftovers."

Nick kept ranchers' hours, so he started work at seven a.m. Kate had woken up a five to give him a "send-off" before he left!

"Is every morning going to be as good as this?" he asked.

"Why not?" she answered. "I have to get up early to also be at work at seven, so we could easily arrange something!"

"Don't forget, I'm coming home for lunch," he reminded her with a grin, his dimples showing!

"Oh, I'll be waiting for you," she answered with a grin, showing dimples of her own!

Victoria buzzed the front door later and joined Kate for coffee. She invited the couple for dinner with the family and the Petersons that evening. Kate accepted, and they arranged to have a pre-dinner sherry in the living room at seven thirty.

"I'll tell Nick when I see him at lunch time," Kate assured her. Victoria enlisted Jeanne's help to take the borrowed dishes back downstairs after admiring all the gifts the couple had received. When Jeanne got back to the flat, she started cleaning and tidying whilst Kate made a start on the thank-you notes, making sure Jeanne left no later than eleven thirty, not being sure exactly what time Nick would come back for lunch. He arrived at noon, but eating was not what was on his mind! When they got dressed, Kate heated up the leftover Chinese food, and he went back to work much later normal.

He had promised not to be home any later than five. Kate returned phone calls and was in the bath when her husband came home early. "Come and join me," she invited him.

"I think I'll just do that," he answered her. In the end, they had to hurry to be dressed and ready to join the family and the Petersons for dinner! Nick wore casual clothes, and Kate one of the day dresses she bought in San Francisco.

Everyone greeted the couple with applause and sherry, which Kate passed on for her usual Sprite. They had brought the gifts for Victoria, Audra, and Esther down with them. The ladies were thrilled with them and promptly pinned them on!

They had a long leisurely dinner talking about the wedding and some of the details of the San Francisco honeymoon trip.

"It sounds incredible," Audra exclaimed. After dinner, they looked at wedding photographs, and Victoria handed Nick and Kate the just-completed wedding DVD. There were copies for the family and Petersons.

"We'll watch ours upstairs," said Nick, looking at his watch. "See you in the morning, Heath. Good night, everyone." As they were picking up the photographs and DVD, Jarrod handed Nick a long envelope.

"This is your copy," he told him.

"Oh, Nick, I almost forgot, your secretary dropped this off at the house after you left the office today as she couldn't get a reply from the flat," said Victoria, handing Nick an envelope. Carrying everything upstairs, they all said good night again and parted.

Nick put his copy of the will into their bedroom wall safe. They got ready for bed and put the wedding DVD in. When they were settled down, before he pressed play, he handed his wife a black credit card.

"What's this?" she asked him.

"It's your new credit card," he answered. "In the name of Kate Barkley. It has no limit, so buy whatever you want."

"I really don't need it," she told him. "I've already ordered a card in my new name."

"Take it," he insisted. "You'll need to buy things for the flat and yourself, etc., and it's up to me to pay for that."

"Nick Barkley, I earn a perfectly good salary enough to buy my own things, thank you very much."

"Now, don't start and take offense. I took vows, and part of them was to take care of you, and that's what I'm doing. Let's not have our first argument about finances," he countered. "Silas has already set up accounts, so Jeanne has just to sign for groceries, plus she has a credit card for all other household expenses. The wines are delivered direct from our winery, and the beer and other liquor, we just make a call and they're sent over. But you'll have other expenses that I want to pay for. What you do with your salary is your business. Just let me take care of you."

They didn't get to see the wedding DVD until later in the week!

The next morning, while Nick was showering, Kate decided that she wanted an apple fritter to go with her coffee, so she left him a hastily scrawled note and took off in her mini. She was only two blocks away from the donut shop, the site of their first date, when a car ran a red light, broadsiding her. The impact spun her around, deploying the airbags. *Oh no*, she thought. *My beautiful mini! What has that bloody jerk done to my car!* Within no time, she could hear the sirens, telling of deputies coming to her aid, but fortunately, she didn't need their help getting out of her car. She was surveying the damage to her left front quarter panel of her car when they arrived.

"Dr. Barkley, are you okay? Should we call the paramedics?"

"No, I'm not hurt, but I don't know about the other driver. The idiot, he caused all this!"

"He's fine," said another deputy coming over, "but is trying to say it's all your fault, Dr. Barkley. However, from the smell of alcohol on his breath, I'm running him in for driving under the influence and whatever else we can think of to charge him with. The sheriff will throw the book at him when he finds out what he did to you!"

Whilst she was still standing in the street talking to the deputies, giving them her statement, and waiting for the tow truck, she looked up to see her husband's Land Rover Discovery speeding down the road!

"Oh hell," she said. "Here comes the cavalry. Who called him?" And she glared at the deputies.

"Ma'am, it's more than our life's worth for Nick Barkley's wife to be in an accident and us not to let him know!"

Nick pulled to a screeching halt, he jumped out, and ran toward his wife.

"Before you ask, I'm fine, and the accident wasn't my fault. I'm just waiting for the tow truck and then I was going to ask the man at the garage to give me a ride home."

"What do you mean you were going to ask some stranger for a ride? What do you think I'm here for? You have any kind of problem, your first call is to me, is that quite clear?" he told her angrily, standing there with his hands planted on his hips!

"Nick, I've been taking care of myself for years, and in war zones, no less. I think I can handle one little accident without your help, and don't tell me what to do in that tone of voice. I'm not one of your ranch hands. I won't be spoken to like that. I just won't have it!" she yelled at him, taking an equally forceful stance.

The deputies were listening to this exchange with grins on their faces. They'd never heard of anyone talking to a Barkley like that, far less Nick Barkley himself!

Nick, suddenly aware that he and Kate had a rapt audience, turned to the deputies and told them if they'd got everything, they could go!

Reluctantly, they left, sorry they were going to miss how the heated exchange was going to turn out, but eager to tell their buddies that Dr. Barkley wasn't some quiet little miss and that she was going to give the hot-tempered Nick a run for his money. 'Bout time someone did, they all agreed.

The tow truck arrived, and Kate pushed her fuming husband out of the way and saw to the details herself. When her beloved mini was on its way to being repaired, she got into the Land Rover, fastened her belt, and sat there with her arms folded. Nick climbed in.

"That's not the repair shop I use," he told her.

"Well, it's the one I'm using," she retorted.

He started the engine and turned the truck around.

"STOP!" she yelled. "You're going the wrong way."

"What are you talking about? I should know which direction my own ranch is in!"

"The ranch may be this way, but the doughnut shop is back in the other direction, and I still want my apple fritter!"

Nick swung his truck around, heedless of other drivers on the road and the horn honking he caused! He pulled up in front of the old doughnut shop and jumped out before Kate could undo her safety belt, coming back a few minutes later with a huge pink box in his hands, which he silently handed to her.

"What's this?" she asked.

"You're goddamned apple fritters."

"How many did you buy?"

"A dozen."

"A DOZEN! Bloody hell! Just what do you think I'm going to do with a dozen doughnuts?"

"I really don't give a damn, but I'll do anything to stop you getting in another accident."

"How is buying me a bloody dozen doughnuts going to stop some lunatic driver from running a red light and hitting me? Nick, I exist in the real world. You can't stop me living in it, no matter how hard you try. I've been through a few things and have come out of it relatively unscathed!"

"Unscathed? You've been blown up and shot! I saw the scars on your fanny the first time I saw you, bare ass and buck naked!"

"Oh, oh, well they're from…um…the bullet wound I got when insurgents tried to overrun our field hospital. I kinda told you about that."

"Kate, that's an injury I want you to tell me all about in detail, 'cos it's not what you've always led me to believe. I do know what a bullet wound looks like, and yours is much more than the simple wound you said it was! But for now, how can I make you understand that part of your life is over. Since you married me, it's become my job to keep you as safe as I possibly can."

"That doesn't mean you can yell at me, especially in front of other people like those deputies this morning. They were hugely enjoying our little exchange, or didn't you notice?"

"I'm sorry, it's just I came out of the shower, and you were gone, then I get a phone call you've been in an accident. All I could think of was you laying bleeding or worse in the street. I jumped in my truck and got here as fast as I could."

"Nick, I left you a note telling you where I was going, and you should have slowed down and asked the deputy what happened. Then you'd have known it was just a minor accident with no injuries. It's just the Barkleys have got people in Stockton so in awe of the family that they report the slightest thing back to you. Now that has got to stop, do you hear me? I won't have my every move reported to you. You're my husband, not my jailor. Is that clear?"

"Yes, it's clear. I guess I overreacted."

"You think? I still want to know what I'm supposed to do with a dozen apple fritters."

"Can't you freeze them?"

By this time, they had reached the ranch and followed Jeanne through the gate. Nick talked to her at the bottom of the stairs, and she got in her car, backed it up, and left.

"Where's she going?" Kate asked.

"Back home, I think."

"What for?"

"So I can have a chance to show you how really sorry I am to have overreacted."

"But what about my apple fritter?"

"The hell with your apple fritter, woman. Come here. I've got something much better than that to give you!"

"Oh, Nick! Oh yes, please!"

Much later that morning, Victoria called. "Could you go over the reception plans with me?" she asked.

177

"Of course," Kate responded, and for the next half hour, they poured over the plans.

"Everything looks great, and the cake will be fantastic," Kate told her mother-in-law. "The cream and peach-colored frosting will match the flowers and my dress perfectly."

"Nick is going to wear a tux, isn't he?" asked Victoria.

"I'll make sure," Kate responded. As she was going back upstairs to meet Nick for lunch, she asked Silas if he could spare her a few minutes.

"Of course, Mrs. Nick," he said and walked upstairs with her. They entered the flat as Nick came in through the deck door.

"Wait here a moment. Silas," Kate said to him and went into the bedroom, returning a moment later carrying a small gift-wrapped box.

"This is for you for all you have done for us, with our love."

"Oh, Mrs. Nick, you shouldn't have," said Silas, taking the box. When he opened it and saw the antique white gold cufflinks, his eyes filled with tears.

"I don't rightly know what to say," he told them.

"Don't say anything," Nick responded. "Just know every time you look at them how much we love and appreciate you."

Silas left with his gift clutched in his hand, and Nick embraced Kate.

"That was a wonderful idea of yours to get a gift for Silas. I don't think anyone has done that kind of thing for him in a long time."

"He's such a kind and thoughtful man. I wanted him to know how much he means to us."

Over lunch, Nick updated her with plans they had for new accommodations. "We don't have enough housing on the ranch for all our hands and staff, so we are going to construct an apartment building. There will be one-room accommodations for those who are single, one-bedroom units for those who are married, and two-bedrooms for those with a family. This means those hands with wives and families would have a place to live on the ranch instead of having to get housing in town. We'll rent them out for less than they would normally have to pay, and of course, it means no commuting to get to work. We are also putting in a clubhouse so they can have social events. This is a radical move on our part. I don't know of any other ranch that offers such accommodations. Can you think of anything we've left out?"

"How about some barbecues?" suggested Kate.

"That's a great idea!" Nick told her. "The Cartwrights are coming for the reception, so we can look over the plans with Adam, who drew them up."

"Now to the real reason I came home for lunch," Nick told her with his most mischievous grin!

"Nick Barkley, you've got a one-track mind!" Kate responded, unbuttoning his shirt!

"Look who's talking," he told her.

Tuesday night, their photographer dropped by with a sample of their wedding album and to take the order of the extra photographs that they wanted. That done, he went downstairs to see the family and to take their orders. Nick, escorting him out, made sure to lock the front door. They relaxed in the hammock, Nick with his brandy and cigar, and Kate with a cappuccino from their new machine.

"When do the guests who are staying for the reception arrive?" asked Nick.

"Friday, same day that the huge marquee goes up," replied Kate. "There will also be a team in the house moving furniture and cleaning. The caterers will take over the kitchen, and then Saturday morning, the florist will arrive. Your mother asked me to remind you that you have to wear a tux on Saturday," Kate told him.

"No problem," he replied.

"Jeanne will help me get dressed unless you're up to fastening the thirty-plus buttons on my dress?" Kate said.

"No, I will leave that up to you ladies. Now let's go inside so I can practice undressing you!"

"Oh, Nick," she said.

Wednesday and Thursday, more gifts arrived, and Kate worked on keeping up to date with the thank-you notes and finding places for all the useful and beautiful things which they had been given.

She suggested that any family members who would be home, plus the house guests, come upstairs for pizza and beer or soda on their deck Friday night. Everyone but Jarrod, who had a prior commitment, accepted their invitation, which kept the main kitchen free for the caterers. She made a green salad and served that on their huge patio table.

They all sat around munching on salad and pizza and guzzling the beer and soda. Victoria was grateful for Nick and Kate's invitation, which gave her a chance to relax. Kate was fitting in well with the family with her thoughtful and kind ways, Victoria mused.

Saturday was bright and clear. *It's going to be a beautiful day*, thought Kate, *and not too hot*. They just hung out in the flat, not wanting to get in anyone's way downstairs.

Before it was time for her to get into her dress, Nick handed her a small gift-wrapped box. When she opened it, laying on a bed of red satin was a bottle of Maison Francis Murdjian Baccart Rouge, Eau de Parfum. "I wanted to get you a new perfume to wear today, and when I saw the name 'Baccart Rouge,' I knew this was the one. For my very own 'Lady In Red.' I hope you like it."

Opening it up, the most heavenly scent issued forth from the bottle.

"Oh, Nick, it's gorgeous. Just what I'd have picked out for myself, and I love the name. I used to use one called Red Door by Elizabeth Arden before I found Guerlian's Shalimar. But now, this will be my special perfume that I use when I'm with you."

Soon Jeanne arrived to help her get dressed. Nick used one of the spare bedrooms to change into his tux and then waited in the living room. The bedroom door opened, and there she stood in that incredible dress, looking as awesome as she had done on their wedding day.

"You take my breath away," he told her.

This time, she had done without the veil, headdress, and bouquet. Jeanne straightened out the train as Kate walked into the living room.

"Just be careful on the stairs," warned their housekeeper.

"I will," replied Kate.

"It's that time," Nick told her.

He made sure she held the banister with her right hand and her dress in her left, his hand under her left elbow as they made their way down the stairs.

"That dress really is a knockout and just perfect for you!" Audra told her.

"Thank you, sister," replied Kate with a grin.

They took their places, with Victoria in the foyer to greet the guests, Audra fussing over Kate's train to make sure it was seen but no one would step on it. They heard cars pulling up. Some of their ranch hands were doubling as valets to take care of the parking.

"Showtime, everyone," Nick called as Silas opened the door and the first guests came into the foyer.

After an hour, Victoria deemed it was okay for them to go and mingle with the guests. "My face muscles are sore with smiling," Nick confided to Kate.

"Only about two hours more to go," she whispered. She put the hook to the train of her gown over the fingers of her right hand and slipped her left hand into Nick's hand and set off with him to mix with the almost three hundred and fifty guests, with stragglers still arriving.

The pile of gifts was huge, and Nick whispered to her, "Think of all the notes you'll have to write!"

"You're going to write some this time, Nick Barkley," she countered and watched the grin fall from his face!

They walked into the marquee amidst applause and finally got to dance together. The tune Nick had picked for their first dance was "Some Enchanted Evening." "It was playing the first time I saw you," he said, "and I knew you were the one I'd waited my whole life for."

For the second dance, Kate had picked the song Gus had played for her, "A Nightingale Sang In Berkley Square." "I felt the same way. Just didn't want to admit it to you or myself," she whispered.

She thought they were through dancing when Nick murmured, "One more," and the band started to play "The Lady In Red." "The first time we danced, this is what was playing, and you wore a real figure-hugging red dress. Then you in that red dress at mother's party changed everything."

"Nick, you are such a romantic," she said with a grin.

Over three hundred and fifty plus guests circulated between the house and the huge marquee. At three thirty, it was announced that the bride and groom were going to cut their four-tier cake. Nick put his hand on the knife, and Kate laid hers on top of his, and they succeeded in slicing the cake amid rousing applause. Silas and his crew stepped in and did the actual cutting of the cake. Again, Nick and Kate fed each other a small piece. The cake didn't only look good but tasted delicious.

"I hope they save some for us," Nick said.

"Silas will wrap the top tier and it will go in the freezer for our first anniversary or the christening, whichever comes first," Kate told him.

"That's something I want to talk to you about when we're upstairs alone."

"Is something wrong?" she asked.

"No, just want to ask you something."

"Hey, you two you look serious. Can't be serious on a day like today," said Eugene. "How about a dance, Kate?"

"Sorry, Gene, this is Nick's day. All the dances are reserved for him."

"In that case." Nick took her by the arm and steered her back on the floor as the beginning notes of 'For Your Eyes Only' were being played.

"Definitely all the gifts I received at the personal shower are for your eyes only," she whispered to Nick. The next song they danced to was "Something Good" from the Sound of Music. "It really says how I feel having you for my husband," she told him. "I'm glad you picked this selection. They're all special to us," she said.

"They are all on the CD in the box of stuff you got at that shower."

"What CD?"

"In the box you gave me was a CD which had been recorded for us."

"What's on it?"

More
The Lady In Red
Some Enchanted Evening
Behind Closed Doors
For Your Eyes Only
In Love With A Wonderful Guy
Something Good
She's A Lady
If You Ask Me To
Eternally
You Made Me Love You
Be My Love
Can't Help Falling In Love
Hungry Eyes
A Nightingale Sang In Berkley Square
I Just Fall In Love Again
Could I Have This Dance
As I Love You

"I didn't even notice it."

"They're all the songs that mean something to us. I'll play it for you later," he said with a mischievous smile. "Heads up, the governor and his wife are here."

"Where?"

"Coming toward us. Governor and Mrs. Hartley, how very nice to see you. Let me introduce you to my wife, this is Dr. Caroline Barkley, otherwise known as Kate!" There was hugs all around, and they chattered for a while before the governor's party moved on.

Five o'clock came and went, and there were still crowds of people. "I hope they don't think we're serving dinner," Silas whispered to them.

"Start clearing the food away," suggested Kate. "And slow down on the champagne service, that may get the message across that the

183

reception is over. In fact, stop serving the bubbly all together and bring out more coffee."

"Good idea," Silas said and promptly passed on the orders to the staff. Soon, all that was left on the table was cake and coffee. Kate caught Silas as he went by again.

"Could you put up a care package for us with plenty of cake in it please?"

"We've already taken care of that. I'll have one of the servers help Miss Jeanne carry it up to your flat."

"Thank you so much, Silas. You're an angel."

Removing the food and champagne worked. A few people hung around for more coffee and cake, but most decided that the afternoon reception was over.

The band stopped playing and set about putting their instruments away. Nick and Kate went over and told them how much they had enjoyed dancing to their music, and in return, the band thanked the couple for a most unusual playlist.

"It had a bit of everything, old and new, and that's what made it interesting. Some of those songs I hadn't played in years, but I guess they all meant something to you?"

"There was a story behind each one," Kate explained.

"We may pilfer some of your list for some of our other gigs," the band leader told them.

By six-thirty, everyone who wasn't staying on at the ranch had left. That basically left Ben and Adam Cartwright and the five members of the Charlton family from Southern California, old and dear friends of the Barkley's; father, mother, one son, Bobby Jr., and two daughters, Amy and Meg.

Victoria suggested that everyone retire to their rooms to give the staff a clear path to tidy up. "Dinner will be served at eight," she told them. "It will be a cold buffet." The Barkleys, Cartwrights, and Charltons all went upstairs, leaving Silas and his staff to do their job.

Unencumbered, Nick and Kate were grateful to return to their flat, where Jeanne was waiting to help her out of her dress. Kate wasn't sure if that was something Nick wanted to do himself and glanced at him. He signaled to let Jeanne help, so the ladies went into the bedroom. In a few minutes, she was out of her dress. "Just hang it up, please, then you can go," she said to their housekeeper.

Nick changed in one of the guest bedrooms and then strolled into the living room wearing jeans, an unbuttoned shirt, and barefoot. Kate came into the living room wearing the new jade green silk kimono which Nick had purchased for her in Chinatown on their honeymoon. In seconds, they were in each other's arms.

"Having to stand beside you and dance with you and behave myself, not even being able to kiss you properly, was almost too much," he told her. They were walking toward the bedroom as they kissed each other with long deep kisses.

"Nick, this will make us late for the dinner!"

"We're not going to the dinner."

"We have to. Your mother has all those guests, and we are supposed to help her entertain them."

"Well, tonight, she's going to have to manage without us."

"She's not going to be very pleased."

"She'll get over it."

"Well, darling, if you're absolutely sure."

"I am, babe."

"Silas has sent up loads of food, and I could put some of it on a tray, and we could have a sort of picnic in bed."

"Now that's a great idea. Let me help me you."

"I can manage if you could straighten up in here." Kate went into the kitchen and put together a little of this and a little of that. The only thing she couldn't carry was the champagne and flutes. She took the first tray through to the bedroom. Nick had tidied the bed up somewhat. As she was leaving, he caught her hand and asked her where she was going.

"Back to the kitchen for the best part," she answered him. When she got into the kitchen, she remembered the cake and put half a pot of coffee on and took the bubbly, glasses, and cake in. Nick took care of opening the bottle and poured them each a glass. They had their picnic sitting curled up on the bed. Nick's phone rang once. He looked to see who was calling. It was his mother, so he didn't answer it! They ate the cake with more champagne. All the alcohol was going to Kate's head.

"I need some coffee," she told Nick, so he cleared up the remnants of the food and put it away, poured Kate a mug of coffee, and they went outside onto the deck.

"Lay down in the hammock," Nick suggested, and he lay down next to her and lit his cigar. The next thing Nick knew, she was sound asleep, her head on his shoulder, and that's the way John found them at around two a.m. when he was doing his rounds and noticed the deck door open.

He went inside and got a couple of blankets that were laying on the sofa, covered them up, turned off all the lights except the white ones decorating the patio roof, closed the door, and whispered, "Good night," to them, which neither heard.

About five a.m., Nick woke up. "Kate," he whispered. "Kate, wake up."

"What?" she murmured.

"We fell asleep in the hammock. Let's go inside."

"Who covered us up?" she asked.

"I bet it was John. He takes a walk around late at night and must have seen the door open, the lights on, and come to investigate."

"How sweet of him. Do remember to thank him."

"I will, but for now, we need to try and catch some more sleep in a real bed."

But sleep wasn't what happened after they lay down!

"We have to talk with Adam about the new accommodations for the hands and their families this morning after breakfast. I'll call him and see what's a good time to get together."

"Invite him up here if you like," suggested Kate.

"Good idea."

So later that morning, after Kate had had a chance to tidy up the flat, Adam came to talk over his plans.

"The apartment looks wonderful," he told them. "You really have made it a home."

"That was all Kate," Nick told him. "Now, let's look at your plans, Adam." They poured over the new plans for a while.

"Any suggestions, Kate? "Adam asked her.

"Well," she responded, "I know that this may be outlandish, but how about a small children's playground?" The men thought for a moment.

"That's doable," said Adam.

"Good thinking," put in Nick.

"Anything else?"

"Well, I thought maybe we could have a complex manager—perhaps a retired hand could do the job—to oversee the whole thing, fix any problems like a plumbing problem or a light out, and generally make sure that the rules were being obeyed. What do you think?"

The guys looked at each other. Nick was the first to comment. "I like it. I like the idea of someone overseeing the property, and having a retired ranch hand doing it seems perfect. That makes perfect sense. See, Kate, you're a natural at this!"

"Adam, you were worried I wouldn't find the right woman. Now what do you think?"

"I think I better talk to these gypsy friends of yours!"

After Adam left, Kate asked Nick what he'd wanted to talk to her about yesterday.

"Oh that. Well, it was just when you said the top tier of the cake could be used for a christening cake reminded me that we have never discussed birth control. Are you using any?"

"No."

"So you could get pregnant any time?"

"That's right."

"Are you sure that's what you want?"

"If you don't mind, Nick?"

"Are you kidding? You'll look beautiful pregnant, I'll have the pleasure of watching your belly grow, putting my hand on you to feel our child move in your womb, and knowing I put a baby inside you. You know I'll be with you during your labor and right there when you give birth, watching as you push our child out of your body.

We'll be a family of three! Mind, how could I possibly mind? When I do get you pregnant, I'll be overjoyed."

"I know that you'll make a wonderful father, Nick. But who knows when you'll get me pregnant. I could be already, or it could be six months or a year from now. I'm not going to get upset near the end of the month if I get my period. When it happens, it happens."

"That's a good attitude to take. In the meantime, we'll just have fun trying!"

"Nick, you'd better call your mother and see if she's still speaking to us after not showing up last night."

"I already have. She's invited us to lunch." No one passed any comment about their absence at dinner the night before. The talk was mainly about the reception and how much everyone had enjoyed it. After lunch, the men went into the library to shoot some pool whilst the ladies returned to the living room.

"Where did you find that wedding dress of yours?" Amy Charlton asked, so Kate told the story about the antique store.

They all continued to chat until Nick came in and said, "Please excuse us, we have things to do in the flat."

"Thank you for the rescue. I couldn't have taken much more of the girl talk," said Kate. "Let's get started on opening these gifts."

Silas had his staff bring them all upstairs whilst they were at lunch.

"Where do we start? There are so many of them?" asked Nick.

"Let's clear off the table first," suggested Kate.

Once again, Nick opened the gifts while Kate wrote in her book what they were and who had given it. They worked steadily all afternoon, stopped for a while to eat the last of the leftovers for dinner, and finally finished up. They were amazed at all the gifts they had been given.

"These sheets are beautiful," Kate said, looking at some pale green Egyptian cotton sheets.

"Talking about sheets," Nick said with a wink. "Let's get between some!"

"You haven't forgotten today is Memorial Day, have you?" asked Nick.

"Oh goodness, I had," replied Kate. "What all goes on?"

"Well, it celebrates the armed forces, who've laid down their lives for this county, and the unofficial start of summer, so we have a huge cookout with all the hands, office staff, and our friends invited. We roast a steer, have all kinds of other food, and games with prizes for the kids, etc. So you'll have to wait to get help putting all the gifts away and getting the trash out until Tuesday. No more work today except on the barbecue."

"When do you start cooking all the meat?"

"We started at midnight. The steer was already dressed and ready to go, and it will go on until about 3:00 p.m. and then it rests for about two hours and then we eat."

"How much meat?"

"Approximately three hundred and twenty five pounds."

"How do you cook it?"

"On a spit, which turns electronically over a pit five feet across and one foot deep."

"Sounds complicated."

"Not really, but think, in the old days, men had to take it in turns turning the spit! How would you have liked that job?!"

"Not at all!"

"Now it just needs someone to check the meat periodically."

"Who provides the other food?"

"We provide all the food via caterers. Again, in the old days, it used to be a potluck. But so many of the men lived in bunkhouses with no cooking facilities, the house ended having to provide most of the food in any case. Now we just make it easier on everyone by having it catered."

"Not many cowboys were married in the old days, were they?" asked Kate.

"No, very few in fact. They were, for the most part, a very transient group of people. Wives just didn't fit in with their lifestyle, and of course, not many ranches had living facilities to accommodate them, not like us having a children's playground!"

"You're going to do it then?"

"Yes, I am."

"Oh, I'm so happy you're putting my suggestion in the plans."

"Not just that one. We are going to work out the details of the complex, the rules, etc., and then come up with what we need in a complex manager and go from there. I'd like you in on those meetings, so I'll make sure they're on a Friday."

"You're determined to drag me, kicking and screaming, into the ranching business!" said Kate, laughing.

"I think you'll find it interesting the deeper you get into it," replied Nick.

"Silly question, but what does one wear to a cookout?"

"Do you have anything western, a shirt perhaps, and of course jeans? You don't have any western boots, do you? I was going to ask you about this days ago, but it completely slipped my mind!"

"I have a Western-style shirt but no boots."

"That's something we'll have to remedy in a hurry. There is a store specializing in boots right here in town, and it's open today. Let's hurry over there now."

"Now?"

"Now!"

After a quick trip to the boot store, they came away with not one but two pairs of boots for Kate. Brown and black. She was staggered a how much a good pair cost, and then Nick wanted her to have the two colors! She told him she didn't need two pairs, but Nick being Nick, insisted she did. He also bought her a kerchief after asking what color her shirt was. "You still don't have a Stetson," he commented, so next stop, a store that sold nothing but western headgear. They found one in a kind of dark cream color so it would go with any shirt. When the store owner mentioned the price, her knees almost buckled. "All this for a cookout!" she said.

"People are going to expect my wife to dress the part," explained Nick.

"Is there anything I can do to help?"

"No, my mother and Silas have been doing this for so long they have it down to a science! So you just show up and look beautiful!"

About four p.m., Nick and Kate went downstairs to be part of the family welcoming committee. By five, there were over two hundred and fifty plus people on the grounds of the Barkley ranch. Marquees had been set up, with rows of tables and benches for eating. Victoria had enlisted the help of every worker in the children's department of the church to set up and run the games for the kids. The church always considered this one of the two biggest fundraisers for the children's department in the year, the other being the Barkley Labor Day picnic. In return for their help, Victoria wrote a donation check to the church's children's fund, which paid for their program for the entire year!

By six, people had eaten, were about to eat, or were getting in line to get their food.

"The main course should be over by seven," explained Gene to Kate. "Then the desserts come out."

"Desserts?" asked Kate.

"Normally, two kinds of pie or cake and ice cream," Gene told her. "Aren't you going to get in line for your food?"

"I'm just waiting for Nick to come back. He had to talk with John. Oh, here he is. Nick, Gene is suggesting we get some food."

"Let's do it. Are you joining us, bro?"

"Sure am."

They filled their plates and found places to sit together. They were still treated as "The Barkleys," but nothing was ever going to change that. The food was delicious; the meat melted in the mouth. Next, they went to line up for dessert and coffee, staying together because Gene was telling Kate that he'd chosen trauma surgery as his specialty.

"Well, I hope you didn't choose it just because of me," she told him.

"You were a huge influence on me," he admitted.

"Another trauma surgeon in the family. Nick, what do you think about that?"

"I think next to ranching, it's the second family business!"

They watched the fireworks display and then made their way home. Staff would come in during the morning to dismantle the tents and store the folding tables and benches. The trash had mostly been picked up during the fireworks and would be hauled away tomorrow.

"Another cookout success," Nick said as they climbed the stairs to their deck.

"Are you going to have your brandy and cigar?"

"If you'll stay on the deck with me."

"Of course I will. Just let me take my boots off." Boots weren't the only thing she took off! The next time Nick saw her, she was dressed in a long black nightgown and matching negligee. She had put on their CD but had jumped ahead to "Wonderful Guy." "Maybe we could actually hear more of the CD by my doing that," she said, laughing.

"Not tonight," said Nick, grinning!

"You thinking of starting your own department store?" Joanne said when she walked in and saw all the gifts piled up in the kitchen, dining, and living room.

"That's our chore today—find places for everything," Kate told her. "But first, coffee." Just then, John arrived to start work on helping them remove the trash. "Why don't you have some coffee with us?" Kate asked.

"That's mighty nice of you, Mrs. Nick," he said. "Just black is fine."

"Jeanne has brought over some homemade muffins. Would you like one?"

"Sure would."

"Just find a place to sit and relax for a minute," Kate told him.

They enjoyed their break then set to work. Jeanne took care of the linens, putting the towels in the washing machine and loading the dishwasher with china, glasses, and flatware. They set out the silver trays, putting on them decanters—which they filled—and crystal glasses after carefully hand washing them. John removed all the trash, and by lunchtime, the flat was getting back to normal.

All the kitchen bakeware, pots, and pans were put away, and the food mixer and toaster oven were set on the counter. A jug full of kitchen utensils was sitting, waiting to be used. "With all these things, I guess I'm supposed to cook." Kate laughed.

Nick was busy with fruit picking cherries and grapes. The itinerant workers were in town, and Kate wasn't sure when he'd be home. It was after seven when he came in looking tired and saying he was as hungry as a bear. Whilst he showered, Kate got a meal on the table and opened a beer for him.

"This place looks a lot differed from when I left this morning," he told her, looking around.

"Jeanne and I worked on it most of the day but nothing like your day has been," commented Kate.

"Mmm, this is good. What is it?" Nick asked.

"Goulash," she told him.

After his second helping, he was visibly relaxed. "The next few weeks are going to be like this," he told her. "One crop after another, barley, peaches, and plums. Heath is doing a pretty good job ramrodding the operation."

"What does that mean exactly?" she asked.

"Boss, or in this case, second-in-command."

"It must be nice to have a family member in that position," Kate commented.

"It is. I know my orders are going to be carried out without any hesitation, and that feels good. Did the Charltons leave today as planned?"

"As far as I know. I haven't talked with anyone other than John and Jeanne today."

"Tomorrow, I have a meeting with the Cartwrights at ten that should take a couple of hours, and then it's back to the harvesting. If you want to sit in on the meeting, I'd love to have you," he told her.

"Are you sure?" she asked.

"Of course. I told you this is a partnership, and I want you to get a feel for what goes on. But for now, I'm going to bed, and I'm hoping you will come with me!

"An early night sounds good to me," Kate said with her saucy grin!

The meeting with Ben and Adam Cartwright was about buying two bulls from a ranch in Montana. Adam had found out about them and had given Nick the heads up. Each of their ranches was purchasing one. According to Adam, these bulls, a strain of Herefords, would help the herds withstand the cruelest of winters. Agreeing to the bull owner's price via a conference call, the deal was made, and Adam would fly up there and supervise the crating for shipment of these valuable animals. After they were through talking about bulls, Adam said he was already working on the plans for the accommodation complex. "I should be back in about two weeks and we can talk further."

"Thank you so much, Adam," Nick said.

"My pleasure. I can see getting Kate involved is going to raise the bar in all your future plans."

"Sure is," responded Nick.

Chapter 11

After the meeting Kate, went back home while Nick, Ben, and Adam had a working lunch at the office.

She was busy writing some of the huge stack of thank-you notes when she heard someone yelling her name. She ran down the hall and out the front door, nearly knocking over Victoria, who was the one calling for her.

"There's been a shooting, and it's Ciego's little boy who has been hit."

"Get my bag out of my car," Kate instructed Silas, who kept keys to all their vehicles in case of an emergency. He grabbed hers and hurried out the front door.

"Where's the child?" Kate asked. "Has anyone called nine one one?"

"He's at Ciego's house, and yes, the paramedics are on their way," answered Victoria.

They raced to the small ranch house as one of the hands came running up carrying her bag. "I can move faster than Silas," he explained, seeing the surprised look on her face.

"Towels. Get me lots of towels," Kate said as she saw the little boy laying on the front porch, his shirt soaked with blood. "We've got to try and stop the bleeding."

Rosita, Ciego's wife, was crying hysterically, so Victoria dashed into the house and came out with an armful of towels. Kate used them to apply pressure to try and halt the bleeding. They could hear the sirens nearing them, and within minutes, as she continued to work on the small child, the paramedics were on the scene. Heath and Nick, hearing the commotion, came running to find out what was going on.

"I'll ride with them," she told Nick as she climbed aboard the ambulance. At the hospital, the ER staff were ready and waiting for the incoming ambulance.

About twenty minutes later, Kate, bloodstained, walked into the waiting room, where it seemed half the Barkley ranch staff was assembled. She saw Ciego and Rosita rise and come toward her.

"I'm so sorry," she said. "He'd lost too much blood. We couldn't save him."

Rosita's knees buckled as she let out an ear-piercing wail. Heath caught her, otherwise she'd have hit the floor!

"I want to see my baby," she kept repeating.

"In a few minutes, a nurse will come and get you," Kate told her and went back through the door, reappearing a few minutes later in clean scrubs. By that time, Ciego and Rosita had been taken to see their son. Kate walked straight over to Nick and just held on to him.

"I know I should be used to this," she told him, "but when it's a child and someone you know…" She let it trail off. Nick continued to hold her, and then Kate asked, "Does anyone know what happened?"

Heath answered, "From what we have been able to find out, the two boys were playing in the woods behind the houses, and Carlos, the younger one, found a gun and started playing with it and accidentally shot his brother. Somehow, they made it back home, where Danny collapsed."

"There was nothing you could do?" asked one of the wives.

"Have you any idea the kind of damage two thirty eight's fired at close range into the body of a seven-year-old does? He was leaking like a sieve, and there was so much damage, we just couldn't stop the bleeding, and I've said way too much," replied Kate.

"I'll stay here with Heath. The rest of you may as well go home," said Victoria. "We'll take care of all the arrangements that have to be made. Audra is looking after Carlos, and he'll stay with us until his parents get home. If someone could clean up their front porch. We don't need them going home and seeing Danny's blood on it."

"We'll take care of that," said a couple of hands and their wives. "Plus we'll organize some food."

"That will be great," replied Mrs. Barkley.

"I have to sign the death certificate," said Kate. "So I'll be a few more minutes." When she came back, most of the ranch hands and their wives had left. Just a few who were the closest to Ciego and Rosita were there, along with Nick and Heath.

"Where's your mother?"

"She's gone back to be with them. Rosita is in an awful state, and Ciego couldn't handle her by himself, so a nurse came and got Mother to help him."

"Should we stay or go?" Kate asked Nick.

"I think we can go," Nick told her. "Heath is staying because he brought Ciego and Rosita here. Mother drove herself, and I came in my truck. The others are going to wait around for a while."

"What a terrible thing to happen. Who would leave a loaded gun just lying around where a child could get hold of it?" Kate exclaimed.

"The sheriff has it looking for any prints other than the kids and running the serial number to see who it belongs to," Nick told her on the drive home. When they got home, Sheriff Madden was at the house.

"Come upstairs with us, Fred," Nick invited him. "You've never been up here, have you?"

"No, I haven't. You've got quite a place here."

Kate explained what she'd been doing when she'd heard Victoria calling for her. "I just dropped everything and ran."

Just then, there was a buzz from the front door. Kate took care of it. It was Silas, returning her medical bag. "I didn't know whether to put it back in your car or give it to you, so I thought I'd better hand it to you directly in case anything has been used up so you can replace it."

"How thoughtful you are, Silas. You did exactly the right thing. I'll check it out before I return it to my car."

He left, and Kate turned to Fred. "Is there anything I can get you? Coffee or a beer?"

"Cup of coffee would be great. Say, what should I call you?"

"At the hospital, it's Dr. Barkley, but anywhere else, it's Mrs. Nick."

"I like that. Well, Mrs. Nick, a cup of coffee, and if you still have some of that great cake they served at the reception."

"I can help you on both counts. I have a pot of coffee just brewed and plenty of cake, so sit down and relax for a moment. What do you take in your coffee?"

"Just black."

"There you go, one cup of coffee and a big slice of cake."

"Thank you, Mrs. Nick. That will sure hit the spot."

"Now what can you tell us about the gun? Any usable fingerprints?"

"No, the only prints on the gun belong to the little boys."

"How about the serial number?" she asked.

"It was stolen from a house during a break-in over two weeks ago." "What it was doing in the woods behind the houses here doesn't make any sense. The break-in was fifty miles from the ranch."

"To leave a loaded firearm in the grass is just asking for trouble, and trouble found it with a capital T," said Kate. "Two little boys out playing find it and don't realize that it's real, and the next thing we have is one kid shot twice by his five-year-old brother. I mean, how is Carlos going to deal with shooting and killing Danny? He's going to need professional help. In fact, the whole family should get counseling. Nick, you'll have to talk to Ciego about putting at least Carlos in counseling. If it's the money, I'll take care of it myself," said Kate. "But that little boy must get help immediately. No screwing around with this. Promise me, Nick, you'll talk to Ciego within the next few days. Promise me!"

"I will, I will, I promise. I can see how important this is to you, and you don't have to pay for it, the family will cover the cost."

"And we must start an education campaign in the schools and in the homes that if you see a gun, you don't touch it, you find an adult. Children must be educated about guns, how dangerous they are, they are not toys. Nick, why are you looking at me like that?"

"What you must understand, Kate, is we're in the heart of gun country. Children are raised with guns."

"Well, if that's so, you are all doing a mighty poor job of education because a five-year-old killed a seven-year-old this afternoon. Wanna tell me what the hell went wrong?"

"It shouldn't, but accidents do happen sometimes."

"That kind should never happen—a family torn apart because the children were not taught to get an adult when they find a gun. Something that simple could have saved Danny's life today, and Ciego and Rosita would still have two sons instead of one! You are all doing a mighty poor job of firearm education, and because of that, you are all responsible for the death of Danny and what Carlos will have to live with for the rest of his life. And when Carlos wakes up screaming in his bed, are you going to be the one who goes in and sits by his bedside and calms him down? Are you going to take it in turns to do that? What if it had been our sons, Nick? What would your reaction be then? Would it still be 'it happens,' or would you be out of your mind with grief and rage that it did happen? Think about it. I know I shall. Now, Sheriff Madden, is there anything else I can get you? More coffee perhaps?"

"One more cup of your great coffee, Mrs. Nick, and then I must be on my way."

"Any other clues?" asked Kate.

"I'm afraid not."

"Was much stolen in the robbery?" Nick said to the sheriff.

"Just some cash and jewelry, which hasn't shown up."

"That's what's so strange about where the gun ended up. I mean, you would have to physically walk it to that spot. It's not like throwing it out of a car window."

"Does that suggest the burglar has a connection to the ranch?"

"It may."

"Not a happy thought, as everyone knows that the children who live on the ranch play in the woods."

"Thank you for the cake and coffee, Mrs. Nick. Now I must be going."

"Nick, I'm so upset about this shooting more than any other I've seen in a long time. I guess it's because I'm so close to it. If they had just told an adult what they'd found instead of picking it up! I can tell you, our children will be raised completely differently. They will not even be allowed toy guns, and they'll be taught guns are dangerous things!"

Nick had a horrified look on his face. "I think that's going too far."

"I don't think it's going far enough, and I've just got started," she said to him.

"My father took me out shooting rabbits the first time when I was about four," Nick told her.

"Four!" she exclaimed "Didn't that bother you taking an animal's life?" she asked.

"An animal which we ate," answered Nick. "It wasn't just for the sport of it. I've never shot like that. I shoot for food or for danger, a bear or a mountain lion attacking people or the herd. I enjoy target shooting, or if I have to, I will shoot an animal to put it out of its misery if it is so badly hurt and can't recover. But most of all, I will use my guns in defense of my family and our home. There are good uses for a gun or rifle, Kate."

"I understand you, Nick, and you do handle guns sensibly. But that does not alter the fact a little boy is dead from two gunshots. Your handling a gun well doesn't help Ciego and his wife this evening. The minute I get pregnant, I expect to see every gun in this flat locked up, not the haphazard way you do that now, and kept that way for the rest of our lives. The same for ammo. All safely under lock and key."

"What about downstairs?"

"I will ask them politely."

"And if they don't comply?"

"Then the children will never be down there alone. The same will apply to any other house they go to."

"You can't do that!!"

"YOU JUST WATCH ME!"

There was silence in the flat. Both thinking where they stood on the firearm issue. The chasm between them as vast as a canyon. The hall door buzzed. Nick answered it, and his mother came in. There was an atmosphere in the flat that could be cut with a knife. Victoria wisely chose to ignore it and instead updated them on Ciego and Rosita.

"They are home, but Carlos is staying the night with Audra. The porch had been cleaned, so by the time everyone got back, there was no trace of Danny's blood. Food filled the fridge and was stacked on the counters. Their friends had been very generous. A doctor at the hospital has given Rosita some sleeping pills, seeing the state she worked herself into. Ciego is making sure she gets into bed and her medication, and then I'm going back to make certain he eats something."

Nick brought his mother up to date on the gun and the rest Sheriff Madden had told them. All through the conversation, Kate sat there like a porcelain doll, not uttering a word.

"I'm going to have my hands full tonight, so what you two can do for me is go downstairs and host dinner for the Cartwrights. It's their last night at the ranch. Audra won't be there, she's looking after Carlos. Heath will be with me at Ciego's. Eugene and Jarrod will be there, but that's it. I need you both to step in and show our guests that, even in an emergency, we can pull together and be polite."

"What time?" asked Nick.

"Seven o'clock for seven thirty dinner."

"We'll be there," Nick replied. "We won't let the family down."

As it was already six forty, Kate walked into the bedroom and changed. Nick followed. Not a word was spoken until he asked her "Do you want me to do up your zipper?"

"I managed," she replied, not looking at him.

Finally, he said, "It's six fifty-five."

"I'm ready," was her response. They walked downstairs together but not touching. The talk at the table was amongst the men. Kate didn't join in at all. Ben Cartwright apologized to her for that, but she told him "it was fine with her, she didn't care, she had a lot on her mind and was trying to work some things out." After dinner she excused herself telling Nick she had her period, went upstairs took a sleeping pill and was sound asleep wearing PJs when Nick came to bed.

He knew by the PJs that she did indeed have her period. She had told him once that she wouldn't wear her expensive nightgowns when she was menstruating! "When you see I'm back in my nighties, you'll know I'm good to go," she'd told him, laughing!

Nick knew that Kate had gone to sleep upset with him over the gun issue. He undressed and got into bed. He tried to hold her, but even in her drugged sleep, she managed to move away from him! He hoped he would see her before going to work the next morning, but she was still sound asleep when he left. As soon as the florist opened, he ordered wildflowers to be sent to her with a card that simply said, "I love you, Nick." When he got home at lunchtime, the flowers were there, but Kate wasn't.

"She said she had some errands to do," Jeanne told him. "I can make you some lunch."

"No, I'll get something at the canteen," he said on his way out.

When Nick came in after work, Kate had returned, he went to kiss her, but she sidestepped him and went into the kitchen. "Mind telling me what I've done wrong?" he asked.

"You and your attitude on firearms," was all she said.

"I know it's hard for you to understand, coming from a country like England that doesn't have any, but—"

She cut him off. "I've lived for years around guns with people who have a healthy respect for them, not some cavalier attitude."

"Cavalier attitude?"

"You heard me."

"How can you say that?"

"I can say that because this time yesterday, I signed the death certificate on a child who didn't have to die."

"That wasn't my fault."

"Not you, but you're part of this ridiculous gun culture. I've told your mother that I won't be going to the family dinner tonight." And with that, she walked into the bedroom, shut the door behind her, took a sleeping pill, got into her PJs and climbed into bed.

"Kate," said Nick, coming into their bedroom. "Can't we talk?"

"No, I've got cramps and I feel awful."

"Can I get you anything?"

"No."

When Nick came to bed, she was asleep. This time, he put an arm around her, and even though she tried to move away, he held firmly onto her, and that's how they slept.

When Kate woke up at eight twenty five, this being Friday, Nick was still home.

"Stay in bed and I'll bring you some coffee," he told her.

"How come you're this late going into the office?" Kate asked.

"Because we are going to get this issue sorted out if it takes all day. Jeanne won't be coming in. I gave her the day off," he told her. "I understand in your profession you see the worst firearms can do. But I need handguns and rifles nearby in case of trouble. You must remember we live on a ranch with all its inherent dangers, miles away from town. I have to be able to protect us and what is ours."

"So where does that leave us?"

"Trying to understand each other, I hope."

"And when we have children, what then?"

"Give me some credit, Kate. Do you seriously think I would endanger our children's lives by leaving a firearm where they could get to it?"

"Yet at times, you carry one of your Desert Warriors in that custom-made shoulder holster of yours and a Glock in your boot holster. You were raised with guns all around you, and I understand you wanting to keep us safe, but there has to be a way that can be done without running the risk of the weapons falling into the wrong hands."

"How about I put a gun safe somewhere in the living room and bedroom? As long as I can reach my firearms in a hurry, I can live with that, and my rifles can go in one of the bookcases in the living room, which I'll have converted to hold them. I'll make sure they are locked away when I'm not using them. Would that suit you?"

"You mean that, Nick?"

"I mean it."

"Thank you so much."

"Come here."

"I've still got my period."

"Since when did that stop me from kissing you? That's much better. Now I'm going into the office, I'll see you tonight. I love you."

"I love you too, Nick, and thank you."

Kate got dressed and sought out Victoria. "Tell me how you raised four children in a houseful of guns," she asked.

"By teaching them early the difference between the real thing and toys."

"Did you let them have toy guns?"

"Of course. How would they ever learn the difference?"

"I don't understand."

"The difference in feel and weight, to start with, and how to check if the real thing was loaded and if it was, to put it down and find an adult."

"I never thought of that."

"You never had to. Guns were never readily available when you were growing up. But in the army, you were taught how to check if a gun was loaded right?"

"Right."

"And there must have been a time knowing that kept you alive?"

"Yes, there was."

"So you take that knowledge and teach it to your children to keep them safe."

"You make it sound so simple."

"It's not simple at all. It takes constant vigilance, but as you can see, I raised four healthy children, so it can work."

"Thank you."

"Anytime."

That evening, when Nick came in tired and hungry, there was a wonderful aroma coming from the kitchen.

"You go and take a shower, and dinner will be on the table when you come back." She had ready for him a steaming plate of beef stew, an ice-cold beer, and a pone of cornbread.

Sitting down beside him, Kate told Nick, "I had a talk with your mother today about how she raised you and the rest of the family, and it gave me a completely different perspective on raising children around firearms. I'm sorry the way I came down on you. I understand you just want to protect us."

"Thank you for the apology, Kate, I really do appreciate it. I've already put those plans we discussed for the gun safes and lock-up cabinets for my rifles in motion, and they should be completed in the next few days."

"That's wonderful, darling. Now eat your dinner and tell me about your day."

"Before I do, I'd like to ask if this girl I know is busy Saturday night, 'cos if she's not, I'd like to take her out for dinner and dancing?"

"Are you asking me out on a date, Nick Barkley?"

"Sure am. Be ready at seven thirty."

"I certainly will. I look forward to it."

Kate treated Nick with breakfast in bed the next day.

"I could get used to this," he told her.

"Today, the curtain people are coming, so we can pick out fabric for the new curtains and they can measure."

"What's wrong with the ones we've got?"

"They don't match the furniture."

"Are we replacing all of them?"

"Yep. Got to try out the new 'black' credit card you gave me!"

"Ouch!"

"Come on, get up so I can straighten up in here."

By the time they had finished picking out the fabric for the blinds and curtains, Nick's eyes were beginning to glaze over.

"I never thought there'd be so many choices."

"Of course."

"Now can we get something to eat?"

"Just a light lunch. I have a dinner date."

"You do? Anybody I know?"

"A tall handsome guy I know asked me out."

"Handsome?"

"Extremely!"

After lunch, the front door buzzed.

"It's Jarrod, he wants to see you," Nick told her.

"I'm sorry I haven't been up to see you before now," Jarrod said, "but it's been one thing after another. Anyway, I have your will ready to be signed. All we need are two witnesses.

"I'll call Jeanne," said Kate.

"I'll call John," said Nick.

Within minutes, both Jeanne and John were coming through the deck door. Jarrod put the will on the table, covering the top half and asking Kate to sign, followed by John and Jeanne. "Thank you both so much," Nick said. He offered Jarrod a beer, which he accepted, and the two brothers settled down to talk about ranch business, which Kate just listened to. She made guacamole dip and put it out with some chips.

"Alas not homemade," she told them. After Jarrod left, Nick got some business phone calls, so by the time she showered and got ready, it was time for her "date" to pick her up. The "handsome" guy was waiting in the living room dressed in one of his best suits with a bunch of wildflowers and a box of Godiva truffles. "You sure know how to make a good impression on a girl," she told him with a big smile.

"Never know what it will lead to," he replied with a grin. They drove to Paul's for dinner. On their table was a vase of red roses.

"Aren't they beautiful?" she remarked.

"They're yours," he told her.

"Mine?"

"I had them delivered here today."

"For me?"

"For you, darling."

"Nick, I love you."

"I love you, too, so go ahead and order your 'well done' lamb chops. This ranch owner won't mind!"

Paul came over and congratulated them on their marriage and had a plate of *hors d'oeuvres* sent over. Gus played "their" songs, and they danced cheek to cheek in the way they reserved for dancing in public, unlike the way they held each other when dancing on their deck! When they got home with her precious vase of red roses, Nick asked, "Is it still PJs, or are you back in nightgowns?"

"Oh, definitely nightgowns."

Nick's eyes lit up as he picked her up and carried her into their bedroom!

On Sunday, they went out to brunch. Kate having mimosa was equally as ardent as Nick in their lovemaking when they got home. As she lay in the circle of Nick's arms, she reminded him that the next day, she was back to work.

"Already," he exclaimed.

"Already," Kate retorted. "I've been off for five weeks. Time to get back to work."

"I must admit, I enjoyed having you home," Nick told her.

"Trouble is, I was running out of things to do," Kate explained. "I don't know how your mother and Audra fill their time," she said. "I guess it's all the committees and boards they are on, but I couldn't do that."

"Kate, what about when we have children? Will you go back to work then?"

"I think so. I would take three months off and then put the baby in the crèche at work. That way, I'd be right on the spot if I was needed and could pop up and see them when the ER was slow. Maybe cut my hours back or work one less day. I haven't thought that through, but I know I couldn't just sit at home and change diapers all day!"

"You don't think it would be fulfilling enough for you?"

"Quite frankly, I don't, but then I've never had a baby!"

"Maybe you'll change your mind?"

"Maybe, but don't count on it, Nick."

They neither said anymore on the subject. Kate got her scrubs and clogs out ready for tomorrow. Nick was on the phone, something about the pickin', and then watched a ballgame on television, and Kate tried her best to follow what was going on without asking him too many questions! They ordered Chinese for dinner with enough to have for dinner Monday night.

Working a twelve-hour shift was more tiring than Kate remembered, but then, she'd never had five weeks off either! By the time she got home, Nick had only beaten her in by a few minutes. They heated up the leftover Chinese food and sat down to eat, each sharing their day.

"It wasn't too busy at all," Kate confided.

"It was nuts," Nick exclaimed.

They sat and talked for the next hour or so, not bothering to watch TV.

"Let's just go to bed," said Nick at nine thirty. "I'm bushed."

"I feel the same way," replied Kate.

They both almost fell into bed and were immediately asleep.

The rest of the week followed much the same pattern, except Joanne left dinners in the crockpot or already cooked and just needed to be reheated. They didn't fall straight asleep every night. Nick and Kate did find the energy to make love a couple of nights.

Sheriff Madden called Nick a couple of weeks later to tell him that the guy who had done the robbery where the gun the two boys found had been apprehended.

"During his confession, he told the deputy that he'd stopped by the Barkley Ranch looking for work and that, while he was there, he'd thrown the stolen gun in some woods on the property. He had no use for it and didn't want to be found with it on his person if he was ever stopped by the law. John McIntire had told him that you guys weren't hiring at that time, so just left. But that's how the gun ended up on your property for the kids to find. Just by chance! When the perpetrator heard what had happened and one little guy shot his own brother, they told me he got really upset. Never dreamed anything like that would happen, just figured one of your hands would find it and turn it in. Well, at least you now know it wasn't one of your people involved in the robbery or of disposing of the gun in the woods. An accident those kids found it pure and simple. Doesn't help Ciego and his family, I know, but at least they'll understand that no malicious intent was ever meant. Just a stupid unthinking act which has resulted in the death a child! Well, I thought you'd like to know. Bye for now."

208

Chapter 12

Very early, on Thursday morning, the front door phone buzzer sounded! "Who on earth can it be at this time," Nick said, answering it. "It's Mother," he told Kate. "She sounds angry." He and Kate quickly looked around, finding where their nightclothes had ended up on the floor in the heat of passion the night before and hurriedly put them on, grabbing robes as they left the bedroom as Nick buzzed his mother in and Kate switched on the coffee pot.

Victoria came in holding the local paper. "I take it you haven't read this yet?" she asked them.

"We've just woken up," Nick responded. "Why what's in it that has you so upset?"

"It's the gossip column which that troublemaking woman Joan writes. Now I know how you get Nick. Grab a cup of coffee and sit down before you read it."

"What has she said this time?" Nick wanted to know.

Whilst this exchange was going on, Kate had picked up the discarded newspaper. "Oh lord, how can anyone be this cruel?" she exclaimed.

Nick took the paper from her trembling hands and read the offending column.

"Where did she get this trash from?" he yelled. "Who the hell said this about us?"

The gist of the piece was that a so-called former girlfriend of Nick's had confided in Joan that "by now, Kate would be starting to regret her hasty marriage to the ranching magnate. For beneath that seemingly charming facade was a control freak with a hair trigger temper who would have his own way in every aspect of his wife's life." Plus, a "confidential source" inside the Barkley mansion had "told this reporter that all was not going well in the bedroom department! Nick wanted to be very active, and his wife was objecting to his nightly demands. The honeymoon was definitely over for this couple, if they ever really had one!"

Kate sat there, stunned that anyone would say this about her beloved husband and print such rubbish! "Has Jarrod seen this?" she asked her mother-in-law. "Can we sue Joan and the paper for libel?"

"Jarrod is in San Francisco, but I'll give him a call and find out what he advises," Victoria told them. "Until then, I suggest we ignore it. Those who know you two won't believe it, and those who believe it, we don't care about!"

After her mother-in-law left, Kate put her arms around Nick and hugged him. "It's someone who has a grudge against us—who resents our happiness. And that Joan, she's been trying to get someone from here to feed her gossip since we got married. But she's had no luck with Silas and his staff, and as for Jeanne, better luck with a clam! Joan's even tried to get the people I work with to give her juicy tidbits about us, but I'm careful what I say so they have nothing to tell her. So instead, she's made up this awful piece. Nothing in that trashy column could be further from the truth. We both know we have really awesome sex!"

"I had no idea the extent this gossip had gotten to be," he said to his wife.

"Joan actually started asking around about me when she first found from one of her 'sources' that we were dating."

"Are you joking? Why did you never tell me? I would have done something about it!"

"You can't stop it. Your family are hot news, and by association, so are the women you see much less marry. Any piece of news about us is eaten up by the good folks of Stockton! Gosh, look at the time. I've got to get ready for work. This is going to be one interesting day."

When they got home that evening, all they had time to do was hurriedly get changed and go downstairs to join the rest of the Barkleys. This being Thursday, it was family dinner night.

Victoria could tell by Kate's face it had been a difficult time for her.

"How did it go?" Heath asked his sister-in-law sympathetically.

"Well, the staff that I work with were very nice about it and said how sorry they were that we were going through this. But those that I don't know were coming out of the woodwork, I swear, just to see my reaction to it all. And I'm certain that half the patients came in for just the same reason."

"Both Nick and I talked with Jarrod this morning," Victoria told them. "And his advice is to 'ignore the piece.'"

"But everyone in town is talking about it!" chimed in Audra. "We can't let Joan print something like that about Nick and Kate and then do nothing!"

"The problem with legal action is that it will keep the whole thing alive for months," Nick informed them. "And how do we sue when she is writing about the state of our marriage? Better to let it be a seven-day wonder and see who Joan uses her poison pen on next week! In the meantime, would my 'downtrodden' wife mind being seen with me for dinner and dancing Saturday night?"

"A hot date with my so called 'controlling' husband? Perhaps you'd like to tell me what to wear?" Kate answered, laughing.

"I'm not fussy so long as it's red," responded Nick with a grin.

On Saturday, the most talked about couple in Stockton showed up at Paul's. She, wearing her rather sexy red spaghetti strap dress, and he in one of his expensive hand-tailored suits. They behaved like the honeymoon couple they still considered themselves to be, much to the amusement of the other patrons in the restaurant. Gus played "their" songs, and they slow-danced, Nick holding his wife oh so tight, and she, with her left arm around his neck, massaging it gently with her fingertips, kissing each other occasionally, softly, and gently.

"If this is the result, maybe I should ask Joan to write something about us every week," she murmured to him as they tried to climb the steps to their deck whilst locked in a very passionate embrace.

"Are you trying to tell me that the romance was going out of our relationship?"

"Oh no, I won't complain about that ever. I was just teasing you."

"You're going to pay a price for that," he whispered to her.

"Anything, absolutely anything!" she replied mischievously as they made it to their bedroom.

"I think it's about time I kept my promise to you and took you shooting. We've been trying to do this for months, and now we are actually going to do it! But first, make sure your rifle is clean. You've had it locked away in its case since you moved in here. I know your sidearm is in good shape because I've seen you cleaning that. My guns are always ready, so we're good to go. We've plenty ammo, and I'll have Jeanne pack us up some coffee and water."

Nick was a good as his word. He sent Sam Williams ahead to set up the targets and to operate the clay pigeon machine. Nick picked him especially because, if Kate's aim was off, he didn't want it talked about by the men, and Sam wouldn't say a word, being very loyal to Mrs. Nick.

He needn't have worried. Kate gave a great showing. She had obviously been well trained, that plus she had a natural gift. Nick beat her but would have been amazed if he hadn't, as he had been shooting so much longer than she and got a chance to practice much more often. He was impressed by her rifle and the way she handled it, even asking if he could use it to fire a few rounds. They really enjoyed their afternoon and decided that, no matter how busy they got, they would try to come to the range monthly. Just one more thing they had found that they could do together.

They were looking forward to Audra's nineteenth birthday party tonight. It was a formal affair, Nick wearing a tux, and Kate choosing her strapless sapphire blue dress. They arrived with the other guests, the house now full of people.

Audra blew out her candles and then cut a slice for her mother and Jarrod, leaving Nick to get his own. He cut a huge piece which Heath tried to relieve him of, after which, Silas and his staff took over slicing the cake. Nick shared the enormous wedge with Kate, feeding her pieces one at a time with an amorous glint in his eye! Afterward, they went back to dancing, and he noticed the arrival of the Miles, Wally and Jenny, accompanied by their son, Evan.

"I thought the son was away at college," Nick told her. "I wonder what happened."

After they danced a couple more times, Nick said, "Do you mind if I ask Jenny Miles to dance? Wally is talking to Jarrod, and Evan is dancing with Audra."

"Of course not. Go right ahead."

Nick asked Jenny to dance just as Evan and Audra went outside. Evan took Audra some punch, after which, he kissed her. When she didn't object, he kissed her more ardently. She tried to shove him off, but that caused a struggle between them which ended up in the garden room, where he went on trying to kiss her. She tried to push him off, screaming in the process, which drew the attention of Heath, who followed the noise and burst through the garden room door. Seeing Evan trying to force unwanted attentions on his sister, Heath pulled him off and punched him twice, knocking him over. Her screams had drawn the attention of others, who came in to find Evan on the ground, Heath standing over him, and Audra with her hair and dress in disarray.

"Heath, what has happened in here?" asked Jarrod.

"Just a slight misunderstanding," said Evan.

"Evan got out of line with Audra," Heath told Wally.

"Did he force you in here?" asked Wally.

"This is not the right time, Wally," put in Victoria.

"I'm sorry," said Jenny.

"They should be apologizing to us!" fumed Wally.

"I'm sorry, this party is over," Nick announced.

Much later, after everyone had left, Victoria was still up when Jarrod came downstairs because he couldn't sleep either. They discussed the fact that the Miles had left without saying goodnight, the first time in over twenty-four years of friendship. Jarrod was sure that when Wally thought it over, he'd see that Evan was in the wrong. Victoria disagreed. Then Audra came down; she also couldn't sleep. She explained to her mother that she had gone outside because she wanted Evan to kiss her, but when he did, she got a cold feeling.

Audra went on to say, "That's why I didn't want him to kiss me again." And she thought he'd sensed it. "So maybe I was to blame for starting the whole thing."

Victoria said they'd had had a long day, and an even longer night, and what they both needed was some sleep.

Next day, Victoria drove over to the Miles ranch and told them part of what Audra had said, that she thought she was to blame for starting the whole episode. Wally agreed and accepted the apology. Ginny wasn't so sure it was Audra's fault and said so after Victoria left.

"Is this the start of something new?" she asked Wally.

"Now, we said we would give him a chance when we brought him home," Wally replied. "And that's what we're gonna do."

Just then, Evan came home with alkali on his jacket. He told his parents he "picked it up somewhere on his travels round the ranch."

What they didn't know was Nick, who was spending a few hours working on the ranch, and Heath, both on horseback, had bought some ponies to a watering hole only to find it had alkali in it. They thought it had come up through the ground and contaminated the water. Heath was having to take the ponies four miles around to another source of water while Nick arranged to have the original one fenced off because horses wouldn't drink it, but the cattle might!

Evan, knowing that they'd want to use the path to the other water which cut through both the Barkley and Miles ranches, fenced it off and put up a "no trespassing" sign. When Heath saw it, he dealt with it by getting a pair of wire cutters out of his saddlebag and cut the barbed wire. In return, Evan fired into the air, scattering the ponies Heath had brought with him, leaving him to barely hold on to his own horse. That did it. When Heath got his horse calmed down, he charged Evan, knocking him over. Evan was no match for Heath.

When he pulled up and stumbled out of his truck, his parents, who were sitting in their front garden, jumped up and ran to him. They decided to press charges for assault, but when Sheriff Madden got the gist of the call, he elected to go out to the Miles ranch himself. He took the report but decided not to act on it until everyone had

214

calmed down, namely the Miles, not intending Heath to be charged with something it sounded like he was goaded into doing.

This all goes back to the incident he had witnessed at Audra's birthday party. Evan just seemed to be trying to get even with the Barkleys, and if it happened to be Heath, so much the better.

Wally decided to fence in all his property, but five Barkley steers knocked down a section of his fence. He was in the midst of having his hands repair it when Nick and Heath, hearing about the incident, rode up to see the extent of the damage.

"Understand you have some of our cattle, Wally. I'd like to have them back," Nick asked.

"They were your cattle," retorted Wally. "Now I'm holding them for costs."

"Don't be stupid, Wally," Nick exclaimed.

"Get your rifles and fire low," ordered Wally. (When hands were out working on the range, they always have their rifles close by to guard against snakes or to scare off the odd mountain lion!)

Nick and Heath got off their horses and moved toward Wally and his men, who started firing, when suddenly, Heath grabbed his arm and went down. He'd been shot in the upper arm.

"I didn't mean for this to happen, you've got to believe that!" exclaimed Wally. "One of you men help me put him in my truck, and I'll take him to the ER.

"I'll take our horses back to the ranch and then I'll join you there," responded an angry Nick. A couple of hours later, Heath was allowed to go home with his arm in a sling and strict instructions not to use the arm for anything. He had been given pain meds and told to consult a specialist within two days.

"The bullet hit the fleshy part of my arm. Missed the bone completely. They just want to check for any possible nerve damage, but by the way it was hurting before they gave me a shot, I don't think that's likely!"

The steam was almost coming out of Nick's ears when he brought Heath home. He was vowing retribution on the Miles.

"No, Nick, no," said his mother. "Where will it end?" She had managed to calm Nick down by the time Kate got in from work.

"I heard about Heath as I was leaving the ER. I've been in surgery for hours. How's Heath doing now?" she asked. "Should I check on him?"

"Let me call Mother first," suggested Nick.

"She says he's in his room, sleeping, the last time she checked, which was just a few minutes ago."

"In that case, I won't disturb him, said Kate. "How did it happen."

"Everyone was told to shoot low, so all I can think of was a ricochet," said Nick." After all, no one would want to hurt Heath deliberately."

Just Evan, thought Kate, but she didn't say anything.

Wally asked his men where the shot had come from, and it was unanimous—it had to have come from the vicinity of where Evan had been standing. Of course it must have been a ricochet, said a couple of his men, not wanting to blame the boss's son outright! When Wally confronted Evan, he agreed it must have been a ricochet.

"Whatever it was, we've got to heal this rift between the Barkleys and us," he told his son.

"What do you want me to do, Pop?" Evan asked.

"I'd like you to go to San Francisco for a while, just 'til things settle down," explained Wally.

"You're sending me away!" exclaimed Evan.

"No, it's not like I'm sending you to school, and you'll have plenty of money," replied his father. "Your ticket will be waiting for you at the airport tonight."

Evan pushed passed him and went in the house to pack. On his drive to the airport, he spotted Audra going home after her ride. He drove to the Barkley ranch, parked out of sight, and went into the barn to wait. Soon, she came in, and once more, he tried to kiss her, and once more, she started screaming. The more she fought him, the more he pressed his attentions. In the struggle, she scratched his face, and that enraged him, so he hit her hard enough it knocked her senseless. Then he put his hands around her throat, murmuring, "I just wanted to kiss you."

It was at that moment Victoria walked into the barn. Seeing Audra's horse, she called out,

"Audra, is anything wrong? I thought I heard noises from in here." She saw what was happening and ran to Evan, trying to get him to let her daughter go. But it seemed that her blows didn't faze him at all! In desperation, she looked around and saw Heath and Nick's rifles by the barn door. Ciego had unsaddled and put up their horses, but normally, they both took their rifles into the house, but in his hurry to get to the ER, Nick had completely forgotten about them. Ciego was going to take them to Mr. Nick when he got home from the hospital; however, truth be told, he had also forgotten about them.

Victoria picked up what was Nick's rifle, aimed it at Evan, and gave him a warning. "Don't make me do this." But he went on choking Audra, and Victoria knew if she was to save her daughter, she couldn't wait any longer. She fired. Evan crumpled to the ground, as did Audra when he let go of her throat. She threw down the rifle and ran to Audra. In a few seconds, Nick, Kate, Eugene, Jarrod, and Silas ran into the barn. "Call nine one one!" Victoria yelled, and Silas went back to the house to do just that.

"What happened?" asked Nick. Seeing his rifle lying on the ground, he went to pick it up.

"Don't touch it, Nick!" Jarrod shouted. "It looks like it could be evidence."

"Evidence of what?" asked Nick.

"I shot Evan," his mother explained. "He was choking Audra." Everyone looked and saw the marks on her neck. She was slowly regaining consciousness.

Kate checked Evan. "He's dead," she told them.

They heard the sirens, and with Silas leading the way, the paramedics came into the barn. One went to Audra and one to check on Evan. "He's gone," was the verdict. They worked on Audra, giving her oxygen and advising she should go to the hospital to be properly checked out.

"Mother, must I?"

"Yes, I think it's a good idea. Silas, could you please get my jacket and purse?"

"Right away."

They left in the ambulance just as Sheriff Madden was arriving. Nick and Jarrod explained as best they could what their mother had told them whilst they had been waiting for the paramedics The police arrived and bagged the rifle, and that was about all they could do except for taking statements from Ciego and Nick as to where the rifle had been and from the others on what they observed when they entered the barn.

"I'll go to the hospital and talk to your mother and Audra," said Fred.

"Don't you think they've been through enough for one night?" fumed Nick.

"Now, calm down, Nick. It's the law," said Sheriff Madden. "I'll just get a brief statement tonight and get a full statement tomorrow when they are feeling better," Fred told them.

Just then, Wally and Jenny arrived. "We want to see our son."

"I'm afraid you can't, not until he's been processed for evidence," said the Sheriff as the coroner's van drew up. When she saw this, Jenny lost it, crying hysterically. They loaded up Evan and drove away, fending off repeated attempts of Jenny's to touch her son.

"I know what happened!" Wally said. "Audra enticed him to come in here, and it was a trap."

"No, Wally," said Jarrod, and he told Evan's parents his mother's version of what had happened.

"That's not true!" yelled Wally.

"I think it is," said Jarrod very calmly.

Fred Madden took some papers out of his pocket. "I don't know if you'll want a public coroner's court when what I've got here would be introduced."

"What have you got there?" asked Jarrod.

"Reports from back east. Reports on Evan burning down a dormitory which you, Wally, had paid to have rebuilt, no charges filed. Various charges of assault where you paid the victims off so, again, no charges were filed. Every situation Evan got into, you bought him

218

out of until this one, when it seems he went too far and Victoria Barkley did the only thing possible to save her daughter and it cost your son his life."

"I'll get a lawyer and fight you," yelled Wally.

"Stop it, stop it, stop it! We knew what our son was. We knew his sickness. We don't have to go on lying and covering up for him any longer. Let him rest in peace," cried Jenny.

And with that, both Wally and Jenny broke down, crying with their arms around each other.

"I'll drive you home," said Fred, turning to the two deputies who had arrived in a second squad car. "One of you follow me in the Miles' car." And with that, they all left.

"Lord, what a night," said Kate as she and Nick went back into the flat. John and Jeanne tapped at the deck door.

"We didn't want to add to the crowd at the barn," they told the Barkleys. "So we watched from a distance, but when we saw Miss Audra and Mrs. Barkley go off in the ambulance and then a body carried out, we just had to know who it was. Tell me it wasn't one of our hands?" asked John.

"And how is Miss Audra?" asked Jeanne.

"Would you like a beer or something stronger?"

"A beer would be great, Nick," said John.

"Me too," said Jeanne.

"I'll have my usual," said Kate.

They all sat down, and Nick told them as much as he knew. "Now, this part, you have to keep to yourselves." And he told them about Sheriff Madden's reports from back east.

"Sounds like he was a real troubled young man," commented John.

"Yes, from what Nick told me before you got here, he's been in trouble for a long time, each deed worse than the last, but Wally always put it down to hijinks or a wild side. Maybe if he'd got Evan help at the beginning of the trouble years ago, he could have been helped, but that's just speculation," mused Kate.

"Well, we'll let you folks go." And with that, John and Jeanne left.

219

"Did you notice how many 'we's' slipped into the conversation?" Kate asked Nick.

"No, I can't say I did."

"Well, take it from me, there were quite a few. I wonder what's going on there."

"Now, Kate."

"Don't 'now, Kate' me, you don't know what she was like when we were dating, and as I remember, she was your inside track to info about me, even down to my ring size! We should call your mother and see if she is still at the hospital with Audra, and if so, what is going on."

Nick called, and Victoria said she was on the point of leaving the hospital and that they were going to keep Audra overnight for observation. "I'll come up when I get home."

"We are just ordering pizza if you're hungry?" Nick told her.

"Famished," was her response.

About forty-five minutes later, almost simultaneously, the front door and the gate buzzed.

"You take the door, and I'll get the pizza," Nick suggested.

Kate let Victoria, Heath, Eugene, Jarrod, and Silas in. "We don't have enough pizza for all of you, but I can order more."

"Don't worry about us, Mr. Nick, we've all eaten except Mrs. Barkley," said Silas.

So in between bites of food, Victoria updated them on the hospital visit. "They ran a CT scan of her head and throat."

"I understand the throat, but why her head?" asked Kate.

"Because when Evan let her go, she hit her head as she fell, leaving a real goose egg, and that could have contributed to the length of time it took for her to come around."

"You mean she was knocked unconscious. Now that makes perfect sense, them keeping her in overnight. They will want to watch for signs of a concussion."

"Well, everyone, I don't know about you, but I'm going to bed," said Victoria, and three of her four sons and Silas stood up and followed her out.

"Now, to change the subject completely about that offer of mine you were going to think about," Nick asked Kate with a gleam in his eye.

"I've thought, and the answer is yes."

Nick gave a *yippee*, swept her up in his arms, and headed for the bedroom.

In fact, the hospital kept Audra in for two days, so Kate checked on her. "How are you feeling?" she asked her sister-in-law.

"Well, my head is still very tender at the back, and my throat is sore, but apart from that, I feel fine. Oh, but I'm so bored!"

Kate chuckled. "Hospitals aren't known for their entertainment value. Just for getting you well enough to go home!"

"I think the doctor is going to let me go today."

"That's great! I'll see you at home. My beeper is going off. I have to run. Bye."

The doctor came by on his rounds when her mother was there. "She can go home on the understanding that she spends the next couple of days in the house," he told his patient.

"But—" said Audra.

"No buts," said her mother. "If these are the doctor's instructions, then you'll follow them, my girl."

"Yes, Mother," Audra responded dejectedly.

"I'll sign the discharge papers, and you'll be good to go in about half an hour," said her physician.

"That just gives me enough time to run down and tell Kate," Victoria said.

When she got to the ER, Kate was nowhere in sight. "Can I help you, Mrs. Barkley?" one of the nurses asked.

"I was looking for my daughter-in-law, Dr. Barkley," Victoria explained.

"She's operating and will be for at least the next two hours. Is there something I can help you with?"

"If you could see she gets the message that my daughter Audra is being discharged from the hospital any time now."

"Sure, I'll put a message in her box, but you could leave her a message on her cellphone."

"Oh, how silly of me. I never thought of that. I'll do just that. Thank you for your help."

"Of course, Mrs. Barkley."

They know I'm on the board, and they almost fall over themselves being helpful, or am I being unfair? Maybe the staff here are just trained to assist everyone, thought Victoria as she made her way back to Audra's room.

Soon, Audra was dressed, the paperwork all signed, and they were on their way home. While she had been waiting, Victoria had texted all four of her sons of Audra's release from the hospital. Eugene had gone back to school Sunday and texted back his congrats at his sister's release. Both Jarrod and Nick said they'd see them at home. As the afternoon passed, all three stopped in to see their sister, just glad she had sustained nothing more than a bump on the head and a sore throat.

"If you hadn't heard a noise from the barn, Nick said "we could have been burying her, so you've got nothing to blame yourself for."

When Jarrod arrived, he had the good news that Fred Madden had talked with the DA, who had declined to press any charges. "Justifiable Homicide," it will be ruled.

"That's a load off my mind, I must admit," stated his mother. "I thought I might have to face a trial."

"No, the DA took one look at Evan's history, even though no charges were ever filed, plus the incident at the party and Heath getting shot."

"You sure that was Evan?" inquired his mother.

"Absolutely. Even Wally admitted all his men said the shot had to have come from where Evan was standing, ricochet be damned—it was deliberate. If his aim was any better, he could have killed Heath! He had severe mental problems, which his parents covered up for years. Kate mentioned if they had gotten him help way back then, maybe all this wouldn't have had to happen."

"I don't know, Jarrod, some kids, sad to say, are just born bad, and nothing anyone does to help them makes any difference."

"Anyway, it's all over now, and you and Audra have to put it behind you."

"I don't quite know how we do that," his mother said.

"Maybe you might think about getting some help for you both."

"It's a thought. I'll see how we handle it."

Kate got her mother-in-law's voicemail and stopped in after she got home.

"Audra had already gone to bed," she told Nick. "So I just had a quick word with your Mother who, by the looks of her, hasn't slept since the whole thing happened. I offered to prescribe sleeping pills, but she turned me down flat. When I go tomorrow night, I want reinforcements with me in the person of you and your brothers. If she still hasn't slept, I'm going to insist she take some pills, but I can only pressure her so far. I'll get some and have them with me, but I need the backup of her sons. Having her outnumbered and out-maneuvered by having an already filled prescription with me. If she doesn't sleep, she can get seriously ill, and she's gotta face that."

"Thank you for doing that," Nick replied.

"I want her around for at least another forty years. You think I want to give up our flat to run this whole house? I want to raise our children and grow old with you up here before I take on this white elephant!"

Nick laughed and hugged her. "After dinner, cowboy," she promised him, and Nick knew Kate always kept her promises!

When she went down to check on Audra the next night, she had Victoria's prescription in her bag. Nick went with her, and his brothers were in the living room. After she made sure Audra was okay, she turned to her mother-in-law.

"You didn't sleep again last night, did you?" asked Kate.

"I slept a little," Victoria told her.

"You're a liar," Kate said bluntly.

"I beg your pardon, young lady?" responded Victoria in icy tones.

The brothers just looked at each other. *Uh-oh*, was the thought transmitted between them.

"That tone doesn't do a thing for me! I've heard worse in my capacity as a doctor, and that's how I'm talking to you."

"You don't have much of a bedside manner."

223

"Surgeons aren't known for their bedside manner. As long as we are good at slicing and dicing, the bedside stuff doesn't matter. Besides, by the time a patient sees me, it's way too late to be polite, and that's exactly where you are headed if you keep this up! Now, I bought your prescription with me, so no nonsense about having to get it filled." And with that, she reached into her bag and pulled out the vial of pills and tossed them to Victoria, who automatically caught the bottle.

Victoria Barkley had, for one of the few times in her life, realized she'd met her match. Kate might be English polite until you didn't do what she wanted, and then watch out. *Oh, Nick,* she thought. *Just wait until you really have an argument with this woman. You're not going to get your own way as easily as you normally do. I imagine she's got a temper to match yours, she just controls hers better.*

"All right, Kate, you win. I'll take the pills."

Back in the flat, Kate said, "Well, you boys were no help at all."

"You did just fine all by yourself. It was when you called her a liar that we were all ready to duck and run for cover."

"Cowards!"

"Well, to my knowledge, no one's ever called her that before."

"I've had to deal with difficult patients normally way above my rank, and I found shock value really works."

"Shock value? Is that what you call it? I call it taking your life in your hands!"

"Never court-martialed yet!"

"To change the subject, I must go out of town next week. I'll leave Tuesday and be back Friday."

"Well, I guess I'll just have to deal with it. Doesn't mean I have to like it though. But I knew, when we got married, that there were times you'd have to be away. Guess the honeymoon is over!"

"Come over here and say that, I dare you!"

"But, Nick, we haven't had dinner."

"Dinner can wait. We are only, what, five weeks married? And just because I have to go out of town for a few days, you have the nerve to suggest the honeymoon is over. Now, get over here, woman, and say that!"

By now, Kate was giggling, but that didn't cool Nick's ardor, and dinner was very late that evening!

Wednesday and Thursday flew by. Audra was feeling better each day, which was a good sign, and the word from the specialist that Heath saw was there was no nerve damage, and he had only to wear the sling one more week. "That way, we'll make sure the wound has a chance to heal and won't reopen. Check with your regular doctor at the two-week mark, and let him examine your arm, but I'm pretty sure he'll agree with me about removing the sling."

Nick had invited his favorite gal out on a date on Saturday.

She mentioned that fact to Jeanne on Friday when she saw her. "So what's the deal with you and John McIntire?" Kate asked.

"Me and John McIntire? Why, nothing!" said Jeanne, but she wouldn't look Kate in the eye—a dead giveaway!

"Bull," answered Kate. "You gave yourself away the other night. It was 'we' this and 'we' that, and just now, you couldn't make eye contact with me."

"You're too good!"

"So how long has 'it' been going on, and what exactly is 'it'?"

"Well, he just has a one-room apartment, no real kitchen, and we got to talking one night, and I just invited him over for dinner. It wasn't anything special, but he ate two platefuls. I had made extra thinking I could freeze some, but there was nothing left after John got through eating! And so, at first, I kinda felt sorry for him and, a few days later, invited him again, and he jumped at the chance. Then he took me out to a little Mexican place that Nick recommended.

Oh, he did, did he? thought Kate. *I'll be having words with Nick about that.*

"When he picked me up, he brought me flowers. Oh, not the fancy ones Nick brings you, but it's the thought that counts, isn't it?"

"It certainly is, Jeanne, and I couldn't be happier for you. When are you seeing him again?"

"Saturday night, he's coming to dinner."

"I have one question. What are you going to wear?"

"They both broke out into laughter, remembering how that was Jeanne's first question every time Kate said she had a date with Nick.

When her husband came in from work, before she fed him dinner, Kate asked, "Giving out restaurant recommendations now, are we?"

"Huh?"

"I said."

"I heard what you said, I just didn't understand it, that's all."

"Think maybe when we go over to Jose's next, we might run into John and Jeanne?"

"Oh, that." Enlightenment dawning on Nick's face, he also knew he was in trouble for not telling Kate.

"Yes, that. Why didn't you tell me?"

"Well, John asked me not to mention it to anyone."

"Well, if you gave your word, Nick Barkley, that's different."

Nick breathed a sigh of relief, thinking he'd just dodged a major bullet. "How did you find out?"

"Jeanne told me when I used my 'bedside manner' on her today."

Heaven help her, thought Nick, having witnessed what his wife's "bedside manner" could be like!

"Anyway, I told you weeks ago they'd make a cute couple."

"I believe you did," said Nick, not wanting to admit he hadn't remembered.

Chapter 13

Nick had decided on Jose's for dinner that night, knowing from Kate that they wouldn't run into John and Jeanne. Kate really enjoyed eating there and had her usual *chile relleno*. Instead of sitting on the patio, they decided to go home and switch the speakers to the deck, and after Nick had his brandy and cigar, they could slow dance by themselves. As Nick was finishing his brandy, Kate excused herself. Coming back a few minutes later, she coughed, and when Nick didn't turn around, she made sure "The Lady In Red" started to play.

"Where are…" If Nick was going to say more, the sight of her stopped him in his tracks. She had changed into a full length red nightgown and matching negligee. For a few seconds, he just stared at her, his beautiful grey eyes wide open!

"I believe this is our dance," he eventually said and took her in his arms.

When they got to "For Your Eyes Only." "I now understand what you meant when you told me the shower was all for my benefit," he murmured in her ear. She just snuggled closer in his arms, wrapping hers tighter around his neck. "Behind Closed Doors" came next on the playlist.

"Okay, Kate, I can't take this any longer. I know you're not wearing anything under that nightgown, and it's driving me crazy."

"I'm never going to hear this entire CD," Kate said. "This is always as far as we get."

"I can remedy that," said Nick, and as they passed the sound system controls on their way to the bedroom, he stopped kissing her long enough to switch the music over to their bedroom and turn the volume down until it was just background music to their lovemaking.

They were just as ardent Sunday and Monday, knowing Nick was leaving Tuesday morning.

They said goodbye before Kate left for work. *I won't cry*, she told herself, and she didn't until she was driving to work when she shed a few tears. "Get a grip, girl," she told herself. "It's only four days and three nights. It's the nights that will be the hardest," she admitted. The song she sent Nick that first night was an old standard which one of her favorite singers, Shirley Bassey, whom Nick had taken her to see in concert on their honeymoon, had updated, "You Made Me Love You." Later that night, she got a text from Victoria, telling her that the family dinner Thursday night would include a man the family co-owned a mine with.

"I know Nick wants you exposed to all our business interests, so I hope you find it interesting."

Jeanne supplied her with dinners Tuesday and Wednesday, Nick sent her a version of "Some Enchanted Evening" by Phillip Quast that she'd never heard before, and that made her cry, it was so beautiful! Kate did get some work done on a paper she was hoping to have published in the AMA journal. Thursday's dinner, as it turned out, was very informative, and she learnt a lot just listening to everyone talk.

Victoria looked much better and pulled her daughter-in-law aside to thank her for insisting she take the sleeping pills. "They really have made all the difference."

Audra seemed back to her old self, except she'd had a couple of nightmares, Victoria confided in Kate.

"Give her one of your sleeping pills, and I'll write her a prescription of her own to get her over the hump. If she's still having nightmares after sixty days, then it's time to seek professional help. I know of a very good therapist she or both of you could talk to."

"Okay, we'll see how it goes for both of us."

She said goodnight to the family and went back to the flat. The first night Nick was away, she'd had trouble staying asleep, waking up so many times and realizing she was trying to find Nick in their bed!

So Wednesday and Thursday nights, she followed her own advice and took a sleeping pill, which made all the difference. She even wore her short cotton night shirts. No point in wearing her fancy long nightgowns when there was no one to admire them. Thursday night, she decided to read until she felt sleepy.

"My goodness, I've fallen asleep sitting up," she said to herself. Kate put aside the book she'd fallen asleep with and got up to use the bathroom. It was on the way back that the trouble occurred. One minute, she was upright, the next, she was flat on the floor. She carefully picked herself up. But Kate was sure from the pain that she had broken the toe next to the big one on her left foot. *Damn and blast, this hurts like hell,* she thought. *Oh, I wish Nick was home. He could have taken me to the ER. As it is, I'll have to wait until Jeanne gets here. I have something in my bag I can take for pain.* She hobbled down the stairs to her car, got her medical bag, and brought it back upstairs. She lay down with an ice pack and gave herself a shot. It helped, but she couldn't wait for Jeanne to come over, so at seven, she called her.

"Do you think you can come over now?" she asked. "I've had a sort of accident, and I need to go to the emergency room."

"I'll be right over."

Jeanne was there in moments. "What did you do?" she asked.

"I misjudged the corner of a chair. I was still half asleep and fell. I'm sure I've broken my toe, but it should be x-rayed and taped up," explained Kate.

"Okay, let's go," said Jeanne.

"What are you doing here on your day off?" asked the intake supervisor.

"I'm here as a patient." And she explained what had happened.

"We'll get you straight in. It's quiet right now."

"Dr. Barkley," said a nurse. "Come with me."

"You go ahead, I'll wait here," said Jeanne.

Kate went into a treatment bay, and soon, the examining of her foot and getting x-rays was in process. "Well, Dr. Barkley, you've done quite a number on your foot," said the attending physician. "Not only did you break your toe, but you hit it so hard that it caused a ligament further down your foot to peel off a piece of bone."

"Oh no, that's why it hurts so much," exclaimed Kate.

"We are going to put a temporary cast on today, but I want you to see an orthopedic specialist on Monday," the doctor said.

The nurse came in and put the cast on after taping up her broken toe to the next one. The cast reached from her toes to just below her knee and went from the back of her leg to halfway round the front and was secured by three ace bandages. "You can take it off to shower, but then it goes right back on. You even have to sleep with it on. I'm giving you a set of crutches. That foot shouldn't touch the ground. No weight bearing at all. In fact, you should get a chair for your shower today."

Oh great, Kate thought. *I'm not going to be able to do anything for myself.* She was taken back into reception in a wheelchair, holding onto the crutches. One look at her, and Jeanne's eyes opened wide.

"I'll bring the car to the door," she said.

When the car was at the door, the nurse helped Kate in and put the crutches in the back seat.

As they pulled away, Jeanne commented, "Worse than you thought, huh?"

"Yes, not only have I broken my toe, but it seems I've broken a bone in my foot, and I'm stuck on crutches for the next six weeks. I have to see an orthopedic specialist, and he'll give me something more permanent to wear."

"Are you in pain?"

"Yes, the shot I gave myself is starting to wear off. But I've got a prescription for pain medication to pick up."

"We'll stop in at the pharmacy on the way home."

After stopping and collecting Kate's meds and buying a shower chair, they got to the ranch. Going through the gate, Jeanne parked as close as possible to the stairs.

"How are you going to get up them on crutches?" she asked.

"I'm not," responded Kate. "I'm just going to walk up as best I can if you'll follow me with the crutches."

"Sure thing."

Slowly and painfully, Kate made her way to the deck with Jeanne right behind her.

"Let me get my breath back a minute," said Kate, sitting on one of the chairs at the table. After a few minutes, she was ready to move again, and she made her way into the flat and sat down on the couch.

"What can I get you?" asked Jeanne.

"Coffee, I would love some coffee. I haven't had any this morning," replied Kate.

"I'll put it on, but wouldn't you be more comfortable in bed?" suggested Jeanne. "I mean, you can't carry anything, and you're supposed to keep your foot elevated."

"You wouldn't mind fetching and carrying for me until Nick gets back?"

"Not at all."

They went into the bedroom, and Jeanne got her settled.

"Before you go, there is a wedge-shaped pillow up in the closet. Could you get it down please?"

Jeanne got it down. "Under the covers or on top?"

"For now, on top."

Joanne left to get Kate her coffee and then fixed her some brunch. "I found one of those thermal jugs which someone gave you as a wedding gift and filled it with coffee, so that should keep you going for a while. You've got your phone and your laptop. Is there anything else you need?"

"No, I've got everything. Thank you so much. You've been marvelous."

"No problem. I'm going to dust and vacuum the guest rooms, but I'll check back in with you to see if you need anything." Jeanne was as good as her word and, about forty-five minutes later, walked in the open bedroom door and asked Kate, "How are you doing?"

"Time to take my pain meds. Could I have a Sprite to take them with, please?"

"What time does Nick get home?"

"About four."

"Does he know what happened?"

"No, and if you talk with him, please don't tell him. I don't want him worried, and there's nothing he can do."

"My lips are sealed."

So at four fifteen, when Nick came in the door, he had no idea what he was walking into.

"Where's my wife?" he asked Jeanne.

"She's in bed, asleep," replied his housekeeper.

"Asleep? Is something wrong?"

"Well, I guess it's up to me to tell you." So she filled Nick in about the fall, the trip to the ER, what they had bought at the pharmacy, etc.

"Is she in pain?" he asked.

"She was until she took her pain meds, but they make her sleepy."

"I'll wait until she wakes up before I go in there. Got any coffee?"

"Sure, I just put a fresh pot on."

Kate woke about forty minutes later. "Nick, do I hear Nick's voice out there?"

Nick went straight in to her. A few minutes later, he came out and told Jeanne how much he appreciated all she had done to help.

Nick went back to his wife. "What can I get you sweetheart?"

"A Sprite would be great."

Nick fixed her drink and got himself a beer. He brought the drinks back into the bedroom, gave Kate hers, and sat with his feet up on his side of the bed, with his arm around his wife.

"I'm sorry you came home to this. I had a special dinner planned and then dancing on the deck—the whole thing. I was going to see if we could get beyond 'Behind Closed Doors.' Now I've ruined it all. I've spoiled an evening like that for weeks." She began to cry.

"Hey, stop it! I took you for better or worse, remember? So we can't dance for four to five more weeks. It's not going to kill me. We can have dinner in bed," he said with a grin.

"But, Nick, I'm going to be off work for at least four more weeks and totally useless."

"Well, you've looked after countless people in your career. Now it's time you were looked after, and between Jeanne, myself, Mother, and Audra, you'll be well taken care of."

"Oh, I don't want to be a bother to your Mother and Audra."

"Kate, I thought more of you!"

"What do you mean?"

"Don't tell me you can dish it out but can't take it!"

"I didn't mean it like that."

"Then let the people who love you take care of you."

"Love me?"

"Of course they do. Jeanne is devoted to you, and Mother is so proud of you, and Audra wants to be just like you minus the doctor part."

"You really think your mother cares about me?"

"I said 'loves you,' and yes, she does. Do you really think she'd have taken the sleeping pills from just anyone? Don't tell her I told you, but she's planning a birthday party for you July first. Now you have to act surprised, okay?"

"I promised to be totally surprised. Nick, there were times I wasn't even sure if she liked me!"

"Well, now you know. And as for a great dinner, Jeanne found the roast in the fridge and is cooking it with potatoes and vegetables. It will be ready about seven. That okay? And as for the other part of your plan, we can switch the music in here and just listen to the CD."

"Nick Barkley, it's my foot that's injured. The rest of me works fine!"

Jeanne served them a delicious dinner, which they ate sitting on the bed. Nick put on their CD, and Kate started kissing him, leaving him in no doubt what she wanted. Nick was worried that he might bump her foot, causing her more pain.

"Just be careful that you don't, or I'll scream, and your family will think we're having wild sex!"

"No pressure," he said grinning.

"Oh Lord, I'm really in pain this morning," Kate said when Nick asked how she was doing.

"Seriously, did I bump your foot last night when we were making love?"

"No, darling, it's the first couple of weeks after a bone is broken that hurt the most."

"What can I get you?"

"Some juice to take my meds with."

"Jeanne has offered to come over and make us omelets for breakfast. What do you think?"

"I think anything that frees you up sounds great."

"I'll call her back and tell her we accept with pleasure. For all this, I'll make sure she gets a large bonus in cash so she won't have to pay taxes on it."

"You think of everything, and I love you for it."

Around six, Victoria popped up with dinner for the couple, followed by Silas bringing Kate's favorite cake.

"Are you up for visitors?" asked Nick.

"Of course," she told him, so Silas popped his head in.

"I'm so sorry to see you like this, Mrs. Nick. Is there anything I can do to help?"

"Bringing me your famous dark chocolate cake is more than enough, Silas."

"Well if there is anything else I can do for you, just let me know. You know there is nothing I wouldn't do for you, ma'am.

"Nick, dinner tasted like you slaved over a hot stove all afternoon!"

"Oh, I did, I did!" he replied with a huge grin on his face.

"Why don't you go have your brandy and cigar?"

"No, not tonight."

"You're just saying that because I'm laid up. Now go, Nick. I'm fine."

"Well, if you insist."

"I do."

He was settled in his usual chair with his back to the door when he heard it open. He turned around to see his wife on her crutches, standing in the open doorway.

"Pull out a chair for me, will you please, Nick, and a bench to put my foot up on so I can be facing you," she asked him.

"What the hell are you doing out of bed?" he asked.

"Well, I had to go to the bathroom, so I thought a change of scene would do me good. No one said I had to stay in bed. In fact, if I do, I'll go stir crazy. Actually, I can still technically drive a car!"

"You damn well won't!" exclaimed Nick.

"Okay, okay, I won't do that, but I have to move around a bit."

"Are you comfortable sitting there?"

"Not really, but it's a change of scene, and I'm with you so I can deal with it. Don't rush your brandy and cigar. Take your time the way you normally would."

They sat and talked about the coming week and the next crop to be picked—apples, starting the middle of July.

"What about going out on your birthday?" Nick asked her. "Will you be able to go out, or should we just celebrate at home?"

"I hadn't even thought about that. It's Thursday, isn't it?"

"Sure is."

"I think going out maybe is pushing it a bit. I'm still trying to work out how I'm going to get to the doctor on Monday."

"Don't worry about that. I've got it all taken care of."

"What do you mean?"

"I'm taking you, and we are going out the front door. John will pull my Land Rover around. You can walk on your crutches to the top of the stairs and then I'll carry you down, with Silas taking your crutches. I'll take you straight out to the truck and load you in! And we'll do the same but in reverse order when we get home. We'll do something similar to get you in and out of your doctor's office."

"But what about your work?"

"There is nothing more important than my wife," said Nick stubbornly. "The plans have been made, and you can't change them. All we need is the appointment time. But you think it would be too much to go out on Thursday?"

"I really think it would. I'm sorry if I've messed up your plans."

"No problem. I'll just think of something else."

"I'm sure you will."

"Now, let me help you back in. I'll get the door for you."

By the time she got back into bed, she was visibly shaking with pain.

"I said it was too early for you to be moving around the way you did," Nick told her. "But no, you wouldn't listen. Now take your pain meds and go to sleep, and from now on, do what I say and forget you're a doctor, please!"

"Yes, Nick," she said very meekly.

The plan to get Kate to the doctor's went smoothly, and he gave her an orthopedic boot to wear. It was held in place by three Velcro straps. The only drawback was it was very heavy and had a two-inch heel to it. "You need to wear something on the other foot that also has a two-inch heel," the doctor told her. "Otherwise, you'll be thrown completely off balance, and it will affect your back. Also, sleep with the boot on, and come back and see me in two weeks."

Kate had to admit, by the time she was back home, she was in pain and exhausted.

"Bed and pain meds," Nick told her.

"But it's not time for the meds," she informed him.

"I don't care. What do doctors know anyway?" he responded.

"Yes, sir," she said meekly again!

The day of her birthday, Nick served Kate breakfast in bed with a little gift-wrapped package on her tray and a card. The card spoke very beautiful sentiments, and she hugged and kissed him. Then she opened the package. It was a very long white gold chain interspersed with channel-set diamonds.

"Oh, Nick, it's absolutely gorgeous," she told him with tears in her eyes. "You give me the most incredible gifts. Thank you, thank you." She hugged and kissed him again and again with more tears in her eyes.

"You're so very welcome, darling," he said. "Now, after lunch, you can't come out of the bedroom because I'm planning a little surprise, and you can't see it until it's ready."

"You sound very mysterious, Nick Barkley, and of course, I won't spoil the surprise. What do I wear to this special occasion?"

"Your PJs will do just fine. It's not formal."

So at seven thirty, Nick opened the door, gave her the crutches, and said, "Your table awaits, sweetheart." When she got into the living room, she couldn't believe her eyes. Their mahogany dining table was beautifully set with antique silverware placed on gorgeous red placemats with matching napkins, red candles in antique silver candlesticks, and a crystal vase of red roses, and standing next to it, she had to look twice, was a waiter from Paul's. When she glanced into the kitchen, there was a man in a chef's outfit.

"Who is that?" she asked Nick,

"One of the chefs from Paul's."

"Nick, what have you done?"

"Well, you couldn't go there, so I brought Paul's to you."

"Nick, this must have cost you a fortune on top of that diamond chain." Which she was wearing with her PJs!

"Now, I don't want to hear that kind of talk."

"If Madam will sit down, I'll take your crutches," said the waiter.

She and Nick sat down, and they were served a plate of *hors d'oeuvres*. A salad was followed by lamb chops—cooked well done—and Nick's rare steak, and for dessert, *crepe suzette,* made at their table. Whilst they were enjoying that with their coffee, the chef and waiter packed up their things and got ready to leave. Nick picked up two envelopes from his desk and paid them. They loaded up their van, and with some final thanks from Nick and Kate, left.

"I can't believe you brought Paul's here."

"Well, you aren't in any shape to go there, so I had to do something for your birthday."

"And more flowers, you had already sent me some this morning."

"Can't ever have too many flowers."

They finished their coffee, and Nick carried their dishes to the kitchen.

"How are you feeling?" he asked.

"Okay. I took some medication just after seven so I wouldn't be in pain during the surprise."

"Would you like to sit on the deck for a while? I could bring you out a cappuccino?"

"Yes, that sounds wonderful."

"Let's get you settled out there, then I'll bring out your coffee and my brandy."

Kate got situated in a chair with her foot up, and after Nick brought out their drinks, he lit his cigar and leaned back in his chair.

"What an incredible evening," Kate told him.

"I'm glad you enjoyed it."

"There is only one thing missing."

"There is? What's is it?"

"Our CD."

He looked at her and grinned that Nick Barkley grin she loved so much. "Then let me rectify that now." And with that, he went indoors, and soon, their music could be heard. "Maybe we'll get to hear the whole thing," he said mischievously.

"I doubt it," said his wife with that Kate Barkley grin that he loved so much.

"Exactly how are we supposed to go to this party?" asked Kate.

"I'm to tell you that Mother wants to see you downstairs," answered Nick.

"So I'm going in my PJs?"

"Well, they don't look like PJs."

Kate had bought Vera Bradley PJ bottoms and then purchased T-shirts to match them. Her orthopedic boot fitted over the cotton pants, which were cool to wear under the hot and heavy boot.

"No, I suppose they don't resemble normal PJs. I'll wear the black and yellow pants and a black tee."

"Just make sure you look surprised."

"I promise."

It was just after eight when Nick carried her down the stairs, with Silas bringing up the rear with her crutches. They got into the living room when a crowd of people yelled, "Surprise!"

"My goodness, what's going on?" asked Kate.

"Everyone's here to celebrate your birthday!" her mother-in-law said.

There was Jeanne and John, friends from the hospital and, of course, family. About thirty people in all. There was a table with snacks and another piled up with gifts.

"Is that the chain Nick bought for you?" asked Audra. "It's beautiful."

"Yes, it is," replied Kate, who had hardly taken it off since he had given it to her.

"Wow, that man of yours sure gives you incredible gifts," said one of her friends from the hospital.

"How's the foot doing?" asked John.

"As long as I'm on my pain meds, it's tolerable," she told him.

They chattered and enjoyed Silas's famous punch and various snacks. At about nine, the lights dimmed, and in walked Victoria, carrying a beautiful birthday cake. Nick helped Kate get to the table to blow out the candles and make the first cut, after which, Silas took over slicing it, his version of a black forest chocolate cake. It was scrumptious, everyone agreed on that. Then it was time to open gifts. She received many charming and useful things. It seemed people knew her better than she thought! After another round of coffee, everyone started to leave, understanding that Kate needed to get her rest. Nick carried her back upstairs while John and Jeanne brought up her gifts. Silas, after leaving a chunk of cake for the family, packed the rest up for Nick and Kate.

"What a fabulous evening that was," Kate told Nick happily. "I can't believe all the gifts I received. It was so great of your mother to do that for me."

"Do you need anything?" asked Nick.

"I certainly do," she answered him. "YOU!"

"You have remembered that today is a holiday? You forgot about Memorial Day," Nick said.

"Give me a break. It's my first year in the United States, and all these holidays are new to me. We don't celebrate Fourth of July in England! What are we doing?"

"I'm going to barbecue steaks and corn on the cob, baked potatoes, and Joanne made a salad yesterday, then Silas will drop off dessert."

"I'm putting on weight just listening to the menu! What time does all this happen?"

"About five, and then you can rest up until it's time for the fireworks. We can see them from the deck."

"What does your mother do?"

"Usually just has family and a few friends over. Having the two big barbecues at the beginning and end of summer takes care of social

239

barbecues for her. By the way, on the fifteenth of August, the family goes camping to Indian Springs for two weeks."

"Camping?"

"Yes, you'll love it. It takes us about five hours to drive there, right in the middle of God's country! There's a logging camp not far away, and we go to their Friday night dance. You haven't lived 'til you've been to one of those dances!"

"What do you do for two weeks?"

"Hike, fish, track, swim in the lake, just enjoy being away from it all."

"Sounds wonderful! But I'll only be back at work a couple of weeks, Nick. I've had five weeks off for the wedding and then another four for my foot. I can't ask for two more weeks on top of that, I just can't." Nick's face fell. She could tell he was bitterly disappointed, but what could she do? She had a job that she would have been absent from for three months!

"I'm sorry," she said.

"So am I," he responded.

He was unnaturally quiet the rest of the day. *I know he's thinking about the camping trip, but I must be firm about this*, she thought.

They enjoyed their steaks and accompaniments.

Silas brought them part of a white cake topped with blueberries and strawberries. The fireworks were awesome, and they sat on the deck to watch them; Nick with his usual brandy and cigar, Kate with her vanilla cappuccino. But something wasn't quite the same, and it made Kate sad. Nick didn't even touch her when they went to bed, and that made her feel even worse.

Chapter 14

Days later, Nick had resigned himself to the fact that they wouldn't be going on the trip to Indian Springs. They had even made love a few times. *But I know something that will put a spring in his step,* thought Kate. She had asked Jeanne to make goulash for dinner, knowing it was one of Nick's favorites. When he came in, she was sitting on the bed with her foot elevated on the wedge pillow and a big grin on her face.

"You look like the cat that caught the canary," Nick remarked when he bent down to kiss her. "What's going on?"

"Here, Nick, congratulations."

"What's this?" he asked, taking it from her with a puzzled look on his face.

"A home pregnancy test. You're going to be a father."

"W-What!" he stammered.

"I said—"

"I heard. I just don't believe it!"

"Believe it, Daddy."

"Daddy!"

"You will be in about seven and a half months."

He sat down on the bed beside his wife, kissing her over and over and hugging her.

"Are you okay? You're not throwing-up or anything are you?"

"Not so far."

"Who else knows?"

"No one. You had to be the first, silly."

"You're absolutely sure?"

"I took two tests a couple of hours apart just to be on the safe side."

"Where did you get them?"

"I've had them in the back of a drawer ever since we got married."

"Can we tell people?"

"Well, it's kind of early, but if you want to, it's okay."

"Jeanne."

"Yes, Nick."

"We're goanna have a baby!"

"What?"

"Kate's pregnant!"

"Congratulations to both of you! I'm so happy for you."

"Thank you," they both said in unison.

"I'm just cooking the noodles, Nick, and then dinner will be ready."

"Okay, I'll jump in the shower."

After dinner, Nick called downstairs and asked his family to come up to the flat. When they were all assembled, including Silas, Nick made the big announcement. "We're going to have a baby. Kate just found out today." There were gasps and then congratulations all around.

"How far along are you?" Victoria asked.

"About five weeks," Kate answered, "so I think March, but I'll find out when I see the doctor tomorrow."

"I'm just so happy for both of you," Victoria told them.

"Decaf coffee from now on," said Kate, laughing.

Which was what Jeanne brought with her when she came to the flat next morning, that and a package wrapped in white tissue paper. It was a tiny pair of white booties.

"Jeanne, thank you so much our first baby gift. I have to call Nick and tell him."

She called Nick and told him what Jeanne had brought them.

"The size of her bonus just went up," said Nick, laughing.

When she went for her two-week checkup on her foot, Kate was pleased to find out it was healing up well and she could now sleep without her boot but still had to stay on the crutches.

Nick was at the start of the apple picking, so he worked long hours between the office and the ranch and the pickin'. Heath helped but still hadn't developed the people skills that Nick obviously had been born with. That, and Nick's memory made him a hard act to follow.

There had been the incident with Brahma, a hand who had worked for the Barkleys for nearly twenty-two years and was getting on in years. During an attempt to catch a wild stallion, Brahma missed a signal given because he was asleep in the saddle. Seeing what had happened instead of going to Nick and telling him about it, Heath had tried to deal with the situation himself. He meant well, but as it happened, Kate, who had been walking by, heard the whole conversation between the two men. What Heath meant to say was one thing, but what he said was to the effect that Brahma was too old and tired to do his job and he could have a job as a handyman! Brahma was naturally insulted and quit there and then! Nick was furious. Kate was in a spot since she didn't want to tell tales on Heath but felt Nick should know what really had happened. So taking a deep breath, Mrs. Nick pulled Heath aside. As gently as she could, Kate told him what she knew he had meant to convey but what she had heard him actually say. Heath was appalled at his blunder and went to Nick himself about it. Nick thought about if for a while and then came up with the idea that Brahma, with all the years of experience he'd had, plus his natural talent, could be hired as the stock buyer of horses. Brahma was delighted, especially as it meant an increase in pay. Situation dealt with, but it showed both brothers that Heath had a long way to go in dealing with the hired hands.

Within a week, the morning sickness had started, and Kate had to maneuver crutches trying to get to the bathroom in time! She kept Sprite and crackers on her nightstand beside the huge floral arrangement in pink and blue Nick had sent her.

When Kate went for her next foot checkup, it was even more good news. She no longer had to wear the orthopedic boot. She was down to a small lace-up ankle support which, again, she didn't have to sleep in, and the crutches were gone. Now she could go back to work.

"Thank you, Lord," she said as she told Nick the good news. Almost back to normal except for the morning sickness, which seemed to go until the midafternoon!

"It feels great to be back," Kate told everyone on her first day back in the ER. They, in turn, were congratulating her on the pregnancy, which she couldn't keep a secret with the almost all-day long morning sickness. The due date, March fifth, end of the first trimester, beginning of September, so Kate was hoping the nausea would end about then.

Nick had been kept busy with the picking of the apple crop which was the best ever. He was trying something new this year, a limited amount of their own cider. They had employed a small rancher who used to make his own but couldn't make it financially viable by himself to oversee the first ever mass production. Nick was eager to sample it, but he had about three months to wait.

Kate was still trying to get him to stop treating her as though she were made of glass and would break if she had to do anything herself. "I'm pregnant, not sick," she kept telling him, but it fell on deaf ears. *Oh, this is going to be a very long pregnancy at this rate,* she thought.

Nick flew to San Francisco to meet with the Itos Tuesday morning.

"I'll be back Wednesday lunchtime," he told Kate. When Kate was getting ready for work Wednesday morning, a huge rainstorm started. *Oh, I wish I had time to sit on the deck and enjoy it,* she thought. Dressed in her raingear, she hurried down the outside stairs and into her beloved mini on the way to the ER. The rain was coming down so fast her wipers could hardly deal with it. Then, just before a bad bend on the ranch road about three miles before it joined the highway, the unthinkable happened. She tapped the brakes and nothing happened. She hit them again, only harder. Still nothing. Then her car, instead of slowing down, picked up speed, missed the bend, and went off the road, rolling at least twice that she knew of before she blacked out.

When she didn't go into work, at first, they put it down to the rainstorm and just thought she'd waited until the worst passed.

But when that happened and she still had not arrived, Ann called Kate's cellphone, but it went to voicemail. "I'll try the house," said Dr. Greene. Silas answered and put Victoria on.

"No, I haven't seen her," she told Kate's boss, "but let me run upstairs and I'll call you right back." She went up and buzzed. Jeanne let her in.

"Is Kate here?" she asked the housekeeper.

"No, ma'am. She left before I got here this morning."

"Are you sure?"

"Well, her car, purse, and raingear are all gone. Is something wrong?"

"She didn't make it to work."

"Then something is very wrong."

"You don't think she might have had car trouble?"

"Without calling someone? No, she wouldn't do that, Mrs. Barkley. Something's happened! We should call the sheriff!"

"I'll call Dr. Greene back, and then I'll call Fred Madden."

She called Kate's boss and got his assurance that he would be in touch if he heard anything. Then she called Fred and explained the situation to him. "We may be panicking prematurely, Fred, but on the other hand, this just isn't like her, and she's now over two hours late."

"What does Nick say?" asked the sheriff.

"Nick's in San Francisco and won't be back until lunchtime."

"Okay, I'll have a squad car drive the road from the hospital to your ranch and see if they notice anything. I just wish it would stop raining. It makes it difficult to see in this downpour."

It was noon, and Nick's plane was about to land when they found the mini upside down where it had gone off the road on a curve, rolling who knew how many times, but stopping short of going down a steep ravine. It had taken that long to find Kate's car because it took that long for the rain to let up so they could make a proper search. They first had to secure the mini to stop it rolling any further and then set about the task of getting Kate out of it. Wearing a C-collar and strapped to a backboard, Kate was very gently lowered from the crumpled mess of steel which had once been her car.

Victoria and Heath were at the crash site, as well as John and Jeanne. Jarrod had taken John's place to pick up Nick at the airport.

"I'd better go and break the news to him," he told John, because at that point, they didn't know if Kate was alive or dead. "Mother will stay in constant touch with me so I can give him the very latest news."

Victoria had made sure to tell the paramedics about Kate's pregnancy. "That's very important to know," they had told her.

As soon as Nick saw Jarrod waiting for him, he knew something was wrong.

"What's happened?" he asked, with concern written all over his face.

"Nick, I'm afraid it's Kate. There's been a car accident."

"How bad?"

"We don't know. They've just got her out of the car and are transporting her to the hospital. We'll meet them there."

"I'll drive."

"Indeed you won't. One wreck in the family is all we need."

"Can't you go any faster?"

"We'll be there in a few minutes, and there's nothing you can do. You have to let them work on her."

When they got to the hospital, Nick had to be restrained by his two brothers and John from busting through to the examining bay where Kate lay. She was going through the process of examination, blood work, and x rays. "She's pregnant," a nurse told the attending.

"Not any longer," he said, pointing to a pool of blood on the floor as they stripped off her clothes and covered her with a gown.

"What's all that noise?" Dr. Green asked a nurse.

"I think it's her husband wanting to come back here and see her," she said.

"I guess all I've heard about Nick Barkley's temper is true," said another nurse.

"He's crazy in love with her" Ann told them. "The waiting must be about killing him!"

"Her blood pressure is dropping. Let's get her into an OR and take care of this bleeding before we lose her."

"Want me to update Nick? I know him." asked Ann.

"Yeah, you can go," said Dr. Greene.

Ann walked out into the waiting area. The whole Barkley clan, plus some of the hands and office staff, were assembled. They all rose as she walked toward Nick.

"She's alive and going into surgery."

"Surgery? What for?" exclaimed Nick.

"I'm afraid she suffered a miscarriage in the accident and is bleeding internally. We've got to get the bleeding stopped and do a D&C."

"What's a D&C?" said Nick in a shocked voice.

"It's a dilation and curettage. Basically remove all traces of the pregnancy," Ann told him.

"But she's goanna be all right?" persisted Nick.

"She's a fighter."

"It's that bad?"

"I'm afraid it is. She's hemorrhaging, and we must get that stopped. It looks like she was in the car upside down for a few hours before she was found, and lack of immediate treatment just made things worse."

"WHAT?!" yelled Nick. "HOURS! Why didn't someone tell me that?"

"Because we're still piecing together what happened, Nick," said Jarrod, the quiet voice of reason.

"Oh god, Mother. I can't lose her, I just can't."

"Now, Nick, you know Kate's a fighter," said his mother, trying to give her son some hope.

"Ann, can I see her for just a minute?"

"Come with me. They may not have taken her to surgery yet."

They both hurried through to where Kate lay. Nick was stunned at how pale she looked.

All he had time to do was kiss his darling and tell her how much he loved her before they wheeled her away. He looked down and saw a pool of fresh blood on the floor. "Kate's?" he asked Ann.

"Afraid so," she replied.

"Oh god," Nick said to himself. He went back to his family and sat down.

"Did you get to see her?" his mother asked.

"Yes but there was a pool of her blood on the floor."

"Must be from the internal bleeding—the miscarriage," Victoria told him. "Nick, I'm so sorry about the baby. I know how excited you were."

"I don't care about the baby. I care about my wife," said Nick angrily.

I know he doesn't mean it, thought Victoria. *Oh dear God, please let her be all right. He can't lose them both, it would destroy him.*

After what seemed like an eternity but was only about forty-five minutes, Dr. Green came to see Nick. "We got the hemorrhaging to stop, but it was touch and go there for a while. Once, we almost lost her, but she's in ICU, resting comfortably. A nurse will come and take you to her in a few minutes. We'll see how she does today, but likely, you can take her home in few days."

"Thank you. Thank you so much, Doctor."

A nurse came to lead Nick to ICU. "Only two at a time," she said, looking at the crowd of people in the waiting room!

"You go, Nick. Alone," said his mother.

Nick stopped at the door of Kate's ICU cubicle and stared at all the equipment surrounding his wife.

"Don't worry," said the PA. "She's not hooked up to everything here. They are there just in case we need them. Right now, your wife is heavily sedated after her surgery. She has I don't know how many bruised ribs and multiple cuts and abrasions but, amazingly enough, no broken bones. She must have been suspended upside down for hours, judging by the injuries to her left shoulder where the seatbelt cut into it. But I'm guessing it was the way she was tossed around and probably slammed into the steering wheel as the car was tumbling over and over that caused the placenta to rupture from her uterus wall and cause the internal hemorrhaging. She can't have been very far along in the pregnancy."

"Just a few weeks," Nick told her.

"Well, I'm sorry for your loss."

"As long as my wife is going to be okay, I don't care."

"Let me warn you ahead of time, she will care a lot, so be prepared for many tears and maybe some depression, and for goodness's sake, don't say, 'You don't care,'" confided the PA.

"Thanks for the heads up."

After about ten minutes, Victoria came to join him.

"I'm the designated visitor," she told him. "I'll tell everyone how she is, and then we'll all go home and leave you alone with her."

He updated his mother on what he'd been told, including the tears and possible depression.

"Makes perfect sense to me," she told him. "Anyway, now I'm going to update everyone and get them all to go home. Call me when you have more news." With that, she was gone.

There was a reclining chair in Kate's cubicle, and Nick dragged it over to her bedside, positioned it so he could sit in it and still hold her hand, and settled back to wait for his wife to wake up.

About an hour later, Kate stirred. Nick was immediately on his feet. He kissed her gently on the lips as she opened her eyes. Looking around, she asked, "What happened?"

"You were in a car accident," Nick told her.

"Mmm…now I remember. I had no brakes, and the car went off the road. It rolled, Nick. It rolled and rolled. I was so scared," she said, gripping his hand.

"It's all right, you're going to be just fine."

"What are my injuries? Have I broken any bones?"

"Er…you were lucky your seatbelt held, but your left shoulder is going to hurt like hell."

"Then what am I doing in ICU?"

She saw the hesitation on his face.

"The baby. What about the baby?"

"I'm sorry, love. So sorry."

"NO!" she cried.

"NOOO!!!" With that, she started to sob, the sobs giving way to wails, drawing the attention of Kate's assigned PA.

"What's wrong?" she asked.

"She just found out about the baby," Nick whispered.

"I'll give her something to help her calm down."

She came back with a shot, which she put in Kate's line. "It will take effect in a matter of seconds."

Soon, Kate's sobs lessened, and she lay with Nick's arm around her and her head leaning against his shoulder.

"I'm so sorry," she said. "I should have been more careful. It's all my fault. The car was due to be serviced. I just hadn't got around to taking it in. I was going to do it Friday. Oh, why didn't I do it sooner. I'm so sorry. It's my fault I lost our child. Nick, can you ever forgive me?"

And with that, the sobbing started again. Nick was trying to tell her it wasn't her fault and he didn't blame her when the PA walked in again.

"Didn't that shot work?" she asked Nick with a puzzled look on her face.

"Yes, for all of about three minutes, but she's blaming herself for the accident and losing the baby."

"I see stronger measures are in order." She disappeared, only to return almost immediately with another hypo.

"This time, I'm putting her out." She put the sedative in Kate's line. Within minutes, Kate's sobs ceased and her head fell back. Nick gently withdrew his arm.

"Thank goodness you gave me the heads up about her reaction to the news or I might have said the wrong thing and made it worse, although how that could have been worse, I just don't know!"

"Her hormones are a mess right now. They were just adjusting to her being pregnant and now, bang, she's not. It will take time for her body to get back to normal. In the meantime, you're just going to have to be patient with her, because it could be weeks before her hormones balance themselves out."

"Just love her," murmured Nick.

"Pardon?"

"That's King Arthur's remedy on 'How to Handle a Woman.'"

"Smart man."

When Kate woke up next, it was the middle of the night, and Nick was asleep in the chair, holding her hand. As she moved, he was immediately awake.

"Hi, sleepyhead," he whispered.

"Hi, yourself. What are you still doing here? Visitors should have gone home hours ago."

"Not in ICU."

"Oh, for a moment, I forgot where I was."

"Well, if you continue to make progress, they should move you to a room later today."

"Nick, I'm so sorry. I really am."

"Kate, I don't want to hear that kind of talk. It was an accident, which means it was no one's fault."

"But..."

"No buts. I could have had John take the car in while you were laid up, but to be honest, I never thought about it. I just had him start it up and drive it around three or four times a week. You're gonna blame me for that?"

"No, of course not."

"Because it was no one's fault, got it?"

'I suppose, but it doesn't make it any easier. Our baby's still gone," and her eyes filled with tears. But this time, she just cried quietly, not the awful sobbing that had worried him so.

Her blood pressure remained steady all day, so at about four that afternoon, they moved her to a room where there was already a vase full of wildflowers from Nick. He hadn't been home since he'd landed the day before, so Kate persuaded him to go home to shower and shave. "I'll go when Mother gets here," he reassured her. After Victoria, John, and Jeanne visited, then Nick was back. He had a few words with Jeanne outside Kate's room.

"Remove anything that would remind her of the baby," he instructed her. "If Kate gets mad, blame it on me."

"I've already got rid of the decaf, and I'll go through her things for those pregnancy tests that she kept, and the booties. That was all she had."

Again, Nick spent the night with Kate. When she asked him why he didn't get thrown out with the rest of the visitors, he answered quite simply, "I'm a Barkley!"

After two more days in the hospital, Kate was allowed to leave. Her doctor had prescribed some sedatives to take if she got badly upset again, and Nick made sure he got them before he picked his wife up from the hospital. "Home, sweet home," Nick said, and he insisted on bringing her in the front way and carrying her up the stairs. Jeanne had already put on a pot of coffee, and a plate of Kate's favorite homemade cookies was sitting on the counter.

"Bed," ordered Nick.

"No," responded Kate. "I'm not sick, Nick. Don't treat me as if I were, please."

"At least rest," pleaded Nick.

"I'll sit on the sofa with my feet up if you'll sit with me."

"Done," he replied.

"Dinner is in the crockpot. It's already cooked and will stay warm as long as you don't take off the lid," said Jeanne on her way out of the door.

Saturday and Sunday mornings, their housekeeper came over and made them brunch, but Nick wouldn't hear of her fixing dinner. "That's what take-outs and barbecues are for," he told her.

Nick went back to work Monday. Kate had been given the week off work despite her protestations. "We want you one hundred percent healthy to do this job," Dr. Greene told her. "And right now, you're not!"

When the family, all except Nick and Kate, left for their annual camping trip, Kate knew Nick was disappointed at not going but accepted the situation. But Kate had a treat in store for him. She had a talk with John about a camping site by a lake an hour from home. "Nick likes to go fish there," said Kate. "This is what I want you to do..." So Friday morning, at seven, instead of Nick going to work, Kate told him they were going camping.

"John packed your truck with everything we could possibly need last night, so all you have to do is get dressed and we're off!"

"And where are we supposed to be going, pray tell?"

"That spot in the local mountains where you like to go fish, Crystal Lake. Everything is ready, and we're gassed up. Come on, let's go!"

They enjoyed the drive, and in just under an hour, they reached the spot.

Nick unpacked, setting up their small camp. "Thank you for doing this," he said for what seemed to be the sixth time.

"Don't thank me again, or you'll spoil it," Kate told him.

"Okay, no more thanks," he said.

Kate had the novel experience of making love under the stars! "We'll have to do this more often," she whispered to Nick. "I never knew camping could be so romantic!"

"See, I told you would enjoy it," Nick murmured to her.

They spent a wonderful weekend returning home on Sunday afternoon. "We can do it again next weekend," Kate assured Nick with a grin.

They decided to do just that and enjoyed the time of being completely alone.

The family came home after their two weeks and were delighted to hear about Nick and Kate's two camping trips of their own.

They all started to get ready for the Labor Day picnic, which was virtually the same as the Memorial Day one, except no fireworks but a concert to replace them.

Again there was a huge cookout and games. "And so the end of summer," Nick told Kate.

"It certainly has been an adventurous one," she commented.

Kate had times of tears over her miscarriage, more in fact than Nick knew about.

Her husband's answer to her lack of transportation was a Land Rover Discovery and, just like his, was totally luxurious, with every conceivable extra on it. Also, like every other vehicle belonging to the Barkley Family Companies, it was black on black, with the Barkley brand embossed on the front door panels.

"I was going to get another mini," she told him.

"I'll feel happier with you driving something more substantial," he countered.

Sheriff Fred Madden called and said he wanted to talk to both Nick and Kate. When he arrived at the gate, he was buzzed in and went upstairs.

"You sounded very mysterious on the phone," Nick told him.

"I have some very disturbing news," said Fred. "The accident was no accident. The brake line had been cut."

"WHAT!" exploded Nick.

"The line had been cut almost all the way, and something like chewing gum was put over the cut. That would stop the fluid draining out until Kate was on the road, then the heat would melt the gum, and out would pour the fluid," explained the sheriff.

"You mean someone tried to kill me?" asked Kate.

"'Fraid so," was the reply. "Well, that's what I'm here to ask you about. Who would want you dead? Do you have any enemies?"

"Don't be ridiculous, Fred. This is Kate you're talking about," yelled Nick.

"How about a patient that died and the next of kin threatened you?"

"It happens, but I don't take it seriously."

"But how would they get to where we park the cars?" asked Nick. "It's a four-digit code to get through the gate."

"Or like me today, someone buzzed them in."

"But you can only do that from the inside the area."

"Change the code and tell John that no one else must know."

"Jeanne will have to know," Nick told him."

"Anyone else?"

"No, but we'll have to explain to them why they have to be the only ones with the knowledge."

Nick called them both and asked them to come over. They were shocked, as shocked as Nick and Kate had been by the news. Neither had seen or heard anything around the car before or since the accident.

"What do we do now?" asked John.

"Mrs. Nick's car must be checked before she drives it," said the sheriff. "I brought over a mirror on a long handle so you check under her car," he continued.

"But you'd think if they were going to try again, they would have done it by now. It's been over a month," said Kate. "Maybe it really was a bizarre accident of some kind."

"Or perhaps your new vehicle is harder to sabotage than the mini," suggested Nick.

"Whatever the reason, we have to be vigilant for the next few weeks. John, change the code on the gate," he instructed, "and only the four of us must know it. Have we hired anyone in the last few weeks?" asked Nick.

"There have been a number of new hands," John told him.

"Get me the list," said Nick.

Nick was given the list immediately. Looking it over, he stopped at one name. "Jeff Scott. That's Mona's brother, isn't it?"

"That's him," John told his boss. "He got back into town about two months ago."

"Why is he working here?" asked Nick.

'The only thing their father left when he died was debts," John informed Nick. "Jeff came back into town, and both he and Mona had to get jobs to pay off the debts and support their mother. It's been tough on all of them."

"I might be crazy, but what if Jeff thinks getting rid of Kate would put Mona back into my life? Then they wouldn't have to work. That, as Mrs. Nick Barkley and my brother-in-law, I'd take care of them!"

"Isn't that a bit farfetched?" said John.

"Not if you knew Jeff Scott like I do, it isn't. He enjoys the easy life, so working for a living must be about killing him!" Nick told him. "He'd do just about anything not to have to work. What do you think, Sheriff?"

"Maybe I could talk to him," Fred said.

"No maybe about it! I'm going to ask Jeff and Mona over here for a face-to-face meeting with you, Mother, Jarrod, John, Jeanne, Kate, and I," Nick said. "I want to see Jeff's reaction and find out what the people closest to this think."

At the meeting, when the Scotts realized that Nick thought they could be implicated in Kate's accident and why Nick suspected them, they seemed shocked. They vehemently denied any involvement. The others just sat and watched the reaction of the brother and sister, all agreeing if the Scott's were involved, they were very good at denying it.

Kate sat quietly and listened to everything that was said. After the Scotts left, she said there was something she had decided it was time to share with them. The current event had forced her hand, but before she did, she had to have their words it wouldn't go any further.

"I was asked to go on a mission with some special forces. They were going to pick up a fugitive from justice. He was to be executed by the team, and I was to confirm his death. It was a short notice action, and I had some unique qualifications, so that's why I was ordered to go. Because of the success of that mission, I was sent on others."

There was a stunned silence in the room.

"In view of what has happened, it is my opinion that the news of my participation in that and other missions, none of which I should be talking about, could have somehow become known by certain parties, and that has caused someone to try and kill me in a kind of retribution This suspicion should be turned over to the Department of Homeland Security and the British Embassy immediately. Sheriff, I'm asking you to take care of that."

"I'll take see to it right now."

The rest just sat and stared at Kate.

"I had no idea, Kate, that you were involved in anything like that," said Victoria.

"Neither did I!" Nick added.

"No one was supposed to know. It's supposed to be classified," Kate explained. "It started by my going on missions where the likelihood of someone on the tactical team getting hurt was extremely high. I was in a chopper, usually a Sikarsky Super Stallion or something similar, typically with an anesthesiologist, a PA, and nurse, all of us ready to give medical attention. We were set up to do surgery and saved lives that way. From there, it just sort of grew. I went on quite a few missions with special forces teams."

"Wasn't it dangerous?" asked Jeanne.

"Yes, but we were able to save lives by operating within minutes instead of hours."

"Some people from DHS and the embassy will be coming to see you tomorrow," Sheriff Madden told Kate.

"Well, that's a start," said Nick.

After everyone left, Nick just stared at Kate. "So this was the 'er…um' when I asked you if there was anything else you had to tell me besides being blown up and shot!" he said. "Now spill the beans, Kate, and I mean everything!"

So for the hour or so… Kate outlined to Nick her military service.

"Just a doctor in the military, huh!" he said when she had finished.

"Well, part of it was I had no dependents. So I didn't have many people who would mourn me if I got myself killed! And when I left the military, my record was supposed to be sealed, but it's possible that, somehow, my service record has become known by some people in dangerous circles! I'm just concerned that if they come after me, they could come after my family!"

"I guess that's something we'll go into with DHS."

The people from DHS and British Embassy arrived Saturday afternoon and spent some time interviewing Kate. But before any conclusions could be reached…

Chapter 15

There were yells of, "NO, NO, NO...wrong way!" Then screams and more yelling as Kate was carried into the ER by a man going the wrong way, and then shots were fired and fired and fired! It seemed to go on forever but was, in fact, just over five minutes before the men who had been dressed as doctors escaped in cars, still firing as they went. There were dead and dying all over the ER, the waiting room, and parking lot!

Incredibly, one of those not hurt was Dr. Caroline Barkley. She sprang into action immediately and was going from one patient to the next, assessing injuries and trying to give help, but so many were dead or dying!

Next, she heard the sirens of the sheriff's cars, and they worked with her and any hospital staff member left standing to find and help the injured.

The killing field was huge. Thirty-four dead and eighty-two injured. That was the day pediatricians doubled as trauma surgeons and the everyday joe on the street became a paramedic! The shooters had been dressed as doctors, and one had picked up Dr. Barkley and used her as a battering ram to enter the hospital, going in the wrong way. There had been witness accounts of three shooters with a collection of weapons all on semi and full auto. This was something they saw on the news happening to other towns and cities not their own!

Patients ended up in beds, gurneys, chairs, cots, and on the floor. Everyone who worked or volunteered at the hospital reported for duty. The entire Barkley family, plus hands and office staff, came to the hospital to volunteer their services. If you could use a mop, you were being used!

The reality of what just happened didn't set in until all the patients had been attended to and the staff left living got a chance to watch the news on television. There were reporters from all over the country in Stockton. All the major networks sent crews. Kate grabbed some sleep on the sofa in the office and then went right back to work.

What was the cause? Ideology? Not in this case! No answers! Just a group of men who got together and decided to do the most harm possible. They had been in the same hunting club, but what had made them go from killing game to killing people? Men, women, and children became the targets instead of the four-legged or feathered variety. The usual gun control issues were heard, but all the men had obtained their guns legally. Not one had raised a red flag. Gun collectors, all of them, owning twenty to thirty rifles and thousands of rounds of ammunition quite legally. How do you legislate against that?

Kate had seen carnage before, but nothing had prepared her for the devastation of people that she knew! Bodies with sheets or tablecloths covering them had lain scattered all over. The FBI had to fly in a team to deal with the ballistics. Sheriff Madden became a nationally known law enforcement officer through his twice-daily press briefings. Elective surgeries were put on indefinite hold, and no one got enough sleep for days.

When Nick and Kate finally slept in their own bed, all he wanted to do was to hold her tight in his arms and thank God she hadn't been hurt or—the unthinkable—taken from him!

She had to explain over and over how one of the shooters had just picked her up and used her as his battering ram and cover for the path of destruction he wrought through the ER, dropping her before going out into the full waiting room area and then, joining with the other two shooters, firing on the parking lots and freeways before going down in a hail of bullets with the state police.

None of them had wives or families. Just three men who had been drawn to each other by how much death and destruction they could leave in the city in the space of five minutes.

"How do we ever recover from this?" The survivors kept asking themselves?

Nick and Kate spent hours just lying in each other arms, hardly believing that they and their entire family had come out of this whole when so many other families hadn't!

It seemed everyone knew someone who either didn't make it or had been injured, and at the hospital, it was so much worse. Kate lost count of the funerals she and Nick attended and the flowers they sent to grieving families.

Slowly, the national press corps went home, and Stockton tried to kid itself that things were getting back to normal, whatever that was! But there was going to be too many empty places at the dinner tables this Thanksgiving for there ever to be normality again!

They all kept asking, "How it could happen here in Stockton. This is our home! What signs did we miss in these men? Did they talk of death and of nothing else? They were doing good in the community, how could it suddenly all go so wrong? How did they go from helping people to shooting them indiscriminately?" There were no answers, only more questions. Neither Kate, Nick, nor his family had known the shooters, so they had nothing to add to the profiles which the FBI were building. People who had known the killers had nothing negative to say about them. Those three men kept the dark side of their personalities well hidden. It seemed that there was not one person who had any interaction with them who had any clue that they even had a dark side! Their behavior was a shock to everyone. Not one single person had the tiniest clue what they were planning to do. They kept their "dark side" to each other only. Goodness only knows what profilers call that.

After a while, the news of the shooting stopped being on the six p.m. news because there was no new news. There was no one to take to trial, so details of the shooting got less and less until it was no longer reported about in the media.

"I guess the bottom line is we'll never know why it happened," said Nick, "and that's what we have to live with."

"Whether we know the reason why or not doesn't make the people any less dead or those hurt any less injured," Kate said. "So the bottom line is, it was three men who wanted to kill and injure as many people as they could before they shot it out with the police. And that's all we'll ever know!"

Chapter 16

"I can't believe that we are going to celebrate our six-month anniversary," said Kate. "Just where are we going?"

"Let Jeanne do the packing," Nick told her. "We leave on our plane in the morning."

"Hawaii. I don't believe it. What a beautiful hotel suite."

"Ours for seven days, and now, I want to see you in one of those tiny bikinis! I thought after what you've been through, you could use a change of scene. Race you for the beach!"

When they had checked in, as soon as Nick wrote Stockton, the clerk asked him if they had been involved in the shooting.

"My wife is a trauma surgeon at the hospital where it happened," Nick told him. "Please don't mention it to her. We've come here to get away from it for a while."

Nick thought he was the one with all the surprises, but he should have known better! On the evening of their second day, she announced to him that she'd talked to the hotel concierge and had arranged for them to go deep sea fishing the next day. This was for him to catch a Pacific blue marlin. And if he did, she'd already made arrangements for it to be stuffed, mounted, and shipped to them! And she had a further surprise. She'd talked to Adam Cartwright about converting the guest bedroom down the hallway into a "man cave." The idea being on the other side of the wall down that hallway was a guest room in the main house that was never used, so the wall could be removed, making the room twice its size. A fireplace, like the ones they had in their bedroom and living room which worked by a remote control, could be installed. Then Nick could have his own space to hang out with his brothers or friends or just be alone if he wanted to. This was her six-month anniversary gift to him. What did he think?

"What do I think? I think you're the most amazing woman who ever walked this earth, that's what I think! A man cave, but what about you? Don't you want a room of your own?"

"No, Nick, I don't. But I think it's very important you do. Guys should have their own space. A place to just go to and hang out with their buddies or be alone. And before you say it, I know you like spending time with me, but be honest, haven't there been times when you've gone out on the deck alone just to think through a problem? Now, wouldn't it make more sense to have a room of your own, furnished just the way you want it, to go hang out in?"

Nick was silent for a few minutes. "Yeah, you're right, babe, a place like that would be wonderful. I'll talk to Adam as soon as we get home, and we'll get the work started as soon as possible. Thank you so very much for thinking of this for me, and I'm so looking forward to going fishing tomorrow. But aren't you going to be bored? What are you going to do? And how long have you chartered the boat for? And who else is going?"

"Boy, you're just full of questions! The charter is for the whole day, and it's a private charter, so it's just us my love. I've already told them you drink lite beer and I drink diet Sprite and to make sure they have plenty of bottled water on board. They will also supply lunch and snacks. As for me, I'm going to wear a bikini and work on my tan, bringing lots of suntan lotion for both of us. I'll also bring a book, which I'm sure I won't get to read as I'll be too busy watching my hunk of a husband fish all day long."

"Well, I'd better say thank you to my wonderful wife for her gifts. Get over here, woman, so I can show you how very much I appreciate you."

"Oh, Nick. Yes, yes please!"

At the end of the next day, they returned to their hotel tired, suntanned, but very, very, happy. Nick had caught a one hundred and twenty pound, seven feet four inch long Pacific blue marlin, which was already on its way to the taxidermist, who would then ship it to them in Stockton when his work was completed. Nick was already planning to hang the marlin over the fireplace in his new man cave. They quickly showered and then called room service and ordered dinner, both too tired to get dressed again and go out to eat. They were even too tired to make love and just fell asleep naked, with their arms wrapped around each other. But next morning, boy, did they make up for it!

Every day except for the day they went fishing, the two of them spent some time scuba diving, both of them getting their certifications years ago and keeping it up. Just another hobby they had in common.

The whole time they were there, they drank 'Blue Hawaii's', swam, lay on the beach, and made love and forgot about crazy shooters and thought only how much they loved each other.

Chapter 17

"Happy Thanksgiving, everyone!" Victoria Barkley said.

"Happy Thanksgiving," replied her family.

The entire Barkley clan gathered for their Thanksgiving lunch. The huge turkey had been cooking all morning, filling the house with an enticing aroma. Another turkey, just for leftovers, had been roasting in a second oven. The sides were set out on the buffet, and everyone was soon consuming their meal. The pies would be brought out later, along with the coffee and liquors.

Football was being watched in the living room by those family members who were still awake.

Nick and Kate took their pies—a sweet potato and cherry—upstairs with them, and they changed into more comfortable clothes. Silas came to the flat with containers filled with enough leftovers to last them for days! They lay stretched out on the sofa, Nick watching the football games and Kate dozing. After a while, Kate fixed pie and coffee, and they fed each other pie topped with whipped cream. Neither had work the next day, so they planned on eating the leftovers in bed!

At about midnight, there came the sound of a loud ruckus going on in the garage area, and John McIntire's voice could be heard shouting for Nick. Throwing on some clothes, he picked up his Desert Warrior, flipped a switch flooding the whole parking area with even brighter lights than normal, and ran down the stairs. John had Jeff Scott pinned down beside Kate's car. He told Nick Sheriff Madden was on his way.

"What's going on, John?" His boss wanted to know.

"I saw Jeff climbing the gate on CCTV and came over here and caught him with these tools going under Mrs. Nick's car. He had the right tools to cut her brake line again! That was when I grabbed him and yelled for you."

"I didn't know we had CCTV on the gate."

"It was my idea. I just did it a couple of days ago. The whole parking area has cameras so I could watch for trouble. The monitor is in my apartment. I was worried about anyone getting over the gate and to her car, so I picked up the components at the store and fixed it up myself. I checked the monitor just before midnight and saw him coming over the gate, got my gun, and came out to see what he was up to. Told Jeanne to call Sheriff Madden direct. Thought he'd want to know about the situation."

"Just what the hell were you thinking, Jeff?" yelled Nick. "Are you really dumb enough to think if you killed my Kate that Mona and I would get back together? You f—ing son-of-a-bitch bastard." And before John could stop him, Nick pulled Jeff up from where he had been sitting on the ground under John's watchful eye, lifted him off his feet, and punched him hard twice. John had to pull Nick off before he hit Jeff again. "Let me at him. Lemme f—king at him," Nick roared. "He tried to kill my wife once, and now the damn mother f—ker was going to try again! I'll kill him! I'll kill the moth-erf—king bastard! Let me at him!"

"Calm down, Nick. I know you're angry, and you've every right to be, but the sheriff is on his way. Let him take care of things," pleaded John McIntire.

"You f—king asshole. After that conversation we had—and I told you that you were on my damn suspect list—no one could ever take Kate's place. Yet you son-of-a-bitch still made another attempt at sabotaging her car!" With that, Nick grabbed Jeff by his collar and spun him around, taking a swing at him, connecting this time with Jeff's jaw. Just then, Sheriff Madden and another squad car with deputies could be heard arriving at the ranch.

"You should thank God that they've arrived," John told Jeff, "'cos I don't know how much longer I could keep Nick from killing you."

"What is going on down there?" said Kate, standing on the deck.

268

"That no good son-of-a-bitch bastard, Jeff Scott, climbed the gate to try and sabotage your car again," Nick told her. "John spotted him on camera coming over the gate and then came and nabbed him just as he was going under your car. John has the bag of tools Jeff brought with him."

At that moment, Sheriff Madden and a patrol car pulled up. John opened the gate to let them in. He and Nick were explaining what had happened when Jeanne came to see if John had "got his man" and was thrilled to find out he had.

"I'm so grateful to John for putting up cameras," said Kate. "Without them, we wouldn't have known that another attempt was being made on me."

"Well, that seems clear enough," said Fred. "We've made a copy of the DVD showing Jeff coming over the gate and then going straight over to Mrs. Nick's vehicle, taking out a saw, and then attempting to get under the car. It's even on camera, John taking him down—none too lightly I might add—but Jeff doesn't have any excuse for what he did, and seeing what happened in the past, we'll find out what the DA is going to charge him with. I mean, after being in your home when you told him you were suspicious of him, he went right on doing it again. That guy is downright crazy! Oh, he did say that you assaulted him, Nick. Not once, but twice."

"I thought he was trying to escape, so I stopped him," said Nick with a straight face.

"I agree," John added.

"I didn't see what happened," said Kate. "But I've coffee upstairs for you all if you want to take statements in comfort."

The deputies had put a handcuffed Jeff Scott into their patrol car and left.

Fred, John, Nick, and Jeanne went upstairs to give statements and drink coffee. Before Fred left, he told them he would get in touch with the American and British authorities. "It would appear that it was no one from your past sabotaging your car, so you can rest easy on that score. I'll tell them we've caught the culprit and they can cancel their investigation."

When they were alone, Kate confessed to Nick that she was glad it was just Jeff Scott who had come after her and not someone from her past. "They would have been much more dangerous and would have kept coming until they got me. Well, I guess we can put that behind us now."

"Let's go back to bed, darling, and get some sleep," suggested Nick.

"Before we go to sleep, can't we open a bottle of champagne and celebrate catching the culprit whose been trying to get me?" asked Kate. "I for one am now wide awake and feel like drinking a few glasses of the bubbly!"

"Um, darling, have you forgotten what you get like after a few glasses of champagne?"

"Nope, have you?"

"How could I when it took over a week before the bite marks on my neck faded."

"Funny, you weren't complaining when I put them there! Besides, no one could see the marks when you had a shirt on. Plus, you did agree to spend tomorrow in bed. It just means we get a head start on our plan."

Nick looked at his wife for a moment and then walked into the kitchen got a bottle of champagne from the wine fridge and picked up two crystal flutes. He sauntered into the bedroom, opened the bottle, poured two glasses, lay down on the bed, and softly called to Kate, "I'm waiting!"

That was all she needed to hear. Kate went right in and laid down next to her husband and began to kiss, nibble, and gently bite on Nick's chest, all the time sipping champagne until he couldn't take it any longer. He pulled off his PJs bottoms—all he ever wore to bed—and had her nightgown removed in seconds.

"I'm taking over from here," he murmured to her.

"Oh, a man of action. I love it."

"Don't mess with me, woman. Your man needs you desperately!"

"Well, what are you waiting for?"

"Nothing, nothing at all."

"Oh, Nick, oh, oh!"

Chapter 18

"Our first Christmas together. Can you believe what has happened since last Christmas?" said Kate. "We hadn't even met this time last year."

"It's almost a year since we did meet," Nick reminded her. "December twenty eight, Mother will be hosting her annual holiday party, and we do have a lot to celebrate."

"Just being alive is a cause for celebration," said Kate.

"I'm glad that the DA is charging Jeff Scott with attempted murder for causing the car accident you had. He really had no defense with that DVD showing him coming over the gate, going straight to your car, and then getting out the tools to cut the brake line again. John did a wonderful job putting in those cameras. Believe me, he got a very nice Christmas bonus for that," Nick told her.

"I take it we will be going to the holiday party?" asked Kate.

"Oh yes, we will be expected to help host the celebration, but I don't see why we have to stay for the whole thing. I was planning on us slipping away about eleven to have our own party with a bottle of champagne. We can celebrate how we met and 'froze' when we saw each other," said Nick.

"We don't do that anymore, do we?" Kate said. "Maybe we should practice in case we freeze again on the night."

"You mean practice shaking hands?" Nick asked her.

"I was thinking of something a little more intimate, and that would fill up the time until the family holiday lunch," Kate told him, trying to keep a straight face!

"I like that idea, and nothing says Merry Christmas like a roll between the sheets!"

"Merry Christmas, Nick!"

"Merry Christmas, Kate!"

It was much closer to lunch time before they got around to opening their gifts to each other. Nick had gone a little crazy buying for his wife, and a total of fifteen gifts had her name on them, ranging from a new medical bag (hers was falling apart) to a beautiful platinum diamond ring to wear on her right hand, to some gag gifts! A whistle so he could come when she really, really, really needed him, and yes, she understood the kind of need he was referring to! Nick wouldn't open any of his pile of gifts from her until Kate had opened every last one of hers!

Obviously, he was curious as to what she'd decided to get him, as she was known as the best gift giver ever amongst her friends. Her choices blew him away! She'd heard from his mother and from something he'd once said that he used to be interested in sculpting but had given it up due to work pressures. Well, Kate had bought him everything he could possibly need to start up again! From a tarp to put on the floor in the soon-to-be-finished "man cave," a pedestal, clay, and on and on went the gifts, so he'd have no excuse to take up the hobby again!

"I was just thinking the other day, now my life is so much more organized, that I might just take up sculpting again," Nick told her, his grey eyes shining as he looked at all his gifts. "Now I have plenty of time before the cave is ready to do some preliminary sketches on the pad you gave me of what I'd like to work on first. I even have choice to use charcoal or pencil to sketch with! Kate, you thought of everything! How on earth did you manage it?"

"Well, I started thinking about this about three months ago. I went online and made a list of everything suggested, and then I called an art supply store in San Francisco and talked to the manager who was very helpful. Then about a month ago, I started ordering everything and had them sent, care of your mother. I wrapped everything down there and didn't bring them up here until we put our tree up. That way, you'd never find out what I was up to! I take it you kept all my loot over at your office?"

"I had all your things that I bought online shipped to the office. Had to keep them hidden from you somehow. I wasn't sure if you'd go looking for your gifts before the big day! Only brought them over here when they were wrapped, so I guess we both did the same thing! Babe, you are the best gift giver ever, and later when we get back from the family lunch, I'm going to show you just how much I appreciate your thoughtfulness!"

"Well, it's shaping up to being quite a day, because I was thinking I'd thank you in the same way! Maybe it will turn into one of those all-nighters!"

Nick gazed at his wife. "This is shaping up to being the best Christmas ever."

Chapter 19

Nick and Kate elected to spend New Year's Eve alone, thinking back over the past year. Where they had spent the last New Year's Eve having dinner with the Barkleys, had a code black, spent their first date over coffee and an apple fritter. Their further dates, his mother's birthday party where they had really kissed each other for the first time, engagement, marriage less than three weeks later, honeymoon in San Francisco, broken foot, pregnancy, car crash, miscarriage, the mass shooting, six-month anniversary in Hawaii, Thanksgiving, Christmas, and Victoria's holiday party. All of that in one year!

They had decided to give John and Jeanne a couple of days to just be together.

Nick and Kate spent their day looking at photographs that Kate had just finished putting together in albums. Some of it gut wrenching, seeing people they had not seen since the shooting. Kate had found it cathartic to put the albums together. She had just picked up the photographs taken at the Christmas party, framing one of the three Barkley women and another of she and Nick in front of their first Christmas tree. She was now up to date in a year filled with photographic events.

The renovations to put in Nick's man cave were well underway. Adam had paid a flying visit right after they had gotten back from Hawaii just to check on load-bearing walls, etc. But finding no problems, he went right ahead with the architectural plans and sent them by overnight service to Nick, who jumped on them straight away. Whilst the renovations were being done, he picked out the flooring, furniture, fixtures, and fittings to go in the room. At first, Kate didn't even want to go with him, saying it should all be his choice, but he persuaded her to go with him, citing he really would like to hear her opinion on his choices, that he wouldn't necessarily go with her opinions, but he would like to hear them. So they had a great deal of fun shopping together, Nick having very definite ideas of what he wanted in his cave. The marlin had arrived, and they took a look at it. Nick, of course, was thrilled with the result, but they left it in its crate until the cave was completely finished and the fish could be hung.

By January twenty first, the man cave was completely finished. The marlin was hung, books put on the shelves, guns and rifles in the locked cases, and all other treasures that Nick had collected over the years on display. He stood in the middle of the huge room and looked around, not believing how wonderful everything looked and knowing he owed it all to his incredible wife because he wouldn't have come up with this idea, not in a hundred years. He heard a knock on the door.

"Come in," he called, and there stood Kate with a beautifully wrapped large box in her hands.

"This is a man cave housewarming gift for you." He took the box and began to unwrap it. Inside, he found an antique decanter and four matching brandy snifters.

"I found them in an antique store in Stockton before Christmas and have had them hidden in my closet until the cave was finished so I'd have something to give you to celebrate your moving in day. Oh, there's one more thing." And out of her pocket, she pulled a silver decanter collar that said "Brandy" on it. "This just arrived yesterday, so I couldn't put it in the package 'cos it's been wrapped for weeks. There's one more thing." And she disappeared for a couple of moments, coming back with a small crate in her hands. "Here, darling, this is to fill your decanter with." In the crate were six bottles of Courvoisier!

"Oh my god, Kate! Will you never stop spoiling me? This is all too much, even for you, the world's champion gift giver!"

"My grandmother used to say, 'You can never spoil a good thing.' And you, my love, are a really, really, really good thing. Enjoy your cave, Nick, and know I'll never come in here unless I'm invited.

It's your space and yours alone. May you spend many happy and peaceful hours in here. Now, I'll leave you to enjoy your room."

"No, you don't. I haven't thanked you for these amazing gifts. You have the most incredible knack of finding just the right gift—everybody says that about you. This decanter, collar, snifters, and six bottles of the decadent Courvoisier, my favorite brandy of all time, are just too much but are perfect for in here. I'm afraid to tell you, though, that cigar smoking will be allowed in the cave! My darling, none of this would have been possible without you." And he took her in his arms and began kissing her as only he could. The room ended up being truly christened that morning!

It was now the end of January, and Kate was getting ready to leave the ER at the close of her shift on Thursday when Ann informed her that there was a call from someone in London looking for the former Dr. Caroline Warner. Surprised, Kate picked up the phone and listened for a few minutes. The smile on her face disappeared as tears welled up in her eyes.

"Is everything okay?" Ann asked. Without answering, Kate picked up her purse and keys and left. Arriving home, she didn't speak to Jeanne, she just shed her jacket and sat down.

"Are you all right?" Jeanne inquired.

"No, I'm not. I had some very bad news from England," she responded, tears running down her cheeks. Then she got up and went into the bedroom.

A few minutes later, Nick came in. "Where's my wife?" he asked.

"She went straight into the bedroom. She's upset about some news she got from England," Jeanne informed him.

Going in, he found Kate laying across the bed, crying. "What's happened?" he inquired as he took her in his arms. "Is it Audrey?"

"No," she sobbed. "I got a call from a former colleague in London who told me the whole of a Special Forces team that I served with were killed on a mission. The whole unit, Nick! Echo team was completely wiped out in one fell swoop. It seems the building they were making entry into was booby trapped and blew as soon as they got inside." She sat up and got a tissue to blow her nose and wipe her eyes. "Six men gone! Six families torn apart. I know what they do is dangerous, but you never think about losing a whole team. The other units must be out for blood. I only hope that it doesn't make them reckless."

"Who was it that let you know?" Nick asked her.

"A member of another unit called me, knowing that Echo was the main force I had worked with, and he didn't want me hearing about it on the news. They instruct you not to get too close to the team members, because on any mission, someone can be killed either outright or die in surgery. You should remain detached, but serving with the same people on a regular basis makes that very difficult."

"I'm so sorry you have lost your friends. Do you want to go back to England for the funerals?" Nick asked, continuing to try and comfort her.

"No, they will all be buried in separate sites. We don't have a place like Arlington. I'll try to find out about the services and send wreaths.

"Do you have photographs of the men? Would looking at them help?" he asked.

"What a good idea. I have some pictures packed away in box which I think is in the hallway closet. I'll go look for it now. Thank you, Nick. You always know just the right thing to say and do for me."

Nick called his mother and told her that he and Kate wouldn't be joining the family for dinner that night. "Kate has been given some bad news and she wants to deal with it privately."

After they ate, she showed him photographs he'd never seen before. Weeping, she pointed out the men who had just lost their lives and told him stories about some of their missions together.

By the time they went to bed, Kate just wanted Nick to hold her, but one thing led to another. "Are you sure this is really what you want to do?" he asked.

"I can't think of anything else I'd rather be doing," she whispered to her husband.

The next morning, she called a friend in London who promised to find out and let her know when and where the funerals would be so she could arrange to send flowers.

"I guess it sort of puts an end to that chapter of my life," Kate told Nick. "I much prefer the one we're writing together," she murmured him.

"You do realize I can call Jeanne and tell her not to come in today so we'd have the flat to ourselves, and I haven't anything important to deal with at the office. How about you? Did you have anything planned for today?"

"Nothing at all," Kate told him with a loving smile. "So we can take up where we left off last night!"

"Just what I was thinking," he said. Putting his arms around her and picking her up, he carried her back into their bedroom. Lying in her husband's arms seemed to put the world into perspective for her as nothing else could. *Nick is what my life is all about now*, she thought. *Nothing else matters to me. The past is just that the past, and I must learn to leave it there and enjoy every moment I have with my husband.* And with that, she nestled even closer to Nick as he kissed her as only he could.

Chapter 20

Jarrod had been in New York on Barkley business, but getting out of there had been a chore. He'd been bumped from two flights already and was wishing he'd taken Nick up on the offer of the plane, but Nick had been in Washington State and needed to get back to the ranch without delay. Finally, Jarrod was offered a seat in coach and jumped at it. When he sat down, he was glad he did. A beautiful young woman was sitting in the window seat. *My luck is changing,* he thought.

After takeoff, before the attendant came around, he introduced himself. The beautiful hazel-eyed brunette was Beth Randall, and she was going to San Francisco to start a new job. They ordered coffee and chatted like old friends. Everything about the west was new to Beth, and she was fascinated to learn that, when in Stockton, he lived on the family ranch.

After nearly six hours, the captain informed them that their two-hour layover in Denver was going to last a lot longer than that. Weather was closing in, and they would be the last plane to be allowed to land. There was a loud groan from everyone on the plane except the two people in row 23, seats A and B! At the airport, Jarrod offered to buy Beth a meal and a real drink.

"That sounds great," she said.

The hours slipped by as the blizzard outside howled. The airport began handing out cots, pillows, and blankets. "No telling how long you're going to be here," the passengers were told.

"It could be days," according to the weather forecaster.

"As long as they don't run out of food, we'll manage," Jarrod told Beth and went on further describing life on a ranch.

Beth, he learnt, came from a small town in upstate New York. Her parents killed in a car crash when she was twenty. She, like Kate, was basically on her own and, like Kate, had decided to move out west. She had applied for and had been hired by a small company in San Francisco. Not far, as it happened, from Jarrod's branch office.

After three days, the storm had subsided enough to start letting planes get out. What Beth didn't know was Jarrod had changed his reservation from Stockton to San Francisco. At home, the family couldn't understand the last-minute change of plans.

Another item they didn't understand was why Jarrod hadn't told them about Cass Hyatt's early release from jail. About nine years ago, Hyatt had been sent to jail mainly on Jarrod's testimony. When the jail term had been handed down, Hyatt had screamed he'd get even with Jarrod if it was the last thing he'd ever do!

"Probably didn't want to worry us," Victoria said.

"I do wish he'd get home soon. I've got contracts I need him to go over," complained Nick.

"Fax them to him," Kate suggested.

"Yeah, I'll do that in the morning, but it's not the same as having him here," Nick answered. "Besides, I've got things I want to discuss with him in person."

Nick had asked Jarrod when he'd be home, but all he got in response was "Some things have come up that I need to take care of."

"To do with the ranch?" Nick responded.

"Oh no, nothing to do with the ranch," he was told.

Five days later, after a family dinner, Nick and Heath were shooting pool and the women were just chatting when they heard a car drive up.

"Was anyone expecting visitors?" asked Victoria as Nick looked out the window.

"It's Jarrod," he said.

The guys went to greet him as the women finished their conversation. Then they too headed to the door to welcome Jarrod.

"Well, am I glad to see you. What took you so long?" was Nick's greeting.

"Good to have you back," said Heath.

"Welcome home," chorused the ladies.

"There's someone I want you all to meet," said Jarrod. "This is Beth, and we're married!"

"What! When?" Nick asked.

"Two days ago in San Francisco," Jarrod told them. "We met on the plane from New York. Now Beth wanted to wait and be married here, but I said no." With that, he introduced Beth to her new family.

They all went into the living room and were asking questions. Jarrod held up his hand and told them of their meeting, stay in Denver, and short time in San Francisco. "And that's basically it," he said.

"Tell us about yourself," Victoria asked Beth, and so it was Beth's turn to talk.

"Where are you going to live?" asked Kate.

"Well, for the time being, we'll move between here and San Francisco until we build our house down by the lake, with Nick's permission of course. Beth, after hearing stories about our growing up, thinks it's a wonderful place to raise children."

"Of course, you have my permission. Just pick out the piece of land you want," said Nick. "No better place for kids, and between brothers and sisters and cousins, the place should be alive with them! Just think, Mother. Most of your grandchildren in one place."

"I couldn't be more delighted," Victoria responded.

"And now we've had a long day, so if you don't mind," Jarrod said.

"Of course we don't," Victoria told them.

"Tomorrow, you must come up and visit with us." Kate invited Nick's brother and new sister-in law. "I'm off."

"Off?" said Beth.

"Tomorrow is my day off, so when you're ready, just buzz the phone. Jarrod will show it to you. 'Til then, good night."

"Can you believe Jarrod getting married like that?" Kate said.

"Yes, I can," Nick replied. "She seems very nice but rather quiet," he continued.

"Maybe she's just shy. We're rather overpowering as a group."

"Did you ever feel that way?"

"Not really, but then, I was introduced to the family a bit at a time, and they knew me via my job, etc."

The next morning, Beth and Jarrod buzzed the front door, and Jeanne let them in. Kate introduced them to her housekeeper and gave them a tour of the flat while Jeanne put on a fresh pot of coffee. When the housekeeper heard they might be having visitors, she'd whipped up a couple of her mouthwatering coffee cakes. After showing them around, Kate and her visitors sat down in the living room in front of the fire, and Jeanne served them with coffee and cake.

"Your home is beautiful," Beth told her. "Who designed it?" Just then, Nick and Heath came in through the deck door.

"Something smells good. Has Jeanne been baking?" he asked.

"She sure has," his wife told him, and they were served with a huge slice of cake and a mug of steaming coffee.

"I'll be back later," her housekeeper told Kate.

The five of them of them chattered; the men talking business whilst the sisters-in-law talked about house design, and Kate told Beth about Adam Cartwright.

"He thought of everything," Kate said. "There isn't one thing I wish he'd done differently. You haven't been outside. It's so cold, but we have an enormous deck. Here you can see it out this door."

"Wow," Beth said. "That really is huge."

"Yes, we have a fire pit so we can sit outside, even on chilly evenings. It's just a few winter days that we can't use it. There are steps down to the pool so we won't disturb anyone when we want to use it or the Jacuzzi."

The front door buzzer sounded. "It's your mother and Audra," Kate told Nick as the ladies came in.

"Would you like some coffee and cake?" offered Kate. "Please sit down. I'll bring it over."

All the Barkleys sat, munching on the wonderful cake and drinking Kate's favorite Kenya coffee, whiling away the morning.

"What plans do you have for the weekend?" Victoria asked her newest daughter-in-law.

"We are going to drive in to Stockton tomorrow, and Jarrod is going to show me his office, but Sunday, we haven't anything planned."

"Then I'd like to have a big family dinner on Sunday, if that's okay with everyone?"

"Sure," they all agreed.

"Do you want me to fix lunch for everyone?" Kate asked.

"We need to get back to work," said Nick. "And, Jarrod, I do need to talk to you about a contract which came in yesterday."

"Do you mind if I go in the office for a while, Beth?"

"Not at all," she told him. "I'll just stay here with the ladies."

"So lunch for the ladies," Kate said.

"Sounds good," they told her.

The brothers left just as Kate's cellphone rang. "Excuse me," she said. "It's Jeanne. Oh, that's wonderful, come right up. She thought I might have lunch guests, so she made quiches, and she's on her way up with them. She makes the best quiches you've ever tasted."

Whilst Kate set the table, her housekeeper made a tossed salad.

"Lunch is ready, ladies," said Kate. They all agreed it was the best quiche they had ever had.

"Where did you find that treasure?" asked Beth, so Kate regaled her with the story of how they met and her housekeeper's participation in her dating Nick.

"What fun!" Beth agreed. "How long did you and Nick date before he asked you to marry him?"

"Well, we dated a dozen times, but he never actually asked me to marry him. He told me we were getting married!"

"What did you say?"

"After arguing with him for a while, I ended up agreeing!"

"I never heard that story," said Audra.

So Kate had to tell the whole dating story, culminating with the events at her mother-in-law's birthday party.

"You really interrupted things that night, Audra," Kate told her.

"I did?"

"Even I saw that," put in Victoria.

285

The Barkley women sat talking until Nick came in from work. His eyebrows rose when he saw his wife, sister, Mother, and sister-in-law still sitting virtually where he had left them.

"What have you four been talking about all afternoon?'

They looked at each other and then chorused, "You."

Nick looked startled. "Me? What have I done to keep the interest of you four all afternoon?"

"You never asked your wife to marry you," said Beth.

"What! Of course I did!" Nick replied.

"No, you didn't," came four voices. Nick looked stunned!

"And on that note, we'd better leave these two to sort out the proposal or lack thereof," said his mother.

Kate and Nick sorted out the proposal problem the way they sorted out most of their problems—between the sheets, where he made a proposal of a different kind, to which Kate immediately said, "Yes, please. Oh yes, please!"

Saturday night, Nick and Kate and Jarrod and Beth doubled dated at Paul's, where two vases of red roses sat on their table. "What a fabulous restaurant," Beth said to Kate whilst they were in the ladies' room. Kate told her about the birthday dinner when Nick had brought Paul's to the flat because of her broken foot.

"He did that?" Beth gasped.

"He sure did, these Barkley men are bottom-line romantic. I mean, look how fast you and Jarrod met and married. I thought Nick and I moved fast, but you've got us beat hands down!"

After dinner, the two couples ended up on Nick and Kate's deck. It was cold, but Nick lit the fire pit and tiki torches. The men enjoyed brandy and cigars whilst the ladies had Bailey's Irish Cream, and all enjoyed mugs of coffee. Afterward, they slow danced to Nick and Kate's CD, neither couple making it much past "Behind Closed Doors" before they said their good nights.

Sunday, everyone met at six thirty for sherry, and even Kate had one. They talked about the night before and how much they had enjoyed it and how they must do it again soon.

"That deck of yours in one romantic place," Beth confided in Kate. "With the tiny white lights, tiki torches, and the fire pit plus the music piped in."

"Giving you ideas for your own deck?"

"Absolutely! With the half roof and partial walls like you said, you can even sit out there when it rains."

"Nick knows how much I love the rain even more when there's thunder and lightning. He had it done when we were on our honeymoon."

"Where did you go?"

"San Francisco, and it could not have been more romantic. Nick thought of everything."

"Jarrod described Nick so differently."

"Oh, I know. two fisted hard drinking, hot-tempered, right?"

"Kind of."

"He's maybe that way, but underneath, he's a pure romantic."

"That's wonderful. You two are so much in love."

"Like you and Jarrod, it was love at first sight. He's my soul-mate. I can't imagine life without him."

"Hello, Mother,"

"Jarrod what are you doing home at this time of day?"

"I'm here to take my wife on a date. Where is Beth?"

"I'm right here, Jarrod. Where are we going?"

"It's a surprise, so get your jacket, and we'll be off."

"Where do we go on a date at two in the afternoon?"

"You'll see soon."

They drove for about fifteen minutes and stopped at a spot beside the lake.

"Well, what do you think?"

"I think it's beautiful."

"This is where I suggest we build our home!"

"Oh, Jarrod. Really?"

"You like it?"

"I love it, but please, let's not have a big house, and do you think Adam Cartwright could design one that wouldn't need a roof? Then we wouldn't have to shut out any of this wonderful sky."

"We'll tell him that's part of the order."

"Look at these gorgeous wildflowers."

As she bent down to pick some of them, a shot rang out, and she fell forward.

Jarrod froze for a few seconds, not knowing what had just happened. "My god, Beth!" he cried. "Beth!"

He picked her up and carried her to his truck, knowing full well there was no cell service where they were, so he couldn't call for help. Jarrod lifted her into his truck and, getting a blanket from the back, gently put it over her. Driving with one hand, he tried to keep pressure on the wound in her abdomen. He went directly to the emergency room and laid on the horn as he pulled up at the ER ambulance entrance. A nurse came running. When she saw through the truck window what was going on inside, she yelled for help. Two orderlies and another nurse, followed by Kate, came dashing out. When Kate saw the truck and Jarrod, her mouth fell open. The nurses were easing Beth out of the vehicle and onto the gurney, hurrying with their patient inside.

"We've got her now," Kate yelled to Jarrod. "Park, then come in."

As soon as they had Beth inside, they started work on her. "Prep her for surgery," instructed Kate as one nurse put a line in, another cut off Beth's clothes, whilst yet another hung units of blood. "We've got to stop that bleeding," Kate said as they rushed Beth to an OR.

"Call my husband and tell him my sister-in-law is here and he's to bring the whole family with him, pronto," Kate instructed a nurse.

About twenty-five minutes later, Kate walked into the waiting room. Her whole family were indeed there. Jarrod jumped up.

"I'm so sorry, we just couldn't save her," Kate told him, fighting to hold back the tears. "She coded twice on the table, and the second time, we couldn't resuscitate her."

"I thought you were supposed to be some kind of a hotshot doctor. How come you couldn't save her? How come you couldn't save Beth?"

Immediately, Nick jumped up, but Kate motioned him back.

"I'm sorry, Jarrod. There was nothing I or any other doctor could have done. She'd lost too much blood, and the damage was too great."

"Where is she? I want to see her?"

"They are moving her to a room where you'll have some privacy," Kate told him.

A couple of minutes later, a nurse came in. "Mr. Barkley." Three men looked up!

"She will take you to Beth," Kate said.

When he left, Kate walked straight into Nick's arms and broke down.

"I did everything I could," she sobbed.

"I know you did," Nick said, holding her tight. "Get your things. We're going home."

"I can't. My shift isn't over."

"It is now. Get your stuff."

"I still have a death certificate to sign." There was silence in the waiting room when she said that.

"Go take care of your paperwork."

"I'll try not to be too long."

"I'll be waiting," he reassured her.

There was a knock at the front door. Silas answered. "Sheriff Madden, come in."

Victoria and the family were in the living room. The mourners had finally left after Beth's funeral.

Jarrod jumped up when he saw Fred.

"It was Jarrod I came to see," said the sheriff. "I had to let Cass Hyatt go today."

"WHAT!" yelled Jarrod, "I had no evidence against him. No ballistics, nothing."

"But he threatened Jarrod!" put in Nick.

"That was nine years ago. If it hadn't been for that, I wouldn't even be questioning him."

"He did it. He killed my wife."

"Now, Jarrod, you're a lawyer. How can you convict a man without any evidence?"

"I'll kill him myself."

"And I'll pretend I didn't hear that."

Jarrod went into a deep depression. So to help him, Victoria called Bret Scyler, an old friend of his and who now ran his San Francisco office, to come out to the ranch.

"Maybe you can get through to him," she said to Bret. After talking for a few days, the friends decided to go on a camping and fishing trip. They planned to be gone for a week.

When Nick and Heath got back in town and heard about the trip, they were very concerned. "The Hyatt brothers go to Indian Lake every year," said Nick. "Jarrod is just going to hunt them down. We've got to go after them. How much head start have they got on us?"

"About ten hours," Victoria told them.

"We'll be faster if we go on horseback. I know a shortcut if we go like that," Nick said.

He, Heath, John, and two others made their plans and left at first light.

Bret couldn't understand why Jarrod was driving at such a blistering pace. "Slow down, good buddy," he kept saying.

"I just want to get to the campsite, that's all."

Not once did Jarrod mention Beth's name. Bret only raised it once and was told he didn't want to discuss her; it was too soon.

It was a game of shortcuts that culminated in Jarrod pinning down the Hyatt brothers with rifle fire. It was only then that Bret realized the trick Jarrod had played on him. He threw down his weapon, saying he wanted no part of this.

Jarrod kept the Hyatt brothers pinned down another two hours until the rest of the Barkley party arrived.

Nick and Heath tackled Jarrod, and it broke the spell. The Barkley brothers "persuaded" Hyatt to confess that he'd tried to kill Jarrod and got Beth instead.

Jarrod was quiet on the way home. So ashamed of the dark place he gone to and grateful for the family and friends who had pulled him back from the brink.

Hyatt received a sentence of life for killing Beth.

Victoria talked with Jarrod late one night, when he was sitting and staring into the fire. "I didn't know that such a dark place existed in me—that I was capable of such rage."

"And now?" asked his mother.

"Now all I want are the good memories of Beth, and to put the rest behind me."

"That's what Beth would have wanted. Good night, son."

"Good night, Mother.

Chapter 21

It was the day after Valentine's, and Nick was getting ready to leave the following morning on a purchasing trip for yearlings and two-year olds with his stock buyer, Brahma. It could take anywhere from nine to twelve days. He had almost finished his paperwork. Just a couple more hours of it, and he'd be done. Anything that came in after today, his brother Heath could take care of, and if he couldn't, and it needed Nick's attention, it could be faxed to him or sent to his laptop. John McIntire was still overseeing the ranch, a position Nick felt very comfortable leaving him in.

Kate had written her letter of resignation to the Regional Support Command of the British Army. She had held her commission for the required eight years, which would entitle her to a small pension and other benefits when she turned sixty-five. Of course, now that she was married to Nick, she wasn't in need of them. She was now just waiting for the honorable service discharge papers to be sent to her.

What this meant for Kate was she could no longer be called to active duty or for two weeks each year to play "war games," feeling that this was now the time to make a clean break with her past army life and concentrate on her new role in the United States as wife to her darling husband, Nick.

What she couldn't bring herself to do was renounce her British citizenship to become an American. "Just think," she explained to her husband when they had discussed the subject. "If I stay British, our children will have dual citizenship. They'll be Anglo-Americans. All I have to do is register their births at the British Embassy in

Washington DC." Nick left the subject alone, understanding what a monumental decision changing her citizenship would be for Kate.

"I don't care one way or the other," he told her. "Only try not to lose that cute accent, and don't go driving on the other side of the road over here!"

What Kate was not looking forward to was spending the next she didn't know how many days—and more to the point, nights—alone! She understood that this buying trip was important. The ranch needed to introduce some new bloodlines into their stock and also pick up some colts that would eventually to be trained as cutting horses. If there was one thing Nick loved besides Kate, it was the ranch and his horses. *It will do him good to get away*, she had realized, seeing many of his friends and catching up on the latest horse and ranching news.

Nick was dictating some letters when he received a phone call from the hospital. Would he please come and collect Dr. Barkley and arrange to have her car driven home?

"Why what's happened to my wife?" he hollered.

"That will be explained to you when you get here," he was told.

"JOHN!" he shouted as he ran to his truck. "Come with me." They drove at breakneck speed to the ER, John hanging on for dear life! The security guard was about to tell Nick that he couldn't leave his truck where he'd parked it when the man recognized him and saw the look on his face and the steely gaze from his grey eyes and thought better of it! Nick struck an imposing figure—long legged, broad shouldered, narrow waisted, six feet three inches, approximately one hundred and ninety five pounds, wearing a leather jacket, large brown Stetson, and his usual brown leather gloves. He went storming in and was immediately buzzed through from reception to the treatment area, with John McIntire hot on his heels. "WHERE'S MY WIFE?" he roared.

Dr. Harry Greene hurried forward. "Now, Nick, Kate's in here. She's not too badly hurt, but I admit it should never have been allowed to happen." With that, he drew back a curtain and showed Nick the treatment bay where Kate was surrounded by a crowd of people: Ann, some nurses, and a couple of orderlies. Nick saw Kate lying on the bed, her left arm in a sling and holding an ice pack to the left side of her face! When she took the pack away, her husband could see how swollen her face was.

"She has a dislocated shoulder, a couple of cracked ribs, assorted cuts, abrasions, and hematomas," Dr. Greene informed him.

Nick almost came unglued! "What in the hell has been going on around here? How did you let my Kate get hurt like this?" His bellow loud enough to be heard by the whole ER unit. He leaned over, throwing down his hat and removing his gloves to tenderly take her in his arms, murmuring softly that everything would be all right, he was going to take her home and then yelling at the assembled staff, "After I find out what the deuce has happened!"

"It was an accident," Kate tried to explain to him. "We had a patient who was so high on PCP and goodness knows what else that he broke out of his restraints and attacked me before anyone could stop him!"

"What exactly did he do to you?" said Nick in a very stern voice. "And I want to know ALL OF IT!"

"He twisted my arm, which dislocated my shoulder, picked me up, and threw me across the room into some wood and glass cabinets and then kicked me repeatedly," she told him in a very small voice.

"WHAT!" responded Nick, who was by now boiling mad! "Why didn't anyone stop him?"

"It all happened so fast. It took a few moments for us to realize what was going on and do something about it, but by then, the damage was done," said Dr. Greene.

Kate had never seen Nick this angry. "Get me her things," he ordered Ann tersely. "I'm taking her home, AND SHE MAY NEVER BE BACK!"

Before picking up his hat and gloves, he gently put Kate's jacket around her shoulders, gave John the keys so he could drive her car home and, with great care, helped the love of his life into a waiting wheelchair. He drove Kate home as though she were made of glass.

"I'll take you in the front way and carry you up the stairs," he told her.

"No, please don't do that, Nick, I can walk up the steps by myself, I just want to get home," she said, fighting back tears.

"Well if you're sure you can manage." He parked close to the steps and helped her out of his truck, walking up right behind Kate, keeping both of his hands on her waist.

John had called Jeanne on his way back to the ranch and told her only that Kate had been hurt not to what extent, so their housekeeper was unprepared for what she saw. "Oh lord, look at your face," she exclaimed.

"I'm going to help Kate get into bed, so would you fill an ice pack for her face and brew a pot of coffee, please?"

"I've already put it on and just call when you need the pack, and I'll bring it in."

"Okay, Kate, let's get you changed into something more comfortable," said Nick. "And, sweetheart, don't get upset. Everything's gonna be all right. I'm looking after you now."

"I know you are, I just feel like such a fool by letting it happen in the first place!"

Nick held her gently in his arms, trying to comfort his love. "It wasn't your fault, darling," he told her. "You weren't to know that something like this would happen. You shouldn't have been left alone in that situation, so no more tears. I'll take care of you."

"You could start by helping me out of this hospital gown. Ann put my bra in my purse when she took it off me to get my shoulder and ribs x-rayed. My diamond lariat necklace is in there as well. She had to remove that for the same reason, but it feels strange not having it on. I've worn it since you bought for me on our honeymoon. Could you please find it and put it back on me?" Kate said, fighting back the tears. "I'd really like to wear a set of those beautiful PJs, maybe the red ones that you had delivered from pajama gram yesterday for Valentine's, but I'll need your help getting the top on."

Nick helped her get changed into her new PJs and tucked her up in bed. He could see the start of bruising and swelling coming out all over her body, especially over the left side of her ribcage.

"He actually threw you across the room and then kicked you when you were down?" he asked, shaking his head still fuming.

"Yeah, he was a big guy, about six feet four inches and at least two hundred and eighty pounds. Totally out of control," she admitted to him.

"What kind of restraints was he in?"

"The zip lock kind, nowhere near strong enough, as it turned out. Next time, it will have to be metal cuffs to keep everyone safe!"

"Are you in much pain?" he asked as Jeanne came in with the ice pack.

"Oh, I'm pretty sore all over. Maybe later you could help me into our Jacuzzi tub. It might help with the aches. Until then, I think I'll try and nap for a while."

"Jeanne, could you think of something I could eat for lunch and dinner which won't need much chewing?"

"Of course! What about something soft like scrambled eggs for lunch?"

"Perfect."

Nick got Kate settled down and went into the living room. John was waiting, and Victoria had just called to say she was on her way up with Heath. John wanted to know if there was anything else he could do to help. There were a couple of things at the ranch that Nick was going to take care of himself that afternoon which John would be able to look after for him. When Victoria and Heath arrived, Nick told everyone he wouldn't be going away and that his younger brother should go on the trip with Brahma. He explained to them what had happened to Kate and that, in the next few days, she was going to be in some serious pain as the bruising and swelling really emerged. I won't leave her like this, and I haven't finished with that damn hospital. I meant what I said. She may never go back there. I need you all to step up and cover for me while I deal with all this."

"No problem, Nick," said Heath. "I know the kind of stock you want to buy."

"And we had already talked about what you wanted done on the ranch while you were away, so I've got you covered there," John told him.

"I'll fix meals where she doesn't have much chewing to do," chimed in Jeanne.

"I don't know exactly how I can be of help here, but if you think of anything, just let me know," Victoria told her son. "One thing I will do is call at special meeting of the hospital board and have the 'restraint' policy reviewed. This must never be allowed to happen again!"

Kate slept fitfully for an hour or so 'til the effects of the morphine she had been given wore off. Jeanne volunteered to go to the pharmacy and pick up some pain meds which Dr. Greene prescribed. Nick made sure Kate took them and helped her sit up in bed when their housekeeper brought in the lunch tray. The scrambled eggs were exactly the right thing for her.

Nick tried not to wince each time he looked at the swollen and bruised face he loved so much. "She's going to look much worse tomorrow," Jeanne warned him. "You'd better prepare yourself for that."

They had an early dinner—large fluffy omelets, a three cheese one for Kate, and a fully loaded one for Nick.

Around eleven, Kate was having so much trouble getting to sleep that Nick helped her into their Jacuzzi bath. That seemed to ease some of her pain, and she dozed for about two hours. Nick, fully aware of every move she made, slept very little. About dawn, they both fell into an uneasy sleep and were still that way when Jeanne came to work. She guessed Kate had had a bad night and tiptoed around until Nick emerged from the bedroom a few minutes later, looking frazzled and wanting coffee, which she had already brewed.

"Bless you, Jeanne," he told her.

"Rough night?" she asked.

"Oh yeah," he replied. "And I don't think it's going get much better any time soon!"

"Is Kate awake?"

"Yes, and she'd like some coffee and more of your great scrambled eggs."

"You got it. By the way, did you get the envelope I left on your desk yesterday? I found it in your carryon bag when I unpacked your things, it looks like it's addressed in Kate's writing."

"No I didn't notice it with all that's been going on, but I'll look at it first chance I get."

The next couple of days were very hard for both Kate and Nick. She, because she was so bruised from all the kicks she had taken to her body and her cracked ribs which hurt so much that finding a place to lay or sit was painful. He, just watching his wife go through this, knowing there was very little he could do to help was frustrating. Nick stayed by her side and helped her take Jacuzzi baths, making sure she took her pain meds on time, and wishing there was more he could do to reliever her pain. They even swapped sides of the bed so Kate could snuggle into him without having to lay on the swollen side of her face. As she nestled next to him, he kept the ice pack on her face, knowing from personal experience it would get worse before it got better! They watched movies, each taking it in turns to pick one.

Nick managed to do some work whilst she napped. Having planned to be away, there wasn't a whole lot needing his attention, and what there was, he could take care of on his laptop. During one of her naps, he remembered about the envelope Jeanne had left on his desk. Opening it, he took out a CD and note in Kate's writing.

The note simply said:

> The songs on this CD are to remind you how much you're loved and adored and how much I miss you when you're away. Maybe hearing this music will bridge the gap between us until your home and in my arms again.

Nick plugged in his headphones, slipped the CD into his laptop, and listened. He made a note of the music as it played.

"Twelfth Of Never"
"I Left My Heart In San Francisco"
"And I Love You So"
"Islands In The Stream"
"Just Another Woman In Love"

"You Made Me Love You"
"Yours"
"Till"
"My Own True Love"
"You'll Never Know"
"Power Of Love"
"Why Did I Choose You?"
"First Time Ever I Saw Your Face"
"You're My World"
"As I Love You"

Nick just sat there in silence when the music finished and marveled at his wife. The time and effort she must have put into finding
just the right songs for him was amazing. Her choice of lyrics had
made him tear up. Each one more poignant than the previous one,
but all telling him how very, very much she loved and adored him.
This CD would be taken on all his travels, bringing them so much
closer when business forced them apart. He walked softly into the
bedroom just as Kate was waking up.

"I found your gift to me."

"What gift?" she asked, still a little groggy from the medication.

"My CD," he told her.

"Oh, I'd completely forgotten about it. Did you like it?"

"It's the second best gift after yourself that you have ever given
me. I don't know how to thank you for it. The songs mean so much
to me because I know they were chosen from your heart. I'll never
travel without it, but once in a while, I'll play it here so we can dance
to it. I'm sure it will have the same effect on us the other CD has. I
love you so, my darling Kate, for doing this for me."

A few nights later, Nick was sitting on the deck, enjoying a
brandy and cigar when he heard the opening bars of "Something
Good" from *The Sound Of Music*. He turned around to see his wife
standing in the doorway, dressed in another new pair of PJs, still with
her bruised and swollen face.

"This is my song to you," she told him.

Nothing comes from nothing, nothing ever
could, so somewhere in my youth or childhood,
I must have done something good.

"That's the only way I can explain having such an incredible
husband," she told him, her eyes filling with tears.

For the first time since she'd been hurt, they danced. Nick
held her oh so gently in his arms, afraid of harming her cracked and
bruised ribs. He was hesitant about him making love to her in case he
accidently caused her more pain, but she persuaded him that he was
just what she needed, and indeed, that night, after they had made
love, Kate slept six hours straight—a first for her since the accident.

She told him the next morning, "Nick Barkley, you are all
the medicine I need to heal. I wish I could prescribe you for me
'three times a day for the next seven days!' How about that? Doctor's
orders," she told him, laughing.

"Well, if they're doctor's orders, I can't argue with them," he
replied with a hugely mischievous grin on his face. "Maybe I can do
something about that!"

When Jeanne arrived, he asked her to make sure the fridge,
freezer and pantry were filled with the kind of food Kate could eat,
lots of eggs, soups, fish and other soft food. Then he announced to
their housekeeper that she could have the next seven days off starting
tomorrow.

She was only slightly surprised, because nothing Nick and Kate
did really surprised her. He explained that they wanted to spend the
next week on their own. He was going to take care of Kate by himself.

Jeanne spent the rest of the morning stocking up the flat with
every conceivable thing they could possibly need, from food to drinks,
including some of her homemade muffins and quiches. "Jeanne, you
have stocked us up for a siege." Nick laughed. "Thank you so much.
Now, take this and go shopping for yourself." He handed her a long
white envelope.

When she looked inside, she exclaimed, "I can't accept all this."

"Oh yes, you can," he told her. "You have earned every penny and more. Now go have yourself some fun, and we'll see you next week.

"Okay, Kate. We have the flat to ourselves for a week, so your prescription for yourself of me three times a day for seven days can be filled without any interruption!"

"Nick, I can't believe you've done that! Oh boy, are we gonna have some fun, and I'm sure going to heal in record time!"

Nick was very hesitant about Kate returning to work. "So much has happened to you. I don't think I could handle it if you got hurt again. It just tears me up inside to see you in pain. First, your broken foot, then the car accident, and now this. Kate will you seriously think about doing something else? Maybe start a clinic for the staff, ranch hands, and their families, and also the migrant workers? A place like that, you know, would be so appreciated and is needed."

Kate was stunned! She knew that Nick was still angry at the way she had been hurt but had honestly thought that, given time, he'd get over it, but that obviously wasn't happening.

"Why don't we have a meeting with Dr. Greene and see what he has to say—what new protocols are now in place for the kind of situation I had faced?"

"Call him and invite him over, if that is what you want to do, but I have to tell you that, right now, I can't think of anything that will change my mind about you going back there."

Kate called Dr. Harry Greene, and he came over to the flat that afternoon. Nick laid his cards on the table with a great deal of force.

It obviously took Harry by surprise. He explained to them both that, now, any patient coming in who is even suspected to be high on drugs is handcuffed to the bed frame for everyone's safety. "I really don't know what else we can do," Greene said. "We are, first and foremost, a hospital, not a jail!"

"Then why can't they be transported to the jail ward over at the county hospital?" asked Nick.

"Because they don't have the staff and equipment we have," answered Harry. "Does that ease your fears about Kate?"

"I have to be honest with you and tell you it doesn't," Nick said.

Throughout all these exchanges, Kate just sat there and listened to her husband and boss state their points of view, which seemed to be a million miles apart. *What am I going to do?* she thought. On one hand, here is Nick, her husband, saying he doesn't want her to go back to the hospital but, rather, start a clinic for the ranch and itinerant workers. Then there's her boss wanting her to go back and do the job she's trained most of her life for! *I'm so confused, I can't think straight!* Suddenly, she realized they were both looking at her.

"I was asking you for your opinion of the situation," said Nick.

"I honestly don't know what I think, I'm so mixed up. I'm going to need a day to think this whole situation through. I won't keep you hanging, Harry, I'll let you know within twenty-four hours what my decision is." He left after reiterating to Nick how safe he now felt the ER to be.

"Nick, have you really thought this through, or is it just the beginning of an idea?" she asked her husband with concern written all over her face.

"I got as far as deciding to ask Adam Cartwright to design a building. We'll need a lot of input from you. The kind of clinic it would be, what patients you would you treat, what would you refer to the hospital, the supplies and equipment needed, what kind of staff you will need, can we qualify for a grant because you'd be treating migrant workers. There are lots of details to be gone into. I'll ask Jarrod to start looking into the grant angle and the legalities of it all. We would make it a 501(c)3—a nonprofit, which means we'll need a board of directors, etc. But we'd keep that in the family. Basically, it would be yours to do with as you please."

"How would it be funded?" Kate asked.

"Well, as I said, grants could play a part in it, and the patients should pay on a sliding scale. I wouldn't want them to feel it was just charity, plus the family would help with the funding. The clinic wouldn't be open every day, maybe one morning, two afternoons, and an evening, something like that. You would be your own boss and set the schedule. Of course, you would draw a salary. I'm not suggesting you work for nothing."

"But that's not going to happen overnight. What do you expect me to do in the meantime?" she asked him. "I can't just sit in the flat all day! Why don't I just go back to the hospital, and we can investigate the clinic idea for the future? Perhaps that's the answer to when we have children. I could be at home with them and work part time. But for right now, being a trauma surgeon is what I've trained for practically my whole life. I can't just walk away from it because of one isolated incident. I understand how you feel, Nick, but you've got to see things from my perspective. In the interim, let's have Jarrod look into the feasibility of opening this clinic."

This wasn't the answer Nick wanted to hear, but he did understand how very important being a surgeon was to her. He partly acquiesced to Kate returning to work, because this was the first time she had ever talked about staying home with their children. This was very important to him, although he had never really pressed her on the subject, instead deciding to leave it until the first baby was on the way.

She called Harry Greene and told him of their decision. He was very relieved to hear that she would be back to work on Monday, when she had healed enough to do her job and that the clinic idea would be for the future.

"Nick, you take such incredible care of me. I hated the thought of going against your wishes, but this way, we have come up with a plan for our future."

"As long as you are safe, that's all that matters to me," he said, taking her in his arms. "How about, after dinner, we put on one of our CDs and see how far we get?" Nick asked with a look that left her with no doubt of what he meant!

"About our original CD, I have to fess up and tell you while you were busy this afternoon, I burned us two more CDs. The first one is our original songs but in reverse order, and the second one are the same songs, but I put them in a random order. I just didn't want our music to get predictable, so this way, we can just put in a CD and not know what to expect."

"What a great idea! We'll use one of the new CD's tonight, but I'll bet you we don't get past four songs," he murmured into her ear.

"The way we dance, that's a bet I won't take! And now we have seven whole days to ourselves to eat, sleep, dance, and make love whenever we want! Could we turn our phones off? Or would that be going too far?" Kate whispered to her husband.

"Well I'm still supposed to be away, and you're off work injured, so why would anyone want to call us? We'll shut them off and see what happens after making sure all the doors are locked," he answered her with a glint in his eye!

"Can we really get away with that?" she asked him.

"We are going to give it a good try. I've turned off your phone, and I'm shutting off mine right now. So as of this minute, it's just you and me. What would you like to do first?

"Do you really have to ask?"

"Race you for the bedroom!"

March thirteenth was Nick's birthday, and Kate had a special gift and evening planned for him. To start with, laying on the dining table was a box beautifully gift wrapped. When he opened it, he sat down with a thump, not believing his eyes! It was a Remington model eighteen fifty eight revolver in mint condition.

'Where on earth did you find this?' he asked Kate with an incredulous expression on his face.

"I looked through your gun magazines, did a lot of research on my own, and came across an antique gun dealer who said he would represent me at an auction which was coming up. I told him specifically what I wanted and voila, here it is! Want to know the details? The province on it says it was carried by a confederate soldier, it has an eight-inch barrel, weighs two pounds and thirteen ounces, is a percussion revolver, powder and ball load."

Nick knew Kate was good at research in her own field but couldn't believe how much time she must have spent finding this revolver for him. Then his wife showed him the paperwork that came with the gun, proving that a southern soldier named Beauregard Jones had indeed carried this historic piece throughout the civil war.

Nick had once mentioned to his wife that collecting firearms from the civil war era would make an interesting hobby when he had the time, never dreaming she'd start his collection off by giving him a revolver so incredibly rare as this one. He just sat there, staring at his gift, then he jumped up and gave Kate the biggest bear hug she'd ever had as he swung her around, lifting his darling off her feet!

"And tonight, I'm taking you to dinner," she told him. "So put your 'glad rags,' on and be ready at seven thirty sharp."

"Yes, ma'am," he replied with a huge grin on his face.

He dressed carefully for this dinner, choosing to wear his new grey pinstripe suit that he'd just gotten from his tailor. He paired it with a south sea island white cotton shirt with French cuffs (one of half a dozen he'd just received), into which he put the cufflinks Kate had given him on their wedding, his tie a Paolo Albizzati in dark red and blue stripes, in his breast pocket, a handkerchief in the same dark red, his new cologne, Creed Aventus Black, and, of course, his Rolex watch. Tucked into his black Lucchese handmade boots was his Glock seven.

That night, Kate, wearing a new low cut red dress—which Nick admired the moment he saw it—drove him to Paul's. "I've already ordered dinner for us," she informed Nick.

"Oh, you have, have, you? I only hope you're not going to make me eat well done lamb chops," he replied, laughing as he leaned over to kiss her neck.

"Now would I do that to you?" She laughed.

They were served *hors d'oeuvres*, followed by a salad tossed in Nick's favorite Roquefort dressing. Then a serving cart was brought to their table. On it was a *chateaubriand* for two, cooked rare, just the way he liked his beef. He couldn't believe her choice as she normally ate her steak medium rare.

"Are you okay eating meat like this?" he asked her.

"Of course," she told him. "Anything for you, especially on your birthday." For dessert, Kate had ordered the pie Nick liked best of all, cherry al a mode, which Paul's didn't normally serve, but at her insistence, they had made it especially.

After dinner, they danced to "their" songs played by Gus, with Nick's right arm holding her oh so tight; with his left hand holding her right up against his chest, occasionally putting it to his lips and kissing her fingers so tenderly. She, as always, had her left arm wrapped around his neck, massaging it gently with the tips of her fingers.

"Let's go home," he whispered in her ear. She'd even taken care of the bill, which was a novelty for him. As she drove him home he, kept leaning over and nibbling on her ear! When they reached the steps to the deck, they were so busy locked in an embrace as they tried to go upstairs it was with great difficulty. They finally reached the deck, and Kate pushed him into the loveseat, went inside to get his brandy and cigar, picking up her coffee, which she'd had the foresight to put on a timer to be ready for when they got back. She took everything outside, not forgetting to turn on his CD. They sat on the loveseat in front of the fire pit and made out like they were teenagers! Finally, Nick got around to drinking his brandy and smoking his cigar. Kate went back in for fresh coffee and quickly changed into a new red nightgown and negligee that she'd bought specially for this evening. When Nick saw her new outfit and heard what was playing—"You'll Never Know"—he finished up his brandy, allowed Kate to finish her coffee, and then swung her up into his arms. They danced cheek to cheek and continued that way until almost the end of the disc, when they heard the start of "The First Time Ever I Saw Your Face."

Nick put his hands on either side of Kate's face and told her, "This song is an anthem to you, my darling." Kate's eyes filled with tears as he kissed her over and over again. The CD finally finished with "As I Love You," which Nick serenaded Kate with.

"Nick, it's your day, not mine. All the focus should be on you, not me."

Finally, Kate broke the silence. "Come with me and get the last part of your birthday gift." She took his hand and led him inside. She seduced and undressed him with great loving precision and then gave him what he considered the best part of the evening, in which she kissed, caressed, and gently bit him as he laid there, hugely enjoying himself until almost the last minute, when Nick decided she'd done enough for one evening and took over! Later, laying in each other's arms, he confided to her it was by far the best birthday he'd ever had!

April was time for the annual Stockton Cattlemen's Association's Ball. This past year, Nick had been the president. The event was a throwback to an earlier time when only men were allowed to be members, and for one evening a year, women were invited to join the menfolk. Now, of course, the meetings were open to women, but there were very few who joined. Maybe it had something to do with the cutthroat games of poker which ended most meetings! Nick used to play in these games, but since Kate came into his life, he much preferred to go home to be with her. Just another way she had changed his life without trying to.

The proceeds of the ball went to a local charity, Victoria, as usual, was leading the steering committee, making all the arrangements. Nick, of course, had to make a speech, and Kate was concerned about the kind of dress she should wear. It couldn't be anything too ordinary but also couldn't be too overly expensive looking; she had to strike the right balance. In the end, she settled on the jade halter neck that Nick had bought her on their honeymoon.

A week before the big night, Nick came home and said he needed to talk with her. He looked kind of serious, and she wondered what could be going on.

"I've just received word that they want to elect me to be president of the Northern California Cattlemen's Association," he told her.

"That's wonderful, isn't it?" she asked.

"In a way, yes, it's prestigious, and I think I can use the position to bring about some changes I've always wanted to see in the association."

"But?" Kate asked. "What's the downside?"

"It means more work and travel for me, which affects you directly, darling," he told her.

"How long is the appointment for?"

"One year."

"Is it something you really want to do?"

"Only if you're okay with it."

"In that case, accept!"

"You really think so?"

"I know the innovative ideas you have for the ranching business, and this would be the exact forum for you to set those plans into motion, wouldn't it?"

"Yes, but, Kate, I'm not sure you understand what you're letting yourself in for," he warned her.

"Then I'll find out as we go, but it won't stop us from being together. When you have to go out of town to functions on Fridays and weekends, I'll be happy to go with you."

"You'll be bored to death listening to the same old speeches!"

"Ah, but I'll be thinking about what follows when we're alone, and that's never boring!"

The family were delighted that Nick had been offered this well-deserved accolade.

"I know he talked it over with you before accepting," Victoria said to her. "I'm so glad you realized how important this is to him. Ranching has always been his first love ever since he was a little boy until, of course, he met you, that is."

"Whatever is important to Nick is important to me," Kate told her. "We're a team. He has always supported me when I've had speaking engagements at Stanford and other universities, even though the subject matter goes right over his head. He flies or drives me to those lectures and then stays in the background, wanting me to have all the attention. The least I can do is return the favor. It will take a little adjusting to get used to our new schedule, but like everything else, as long as we work together, we'll manage.

She really is an extraordinary young woman, Victoria thought. *Nick sure knew what he was doing when he fell in love with her. Not every wife could deal with his work schedule and absences from home the way she does. They seem to have some to an understanding which allows for them both to have demanding careers. I can understand why, when they're together, they just want to be alone, they do so enjoy dancing on their deck! Not at all the jet set kind of couple that some of the women he had dated would have wanted to become who would have married Nick for the Barkley name, whereas Kate married the man himself. I know they'll make his new appointment a huge success.*

Chapter 22

Nick was away on a three-day business trip to talk to the main buyers of their crops. Spring signaled the beginning of an even busier time than usual for him. Starting in April with strawberries, cherries, and grapes, which took him to the start of summer with barley, peaches, and plums.

He put Heath in charge of the branding, and John McIntire was still overseeing the day-to-day running of the ranch. Nick knew he was taking a chance putting Heath in direct contact overseeing men, normally keeping him away from dealing with the ranch hands and instead keeping him in the corporate offices as a sort of "right hand man vice-president," but his brother had been with them long enough to establish himself as a true Barkley. Not having the kind of ranching management experience his brothers were born and raised to had been a huge drawback for Heath, who had to try to play catch up. The problem was there were many hands who had been at the ranch for many years. The family had an excellent reputation as employers, and the accommodations were better than anything other ranches had to offer, all that plus top pay. So men stayed with them for years, and some clearly remembered Heath arriving.

Most of the hands agreed if Mrs. Barkley said he was her son; that was good enough for them. But there were those who resented Heath and the way he tried to step in and take up his position as a part owner. The running joke with some was the B brand that was on Heath's horse, Charger, stood for Barkley, but for Heath, the B stood for bastard! Nothing was ever said in Nick, Jarrod, or Eugene's hearing; that would cause a fight with Nick and with all the brothers' immediate dismissal.

Nick and Kate were looking forward to their one-year wedding anniversary. They had decided to go back to Hawaii for ten days. This time, Nick had rented a private villa with its own pool and beach. They were going to leave Friday; their anniversary wasn't until Sunday, and they wanted to be settled in by then.

His plane was due to land Thursday afternoon, and John went out to pick him up at the airport. Kate finished her packing. She had left work early so they wouldn't be rushed, having already got her manicure and pedicure. It wouldn't take Nick long to pack his things. They both had been so looking forward to this trip for months.

Time passed. Kate looked at her watch. He was late. *Wonder what the holdup is?* she thought. Just then, the front door phone buzzed; it was her mother-in-law.

"Can I come in?"

"Of course."

She came in with Jarrod and Heath. Kate could tell by the expressions on their faces something was wrong.

"What's happened? Where's Nick?"

"His plane is missing. One minute, it was on the radar, the next, it was gone. They have sent out search planes and helicopters," Jarrod told her. "There was no mayday, no distress signal. There is nothing we can do but wait. They will let us know as soon as they have any news. We have given them your cell number as the main contact," he continued.

"Do they have a specific area to search?" asked Kate.

"Yes, but it's a large area. It's going to take time."

"Who is on the plane?" Kate inquired.

"The pilot, copilot, and Nick."

"What would you like us to do?" Victoria asked her. "Stay with you or leave you in peace?"

"I would like to be left alone right now," Kate responded.

A few minutes after the family left, there was a knock at the deck door. It was Jeanne. John, who was on his way back from the airport, had called her with the news. She came in, and without saying anything, gave Kate a hug and then put on a pot of coffee.

Now came the waiting.

Three days later—their anniversary—they were still waiting. Kate had called the place in Hawaii Friday and cancelled their booking. When the owner heard what had happened, he wouldn't charge them a cancellation fee. "Maybe when you find your husband, you'll call me, and we'll try to rebook for you."

"Three days, Jeanne. Three days without food or water, to say nothing of the medical help they must need."

Kate hadn't slept properly since Nick had been missing, afraid of not hearing the phone ring. Instead, she dozed on the sofa for a few minutes at a time. She lived mainly on coffee, although Jeanne made finger food so she could pick at it. She looked awful, the sparkle had gone from her eyes, and she jumped every time the phone rang!

Victoria talked with Jeanne, "I'm worried about her. She can't go on like this. It's the not knowing that's killing her. They've got to find that plane. It's the only way she'll be able to come to terms with the result if Nick should be dead. But it's such a huge search area, it could take weeks."

Their anniversary came and went, and so did another three days. Then came the call she had been waiting for. A search plane had spotted some wreckage.

"Any survivors?" she asked.

She was told they couldn't tell. Choppers were headed in. They would be able to land.

Kate was in agony waiting for the choppers to land and assess the situation. The word came through that the pilot and copilot were dead.

"Oh, dear Lord, please let Nick be alive."

"We've found him! The pulse is faint, but it's there! We are putting him in a collar and on a backboard and then transporting him to the nearest hospital, which is Stockton General."

When Kate heard that, she grabbed her keys and jumped into the car and raced to the hospital. She was on the roof when the chopper landed. He didn't look at bit like her Nick, with a week's worth of beard and his skin a chalky color. He had a nasty gash on his forehead, and his breathing seemed to be labored. Kate knew she couldn't treat her husband, so all she could to do was touch him gently and tell him how much she loved him. She rode down in the elevator with Nick and then regretfully left him and went into the waiting room, which was full of family and employees.

"I've never been in this position before," said Kate. "I'm always on the other side of that door. I hate this feeling of helplessness just sitting here." After a while, she couldn't stand it any longer and went back into the treatment area and into the cubicle where Nick was just as Dr. Green was calling time of death.

"NO!" she screamed, pushing him aside and bent over Nick.

"NOOO!" She grabbed her husband's shoulders and began to violently shake him, at the same time, yelling, "Nick! Don't leave me! Don't you dare leave me! Nick Barkley, come back! Please don't leave me! Please, please, Nick!"

Dr. Greene had stepped away to let her be near her husband. Two nurses standing in the cubicle were going to stop Kate, but he said, "No, let her be."

Then he froze. "Listen," he said.

There was a faint beep, and then another. A nurse said, "That's his heart monitor. The patient's heart is pumping!"

Dr. Greene went to Nick and examined him. Kate just stood there, holding Nick's hand with tears running down her face. Harry Greene was stunned. "He's breathing on his own. She's brought him back. I've heard about it, but now I've actually seen it!"

"What did happen?" asked one of the nurses.

"He somehow heard her voice and felt her shaking him and responded. She brought him back, he's breathing normally! He has a nasty gash on his forehead—I suspect a concussion—and is dehydrated, but that's all that I can find wrong with him." The nurses tried to get Kate to leave, but Harry Greene stopped them. "They belong together. I'll go talk to the family."

He went through to the waiting room and, with Kate's permission, told them what had occurred and about Nick's medical condition. "He's weak, and it will take time for him to recover and build his strength back up, but I'm sure he'll be able to go home in a matter of days. Kate will stay with him, and when we get him into a room, you can visit with them."

"Harry, let me understand this, you thought Nick had passed away, but when Kate got to him, somehow, he responded to her, and now you're saying he could be home in a few days?!" Victoria asked, thunderstruck by what she had just heard.

"That's exactly it! I've heard of couples having such a deep bond that they have defied even death, and your son and daughter-in-law obviously have such a relationship."

About an hour later, Victoria was shown into Nick's room. Kate was sitting in a reclining chair next to his bed, holding his hand. Victoria was startled at his pallor and the seven-day growth on her son's face.

Kate looked up and smiled. "He's sleeping naturally without any sedation, which is a wonderful sign."

"Harry Greene told us what happened. How can we ever thank you?"

"I did the only thing I could think of. I couldn't let him go, and I had to tell him that. He was so exhausted he couldn't fight any longer, so I had to fight for him."

"Can I get you anything?"

"No, thank you. They are going to send me up a tray of food, and then tomorrow, Jeanne will bring me some things from home. I'll stay with him until he's discharged."

"I'll tell the rest of the family what's going on. You don't mind if they visit for a few minutes?"

"Of course not. They can visit him now if they like."

One by one, Jarrod, Heath, Eugene, and Audra came to spend a few minutes with Nick and Kate.

Two days later, Jarrod's barber came to the hospital to shave Nick. "Now you look like my husband," said Kate, laughing.

"Now I feel like your husband," Nick responded. "Why don't you go home and get changed. I'll be fine on my own."

"Okay, just don't get up to any mischief while I'm gone!" When she came back, Nick looked very serious.

"You didn't tell me what happened, that I was pronounced dead and you somehow brought me back."

"Who told you?" asked Kate.

"Dr. Greene thought I knew and ended up telling me the whole story."

"You were so weak you couldn't fight for yourself any longer, so I had to fight for you. I couldn't let you go. If you left me, my life was over, so I had to shake you and tell you what was happening. We are two halves of a whole. Without you, I have nothing, an extreme case meant extreme measures."

"The biggest fight of my life, and I missed it!"

"You had fought for a week after the crash to stay alive—that was enough. What I did was just help you when you were too weak to fight any longer. We're partners, right?"

"Kate, I owe you my life."

"Nonsense, you did the hard part that whole week staying alive. I just reminded you that you had won. The way you are improving and regaining your strength, I'm sure you'll be released from the hospital soon. It's very hard to have you in a bed and not be able to jump in beside you, but there are no locks on the doors!"

"Don't think I haven't thought the same thing!"

A few days later, Nick was back in the flat where he and Kate spent some quality time in bed together, not just making love, but just holding each other and relishing in the fact that Nick's injuries were so minor and that, indeed, he was still alive!

Somehow, the story of what had happened in the hospital had spread, and it seemed everyone knew about it. Jeanne was in awe of them. "I always knew you two had a unique connection, but I never dreamed it was that close," she said to Kate.

"We really don't want to talk about it, it's very personal to us," Kate told her.

Nick quickly regained his strength and the weight he had lost. Soon, all that was left of the crash was a memory of being trapped in the wreckage and then waking up in the hospital with Kate by his side. But the story of dying and being brought back because of the deep bond he and his wife share would stay with him forever. He understood what she had done. He would have done the same in her situation. Life without the other was unthinkable.

"Babe," Nick announced. "I still have to give you your anniversary gift." He went into the bedroom, coming back with a beautifully gift-wrapped box.

"Nick, I'd almost forgotten about exchanging gifts!" Opening the box he had given her, she found inside a white gold anklet with the Barkley brand on it and a matching toe ring. "Oh, they're wonderful, and you remembered I broke the one I used to have. Put the anklet on for me please." Nick carefully placed it around her ankle, and she put on her new toe ring. "Nick, I love them, so much nicer than the ones I used to have. Now, wait here and I'll get your gift." She called from the bedroom, "Close your eyes and hold out your hands!" Very carefully, she placed a guitar in his hands! He opened his eyes and held onto it, a look of pure surprise on his face.

"I've so missed you sitting on the deck playing, and since your old one got that crack in it and you never got around to replacing it, I thought I'd do it for you."

"Kate, I don't believe you did this! It's a Taylor, isn't it?"

"Yes, something called a K24CE, whatever that means! Now you have no excuse to not serenade me, or just to take it into your cave and play to your hearts content."

"My darling, you've done it again! You give me the most amazing gifts, and yes, I'll play for you tonight as we sit outside. Now come over here and let me really thank you!"

Unbeknownst to Kate, Nick called about the house in Hawaii that they had booked for their anniversary. The man who owned it said he could rent it to them for ten days starting tomorrow. Nick called Dr. Greene and explained about the short notice.

"Go. You two deserve some time on your own."

"Jeanne, pack Mrs. Nick's bags for Hawaii. Kate, we are leaving in the morning for ten days. It's all taken care of with the hospital, and Jeanne is packing your bags."

"When did you organize this?"

"About fifteen minutes ago. The plane is leaving tomorrow morning at eight thirty. While Jeanne is packing your bags, come with me onto the deck so I can try out my new guitar."

"Sounds good to me."

They settled down on the deck, and Nick spent the next hour playing and singing to his adoring wife.

Nick and Kate flew to Hawaii the next day. After what they had been through during the plane crash and the time it took to find the wreckage, it had taken its toll on them each in their own way, both physically and emotionally. They spent some time talking about their experience, both during and after the crash, being brutally honest about the way they had felt. They enjoyed just being together as they lay on the beach, swam, went sailing, scuba dived, and made love. They even rented a boat, and Nick caught another Pacific blue marlin. This time, a whopping one hundred and thirty two pounds and seven feet four inches long! Nick was delighted and planned to have this one also hung in his "cave" when it was sent to him after it was stuffed and ready for mounting on the wall. The food was exceptional as were the accommodations, and now both felt they could put the whole experience of the plane crash behind them and move on.

When they came back, Nick was ready to pick up the reins of running the family businesses full time. He made John McIntire the permanent ranch foreman after seeing the job he had done. Even Nick could see how close John and Jeanne were getting. Most of the time, John could be found at Jeanne's house. Soon, Nick and Kate were back to their normal routine, spending as much time as they could together either going out to their favorite restaurants or staying home working in the kitchen, trying out new recipes or barbecuing, finishing their evenings by dancing cheek to cheek on the deck, or Nick serenading his love. Nick gave Kate a beautiful sculpture of the horse, Jingo, that she always rode that he'd started to create after he got home from the hospital. It was his way of thanking her for all she had done for him and how much he loved her. Kate proudly displayed the sculpture on her desk in their living room, a positive reminder that out of what appeared to be a tragic situation can come great joy.

Chapter 23

The beginning of July was one of the busiest times of the year. The peach and plum crops were ready to be picked. Beside the itinerant workers, Nick hired any other farmhands that he could, along with the other ranchers in the area. Nick went into town to see how Jarrod was doing as he was helping by recruiting the extra workers. As Nick passed the sign-up storefront for the McGarrett ranch, he looked in and saw it was crowded with men eager to be employed. But when he got to the Barkley storefront, it was empty except for Jarrod, who was sitting there with his feet up on the desk, drinking coffee.

"There's something wrong with our sign," complained Nick. "I just passed McGarrett's place, and he's signing them up like he was giving something away!"

"There's nothing wrong with the sign," his older brother told him.

"Jarrod, the word around town is you're questioning them like you were getting them ready for jury duty!"

"You said to get you the right kind of men, and that's what I'm trying to do."

"Forget what I said, I want men any kind of men. Now just sign them up, and no more questions."

Kate was down by the corral watching a new hire, Don Garvis break a colt. Hearing an engine, she turned around to see an old truck pull up close to where she was standing. A man got out and came toward her.

"Is this the Barkley ranch?" he asked.

"Indeed, it is. I'm Kate Barkley, can I help you?"

"I just signed up in town and need to see the foreman."

"Well, he's not around, but here comes my husband, Nick Barkley, he's the ranch owner. I'm sure he can help you. Nick, can you come over here for a minute? This is a new hand, and he needs to know where to go."

Nick walked over and shook hands with his new employee.

"I'm Waldo Defendorfer," he said. The look on Nick's face was priceless, and it took all Kate's self-control not to laugh.

"I have a short speech I give to all the new hires. We expect this to be our best season and expect all our people to work long and hard and fast and to get along with the person next to them."

"I like other people," Waldo told him.

Nick's eyebrows rose. Kate was grinning from ear to ear. Just then, John McIntire walked over.

"This man is a new hire. What bunkhouse do you want him in?"

"We have a bed in number seven." He told the new man where to find the building.

"What was Jarrod thinking to sign him up?" Nick said to Kate. "I told him to get me men, but that's ridiculous. I bet he doesn't know a peach from a ripe tomato!"

"Now, Nick, don't be so judgmental. I'm sure he'll work out just fine."

"I hope you're right!"

Waldo got to the bunkhouse and introduced himself to the three other men he was sharing with. One of them, Hank Demers, showed him the bunk he was to occupy.

"I'm sure I've heard that name Defendorfer before," he said to one of the other men, Sid, "but I can't think where."

"How are things going?" Victoria asked her son at the family dinner.

"Well, let's see. First, the transport wagon's engine seized up, and it's only two years old! Next, a ladder folded up, and one of my men broke his arm, and then today, a truck backed up, crushing fifteen crates of freshly picked fruit! Do you have any idea how many man hours have been wasted and how much money it has cost us?"

"Accidents do happen," his mother responded.

"It's that Waldo Diefenderfer…"

"Defendorfer," Kate corrected him.

"Whatever his name is, word is out that he's a Jonah."

"Oh, what rubbish, Nick. You can't really believe that," Kate said.

"Well, I asked him to come by tonight for a little experiment."

"What kind of experiment?" Jarrod asked.

"You'll see," said his brother.

Sure enough, after dinner, Silas announced, "Mr. Defendorfer."

"Come in and sit down over here," Nick said, who had been sitting at a small side table playing with a deck of cards since dinner. "I want to try a little experiment, and I thought you could help me."

"Of course, Mr. Nick. What do you want me to do?"

Nick shuffled the deck of cards. "We're going to cut for high card."

"Oh, Mr. Nick, I don't gamble."

"It's all right. There's no money involved."

By now, they had garnered the interest of everyone else in the room who came over to watch. Nick cut the cards and drew a five. Waldo drew a four.

"That proves nothing," Jarrod told his brother, having worked out what Nick was doing.

"We'll do it again. You draw first this time, Waldo."

He drew a six, and Nick, a ten.

"Jarrod's right, this doesn't prove anything," said Kate, who had also caught on to what her husband was doing.

"One last time, Waldo. You draw first again."

"Oh, you drew a queen. That's wonderful, Waldo," said Kate.

"Well, would you look here at what I drew," said her husband, showing them a king!

"You can't tell anything from three cuts of the cards," said his mother, who also had finally caught on to what her son was trying to prove.

"Would you like some coffee?" offered Kate.

"No thank you, Mrs. Nick. I better be getting back to the bunk-house. Need a good night's sleep to be able to get my work done tomorrow. You don't have to show me out. I can find my own way."

"What did I tell you? He's a Jonah. He's bad luck. He doesn't mean to be but—"

He was interrupted by a loud crash. They all looked at each other.

"No, it couldn't be," said Victoria as they all hurried into the foyer where they found Waldo surrounded by the pieces of the five-foot large vase that used to stand there!

"I'm sorry. I guess I didn't notice it!"

"That's all right, someone must have moved it," Kate said, and with that, Waldo left.

"Now what do you think?" said Nick. "A Jonah."

"It's broken," Jarrod.

"Accidents happen," said Victoria.

"Doesn't move like a ballet dancer," said Jarrod.

"He's willing to work," said Kate.

"Honest and loyal," said Victoria.

"And…um…polite," said Kate.

"Whose side are you on anyway?" said Nick.

"Just trying to be fair," his mother responded.

"Well, okay. We'll give it another day or so," Nick told her.

"Atta boy, Nick. After all, it can't get any worse," his big brother added.

"Who said?" Nick replied.

When Waldo got back to the door of the bunkhouse, there were his things, packed up and lying outside.

"Not again," he said to himself. Just then, Victoria Barkley and Nick came out of the house to head down to the stable to check her horse, Misty Girl, who had pulled a tendon in her leg. Seeing Waldo putting his bags into his truck, she went over to see what was going on. He explained that the boys in the bunkhouse no longer wanted him there.

"Then you'll stay in the room off the main stable," she told him. "No one uses it now that Ciego has a house and doesn't need it." Nick just stood there. There was little point in arguing with his mother when she was in this kind of mood. "Walk with us and we'll show you where it is. Bring your bags with you."

"Are you sure, Mrs. Barkley?"

"Of course. We won't have hands dictating who we hire and who we fire on this ranch."

The men in bunk house number seven had observed Waldo walking off with Victoria and Nick.

"He's not leaving," Hank told the other men. The next morning, a delegation of hands talked to Nick and gave him an ultimatum that if Waldo wasn't out of the orchards by noon the next day, they'd go on strike.

Nick was furious to say the least.

"We'll, take him out of the orchards. There are plenty of other jobs around here at this time of year," his mother said when she heard. But when the men found out that Waldo wasn't leaving the ranch, they elected Garvis to tell Nick that they were going to walk out if he didn't get rid of Defendorfer.

"I'll go along so far," his boss told him, "but you've gone too far. This is my ranch, and no man tells me how to run it."

"You've got 'til two p.m. tomorrow or we walk," reiterated Garvis.

Nick talked the situation over with Heath. "Do you have any ideas on how to handle this, bro?"

"Well what would happen if you just ignored the ultimatum?" Heath asked. "Do you really think the men would walk? After all, we pay top dollar and have the best accommodations of any ranch. That's a lot to give up for a superstition."

"But if they really walked, we'd be in a hell of a bind, crops ready to be picked and no one to pick them! We'd sure lose a ton of money. Oh, I know we can afford to take the loss, but it's the principle of the thing. The idea of a bunch of hands dictating to me how I should run this ranch pisses me off no end! It's like I'm damned if I do and damned if I don't! That's it! Hell, I'm not going to do anything! I'm not firing what's-his-name, so Garvis and his cohorts can kiss my ass and do what they want. I'd sooner let all those damn crops rot than be told how to run my own ranch. We'll see if Garvis and the rest of them live up to their word tomorrow. Now, I'm taking the afternoon off. I'll see you at family dinner tonight, and now I'm putting this whole mess out of my mind until tomorrow."

Kate was getting ready to go downstairs for dinner when Nick held up his hand. "Do you hear that? It's raining. I hope it's just a light shower or it'll interfere with the pickin'." But the rain continued all night and showed no signs of letting up. There was no way any fruit could be harvested that day.

"Well, that settles the dilemma. Nobody wins! No point in firing what's-his-name, and no point in Garvis and company walking! The crops may well rot yet! We never have rain like this at this time of the year," he told Kate, who was home as it was Friday. "Our rainy season is October through April."

Of course, the hands were blaming the rainstorm on the "Jonah." Garvis decided to take matters in his own hands and went into the stable to have it out with Waldo.

"We want you out of here," he told him and started to work him over. Unfortunately for Garvis, Nick chose that moment to walk into the stable. Seeing what was happening, he pulled Garvis off the much smaller man and told him, "You wanna fight? Why don't you try it with someone your own size," and proceeded to give him the workover he had planned for Waldo.

"I'm sorry, Mr. Nick. I didn't mean to cause you so much trouble," Waldo told him apologetically.

Nick just shrugged his shoulders and left.

When Kate saw her husband, she got out an ice pack and checked him over despite his protestations that he was fine!

"I'm going down to the stable to check on Waldo to make sure he didn't get hurt," she told Nick. He knew it was pointless to argue with her when she was in doctor mode!

Walking into the stable, she bumped into Waldo, who was on his way out with his bags. "I came down to make sure you weren't hurt," she told him.

"I'm fine, Mrs. Nick. I was just leaving. I've caused too much trouble around here."

"Waldo, you want to know something? You're your own worst enemy. When are you going to have some faith in yourself? You can't go on like this, running from place to place, believing you're a Jonah. There's no such thing. It's all in your head. Oh, I'm so angry with you. You've got to stand up for yourself sometime." And with that, she turned and marched back to the flat.

He thought about what she'd said but didn't think he had the courage to go back to the bunkhouse and face down the men. Instead, he picked up his bags and, trudging through the rain, headed for his truck. He was nearly there when Kate's words came back to him. *Have some faith.*

"I've tried everything else, why not that?" Right where he was, he dropped to his knees on the muddy ground and started to pray. Hank Demers was looking out the bunkhouse window to see if there was any sign of the rain letting up, saw Waldo, and called the others to come and see what was going on. They all crowded into the doorway and watched. Men in the other bunkhouses had seen the same thing and were also standing in their doorways. Waldo was quite oblivious to his audience. He continued to pray. Then the unthinkable happened—the rain stopped, and within minutes, the sun broke through, and there in the sky was a rainbow. The watching men broke out in applause. Waldo looked around as they poured out to shake his hand and slap him on the back.

"You saved the harvest!" they told him. "You're not a Jonah, you're our good luck charm!" Hank immediately asked Waldo to move back into number seven.

When Nick heard from the men what had happened, he was dumbfounded. "They can't really believe he stopped the rain?" he said to Kate.

"Why not? They were more than willing to believe he was a Jonah. Why not a good luck charm?"

The rest of the long harvest went on without any further incident, Waldo now considered a good luck charm, the Jonah tag being long forgotten.

Chapter 24

Geoffrey Peters had worked at the Barkley Ranch for six months, and now he was dead! Found by John McIntire in Geoff's single-room apartment in the newly opened housing unit when he hadn't shown up for work and hadn't called in to say why he wouldn't be there. John immediately reported his grisly find to Heath as Nick was away on business. Heath, in turn, called Fred Madden because Peters had died of a gunshot wound, which didn't look to John self-inflicted or an accident, but murder! Fred, some deputies, and scene-of-the-crime investigators arrived and sealed the crime scene. Victoria and Audra, seeing all the activity, came down from the house to join Heath and find out what was going on."

"This is terrible," the matriarch of the Barkley family said. "We've not had a shooting like this for years and years."

Heath put in a call to Nick to keep him apprised of what was going on. "You've got to handle it, bro. I've got way too much on my plate to take on one more thing this week. In fact, I'm going to be gone two more days longer than I first thought. I won't be back until late Sunday night instead of Friday night. Next, I've got to call Kate and tell her about the change in plans. Fortunately, my darling woman just rolls with the punches, God bless her wonderful attitude. I'm so very blessed to have a wife with that kind of easygoing nature! A couple of the guys here are catching hell from their wives for the extended time we've got to be here! Talk with Mother, she'll help you. Gotta go, bye."

"Do you have an office we can use to take statements?" Fred asked Heath.

"Why don't you come up to the house and use the library?" Victoria chimed in. "It's getting on for lunchtime, and I'll have Silas prepare sandwiches for you and any of your men who want them."

"That's very kind of you, Victoria. Lunch would only be for myself and the two of my deputies who'll be at the house with me. We'll come up with you, get set up, and start interviewing everyone who knew Geoffrey Peters. It doesn't matter how slight. I could start with you, then your family, and then move on to hands and any office staff who knew him."

"Sounds like a plan," Heath said.

Fred and his deputies used the big table in the library, and then Heath came in and joined them, followed by Silas bringing in coffee for everyone.

"Okay, Heath, tell me what you know about Geoff, as you all called him?"

"I brought you a copy of the application he filled out when he applied for a job here. We ran a background check like we do on all our employees, and it came up pretty clean. Just a couple of drunk and disorderliness and a few traffic violations. Much as you'd expect, nothing to stop us hiring him. As you can see, he was born in Helena, Montana, but moved to Conrad when he was a baby and grew up on a small ranch just outside of town. His mother died when he was about twenty, and that's when he left home. Since then, he's worked on ranches between Montana and California, ending up here about six months ago. He was a real good worker, kept to himself. I guess you'd call him a kind of loner. Never heard of him going to any of the social events that have been held over at the clubhouse ever since the complex opened three months ago, although I know he was invited to all of them. The hands and staff who live on the ranch are a friendly bunch and would never have left him out of any activity they had going. That's all I can tell you."

"Okay, Heath. Thanks. I'm afraid it doesn't give us much to go on. You don't know of anyone that had a beef with Geoff or anything like that?"

"Sorry, Fred, I don't. Like I told you, he was somewhat of a loner, hardly ever saw him talking to anyone outside of work, and never heard of any problems during working hours. Just seemed content to stay in his unit, play his guitar, or watch TV. Ate his breakfasts and lunches mostly over at the canteen. Must have fixed dinner in his apartment. Hardly ever went into town, used his truck for work, and we gave him an allowance for doing it. I honestly can't think of anything else I know about him."

"If you do, please call me. Could you ask your mother to step in? Now, Victoria, is there anything you can tell me about Geoff Peters?"

"Not much, Fred. I introduced myself to him when he first arrived here, like I do to all the new hands when I see them. We had a brief conversation. I think he said that he was originally from Montana, that's right, because he liked the winters here much better! I really can't remember what else we talked about. Just surface chit-chat, you know how it goes. Since then, it's just been the 'hi, how are you doing, are you settled in all right, hope Nick isn't working you too hard' type exchanges. Any idea what happened?" Victoria asked.

"All I can tell you is he was shot to death provisionally between eleven last night and four this morning, and he was shot with, we think, a thirty eight, but I'll have to wait until the post-mortem for complete details, and then I'll get the report from the scene-of-the-crime boys, and we'll find out about finger prints, fibers, etc. Not much to go on so far. We do know it looks like his room was searched, but we don't know if anything was taken! Even his application is of little help, he lists no next of kin. I know his mother is dead. He doesn't even list anyone where it says 'in case of an emergency.'"

"That's not so unusual for iterant type workers which so many ranch hands are," Victoria reminded him. "What could he have done that was so bad that it got him killed, and how come no one heard the shot at that time? During the early hours of the morning, it's so quiet out here. A shot would sound like a cannon going off! Do you think whoever did it could have used a silencer?"

"If they did, that would make it premeditated, because they would have to have brought the gun and silencer with them intending all along to kill him. In other words, first degree murder, not just manslaughter," Fred told her.

329

"And if anyone were to drive here in the middle of the night, their vehicle would have been heard. Oh lord, that means the killer lives right here among us? This can't be happening, not on the Barkley Ranch!"

"Now, Victoria, don't start getting ahead of yourself. The killer could have parked a mile or two away from the main compound here and walked the rest of the way, so it doesn't necessarily have to be someone in your employment."

"I didn't think of that, Fred. You're right, the killer must have come from the outside. Maybe someone that Geoff had a problem with at another ranch that he worked at and the guy followed him here. That sounds more like it, doesn't it?"

"They are all avenues of investigation we'll look into. Now, if there's nothing else, you can tell me. I'll have a quick word with Audra, and then, if you wouldn't mind, those sandwiches would be great before we start interviewing the hands and office staff."

Audra had only said a few words of greeting to Peters, so there was nothing she could add to the picture Fred was building of the young man. Jarrod and Gene said the same thing; they just passed the time of day with the hand. After Fred and his deputies had eaten, the office staff came in one at a time, but again, there was very little they could add. Geoff had always been very pleasant and polite but never talked much about his personal life, just about ranching itself. It was much the same story with the ranch hands that Fred interviewed as they came home at the end of the day and heard for the first time the shocking news. All except one, Charlie Jackson, who told the sheriff that, once, when he and Geoff were sitting out late one night having a cigarette and just shooting the breeze about their ranching experiences, there seemed to be a four-month gap in Geoff's working history. When he had asked him about it, Geoff hastily brought the conversation to a close and went off to his apartment. Maybe if the sheriff were to take a close look at the work history, he could figure out where Geoff had been for those four months he had been so reluctant to talk about!

Fred immediately got in touch with Heath and asked him if Geoff Peters had given them a resume.

"As a matter of fact, he did, Fred. I forgot it this morning. I was going to give it to you tomorrow, but I'm leaving the office right now, and I'll bring it home with me for you."

When Heath got home, he and Fred poured over the resume, and indeed, there was a four-month gap at the beginning of the previous year. Geoff had worked at a ranch in north Wyoming before and south Wyoming after, so maybe he had spent the missing four months at a ranch somewhere in between. On his resume, he'd covered the missing months by saying he was unemployed.

"I'll get in touch with the Feds in the morning and see if FICA was deducted for him during those four months. Then we'll know if he worked and where. Until then, there is nothing more we can do. His apartment is still a crime scene, so it remains sealed up. So I'm leaving. I'll talk to you in the morning. Night, Heath."

It was three days later that Fred called Victoria to update her on the progress of the investigation. She suggested that he come to dinner that evening, and that way, he could talk to the whole family at the one time. Assembled were Victoria herself, Audra, Jarrod, Heath, Kate, and even Gene, who was home on summer vacation from university. They decided to have dinner, and then after, when they were settled with coffee and liquors, Fred told them of his progress. The bullet recovered during the autopsy was indeed a thirty eight and had been run through the FBI database but with no luck. That meant the gun which had fired the fatal shot had never been used in a crime. The fingerprints recovered were all Geoff's, and the fibers were just what you'd expect to find in an apartment, so no leads there either. The Feds hadn't gotten back to him about the FICA information, and as it was Friday, he wouldn't hear anything until at least Monday, maybe longer.

"Not much progress at all I'm afraid!"

The family continued to chat about the situation, so Kate excused herself and went back up to the flat.

When Nick was away, they played a little game. Each night, they sent each other a song to say how they felt, and tonight was her turn. This had started the first night Nick had been away from her and she had surprised him by sending him the old song, "You'll

Never Know." The next night, he had sent her a song, and so the game had been born. This evening, she was sending him the song she'd been going to play to him that night when he got home, "Tonight Cowboy You're Mine." She'd also leave him a message telling him Sunday night he was hers, all hers! He wouldn't get either his song or message 'til very late, but she knew he'd appreciate them both! Tomorrow was his turn, and then Sunday, she'd be back in his arms. This was the longest he'd ever been away, and she couldn't wait to feel his lips on hers.

Monday, Sheriff Madden got a call from an agent in the federal government to let him know that Geoffrey Peters had indeed been employed during the dates supplied, and FICA had been deducted from his salary. The name of his employer had been the Bar H Ranch in a town called Redstone, Wyoming. The agent hoped that would be of some help to the sheriff.

Fred put in a call to Heath and asked him if he knew anything about the Bar H Ranch and who owned it. "Sorry, Fred, never heard of it, but hang on a minute, let me walk down to Nick's office and ask him. He knows more ranchers than I do. Fred, he says he's heard of it but knows nothing about it or even who owns it. But he's going to make a few calls and see what he can find out. He'll get back to you."

"Thank him for me. Bye, Heath."

The next day, Nick called Fred with the information he'd been able to find.

"The name of the owner is Boris Harrison, hence the name Bar H Ranch. It's a medium-size ranch he inherited from his father about twenty-five years ago. Seems to be doing okay financially, which says a lot these days, but here's the interesting part. Boris is a very unpopular guy according to my source who happens to be the president of the local cattleman's association out there. Boris argues with everyone. It's his way or the highway! So much so that his wife left him about ten years ago, but he wouldn't let her take their only child, a daughter, with her! The wife was much younger than he, so the daughter is only about twenty. He has a foreman that has worked for him for years, but the rest of his hands come and go partly because he doesn't pay too well, but mainly because he's such a nasty piece of work! Hope this info helps you, Fred. Call me if you want to know anything else and I'll see what else I can find out. Gotta go, Kate is taking the afternoon off work so we can spend some time together after my being away for a week, and I'm taking her for a ride. We just need some time alone."

"Sounds like a good plan, Nick. Give her my best, and thanks for all your help. I think I can take it from here, but I'll call if I need any extra help."

Fred's next call was to the local sheriff of Redstone. He explained who he was and the reason for the phone call. "This guy, Geoffrey Peters, would have been in your neck of the woods mid-December 2016 through mid-April 2017."

"Oh, yes, I remember him. I got a call to come out to the Bar H. Boris and Geoff were involved in a very heated shouting match, but by the time I got there, it had escalated, and they were taking swings at each other! I separated them with some difficulty and tried to find out what in hell was going on. Bottom line, the old man had found out that his daughter Alice had been sneaking out the house to meet up with Geoff in the stables. Boris went ballistic when he found out and fired the young man on the spot. Told him to get off the property. Problem was, Geoff wanted to take Alice with him, and I think she wanted to go, but she was scared to death of her old man and what he'd do if she left. He was threatening to hunt them down and kill them both if she tried ever tried to leave home. I eventually made Geoff leave, telling him he was only making trouble for Alice if he stayed. He left, and I never saw or heard of him again. About a month later, Alice married the only son of Boris's foreman, and the couple live with Boris at the ranch house. They've got a little girl now who was real sick there for a while, but she got a liver transplant, and she's fine now. But I don't suppose any of that helps you.

"I really don't know what helps and what doesn't at this point. Let me think over what you've told me and maybe I'll get back to you, if I you don't mind, that is?"

"You call me whenever you want. I'll be happy to help in any way I can," Sherriff Anderson, the chief law enforcement officer of Redstone, Wyoming, told Fred.

Fred ran into Heath in town, and together, they sat down in the sheriff's office so Fred could give him the latest information.

"Doesn't seem to help you much," Heath said. "Except, oh, I guess it's nothing."

"Except what? What were you going to say?"

"Well, doesn't it strike you as a little strange that the daughter, Alice, wanted to leave her father and go off with Geoff and then a month later, she marries another guy? Maybe it's nothing, but it just struck me as peculiar."

"Now you come to mention it, it does seem odd that she's willing to risk the wrath of her old man to sneak out of the house to meet Geoff, want to leave with him, and then the next thing, marry some other guy. I've got no other leads to follow up. So I'm going to call Sheriff Anderson back and just see if there is anything to this hasty marriage thing. Thanks, Heath, I'll let you know what I find out."

As good as his word, after Heath left the office, Fred called the sheriff of Redstone back. "I know this might sound off the wall, but bear with me. What can you tell me about Alice's marriage so soon after Geoff left?"

"It was a might strange at that. George, that's the name of the guy she ended up marrying, had asked her old man for her hand in marriage months before, but Boris said no. Guess he thought his foreman's son wasn't good enough for his daughter. Then suddenly, a month—no, less than that—after Geoff left, Alice and George were married up at the ranch house. There were only a few friends invited, but that wasn't surprising with the kind of man Boris is. He doesn't have that many friends! Alice got pregnant straight away, but the baby was born prematurely and, a few months later, developed liver problems. They really thought they were going to lose the little one, but the whole family got tested, and of all people, Boris was a good match. He donated a portion of his liver to his granddaughter, and she's fine now, but I think she'll be on medication for the rest of her life though. It did seem kind of strange that neither of her parents were a match, but then, I don't know much about that type of thing. That any help to you?

"I think it just might be. Thanks, Sheriff. I might be paying you a visit in person in the next few days!"

"Fine by me. I'd enjoy meeting you and showing you around. Let me know when you're arriving."

Fred drove out to the Barkley ranch that evening after calling Heath and making sure the young man would be home and free to listen to the idea that was forming in the older man's head.

"Okay, Fred, tell me what you're thinking."

"I know this may sound off the wall, but here goes. Geoff had a thing going with Alice Harrison. It must have been serious because he wanted to take her with him when he was leaving.

"Well, what if after he left, Alice finds out she's pregnant and tells her old man? He'd never have let her marry Geoff, a hired hand. Besides, he was long gone, but there was the son of his foreman who was already in love with her and wanted to marry her. So Boris tells George that he can marry Alice, tells her it's the only way to give the baby a name and a father, and they tell everyone the kid is born prematurely. Everything goes according to plan until the baby gets sick and everyone gets tested to find a DNA match to help her. At that point, George discovers he's not the baby's father! Imagine how that must have made him feel! Maybe he left things until he knew the baby was going to be okay and then worked out who 'his daughter's' real father was—Geoff Peters! It must have made him crazy with rage. He'd been tricked into marriage, and his old rival had fathered the child Alice had told him was his! So he sets about his revenge on Geoff, but it takes him a few months to find out where he's working. When he does, he comes down here one night, leaves his truck a ways outside the compound, and walks in. I'm sure he'd already scoped the place out and found out where Geoff lived. George confronts Geoff and tells him about the baby and how ill the little mite has been, and that's the way he found out he's not the father and Geoff must be. Geoff tells him that he wants to see his daughter and claim parental rights, and that's when George loses it, pulls out his gun, picks up a pillow, and uses it as a silencer and shoots Geoff. He then searches the room to make sure there is nothing in it to lead the authorities back to the Bar H Ranch. Then he leaves the way he came, taking the pillow with him. What do you think?"

"Wow, that's some story! But you know what? It all makes sense. Thing is, how you gonna prove it?"

"I'm gonna fly up to Wyoming in the morning, and Sheriff Anderson is going to arrange for Alice to meet me in his office without telling her father or husband about the interview. Maybe if she really was in love with Geoff, she'll help us bring his killer to justice, even if it is her husband!"

Fred's plan worked! Alice met him in Sheriff Anderson's office and dissolved into tears when she was told of Geoff's death and the circumstances. When Fred Madden outlined to her what he thought had happened, at first, she denied it all. But as the two sheriffs talked to her, and the more she thought about the death of her daughter's real father, she decided to tell the truth. Yes, it had all happened just the way they had guessed. Three weeks after her father had thrown Geoff off the ranch, she found out she was carrying his child. When she told her father, she begged him to find her lover so they could be married, but her father flatly refused. Instead, he insisted she marry George, who had been wanting to marry her for as long as she could remember, but her father never thought he was good enough. Now, of course, circumstances had changed! She had reluctantly agreed to the union to give her baby a father. Everything was going okay until Becky got sick and the parents had to be tested to see if they were a good match to donate part of their liver to save the baby's life. Of course, the test came back that not only was George a negative match, he was not even related! He went wild when he saw the results and demanded an explanation from her and her father! When he found out what had really happened and that Geoff Peters was Becky's biological father, he vowed revenge on him.

"The night you say Geoff was murdered, George was not at home. In fact, he'd been gone one day prior and one day after!"

"Would you be willing to give us a written statement to that effect?" Sheriff Anderson asked her. Without hesitation, she answered in the affirmative. "By the way, what caliber handgun does your husband own?" Anderson asked as she was signing her statement.

"A thirty eight. Why? Is that the caliber gun Geoff was shot with?"

"Yes it was, and now we have enough evidence to get a search warrant to obtain his handguns and any other evidence we can find that would help us close our case," Anderson told her. The Redrock sheriff led a team out to the Bar H ranch house and searched the entire place. Removing from it, amongst other things, four thirty eights handguns and receipts from gas stations in Utah, Nevada, and Stockton itself. Based on the evidence they obtained, George was arrested and charged with the murder of Geoffrey Peters! After ballistic testing was done, one of the handguns seized proved to be the murder weapon. Although the attorney Boris hired for his son-in-law tried to fight extradition, George was transported to Stockton to stand trial for first degree murder.

Everyone at the Barkley ranch breathed a sigh of relief that the murder of their ranch hand had come from the outside. Victoria arranged a memorial service for Geoff after she had his remains cremated. It was attended by all the family, hands, and most of the office staff. His ashes were scattered on the range later by Victoria, Heath, and a couple of the hands who had known him best.

Chapter 25

Jarrod's old friend, Scott Breckenridge, was visiting again. He was here to do more business with Barkley Family Enterprises, but this visit, he was staying in town. Nick wasn't too thrilled having Breckenridge around Kate, especially after him calling her when she was on her honeymoon. If truth be told, there still existed in Nick anger toward Scott for the man even thinking he could break up the Barkley marriage after less than twenty-four hours! The nickname—Midas man—that Scott had was justified; he had a knack of knowing when and how to invest to make a killing!

There was the start of a drought going on in the area, and whilst the Barkleys had several sources of water, most of the small ranchers were hurting for it, and the cost of drilling for water was expensive. They had used up most of their cash reserves and needed money to buy supplies for their herds, but when they went to the local lending institutions to seek short-term loans, the bank officials turned them down.

Scott heard about their situation and offered to loan the ranchers the money they needed with their land as the collateral at almost twice the interest the bank would have charged but less than other money lending facilities. At first, they balked at the deal and turned to the Barkleys for help, only to be told that they just couldn't come up with such a huge amount of cash for all the small ranchers on such short notice, so the ranchers reconsidered Scott's offer.

Jarrod and the other Barkley brothers warned them about the conditions of a short-term loan like this when they were going through a drought. "If the drought continues and you lose your herds, then you'll lose your land," Nick told them. "The agreement is contingent upon you selling your herds to pay back the loan, but if you don't have the herds, then you'll lose everything! I counsel you not to take this offer."

"You Barkleys won't help us, and now you're telling us not to take the only deal that will. We can't afford to listen to you. Draw up the agreement, Jarrod. We are desperate for help, and none is coming from your family. Scott is the only one who has any faith in us."

"We'll take the deal, Mr. Breckenridge."

After dinner, the guys played pool, and as the three Barkley women watched, the subject of conversation was Scott Breckenridge. Jarrod was concerned that Scott went into these deals to get the land, but Audra thought he was just helping the ranchers and was wonderful.

"Most women do," said Jarrod.

"What do you mean?"

"He's irresistible, just like me," kidded Nick as he winked at Kate.

"He has his choice of women from San Francisco to Paris, so I don't think he'd be interested in you, little sister," said Heath.

The next day, Audra went into town to "accidentally" bump into Scott, which she managed to do. After spending the afternoon together, she invited him back to the ranch for dinner. From then on, they started dating regularly.

"Does Audra know what she is getting into?" asked Kate "She is playing in the big leagues now, and she can't have any experience of that. She could get badly hurt."

"Maybe you should talk to Mother," said Nick.

Kate voiced her concerns to Victoria, who agreed with her daughter-in-law. "I intend to have a word with Scott in the next few days."

She chose early morning to go to his hotel to speak with him. They found a quiet place in the foyer and sat down. Victoria told him of her concerns, that he was a man of the world and her daughter's experience was limited to provincial Stockton.

"I never take unfair advantage of an opponent," he told her. "I will lay my cards on the table with Audra. She'll know exactly where I stand."

"Thank you, Scott. I appreciate you doing that."

The drought was getting worse, and the ranchers were starting to lose cattle.

"Jarrod, can't you renegotiate our loans for us?" the ranchers asked him at a meeting with them, Jarrod, and Scott.

"The loans are not up for renegotiations," Scott told them.

"But the way we are losing our cattle, we won't have enough to sell to pay you off, which means we'll lose our land."

"You should have thought of that before you signed the agreements," Scott told them.

"Jarrod, can't you do something?"

"You signed a legally binding contract, there's nothing I can do to change that. I'm sorry."

Jarrod told his family about the conversation at dinner that night.

"He's hoping the drought continues, that way, he'll get some very valuable land for a song, and then, when the drought is over, he can sell it and make a killing," Jarrod told them.

"Is there's nothing we can do?" asked Victoria. "No way to get him to lose his hold on the ranchers?"

"No, I've offered him various deals to get them out of their contracts, but he's not interested."

"He's such a snake," said Nick, his suppressed anger toward Scott rising to the surface.

Audra just sat and listened to the conversation. The next morning, she went into town to talk to Scott herself. She tried to plead the case for the ranchers, but he wasn't interested.

"What do you want?" she asked him.

"How about you?" he said jokingly.

"What do you mean?" she asked.

"Well, if you were to come away with me for, say, six months, I'd be willing to renegotiate with them."

She thought for a few minutes and then told him, "I'll do it!"

341

He was more than surprised at her response. "Are you sure?" he said.

"Absolutely," she told him. "I'll go home and pack. Come by the house and see Jarrod about the contracts, and then I'll be ready to leave." And with that, she left, but not without attracting the attention of some of the ranchers, who decided to follow her back out to the Barkley ranch to find out what was going on.

When she got home, she went upstairs to pack. The ranchers burst in to confront Jarrod and the rest of the family as to what kind of deal they had made with Scott behind everyone's back.

They were in the middle of this argument when Scott himself walked in. When they saw him, they were even surer that the Barkleys were making money out of the deal which they had made with Scott. Scott decided to tell everyone why he was there and the deal he had made with Audra. There was stunned silence. Her brothers said she was not going to keep that kind of deal, but Audra herself had joined the group and told everyone that she was of age and had made the agreement willingly, and no one could stop her, and if Jarrod would take care of the new contracts. The ranchers, to a man, had a horrified look on their faces and told Scott if this was the price of the new contracts, they didn't want it. Audra went back upstairs to pack, and Scott told Jarrod to rewrite the contracts, but he would not be taking Audra with him! And with that, he left.

"Do you really think Audra knew what she was doing?" Kate asked Nick.

"She probably thought it was some kind of romantic adventure," Nick told her. "But whatever her motive was, it got Scott to rewrite those blasted agreements!"

Two days later, the drought was broken when heavy rains came. Nick greeted them with a loud yahoo and picked Kate up and swung her around. When he came in a few days later, he told her, laughing, that he was going to trade his horse in for a boat. It was the first good drink most of the cattle in the valley had had in in weeks. Now the ranchers would be able to pay Breckenridge off at the cattle sales and get him off their backs for good!

About nine p.m. one Friday, just as Nick and Kate were planning on having an early night, Silas called Nick's cellphone. "Have you heard from your mother this evening?"

"No, I haven't talked to her at all today. Is something wrong?"

"Well, she left about seven to have dinner with Ms. Liz Thompson but never arrived at the restaurant, and she's not answering her cellphone."

"No one else has heard from her?"

"No, Mr. Nick. I think something is wrong. Do you think she could have had an accident?"

"What restaurant was she going to?"

"They were supposed to meet at The Stagecoach Stop at seven thirty."

"We'll drive that route and see if we can find her. Call me if you hear anything. Have you let Heath and Jarrod know?"

"Yes, sir, they had the same idea as you and are leaving now."

Kate had heard some of the conversation and told Nick, "I'll get my medical bag out of the car just in case your mother is hurt, and then I could give her medical attention until more help arrives."

The four of them set off in two cars going the way which they knew Victoria would have taken into town. The road was dark and winding as it went across the ranch property until it reached the main highway. Halfway along the ranch road, they saw her four-wheel drive parked with its lights on and engine running. They screeched to a halt, jumped out, and ran to it. The vehicle was empty, her purse and cellphone laying on the front passenger seat. All of them immediately began to search the surrounding area by flashlight, calling her name as they looked.

"This is no good," Jarrod said. "We need searchlights and maybe a tracker dog. I'm calling Fred." Within half an hour, Sheriff Madden and a group of deputies, one with a bloodhound, had arrive on the scene.

"We'll start a grid search," Fred informed everyone as all the ranch hands showed up, eager to help. They searched all night but could find nothing. It was as if Victoria Barkley had vanished into thin air! The ground being dry, there was not even a sign of other car tracks.

"What the hell could have happened to her?" exclaimed Nick, the worry showing on his face.

Silas called and said he'd prepared coffee and food for everyone when they were ready to take a break.

"Let's call a halt to the search for a little while, get something to eat, and then regroup," said the Sheriff to everyone who had converged on the ranch to help.

"There's a special delivery envelope for you, Mr. Jarrod," one of the kitchen staff told him. Jarrod opened it and immediately asked his brothers, Kate, and Fred to go with him into the library.

"It's no wonder we couldn't find her," he told them. "She's been kidnapped! This is a ransom note. They want one hundred thousand dollars."

"Put it down on the desk along with the envelope," Fred instructed him. "There may be fingerprints."

"I highly doubt it, who knows how many people handled it before it was given to me. But I'll put both in this folder, and you can try to see if there's anything usable."

"It says if we don't obey the instructions, and that includes not telling the authorities, she'll be killed. We can't take that chance, Fred," said Nick. "So on behalf of my brothers, I thank you for your help up to now, but I have to ask you to take your deputies and leave."

"You can't be serious, Nick? Now is the time you really need my help."

"I have to go along with my brother," chimed in Heath.

"Me too," said Jarrod. "And I know Eugene would agree with us if he were here. We won't let Audra know what is going on. She's in Denver, visiting Mother's sister, and we don't want to worry either of them unnecessarily. Of course, whatever help we can give you once we get Mother back, it goes without saying you'll have it all, but until then, we can't risk her life by doing it your way."

"I'll make a phone call and arrange to get the cash," Nick told them.

344

"You've not said a word, Mrs. Nick. What is your opinion?" the sheriff asked her.

"I have to go along with the wishes of my family," she answered. "It's their decision to make after all."

"All right, I'll take my deputies and leave. Let me know when you make the drop. Good luck to you all."

"What exactly does the note say?" Kate asked.

"That tomorrow morning at eight, we are to put the ransom money, which has to be in small bills, in a sack and leave it at a place called Indian Springs," her husband told her. "What I don't understand is why they have asked for so little."

"That had occurred to me," put in Heath. "Who's going to deliver it?"

"I will," said Jarrod. "The note was addressed to me."

"Why don't Heath and I go out there just before daybreak and watch for whoever comes to pick up the money? If they let Mother go, we can nab them, and if they don't, we can follow them to where they are keeping her. We'll go on horses. I know that country pretty well. There are plenty of places to hide round the spring."

Kate was about to object to Nick's risky plan but thought better of it and kept her mouth shut.

"Just the two of you could pull that off," Jarrod told them. "Do it."

Right before the sun came up, Nick and Heath concealed their horses in the rocks not far from Indian Springs and then settled down to wait. What they saw surprised them. A pair of young men, not more than sixteen, drove up in an old battered truck, with Victoria wedged between them, her hands tied. They got out, looked around, spied the sack, picked it up, checked the contents, and went back to the truck, pulled Victoria out, untied her, and told her to start walking. Getting back in their vehicle, they drove off. Nick and Heath hurried over to their mother, hugging her and making sure she was unharmed.

"Do you know who they are? "Nick asked her.

"No idea," she replied. "I've never seen them before in my life. They staged a car accident, and when I stopped to help, overpowered me and threw me in their truck. One of them sent that ransom note from an overnight drop off in town, and then they took me to an old line shack not far from the springs, and that's where they've been holding me."

"I know the place you mean," Nick told her. He pulled out his cellphone. "I have service, so if you don't mind, Mother, I'm going to call Jarrod to pick you up and the sheriff to tell him we're going after those young thugs. Come on, Heath, before they get away. I know a shortcut to that shack. Let's hope that's where they've gone."

The brothers got to the shack, hid their horses, and were waiting when the young criminals walked in the door, laughing at their apparent good fortune, only to find themselves looking down the barrels of two large shotguns in the hands of two very angry brothers.

"Hands up and down on your knees," ordered Nick with a look on his face that told them that he would have no trouble using his rifle. By the time the sheriff and some deputies arrived, the youths who had dared to kidnap Victoria Barkley were not just tied up, they were hogtied by men who were experts at doing just that!

"All I want is a hot bath," Victoria told her sons and Kate after they all had breakfast. "And I owe Liz Thompson a dinner!"

"Do you remember Sam Williams?" Nick asked Kate. "You operated on him last year after he was shot by some rustlers."

"Yes, of course. How's he doing?"

"Well, I thought he'd make a great complex manager because he can't go back to ranching. He's been helping John, and we found out he's a really good handyman. Since the shooting, ranching is just too much for him, and to give him a job with responsibility would be good for him. His daughter, Rosemary, had applied for a job in the ranch office, and one has now become available. We could put them in the new units so they'd both be living on site. No commuting for either of them. What do you think?"

"It sounds perfect. What does Rosemary do?"

"She is an administrative assistant and is excellent with computers, I had Trudy check her out when she was here after her father first got hurt. In fact, she came in and helped us out a couple of days whilst she was here, and Trudy was most impressed with her skills and told me then if Stella ever left, Rosemary would make a perfect replacement. Well, now Stella is leaving, so it seems the right time to offer Rosemary the job, the new housing, and Sam, the complex manager's job. By living on site, he'd be able to know firsthand what is going on, and most of the repairs, he can do himself. It wouldn't be too hard for him physically, and that was the problem with him going back to ranching. They can each have a one-bedroom unit or a two-bedroom, whatever they want so Rosemary will be able to keep an eye on him, which is what she told me she wanted to do. I'm going to call her today and offer her the job and housing, and then I'll talk to Sam. John will be sorry to lose his help. They have worked well together."

"It all sounds perfect. Let me know what happens," Kate told her husband.

That night, Nick told Kate, "I talked with Rosemary today, and she's handing in her two weeks' notice and starting to pack up her stuff. I'll arrange with John to have her boxes and furniture moved here and Sam's things transferred over. Then I'll give them some time to settle in before they start work."

"You must be a dream of a boss," Kate said, laughing.

"By the way, we are going to have a wedding on the ranch."

"Oh, who's getting married?" he asked her.

"John and Jeanne," she told him. "I called that months ago!"

"They are! That's wonderful!" he said. "Do they want to have the wedding at the house?"

"I'll ask Jeanne what their plans are and how we can help." She talked with Jeanne. She found out they wanted to have a small wedding but a larger reception.

"Why don't we take care of the reception for you?" asked Kate. "That way, you can invite the whole ranch and office staff if you want. We'll get the cake and everything. Just tell me what color and the flavor."

After talking with John, Jeanne told Kate that they would like a small ceremony at the town hall, with Kate and Nick as their witnesses and then the reception at the ranch. But not a champagne reception—a beer and soda one.

"Nick and I would be honored to be your witnesses. Thank you for asking us. I'll talk with Silas, and we'll take care of the reception. Don't give it a second thought. Are you going to live in your cottage, or do you need something bigger?"

"John and I have talked it over, and my place will be plenty big enough for the two of us. He doesn't have much stuff, and we'll start and move his things over in the next week or so."

"What is the date of the wedding?"

"Well, that really depends on when you can do the reception."

"I'll talk with Silas today and get back to you."

"Silas, I need your help. John and Jeanne are getting married, and I offered to do the reception for them. It would be for all the ranch and office staff. They don't want anything fancy, no champagne, except maybe for them to toast each other. It would be beer or soda for everybody else. No fancy finger food. What do you suggest?"

"Well, ma'am, we could do sandwiches—ham, turkey, and roast beef—plus potato salad, coleslaw, that kind of thing, something more substantial. And then the cake, do you know what kind they like?

"They like chocolate, and that menu sounds wonderful. One more question, what is the earliest we can do this?"

"Well, Mrs. Nick, how about two weeks on Saturday? Would that be all right?"

"That would be wonderful. Okay, Silas, put the plans into action."

"Jeanne, I've been talking to Nick, and he wants to build an attached double garage to your cottage so John will have a place of his own to keep tools and work on his projects. He said to tell John to go right ahead with the construction. And while you're at it, have your front porch enlarged to accommodate the rocking chairs, side tables, plants, and wind chimes which the ranch hands are buying you."

"They are?"

"They sure are. I've often heard you say you'd like to sit out on your porch at night and just relax. Well, now you'll be able to."

"Nick also said to tell John to use as many men as he needs to get the projects done before the wedding." Then Kate told Jeanne of the menu Silas had come up with and the date.

"Oh, Kate, that sounds terrific, and just what John and I had in mind. Two weeks from Saturday it is. I'll call the town hall and book a time, and then I'll let you know what it is. Then we'll put up notices round the ranch and offices inviting everyone to the reception."

Kate told Nick of all the plans. "We'll give them two weeks off for a honeymoon," he told her. "Anything else we can do for them?"

"Why don't we give them a check as a wedding gift, and then they can get what they want," suggested Kate.

"Good idea, darling. Now, let's be honeymooners ourselves!"

The extended front porch and garage were finished the day before the wedding. Jeanne and John were thrilled at the way their cottage now looked.

John and Jeanne's wedding was at eleven a.m. They were back at the ranch by noon, and the reception began. As usual, Silas did them proud. It struck just the right note, not too formal. The sandwiches on mini rolls were delicious, as were the salads. The cake, a beautiful two-tier, was big enough to feed the all guests with enough left over for Jeanne and John to have for themselves. They had decided to take only one week off as the ranch was busy and take the other week in the fall and perhaps go away then. They didn't want to accept the check that Nick and Kate gave them, saying it was too large, but Nick insisted on them taking it. So they were able to afford some new things for the cottage.

Chapter 26

"You've seemed very restless these past few days, Nick. Is something wrong?"

"Not really. It's just that I miss being out on the ranch. I've been so busy in the office these past couple weeks that I haven't had a real chance."

"How are things now?"

"Better. I have arranged it so I'm free to work today and tomorrow, getting my hands dirty again!"

"Tomorrow?"

"Oh, damn it, I'm sorry. I forgot we'd made plans."

"That's okay, it was nothing we can't change to another day. Just one of our 'lock the doors, turn off the phones, we are being honeymooners' days! We can do that on Saturday. Go on, get out on the ranch. I know how happy it makes you."

"You sure you don't mind?"

"Nick, go. No more talking about it."

When he came in that evening, he had more color in his face than Kate had seen in a while, and his mood was lighter.

"Enjoy yourself?" she asked.

"You don't know how much I miss working with the ranch hands and doing some physical labor. It's the greatest way of life I know."

Nick left early Friday morning before Kate woke. She kept herself busy putting the final touches to a lecture she was scheduled to give at Stanford University of Medicine on Wednesday morning. This was a special guest lecture she was giving and was set for ten am. She later found out, after being asked, that this was a very prestigious speaking engagement which made her feel greatly honored. In addition, there was an important faculty dinner to which she had also been invited to on Tuesday evening, so she was traveling to Palo Alto Tuesday lunchtime, flying with Jarrod to San Francisco, and then driving the rest of the way to the university.

Because of the plans she and Nick had previously made to spend the day by themselves, she had given Jeanne the day off and saw no reason to change it. So she was alone when Heath called to tell her Nick had been attacked by a mountain lion and was now in the emergency room. Her imagination was running wild at the kind of injuries he could have sustained in such an attack as she raced to the hospital. Dashing into the ER, a nurse she knew pointed to the cubicle where Nick was being treated. Pulling aside the curtain, she breathed a sigh of relief when she saw her husband lying on the bed, appearing not to have been badly hurt, nothing like she'd imagined! "What are the extent of his injuries?" she asked the attending.

"Those scratches on his upper body and arms are deep, and he's suffered three broken ribs, but apart from that, there's else nothing wrong."

"I'm not staying here any longer," an impatient Nick told her. "Get me my shirt and I'm outta here!"

"How did you get him here?" she asked Heath, who was standing in the background.

"We rode 'til we found some of our men who had a truck and left the horses with them so I could drive Nick here."

"He rode a horse in his condition. He could have driven a rib through a lung!"

"Hey, I'm not in that bad a shape," Nick chimed in. "Stop making such a fuss, all of you. I'll be just fine in a couple of days."

She knew from experience, when he was in this kind of mood, that arguing with him was pointless, so she helped Nick get dressed, getting the top from a set of scrubs as his shirt and jacket had been shredded by the cat's claws. Driving home, he was unusually silent, but she chalked that up to the pain she knew he must be in. Heath came up to the flat to make sure Nick was doing okay.

"What exactly happened?" Kate asked her brother-in-law.

"We were out chasing strays when we spotted some buzzards circling. As we went to investigate, we spotted a steer down. Nick got off his horse and went into the gully to check it out when the cat, who must have brought it down, got the jump on him. I couldn't get a clear shot at the puma, so I had to fire in the air as I ran to help. I guess the noise was enough to scare it, because by the time I reached Nick, the cat had run off."

"Lord, I dread to think what could have happened if you hadn't been there, Heath, he could easily been have been killed. Do mountain lions usually attack like that?" she asked.

"No, I would hazard a guess this one has been hurt by a man and now he's running totally rogue. I'll inform the Department of Fish and Wildlife what's happened and see what they want to do about it. Like I said, it's now especially dangerous, and we can't have it roaming around and attacking people like that."

Jarrod, who was at home when he heard what had happened to his younger brother, felt they were obligated to do something about the situation themselves as the attack had happened on Barkley land. He immediately put in a call to a hunter he'd heard about who had a good reputation. The man was between assignments and said he could come in the next couple of days.

That night, Kate was awoken by Nick having a violent nightmare, screaming and thrashing around so much so that he nearly knocked her out of bed. He was yelling, "Get it off me, get it off me, Heath!" She grabbed him by his shoulders and, with all her strength, tried to hold him down whilst at the same time saying his name over and over, telling him that he was safe. When Nick finally woke up, he was drenched with sweat and seemed disoriented, as it took him a moment to figure out where he was.

"You had a terrible nightmare, but you're all right now," Kate told him, holding onto her husband and trying to reassure him.

"I'm so sorry. I didn't hurt you, did I?" he asked when she explained to him what had just happened.

"No, you just scared me half to death. I think you're suffering from a mild case of post-traumatic stress disorder. That was a terrible ordeal you went through. I'd be amazed if it didn't have some kind of after-effect on you."

He didn't pass comment on what she had just said but got up and took a shower. While he did that, Kate hurriedly changed the sheets, which were drenched with sweat like Nick had been. When he came back to bed, for a long time he just lay there, holding onto her as if he were afraid of what might happen if he slept again. When he did sleep, they passed the rest of the night without further incident.

The next morning, Nick had promised to have breakfast with his family, mainly Kate though, to show them he had no after-effects of the attack. On the way down, he asked her not to mention the events of night before.

"Of course not," she replied. "That's between us."

He was not walking with his usual forceful stride, so she could tell the broken ribs were hurting him, but with the mood he was still in, she was hesitant to say anything about them to him. During breakfast, Jarrod mentioned that they'd have to get the cat before it struck again. It had now brought down nine steers, to say nothing of the risk of it attacking another person.

"I'll get it myself," Nick said, a statement which was met by stunned silence at the table.

"Well, you can't have it," Jarrod told him. "Tanner will be here tomorrow."

"Who's Tanner?" Nick asked.

"A professional hunter I called yesterday."

"We don't need him. I told you, I'll get the cat myself!"

"Don't be ridiculous, Nick, if you tried in your condition, you'd stand a good chance of pushing a rib through one of your lungs, am I right, Kate?"

"Indeed, you are, Jarrod. That's one a crazy idea, Nick. Leave it to this Mr. Tanner."

Nick passed no more comment on the cat, and the talk at the table turned to other things. The rest of the day, he spent time in his cave, sculpting, so Kate let him be, but Nick was unusually quiet during dinner. *His ribs and those scratches must really be bothering him*, thought Kate. She tried to ask about his pain level, but he just brushed her off. There was no repeat of the nightmare of Saturday.

Monday, Mr. Ed Tanner, the hunter Jarrod had hired, arrived. Heath updated him on the events of Friday and the fact no further sightings had been reported. That evening, the entire family met for dinner with their guest. Nick listened as Tanner outlined his plan to hunt down the rogue cat, passing no comment at all. That night, he didn't even respond when Kate made romantic advances toward him—a first for Nick! *This attack has sure had an adverse effect on him, not just the injuries themselves, but the way he was acting*, she thought. Kate had never known him to behave the way he was doing, it's not like him to be moody or short with her, but considering all he'd been through, she thought it prudent for the moment to leave him alone. He spent most of his time holed up in his man cave, only coming out for meals and to go to bed.

Monday night, although he didn't again have a nightmare, he was very restless and was murmuring something in his sleep she couldn't quite understand. When she asked him about it in the morning, he told her it was nothing, she shouldn't worry, to have a good trip, that he'd see her when she got back, gave her a quick kiss, and left. This behavior was so unlike Nick that Kate was now very concerned. He obviously didn't want to discuss anything. But when she got back, if he was still acting this way, they were going to have a serious talk whether he liked it or not! He was dressed in his ranch work clothes, so she worried that he would overexert himself out with his men and do more damage to his already hurting body. But there wasn't anything she could do about it now. Jarrod was waiting for her in the car, and it was time to leave for the airport.

She and her oldest brother-in-law flew out at eight, he having to get back to his San Francisco office earlier than he had been planned to deal with some minor emergency. After driving to Palo Alto, she checked into the hotel and was given the room the university had booked for her. Having plenty of time on her hands, she went back to looking over her already completed and polished lecture. *Leave it alone,* she told herself, *I'll give Nick a call and see how he's doing.* When she called, it went to his voicemail. *He must either be very busy or out of cell range somewhere on the ranch*, she thought as she left him a message. *He'll call me back later.* She still hadn't heard from him by early evening, but by then, it was time for her to leave for the faculty dinner. *This is not like him at all*, she thought. *He must be extremely busy not to return my call.* When she got back to her room, it was late, and even though there was no message from her husband, she chose not to call Nick in case he was already asleep. *I hope he's not overdoing it! I know how he can get if I don't remind him to take a break.* But she still thought it strange he hadn't at least called to say "good night" or leave her a song. *Maybe he'd forgotten it was his turn! Perhaps he just doesn't want to hear me nagging him not to overdo it when he's hurt*, was the only thing she could think of.

The lecture was very well received, drawing a bigger audience than even members of the faculty had expected. After all the niceties and the lunch the school president insisted on giving her was over, she drove back to the airport in San Francisco. She flew home with Jarrod, who had taken care of the "emergency" in his office and was going back to do some work at the family corporate offices. John sent one of the hands to pick them up. When she asked how Mr. Nick was doing, he replied, "As far as I know, okay."

When they got home, Kate went straight up to the flat to find out why she hadn't heard from her husband since she had left.

"Where is he?" she asked Jeanne.

"Um, well…er…he's not here," was the response.

"Is he over at his office or at the ranch?" Kate asked.

"Um…er…I hate to be the one to…um…tell you but…er…" Just then, the front door phone started buzzing.

"Yes," Kate said answering it.

"We need to talk to you," said Jarrod. When he came in, he was followed by Victoria and Heath. Taking one look at their faces, she knew something was very wrong!

"Oh lord, what's happened to Nick now? Where is he? Is it his ribs? Is he in the hospital? Is that why I couldn't get hold of him? Why didn't one of you call me?"

"Now, Kate, it's nothing like that," Victoria told her.

"Then what is it? Why can't I reach him?"

"He's gone after the cat with Tanner," Heath blurted out.

"WHAT! Has he lost his damn mind? When did he go? Why did you let him go? Why didn't one of you stop him?"

"He waited until you'd left, and I didn't know he'd gone 'til a hand told me," Heath said.

"He was determined to hunt down the cat himself. It was something he said he just had to do," Victoria told her. "Have you ever tried to stop Nick from doing something he was rock solid determined to do?"

"I just can't believe that he'd ignore my advice, but most of all, to wait until I was gone before he went off to do something he knew I would be vehemently against! Whose truck did they take?"

"Not a truck," answered Heath. "You can't track that way. They've gone on horseback, and Tanner had his mount trailered in."

"Bloody hell, do you mean to tell me that fool went on this trip on horseback, he could kill himself! If he punctures a frickin lung and there's no damn medical help it could be fatal! I can't believe Nick cares so bloody little about what we've got that he'd risk it all just to get revenge on a damn stupid mountain lion."

The family and Jeanne just looked at each. They'd never seen Kate look or sound this way before. Her face was white with anger, her eyes looked like two emeralds staring at them, a most unnerving sight!

Oh, Nick, thought his mother. *Now you've really done it. You've crossed a line in the sand with Kate, and now you're going to pay a high price! There will be no sweet talking your way out of this! I always knew, with her red hair and ancestry, that somewhere underneath, very well controlled, was a real Irish temper. Well, she's kept it under wraps for as long as I've known her, but here it comes, and it's all aimed at you, Nick my boy! You'd better look out, but it's not like you don't deserve all that she's going to unleash on you! Just don't come to your mother for sympathy, because you certainly won't be getting any from this quarter. You got yourself into this mess, and you'll have to get yourself out! After all, you've only got yourself to blame!*

Victoria gave a signal, and she, along with her sons, left the apartment, leaving Jeanne unsure of what to do next.

"I'm sure he didn't think—"

Kate cut her off in mid-sentence "That's the whole damn point—he didn't think, he just acted. It was something he wanted to do, so he just bloody well did it with no thought of how it would affect me. Hell, I thought we had moved way beyond that, but I've just been goddamn kidding myself. Oh bloody hell, I'm so frickin angry with him, I don't know what to do. It's like he's pissed away all I thought we'd built on some crazy bloody whim, thinking—if he thought at all—that everything would be frickin the same when he came home. Well, it bloody well frickin' won't!"

After the time Nick had been hurt in the plane crash and technically died, being resuscitated by his wife's screams and touch, Jeanne didn't think anything could ever come between them, but his behavior had affected Kate more deeply than their housekeeper was certain Nick could have imagined. *I'm positive he wouldn't have done this*, she thought. *It must have been him going away after she had left that's got Kate so angry and hurt. I don't blame her though, I'd be pretty pissed off if any man I trusted did that kind of thing to me!*

"Jeanne, do you mind leaving? I've some bloody serious thinking to do, and I'd rather be damn well alone."

"Sure, Kate. Just one thing."

"What's that?"

"Don't do anything while you're so angry. Whatever you decide, sleep on it, and let the light of day help you make sure you've reached the right decision."

"Yes, all right, I'll do that."

Nick, aware that Kate would not be pleased by his absence but totally ignorant of how hurt and angry she in fact was, was having a problem of his own.

He had caught up to Tanner on Tuesday morning. The hunter was not at all happy taking an injured man along.

"This is no place for a man with busted ribs," he had informed Nick. "Go back to the ranch and be sensible!"

"I'm going with you."

"I work alone."

"Well, today you have company."

"Look, Barkley, that cat has been wounded by a man or he wouldn't be attacking like this. Having you along makes a dangerous situation even more so."

"I can handle myself. You don't have to worry about me."

"Go home, you're just a liability."

"I'm going after that cat whether you like it or not."

Tanner looked at him long and hard. "Come on then, let's track cat," Tanner finally said.

They tracked the animal for two days, never once catching sight of it. The riding was tougher on Nick than he would care admit to anyone. His ribs were hurting like hell, but he wasn't about to give up before he got that damn cat.

Although Nick did try to call Kate many times out where they were, there was no signal for their phones. *I know she'll be mad when she gets back from Palo Alto but I'll make it up to her,* he thought.

On the fourth day, after staking out some fresh meat, the cat made its appearance. Before Ed Tanner could get even get to his rifle, Nick had the cat in his sights and brought it down with a single shot.

"I guess it was your cat from the beginning," Tanner conceded, laughing.

"I guess so," said Nick with a huge grin. "Let's go home."

But on the way back Saturday morning, Nick's horse, Big Duke, stumbled in a chuck hole and went down, throwing Nick to the ground. As he struggled to stand up, his companion dismounted and went to find out how badly hurt Nick was.

"Sit down before you fall down while I check out your horse."

Knowing he'd really hurt himself, his ribs feeling worse than when he'd originally broken them, all he could think of was, *Kate's gonna hit the roof when she finds out!*

"I think your horse has pulled a tendon, so he won't be carrying you anywhere for a while. I saw a house a couple of miles back. We'll go there and get some help." Putting Nick on the healthy animal and leading the injured one, Tanner got them to the house.

The couple who lived there came out to meet them. Tanner explained what had happened and how Nick had been hurt. They immediately invited them into their house giving them coffee, food, and Nick a place to rest. The husband told them that there was some spotty cell service in the area. Nick managed to get a call through to the ranch office and asked John to send a double horse trailer and also his Range Rover to take him and Tanner home. They weren't that far from civilization, so it shouldn't take more than a few hours to reach them. Next, he called Kate, but even though it was Saturday, her phone went to voicemail. *I guess she's still mad at me*, he thought. *I'll have to put things right with her when I get back.*

By the time he arrived home, it was dark, but strangely, there were no lights on. In fact, there were no signs of Kate at all. He checked downstairs at the main house, but no one in his family had seen her for days. She hadn't even joined them for dinner on Thursday night, which was so unlike her.

Next, he called Jeanne. "Do you know where my wife is?" he asked.

"She's gone," was the reply.

"Gone? Gone where?" he asked.

"I don't know, she came in from work early Thursday and threw some clothes in a bag," his housekeeper told him. "Then she got in her car and peeled outta here like the proverbial bat outta hell!"

"But she must have given you some idea where she was going?"

"She didn't. And I'm gonna tell you I have never seen her so upset and angry as she's been these past few days since you left, not only going against her medical advice but going behind her back in the stupid and thoughtless way you did," Jeanne informed him. "Leaving when she was out of town and couldn't stop you, how could you do that? I don't care if you get mad at me or not for my plain-speaking, Mr. Nickolas Jonathan Barkley, but that was wrong of you. You hurt your wife deeply, and she doesn't deserve to be treated like that."

He was stunned at what he'd just heard from Jeanne. He had just thought Kate would be mad at him for a little while but soon get over it. That he could talk his way back into her good graces the way he usually did with women. Now he realized his mistake, he had mis-judged Kate's reaction badly and was now obviously paying the price. But where was she? He couldn't begin to imagine. He tried calling her again. Again, it went to voicemail. He left a message telling her he was sorry for what he'd done. If she would just tell him what he could do to make things right, he'd do anything, if she'd only let him know where she was, and that she was okay. He didn't sleep at all that night, worrying about Kate, where she was, and if she was all right!

How could I have been so thoughtless? All I could think of was getting that damn cat. Nothing else seemed to matter! I should have known better. I do know better. I don't know what came over me! She would never have done anything like that to me. She always puts me first. All my talk about us being partners, and then I go and do this! Oh, Kate, just come back. I'll make it up to you. I'll never do anything like this again, I swear. Just give me the chance to prove it to you! Oh, Lord, where has she gone? She couldn't be planning to go back to England, could she? He wrestled with his thoughts all through Sunday, falling into an uneasy sleep that night.

Nick went into his office Monday morning, mainly because he couldn't stand being in the empty silent flat one more minute. There were some problems that Heath was unsure how to deal with that needed Nick's attention. It was almost mid-morning before he had some time to himself to call Kate's phone. Voicemail yet again, he was sure she must be screening her calls. He left yet another message. *I wonder if she's gone to work?* he asked himself. *I'll find out.* He called the emergency department, asking for Dr. Barkley.

"Who should I say is calling?" a voice asked him.

"Tell her it's her husband," he said, holding his breath.

"She says she's busy right now," the voice told him. "Do you want to leave a message?"

"Please tell her I love her and I'll see her tonight."

Well, at least, I know she's safe, he thought. *Now to see if she comes home after her shift.*

He was showered and freshly shaved by six thirty. Jeanne left dinner in the oven. "It will be ready at seven o'clock," she told him. "Just take it out of the main oven and put it in the warming oven to keep it hot until she gets in, if she comes in at all, which, if I may say, you don't deserve!" Reminding Nick how he'd fallen in their housekeeper's estimation and that she was totally siding with Kate! Seven thirty came and went. So did eight thirty, but around nine o'clock, he heard the gate open and Kate's car drive in. He breathed a huge sigh of relief! She came in through the deck door, and without looking at him, went straight into their bedroom, and then he heard the door from the bedroom into the hallway open and close. After a few minutes, he could faintly hear a shower starting to run, but he knew it wasn't theirs. When the shower stopped, he waited until she'd had time to get dressed, but then she didn't come back into the living room. In fact, there was silence in the flat. Puzzled, he went to find out what was going on and was just in time to see the light from under a guest bedroom door go off. He realized she'd used the bathroom attached to the guest bedroom. Obviously, she'd moved out of their master suite completely! He couldn't leave things like this. He had to speak to her, so he knocked on the door.

"What?" she answered tersely.

"Can I come in?"

"No, I'm tired, I need to sleep, just go away."

"Please, Kate, give me a few minutes to explain."

"I'm not interested in hearing your explanation, Nick. Leave me alone."

"Kate, I'm coming in. I won't have you going to sleep like this without us even having a chance to talk."

And with that, he opened the door and went in. Kate put on the bedside lamp; she was wearing PJs, even though he knew it wasn't time for her period. It was her signal to him she definitely wasn't about to have sex with him! All he had wanted to do was put his arms around her, but one look at the expression on his wife's face told him that would be the wrong thing for him to do! Her face was white with anger, her eyes like he'd never seen them before, were not the beautiful loving green ones he knew so well but harsh hard emerald-like glistening orbs staring at him.

"What can I do to make this up to you?" he asked.

"I honestly don't bloody know," she answered him. "Gawd, I never would have believed it damn well possible you'd go behind my frickin' back the way you did. Not only did you ignore my medical advice, but you risked your bloody life doing it! You violated the frickin' trust I had in you, and I don't know how you'll ever damn

362

well get it back. I'm not sure where the frick we go from here, Nick. I must be honest, I've even thought of just packing the hell up and bloody going back to England."

This was worse than he'd imagined. He'd never seen her looking or talking like this! That, plus the fact that she'd even considered calling it quits on them and returning to England, scared the hell out of him. Losing her was unthinkable. What would he do without her? She was his world. How could he have been so thoughtless?

"There must be a way of showing you how sorry I am and to get back to where we were. Kate, I'll do anything. How about we go away would that help?"

"Bloody hell! Do you seriously think if you get me away from here, it'll make it frickin' easier for you to talk me into jumping back in the bloody sack with you so you can screw the hell out of me and that'll make everything all right again? How bloody typical, just like a man! You son of a bitch, go to hell!!"

"No, I most certainly didn't mean it like that. I just meant if we got away from here for a few days, we could really talk, and we'd straighten out this mess and get back to where we used to be. My going to bed with you again, Kate, will be on your terms only, but I don't ever want to hear you refer to my making love to you as 'screwing the hell out of you,' is that clear! I've never used that god-awful term about us sleeping together, and I never will. And I don't think it would be wise for you to ever let my mother hear you call me a son of a bitch!"

"Nick, I'm too bloody tired to have a serious conversation about us tonight. Please leave me alone so I can get some sleep. And I don't give a rat's ass what your mother thinks about what I call you!"

"All right, Kate, if that's the way you want things, I can tell you're not in the mood to discuss anything rationally! So I'll see you in the morning. I love you." There was no reply from his wife as she put out the light.

He closed the door and went back to their empty bed. The only solace he had was she had still used the word *us* when she'd talked about them.

The next morning, she didn't have anything to say to him as she poured herself a cup of coffee and got her jacket.

"I'll see you tonight," he said to her, but all he got was a nod in response. This time, Kate got home at her usual seven thirty, and they ate the dinner left over from the previous evening. Nick did the talking, Kate, if she answered at all, was in mono symbols.

After days of this kind behavior on her part, and her still sleeping in the guestroom, Nick couldn't take it any longer. Friday was Kate's day off and he was determined to put an end to the kind of stalemate they were in. When Kate got up, Jeanne, who should have been there was nowhere to be seen; instead, Nick was leaning up against a counter in the kitchen drinking coffee. Knowing he normally went to work in the office or down at the ranch about seven o'clock, and as it was now going on eight thirty, she wondered what was going on, and more to the point, what was he up to!

"Sit down, Kate. I'll get you some coffee," he told her firmly. "We are going to talk this out and get to a resolution, no matter how long it takes us. I've given Jeanne the day off so we won't be disturbed." She sat down passing no comment.

"You've given me the silent treatment these past few days, but apart from making life a living a hell for me, it's done nothing toward resolving our problems. Now I want you to explain to me how we are going to move forward. I've already told you I'll do whatever you want, trouble is, I'm not sure you know what that is! So please start talking, Kate, now's your chance to tell me what a horse's ass I've been and how much I hurt you. I've already gotten an earful from Mother and Jeanne. so have at it. It can't be any worse than the things I've already said to myself!"

Kate continued to drink her coffee and sit there in stony silence.

I'm just not getting through to her, Nick thought. *It's as though she's built a wall around herself and I don't know how to break through.* The silence continued for the next few minutes! *What do I do next? I'm almost at my wits end. I just don't know what else to say*, were the thoughts racing through Nick's head.

Kate got up and went into the kitchen to get more coffee. Whilst she was there, she started to put on a fresh pot. *I've tried everything else, so why not this,* Nick thought as he moved over to stand behind his wife. Before she realized what he was doing, he had slipped his hands around her waist and started to kiss her neck, something she normally thoroughly enjoyed and encouraged him to do.

"DON'T!" she said angrily, moving away from him. Her reaction came like a bucket of ice water in the face to Nick. He took this to mean she couldn't tolerate his kiss or even his slightest touch. This got to him the way nothing else had, after all the very intimate times they'd shared, now she didn't even want him to lay a hand on her!

"What do you want me to do, get down on my knees and beg? Is that what you expect from me?" He asked, stung and confused by Kate's reaction to his romantic advances. "If it is, don't hold your breath waiting for it to happen!"

"Don't be ridiculous, Nick. Just leave me alone."

"And if I do, what then, we go on like this with you barely speaking to me and sleeping in the guestroom? How much more of this do you think I can take? I'm a flesh and blood, very healthy male who has a lot of testosterone, married to a beautiful and very desirable woman, and I've gotten used to having certain of my needs met, and you know exactly what I mean! Kate, how do we start over, or have you decided that we don't? Is that it, have you given up on me? Is what I did so terrible in your eyes that I can't make it right with you? Don't I have any say in the matter? Don't I deserve that much? What about the times we've shared together in bed and out, don't they count for anything? Are you seriously planning on going back to England? Why won't you give us another chance? I think we deserve that much. Talk to me, damn it, say something, Kate. Will you please say something to me?!"

"What you did has made me damn well question all that I thought we had in our marriage because I was under the bloody impression we had a partnership, that you led me to believe you'd never frickin' do anything without first talking it over with me. That my goddamn opinion really mattered to you, and that you'd never bloody do anything which would deliberately hurt me. But the moment my damn back was turned, you went off and did something that not only went against my medical advice but could have cost you your frickin' life! Don't you realize, you goddamn fool, if you'd punctured a frickin' lung, miles away from help, with no way to call for bloody medical aid, you'd be dead by now? You had planned all this before I damn well left, and you let me frickin go out of town knowing what you were bloody going to do. I was so worried when I couldn't get hold of you while I was in Palo Alto, imaging all kinds of terrible things that might bloody have happened. When, in fact, you were chasing all over the bloody countryside on horseback after a frickin' damn stupid cat! And you have the goddamn frickin' nerve to want everything to go back to 'normal!' Well, the truth is, Nick Barkley, you scared the hell out of me knowing what could have happened to you, but you don't seem to give a goddamn about doing that! So to answer your questions, hell, I'm not sure you've left us with enough of a bloody relationship after what you did, to do any-thing with, and if you have, do I really want to bloody put in the effort to save us? Right now, Nick, I'm so frickin' pissed off at you I can hardly think straight. Do you bloody understand what I've just said?"

"Yes I do. I'm sorry, Kate. I never fully realized what the con-sequences of my actions would be and that what I did would upset you like this. But can we please have a conversation with you not swearing like you're doing? It's most undignified and not a bit liked you, and quite frankly, I abhor hearing you talk like that! So to get back to the subject of 'us,' tell me what happens now?"

"I don't know."

"Aren't you willing to give me another chance?"

"I just don't know, Nick, I'm so tired, I've hardly been sleeping, so I'm going to lay down. I'm sorry I can't give you a better answer. And as to my language, I'll talk anyway I want, I don't care if you like it or not, so you can just kiss my bloody frickin' ass! And in any case, just so you know, living with you would make a Catholic saint swear!" And with that, she went back to the guest bedroom she'd been using, slamming doors behind her!

I can't hang around here or I'll lose my mind, Nick thought. *I'm going to saddle Big Duke and go for a long ride to try and clear my head, I don't care how much it hurts my ribs!* He wrote Kate a note telling

366

her what he was doing and that he had decided he wouldn't be back until morning. He took along beef jerky, bottles of water, a flask of coffee, and a bedroll so he could spend the night out on the range. He couldn't face one more night alone in their bed, which felt so big and empty without the love of his life lying in his arms.

When Kate woke up, she found his note. *Oh Lordy, what a bloody mess we're in*, she thought. Just then, the front door phone buzzed, it was her mother-in-law, bringing the mail which had been delivered to the main house instead of the flat. Victoria knew that her son and his wife were still at odds. She'd seen Nick the day before and could tell by his demeanor and lack of humor that Kate still hadn't forgiven him.

"Do you want to talk?" she asked her daughter-in-law. "I know you and Nick are having problems, but maybe if you were to use me as a sounding board, it might help."

"Things have gotten so bad between us that I've been thinking of packing up and returning to England," Kate confided, and with that, she told Victoria all that had just passed between herself and Nick."

"I had no idea the situation between you two had deteriorated to this level," said Victoria. "The only question I have is, do you still love him?"

Kate thought for a few moments. "I'm just not sure."

"Things are really bad if that's your answer, because it is all that really matters."

"There are so many issues like trust to be dealt with now."

"That's where I think you're wrong, Kate. I believe it comes down to only one thing," said her mother-in-law softly.

"Which is?"

"Do you still love him?"

Kate thought for a few minutes more. "I suppose so."

"There is no suppose about it. Either you do or you don't. Which one is it?" Victoria asked her daughter-in-law, pressing her even harder for an answer. "Do you still love Nick?"

Kate thought a little longer and, giving a little sigh, said, "Right now, it's something I really don't want to admit to, but yes, I still love him."

"Enough to forgive him and move on?" asked Victoria. "Because neither of you can go on living the way you are. I know he's truly sorry, and I believe he's learned his lesson and will never do anything like that again. What is it that's preventing you from forgiving Nick and stop punishing him? Are you going to let your pride that he went against your medical advice come between you and the wonderful marriage that you and he had up to a few days ago? Is it so important to you to continue to punish Nick for going after the cat behind your back that you're willing to throw away all that you've both built over the one stupid decision he made?"

"Is that the way it looks to you?"

"I think you've got to come to a decision and quickly. What's more important to you, Kate? Choosing to let go of the hurt—which I completely understand Nick caused by his actions but won't keep you warm in bed at night, and that means completely forgiving him—or saying goodbye to Nick and your marriage and all you and he have shared together by your continued insistence to sleep alone. He's way too much of a virile man to put up with that for much longer. You know what I'm trying to tell you, Kate, you'll have to reconcile or make your separation permanent and one of you move out of the flat!"

"Doesn't anyone understand it wasn't just what Nick did, it was the implications behind his actions! What he's said to me about always considering what I think doesn't mean anything, so nothing he has ever promised me means anything. Why doesn't anyone see that!"

"Yes, I can understand your frustration, but Nick didn't foresee the effect what he did would have on you and his every thought and action, so you have to understand his point of view!" And with that, Victoria left the flat, leaving Kate to think over everything that her mother-in-law had said.

Nick, by not coming home that night, gave Kate more time to be alone with her thoughts. He returned early Saturday morning, hoping that what he was walking back into was different, but it seemed to him nothing had changed, and he felt totally helpless, not knowing what to do next. Kate, coming into the living room with her coffee, nodded in his direction but was just as silent as she had been before he'd left. She proceeded to sit down on the sofa and began doing some work on her laptop. More of the same silent treatment, he thought standing in the kitchen. *What is it she wants from me, what should I do next?* He was a man used to action. Not knowing what to do next was new to him, and he didn't like the way it made him feel.

Kate got a phone call. *Obviously about a patient,* he thought, judging by her end of the conversation. She talked for a few moments, and when she was through with the call, she got up to get a refill.

"How much longer are you going to keep this up?" he finally asked as she poured herself more coffee, standing in the kitchen just inches away from him. All he wanted to do was scoop her up in his arms and hold her, but remembering what happened the last time he tried that and the response she had given him, he resisted the urge.

"Have you made a decision where we go from here? Because I can't take much more of you keeping me at arm's length. I'm not going to have my wife sleeping in a guest room for much longer, and all that it says about us as a couple! The way I see it, married people either sleep in the same bed or I don't see how they can call themselves married! I've told you, I'll do anything to make it up to you, but the way I see it, you won't even meet me halfway! So there's a horse auction in San Diego that Brahma is going to, and now I've decided I'll go along with him. I'll leave first thing in the morning and be gone a week, maybe even longer. I'm sure having me out of the way will make things easier for you for a while!"

"You still don't get it, do you? It wasn't just you going after the cat! That action colors everything you've ever promised me. What else have you said that you'll thoughtlessly change whenever you feel like it? It isn't a partnership when one of us can change the rules arbitrarily."

Nick's cellphone rang, it was Victoria. "I'm sorry, Mother, I won't be able to do that for you tomorrow. I'm leaving town for a week or so. Yes, I'm going to the horse auctions in San Diego. Yes, it's a last-minute decision. Brahma is going, and I just decided I'd go with him, I'm sure Heath can help you. Yes, Kate knows I'm going, why? Okay, I'll see you when I get back." He went into the bedroom to pack his things for the trip. He was only in there a few minutes when the buzzer at the front door sounded. Kate answered.

"Of course, come in. Nick, it's your mother, she wants to talk with you."

"Yes, Mother."

"Well, as you are going out of town and will miss family dinner on Thursday, and seeing neither of you could make it this past Thursday, I've talked to everyone, and we're going to have the dinner tonight, so I'll expect the two of you at seven thirty sharp."

"Er...Mother, I don't think a family dinner tonight is a very good idea."

"Now give me one good reason why not?"

"Look, Mother, it's just not—"

"Just because you and Kate can't get along doesn't mean we can't sit down as a family and eat together. Like I said, I'll expect you both at seven thirty." Before they could offer any further argument, Victoria left the flat.

"I'm sorry about that, Mother's just being Mother."

"I have no intention of going tonight. Tell your mother whatever you like." She picked up her mug and laptop and went onto the deck to continue the work on the paper she was writing.

Nick finished packing his bags and, bringing them out of the bedroom, left them by the door to the deck.

Jeanne called to see if Kate wanted her to bring them up a couple of quiches she'd just made.

"That would be nice, thank you." When their housekeeper came up with the food, she nearly tripped over the bags lying just inside the door.

"Is someone going away?"

"Nick is going to some horse auction."

"Kind of last minute isn't it?"

"I guess so."

"Are you two still not speaking?"

"Stay out of it, Jeanne."

"You can't let him go with things the way they are between the two of you. Is that the reason he's leaving?"

Just then, Nick came out of the bedroom. "Hello, Jeanne, what have you got there?"

"I made you and Kate quiches for lunch, or maybe even dinner."

"Not tonight, it's one of mother's family dinners."

"Oh, that'll be interesting with you two not speaking. Does your mother know about that situation?"

"I told you to stay out of it, Jeanne," said Kate with a defiant edge to her voice.

"Excuse me! I better go and leave you two lovebirds alone! Maybe you'll be able to work things out before you have to go to dinner!" said Jeanne sarcastically.

Kate went back to her work on the laptop, and Nick decided to go down to the stables. She ate lunch alone and at about five, went back to the guest room she was using. Tired, she laid down and promptly fell asleep. She was awoken by a knock on the door. She glanced at her phone, it was just after seven.

"Yes," she said.

"Are you going to the dinner?"

"I told you this morning no."

"Can I come in?"

"If you must."

"I thought you might have changed your mind. You've still got time to get dressed."

"I said I'm not going."

"Okay, I'll pass along your regrets. By the way, I do understand what you said earlier about my going back on everything I've ever told you, and I can promise you that won't happen. I think you're reading way too much into this isolated incident! But if that's the way you're intent on seeing things, there's obviously nothing I can do to change your mind. So in case I don't get to see you in the morning, I'll just say goodbye now. I'll be gone at least a week, maybe ten days. Call me if you need anything, otherwise we'll attempt to talk again

371

when I get back. Take care of yourself, Kate, I do love you." And with that, he shut the door, and she could hear his footsteps receding down the hallway.

That night, for the first time since she was a little girl, she cried herself to sleep. She woke up about five and knew she wasn't going to be able to get back to sleep. She quietly got up and went into the kitchen, taking her laptop with her. Nick had programmed the coffee pot to start brewing at seven, later than the normal time because he and Brahma weren't leaving until about nine. She overrode the timer and pressed brew. Taking her computer and a mug of coffee, she went out onto the deck to work on a paper she was hoping to have published, but she couldn't concentrate, knowing she had a big decision to make. Nick was leaving in a few hours, and they still hadn't resolved their problems. What was standing in the way of her forgiving him and them moving on? She thought over all that her mother-in-law had said to her. How had the situation gotten this far out of hand? All she wanted him to do was take her in his arms and hold her tight, but she knew that wasn't going to happen! She remembered how she had behaved the last time he'd tried that and the shocked look on his face when she'd rejected his advances. Nick was a proud man. He wouldn't give her the chance to treat him like that a second time. As she sat there, she reached a decision, not knowing that she had been watched by him for quite a few minutes, but suddenly hearing a slight sound, she turned around to see Nick standing in the open doorway with a mug of coffee in his hand.

"I'm sorry, I didn't mean to wake you," she said.

"I could smell the coffee and came to find out what was going on at five a.m. on a Sunday morning."

"Couldn't sleep, so I came out to work on a paper I hope to have published in the AMA journal."

"Do you know that's the most you've said to me in days since you gave me the lecture about the consequences of my actions!"

"Excuse me, it's kind of chilly out here. I should go back inside." She brushed past him and went into the living room with her computer and mug and sat down on the sofa.

"Kate, please don't shut me out again," he said in an exasperated tone. "Let me ask you one question—do you want me to go to San Diego or not?"

Silence was the answer.

"It's a simple question with a simple answer. Do you want me to go out of town? Yes or no?"

Once again, her silence filled the room. After a few minutes, she spoke, "Nick I've been thinking, and I've reached a decision. I was going to call you in San Diego because I didn't think I'd see you this morning. But as you're here, I as may as well tell you in person."

His blood ran cold. He was sure he knew what she was going to say and wanted to head her off from actually saying it.

"Kate, don't make any decisions now. Give yourself time while I'm away to really think about what you want to do."

"It's no use. I've thought and thought, and I'm not being fair to you by just prolonging the inevitable, so by the time you get back from San Diego, I'll be gone."

"Then I won't leave town."

"Don't make it harder on either of us, Nick. Please just go and give me a chance to clear out my things. What I don't take with me, I'll have Jeanne donate. Most of my clothes carry too many memories for me to take them. I'd rather just start out fresh."

"I can't believe one stupid act on my part has brought us to the point where you are about to throw away what I was under the distinct impression was one of the happiest marriages I've ever heard of. Think about what you're doing, Kate!"

"Don't you think I have? That's all I have been doing. I don't know why I just can't forget the entire thing and move on, but I can't."

"But you fought so hard to save me when you thought I'd died, you said we were two halves of a whole. What's happened since then?"

"Nick, I wish I knew."

"What does it take to get you to change your mind? Be prepared, I'll fight for you with everything I've got, you'll be surprised how far my reach is."

"That's why I'm not telling you where I'm going. In fact, I'm not sure myself."

"Just as long as it's away from me, that's what you're saying, isn't it?"

"I didn't mean it like that, Nick."

"Have we gotten so far apart that you are going to leave and not at least tell me where you are so I'll know you're all right? Kate, how can you do this?"

"I knew I should have just left it and called you when you were away. I didn't want my telling you to hurt you any worse than I already have. I'm so sorry, I didn't mean for us to end like this."

"I go off and chase a stupid cat without you knowing about it, and the result is it's costing me my marriage. Now, does that seem logical to you? Because, to me, it's nothing short of crazy. I don't see why you can't accept my apology and let us move on past this. Is there something else going on that you haven't told me about? Is there someone else? That's it, isn't it? You've found someone else?"

"No, no, there's nothing else going on, and there's definitely no one else. I can't deal with the man I've got. You'd think I'd be fool enough to get involved with another one! I never said it made sense. It doesn't to me! Now I'll get out of your way until you leave." And with that, she picked up her things and headed for the guest room she was using.

A little after nine, she opened the door from the hallway and looked at the deck door. Nick's bags were gone. She breathed a sigh of relief, he had gone to San Diego with Brahma. She'd feared that, at the last minute, he might change his mind and stay. It was far better this way, now she could go back in their bedroom to sort out her clothes without fear of running into him.

But first, she had to sit down and compose a letter of immediate resignation. She didn't like doing it this way, but couldn't stay and work out any kind of notice without running the risk of seeing Nick again. She went to get some coffee and took it along with her computer out to the deck and sat in what was usually Nick's chair with her back to the door.

She spent time trying to compose a letter of resignation in such a way that her personal life was kept out of it, which proved an impossibility. *Back to square one. If I can't keep my personal life out of the letter completely, then at least to a bare minimum.* That didn't work either. Letter number three contained a few more references to her personal life in regards as to why she was resigning her position at the hospital, much better. She spent time polishing the final draft and then sent it to Victoria Barkley, the new chairperson of the board of directors. Only on her say so in her new official position could Kate send copies to the rest of the board and Dr. Greene.

She didn't get an answer via email from Victoria. Instead, a loud buzzing from the front door. *Like I can't guess who this is,* she thought! She buzzed her mother-in-law in, who came barreling into the living room waving a print out of the email in her hand.

"This can't be a joke because it's not your sort of humor. So would you mind explaining exactly what this means?"

"I would have thought it's self-explanatory—it's a letter of resignation effective immediately. I would have liked to have given at least two weeks' notice, but owing to pressing personal issues, I have to leave Stockton this coming week."

"You're leaving Nick?"

"Yes, ma'am."

"I thought when we talked it was all resolved."

"No, Mrs. Barkley, you lectured, I listened."

"I'm sorry if you thought I was lecturing you. I thought I'd given you some practical tips for marriage."

"What you told me was how to 'stay warm in bed at night' and 'to stop punishing Nick for the hurt he had inflicted.' Hardly 'how to' gems, if I may say so!"

"I'm sorry that's all you got out of our conversation. But to leave Nick and throw over a job which you appear to really enjoy just when the hospital is nearing trauma one status is very serious. Nick is beside himself with worry. He doesn't know what to say or do! I understand from your email you are leaving this week?"

"Yes, I'll start going through my things tomorrow. What I don't take with me, I'll have Jeanne donate. I have lots of clothes that hold too many memories, so they'll be quite a few boxes to go.

"Kate, you can't do this. You're destroying both of your lives over what amounts to one stupid mistake on Nick's part. But now you'll be guilty of an even bigger mistake if you leave him. I don't know if I've told you before, but in all my years, I've never seen a man as much in love with a woman as that son of mine is with you. Doesn't that count for anything with you?"

"It just makes what I know I have to do that much harder. You should be telling me he'll be well rid of me, that he'll soon get over me and move on. I can't talk about it anymore, Mrs. Barkley, my minds made up. If that email has your approval, I'd like to send it to the board and Dr. Greene."

"Tell you what I'll do. I will send out the emails. I want to put a personal note on them, and you seem to have a lot to do."

"Oh, that would be wonderful, and one less thing for me to do. You're sure you don't mind?"

"No problem at all. Well, I guess this is goodbye, Kate. I must tell you, you were all I could have asked for in a daughter-in-law, and you did make my son so very happy. I will truly miss you, my dear." She gave Kate a quick hug and left.

"How could I make her son happy when I'm leaving him?" Kate said out loud. *It would be nice to leave with the chance of one last article published in the AMA journal, and I'm so close to finishing. I'm going to spend the next couple of hours on it*, she thought. She put another pot of coffee on and settled down at the table on the deck in Nick's chair and set to work. Except for getting up for more coffee, she worked steadily for the next two hours. *Almost there*, she thought. *I'm going to stay with it and finish it and send it in this afternoon. That will be another thing taken care of.* She realized she was hungry. Looking at her watch, it was getting on for lunchtime. *I'll just grab a slice of quiche to keep me going*, she thought and went into the kitchen. Getting the pie out of the fridge, she turned around, and standing not eighteen inches in front of her, was Nick! She almost dropped the quiche in shock!

"I thought you went to San Diego this morning?"

"I decided not to leave until later in the week."

"Where have you been all morning?"

"At the stables and then downstairs, talking with Mother. I'd just come up here when I heard you in the kitchen."

She got her food and went back outside.

"I can move if you want your seat back?"

"No, stay where you are. I'll sit in the other chair."

Nick had brought a bottle of rye whiskey and a glass out with him. He broke the seal on the bottle and proceeded to pour one glass after another. Kate could feel his eyes almost constantly on her, which made her feel very uncomfortable, something Nick had never done in the past, but this was a different Nick, one that she didn't know. She'd heard stories about Nick being a "two-fisted drinker," but never, since they'd met, had she ever seen any evidence of it except that one time on their honeymoon! At long last, her article was complete. Now, all she had to do was write a cover letter and she was done. She stood up to stretch and fetch another mug of coffee.

"Sit down, I'll get it for you." He brought the coffee and put it down on the table in front of her. "Shoulders tight? Let me help." And before she could say or do anything, he put his hands on her and started massaging her shoulders and neck just the way he knew she liked him to.

"Please, Nick, please don't do that. Stop it now, please, I'm begging you."

"That's right, I'm not allowed to touch you anymore, who is he, Kate? Who have I been replaced by?" He sat down, picked up his glass, and started drinking again.

Unsure of how to deal with Nick in this kind of mood, which she'd never seen before, Kate picked up her things and took them inside, leaving them on the coffee table. She went into the bedroom she was using and called Victoria. "I need your help."

"What's wrong?"

"He broke open a bottle of rye about an hour ago and he's drunk a third of it already, and there's no sign he's going to stop. What do I do?"

"Kate, this is all your fault, Nick's your husband, you deal with him." And with that, Victoria hung up on her!

Oh, great, she thought. *He's going on a bender and it's my fault. Well, to hell with that. He wants to drink, let him drink!* She went back to the living room, wrote the cover letter, and sent it and the article to the journal.

"I take it you're going to drink all afternoon, so I'm going to take a slice of quiche with me and go in my room."

"Don't go yet, Kate, I could use the company, I really hate to drink alone. I could open a bottle of champagne for you, and you could celebrate dumping a husband! I'd just like to know who you're replacing me with. Who is he, Kate?"

"Nick, I've told you before, there is no one else, and I'm certainly not celebrating anything, least of all us splitting up. Please stop drinking, I'll stay out here with you for a little while if you'll just please stop the drinking."

"Why do you care if I drink or not?"

"I just hate to see you do this to yourself."

"I repeat, why?"

"Because I've never seen you like this before, and I'd hate to think you're doing this because of me."

"I'm losing the love of my life, you little fool. I'm gonna drink today and every day in the foreseeable future. Of course it's your fault, who else should I blame? You say you've never seen me like this before? Well, I've never had a reason to drink like this since I met you, why would I? I had everything in the world I wanted with you, but now you tell me you're leaving and taking my world with you, so what do I have left? Nothing, absolutely nothing. What do you care if I drink? Well, why do you care? Answer me, damn it."

"Nick, of course, I care what you do to yourself. You've got the family business to run, you can't do that drunk."

"The family business! I don't give a damn about it. Let somebody else worry about it! My wife is leaving me because I screwed up and went after the damn cat that attacked me. Can you believe it? That's all I did wrong and it's costing me my marriage! Other men have affairs and are forgiven, but all I did was hurt my wife's pride over one lousy cat and I get kicked to the curb. Go figure." By now, Nick had finished more than half the bottle of rye and was still steadily drinking.

"I can't stay and watch this any longer. I'm going to bed."

"That's right, run away, you're good at that, aren't you, Kate? Things get rough, and off you go and leave me."

"I'm sorry."

"You're sorry? Is that all you can say? You're sorry. You're destroying our lives, and all you can say is you're sorry."

"What do you want me to say, Nick?"

"What I want is for you to say is this has all been a nightmare that I'm gonna wake up from and we'll be back the way we used to be, that's what I want."

"I wish I could."

"So what's stopping you?"

"Nick, we've been over this so many times."

"And we'll keep going over this 'til it makes some sense. I love you, Kate, please don't do this."

By now, he had finished almost three-quarters of the bottle.

"Please stop drinking."

"Why should I?"

"This conversation is going around in circles. I'm going to my room."

"It's not your room, it's a guest room. Your bedroom is in there with me, but that's right, I'm not allowed to touch you now, am I? That's not what you said less than two weeks ago when we couldn't get enough of each other! What's that look for? You don't like being reminded of that?"

"That was a whole other world away."

"Yes, back when you still wanted me to take you to bed!"

"Enough, Nick. What will it take to get you to stop drinking?"

"How about we make love?"

"Don't be ridiculous!"

"Well, you wanted to know, so I'm telling you."

"Nick, I'm leaving you."

"So you say. Kate, do you realize this is the longest we've talked in two weeks?"

"You're drunk."

"And whose fault is that?"

Kate went storming out to the guest room, slamming the door. Nick just chuckled. *I'm sure getting under her skin, and she doesn't like it,* he thought to himself. *Now what else can I do,* he wondered. *I know,* and he went to the music unit and put on the CD she had made for him and turned up the volume. Within seconds, the opening bars of the "Twelfth Of Never" could be heard throughout the flat. Minutes later, he heard her rushing down the hallway. She burst into the living room.

"Turn that blasted thing off," she yelled at him.

"No, I won't, it's mine. I'll play it if I want to. The woman who used to love me recorded it especially for me. It's just the thing to play to get drunk to."

"How could you be so insensitive?"

"Me, insensitive? That's a laugh. Take a good long look at yourself, young woman!" And he started to sing the next track. "I left my heart in San Francisco." If Kate was mad before, now, she was seething! He played the CD through in its entirety three times in succession. *We'll see what tomorrow brings, lady, I have only just begun to fight to keep you,* he planned.

What Nick did as his CD played was write down what Kate had said to him directly during each track.

Twelfth Of Never, I need you like roses need rain, I'll love you till the Twelfth Of Never.

I didn't just give you my heart in San Francisco I gave you myself completely.

How did I live before till now, I don't know.

Islands In The stream, in love forever.

I'm Just Another Woman In Love, I tremble at your name.

You Made Me Love You, you have the kind of kisses I'd die for.

Yours, I never loved anyone the way I love you how could I when I was born to be just yours.

Till you are my reason to live.

My Own True Love, at last I've found you.

You'll Never Know if you don't know now how much I love you.

Power Of Love, I'm your lady and you are my man.

Why Did I Choose You, I lost my heart willingly and lovingly to you.

First Time Ever I Saw Your Face I thought the sun rose in your eyes.

You're My World, if our love ceases to be then it's the end of my world for me.

As I Love You, every kiss from you to me all ways seems so new to me each one warmer than the one before as I love you more and more and more.

My darling Kate, as I play the tracks on the CD you recorded for me, I put down a brief note of what I think you were saying to me at that time. Perhaps if you read this it will give you some perspective of what you felt for me only a short time ago!

He put the note in an envelope and pushed it under her door. That night after reading it, Kate cried herself to sleep!

The next morning, after going back to giving him the silent treatment over breakfast, Kate got two pieces of her luggage out of the hall closet. She went into the master bedroom after first announcing to Nick, who was standing in the kitchen, what she is doing. He followed her into their room with a smile on his face. *What's he up to now?* she wondered. She set about packing her bags with the basics in clothes. All the time, Nick sat on the bed, watching her every move.

"Get my note?"

"Yes."

"Did it help you any?"

"It just confused an already confusing situation," she told him.

"You said all those things to me just a short while ago, you can't have changed your feelings for me so quickly, can you, Kate?"

"Nick, I'm not talking about it anymore. Now I have to get back to my packing."

"Not taking very much, are you?"

"I'll buy anything else I need when I get there."

"Which is where, or am I still not to know where you're going?"

She ignored him, going to the safe and opening it, she started rummaging inside.

"Where's my passport?" she asked him.

"How would I know it's your passport?"

"Have you taken it?"

"Me?"

"You son of a bitch, you're enjoying this, aren't you? Never mind, I'm sure I can get another one on some kind of an emergency basis from the embassy in DC."

As he watched, she took off her engagement and wedding rings, then the diamond lariat pendant and, lastly, removed the matching earrings which Nick had bought her on their honeymoon, and put them all on the dresser. He had not been expecting her to do this, and the smile faded from his face.

"You're not getting this back, if that's what you were hoping for," he said as he fingered his own platinum-braided wedding ring. "You put this wedding band on my finger as you made promises to me, and that was after you took your vows. No matter what happens to us, I'll wear this forever!"

"I don't give a rat's ass what you do with it. I'm leaving."

Knowing it was pointless to ask him to help, she made two trips down the stairs as she toted her bags to her car but was back up again in a few minutes.

"Okay, what have you done to my bloody car?"

"Why, what's wrong with it?"

"You damn well know what's wrong with it. It won't friggin' start!"

"Must be the starter motor. I'll have to get it towed into the shop."

"I don't suppose you'd loan me your truck?"

"You suppose right."

Next, she called John. "Could you please give me a ride to the airport? WHAT? NICK SAID WHAT? Thank you anyway. I understand it's not your fault!" She had gone from scarlet with temper to white with rage!

"You told John that no one on this damned ranch or in the offices is allowed to give me any help or a bloody ride, and if they do, you'll fire their asses. Who do you think you frigging well are?" she yelled at him. "And wipe that stupid ass grin off your face."

"Well, first of all, I'm the 'frigging' boss, and the men and women who work for me will obey my orders if they want to keep their jobs, and second, I find your attempts to leave me rather humorous. I told you it wouldn't be easy."

"I'm calling a taxi. Why do you think that's so bloody funny?"

"No reason. Go ahead make your phone call, Kate."

She called a taxi and waited and waited, but it didn't show up. So she called the company back, only to be told the cab had tried to come out but was turned away when it reached Barkley land. The driver was told the private road was closed to all traffic.

"How bloody dare you try to keep me a prisoner?" she ranted.

"I told you I'd fight to stop you leaving me with everything I have, and as you're finding out, I have lots of ways to fight."

"So you're going to keep me here against my friggin' will, is that it?"

"No you can start walking, I keep telling you it's only ten miles to the highway."

"That is bloody crazy."

"No crazier than your reason for leaving me in the first place."

She stormed out of the living room. Let's see how long she can put up with this, he mused, and he put on "their CD." The sound of "The Lady In Red" filled the flat.

"How dare you!" she screamed at him from the doorway. He just ignored her outburst and instead answered the knock on the deck door. It was John with a case of rye whiskey which had just been delivered.

"You're buying it by the case now?" she yelled at him, the only way to make herself heard over the volume of the music.

"Didn't want to run out," he yelled back.

"You're impossible!"

He played "their" CD all day with the volume set at loud, so she kept up the silent treatment with him. They were back to stalemate.

Jeanne came into work the next day. "Is England still having diplomatic difficulties with the Colonies?" she asked. "You know something, you're the most passionate couple I've ever met. Your reconciliations must be the most epic to behold!"

Kate said, "There'll be no reconciliation this time, passionate or otherwise. I'm through with him, and more to the point, what the hell happened to you yesterday?"

"Nick gave me the day off, and no one has told him about no more epic making up sessions!"

Kate ignored her comment and instead asked her, "Now that you're here, will you please give me a ride to the airport?"

"No, I sided with you when you started all this. I thought you were right to teach Nick a lesson for the way he behaved, but you've carried things way too far. I wouldn't be a friend to you if I told you anything different."

"Don't you start."

"Why don't you two just kiss and enjoy your reconciling, if you know what I mean!"

"Jeanne, please knock it off, I don't know how to turn back. I've gone so far down this road. What the hell is wrong with me? It's all gotten so out of hand, and I don't know how to put it right."

"It's not me you should be saying all this to. Hasn't he tried every which way he knows to tell you he loves you? Why won't you admit that you still love him? Is that so very hard?"

"For no very good reason, yes it is, he'll be much better off without me."

"Is that why he's hitting the bottle?"

"Who told you that?"

"John told me Nick is buying rye by the case. That's hardly a sign of a happy man!"

"If I could just get out of here, he'd adjust. I've put him through hell, and the longer I'm here, the worse it's going to be for him."

"Try telling him that, most men would have given up on you by now, but not him, and he won't hear a word said against you! Now I'm going to make some sandwiches, and there's potato salad in the fridge. He said he'd be home for lunch."

"Then I better make myself scarce."

When Nick came in for lunch, he asked Jeanne where Kate was.

"She's hiding out in the guest room."

"Did she ask you for a ride? I don't know how much longer I can keep her here, I made her cellphone disappear this morning, and I don't think she's even noticed. She's just going to wait me out Maybe I should just give up and let her go."

"Don't you dare do that. I detected a distinct chink in her armor this morning! Hang on, Nick. I don't think it'll be much longer before she'll be back in your arms again."

"Do you really think so?"

"I'm sure of it."

About an hour later, Kate came into the living room.

"Has he gone?"

"What, can't face him now? Not so sure you should be leaving him, huh? Think if you see him you'll change your mind and fall into his arms?"

"What nonsense. Have you seen my cell phone? I've looked all over and can't find it. NICK!!! I bet he's taken it! He just won't give up."

"Are you sure you want him to?"

"Don't start that again." Kate didn't have anything special to do that afternoon, so she tried to concentrate on a movie whilst keeping an ear open for the sound of Nick coming up the steps. But instead, he came in through the front door, so she didn't know he was in the flat until he walked into the living room.

"Have you seen my cellphone, or has that disappeared into the black hole like my passport?"

"Don't know what you're talking about."

"I'll just bet you don't!"

"Is the silent treatment over for the day?" he asked as he got a fresh bottle of rye and a glass and sat down near to her on the couch.

"If you intend to drink your dinner, I'll leave you to it," she said as she stood up to leave.

"What, can't face me now, or are you having second thoughts about leaving me?"

"Have you been talking to Jeanne? No, that can't be right. That conversation was after you left."

"I saw her at lunchtime when I came home to eat and you were nowhere to be found. Why? What did you two talk about after I left?"

"Nothing, just something you said sounded very familiar. Nick, when are you going to stop this game and let me go?"

"GAME?! Is that what this is to you? A DAMN GAME? HOW DARE YOU, KATE!" Nick shouted. She was so startled. He had never shouted like that at her before! She took off down the hall and into the bedroom she'd been using.

Nick went onto the deck to cool off just as Jeanne was coming up the stairs.

"What's wrong, boss? You look upset."

"I yelled at Kate. I've never raised my voice to her like that before today, but she got me so damn mad with something she said."

"Well, it's about time! You've been letting her call all the shots. I was wondering when you were going to wise up and give her a taste of her own medicine!"

"What do you mean?"

"It was one thing to let you know how unhappy she was with you for what you did, leaving town and going after the cat, but now she's just plain gotten out of hand! Personally, I think it's a wonder you haven't turned her over your knee and paddled that cute little ass of hers! It's high time you tried some stuff on Kate, like giving her the silent treatment, and how about really standing up to her!"

"I never thought of that!"

"What, paddling her ass, the silent treatment, or standing up to her?"

"Any of them, but I'll start with the silent treatment and getting under her skin a lot more than I've been doing. I'll leave paddling her, what did you call it, cute little ass as a last resort!"

"You know your problem, you don't have a devious enough mind to think as a woman! Just remember, Nick, no more telling her you love her, no more Mr. Nice Guy. From now on, it's war!"

"Kate, dinner is ready."

"I'm not very hungry, Jeanne."

"I've made one of your favorites, pork loin."

"Oh well, maybe I'll eat just a little."

Jeanne told Kate that, as John was busy, Nick had asked her to stay to dinner. All through the meal, they kept up a conversation, which Jeanne tried to include Kate in, but Nick didn't address one single remark to. For dessert, Jeanne had made Nick's favorite pie, cherry, and she continued to chat and laugh with him. To say Kate was annoyed was an understatement. As soon as the coffee was ready, she poured a mug and left the room. Jeanne winked at Nick, and they both laughed softly.

Kate hardly slept, she was so angry at the way Nick was treating her, and so she got up just after five. *If I can't sleep*, she thought, *the least I can do is get some more work done.* She brewed some coffee and sat down on the sofa with her mug and began to type. The next thing she knew, she felt a hand grab her upper left arm and heard Nick's angry voice.

"You little fool! You were falling asleep sitting up, you're not taking care of yourself, not eating or sleeping properly. Jeanne's right, I should paddle your 'cute little ass.'" And with that, he sat down beside her and yanked the laptop out of her grasp and, setting it down on the table, started to pull Kate over his knees.

"Put me down! Don't you bloody dare!" she yelled as he hauled her across his lap and raised his hand to spank her just as her phone started to ring.

"Saved by the bell," he said as he threw her roughly back onto the sofa, stood up, and headed back toward the bedroom.

"I can't believe what you frickin' were going to do, Nicholas Barkley!" she yelled.

"Answer your damn phone!" he yelled back at her.

She picked up her phone and shouted, "What!" into it. It was the hospital, calling about a patient of hers. She talked for a few minutes and then hung up, still steaming mad at what Nick had tried to do to her, and more than a little afraid that he might try it again! She decided the safest thing would be to lock herself in the bedroom until Jeanne got there. The minute she heard their housekeeper's voice talking to Nick, she came storming out of the room.

"Did you suggest to him that he should paddle my ass?"

"Don't tell me he actually did it? Good for you, Nick!"

"I was interrupted by her phone ringing!"

"You should have let it ring," Jeanne said, laughing.

"You mean you did suggest it to him, and no he didn't, but he was bloody well going to."

"Next time, I will."

"Next time? There'll be no damn next time, Nick Barkley, or I'll have you frickin' arrested for assault!"

"Who by? My good friend, the sheriff? Not likely! I'm going into town. Jeanne, anything you need?"

"No, I've got everything."

"Then I'll see you later."

"What the bloody hell is up with him?" Kate asked after he left. "There's been a change in him ever since yesterday afternoon."

"What happened then?"

"Something I said made him so angry that he shouted loud at me. Actually, he was yelling!"

"Does he do that often? Yells, I mean?"

"He's never yelled at me before."

"Well, whatever you said must have got him plenty mad. Maybe you should apologize."

"I'll apologize to him when he apologizes to me for keeping me here against my will!"

"I guess that's what they call a stalemate."

Nick kept up the silent treatment the whole day.

"Okay, what's got you so bloody miffed?" Kate eventually asked him.

"I've got nothing to say to you," he answered her as he turned the television on and opened a fresh bottle of rye.

"Nick, when the hell are you going to let me leave?"

"I'm not stopping you. I told you, it's only ten miles to the highway, so you can start walking whenever you want!"

"You're bloody impossible."

"So you keep telling me."

"At least let me have my damn phone back?"

Silence.

"Did you damn well hear what I said?"

Silence.

"NICK, answer me! Give me my bloody phone back!"

The volume of the TV went up!

"How dare you ignore me like this! ANSWER ME, damn it."

"Do you want some cheese with that whine?"

"How dare you friggin' talk to me like that!"

"I dare. That's been your problem, everyone has always let you away with your bad behavior, so afraid of incurring your almighty wrath. Well, it's not happening any longer, Kate. Not in my house!"

She went to the bedroom, slamming doors behind her. "Now why didn't I think of this treatment earlier," he said to himself with a grin on his face.

Kate paced in her room up and down, up and down, all the time trying to think of a way out of her predicament. She could walk to the road, then what? Hitchhike into Stockton? When she'd checked her bag, her wallet was missing. Nick, damn him, double damn him, must have taken it. She had no cash, debit, credit cards or ID. All she could hope for would be to hitch a ride to the bank, where maybe she could withdraw some money, but how much would they let her have with no identification? Maybe if a teller recognized her, she could get a couple of hundred, but how far would that take her? She wouldn't put it past Nick to have somehow frozen her bank accounts. After all, the Barkley name was all powerful in these parts. He said he was going to fight to stop her from leaving with everything he'd got, and she was just finding out what he meant by that! *It's like living in some third-world country*, she thought. *How'd I ever get myself into this terrible mess in the first place?*

I fell in love at first sight, she admitted to herself. *And after he did something really stupid, not to say dangerous, and I set out to teach him a lesson, and somehow, without my knowing why or how, I ended up in this awful situation. Where did it all go so wrong? Now he's so mad at me that he's hardly even speaking to me and wants to paddle my ass! I know Nick's trying to teach me a lesson, but I think it's gone way beyond that for him too. He doesn't really want me back, he's just showing me he's got the upper hand. Spank me, indeed. I've never heard of such a thing! Soon, he's going to give me my things back, tell John to take me to the airport, and consider himself well rid of me.*

"Dinner's ready," Jeanne called.

"I'm not hungry."

"It's roast beef and Yorkshire pudding."

"I don't give a rat's ass what it is I don't want it!"

"Kate, you've got to eat, you didn't have any lunch," came the sound of Nick's voice.

"I said I'm not frickin' hungry."

Silence for a while.

"You've got to eat, I've fixed a plate for you. I'll leave a tray outside the door." Nick's voice again.

An hour later, the tray was still sitting where he'd left it.

The next day was much the same. Kate only came out of the room to get carafes of coffee and refused all offers of food, both breakfast and lunch.

When Nick came in from the office, he asked Jeanne what Kate had eaten.

"She's only had coffee. For a doctor, she takes mighty poor care of herself!"

"Take her a tray of dinner," Nick said. But like the night before, the food was left to grow cold.

"It's not working Jeanne, she's too stubborn a woman. She's not going to give in. I can't have her not eating like this. She's going to make herself ill."

"Nick, hang on a while longer, I know her, she'll give in. She just needs a little more time to see what's right in front of her face—that she's as crazy in love with you as you are with her."

"No, Jeanne, I've said and done everything I can think of to keep her, but now it's time I give in and let her go. Here, give her these." He handed their housekeeper Kate's phone, passport, and wallet. "Tell her you'll take her anywhere she wants to go in the morning, I'll stay out of the way 'til she's gone, it'll hurt too much to watch her leave."

Jeanne knocked on the guest bedroom door.

"Go away."

"It's me."

"Okay, come in."

"Nick asked me to give you these and to tell you I'm to take you anywhere you want to go in the morning, except I won't do that. I'll not help you leave because what you're doing is just plain wrong. You'll have to ask John for a ride. Nick said he'll stay out of the way 'til you're gone. You've won, young lady, and I hope you're proud of yourself. You've just about destroyed one of the finest men I've ever known, and you'll never find another man as understanding and patient to take his place. I never thought I'd ever say this to you, but I'm disgusted with your behavior. Good night. I hope you can sleep knowing what you're doing to your husband!"

Lordy, now everyone's mad at me, how did I get myself in this situation? I wish I'd never come to Stockton in the first place. I could have taken that nice safe job in Pasadena, but no, I had to follow my heart and come here. I still remember the first time I saw Nick, how my heart skipped a beat and I got butterflies in my stomach. And the day we got married was the happiest of my life. Nick, I'm so sorry I've caused you this much pain and grief. The sooner I'm out of your life, the better it will be for you. How could everything that started off so right end up in this dreadfully mess? What have I done? Is everyone right and I'm so wrong? These thoughts went racing through her mind.

But he'd never have me back under any circumstances. What am I suggesting? I'm in here, crying myself to sleep at night, and he's through there, drinking himself into a stupor!

Is Jeanne right? Would he really take me back if I fell into his arms? Could it be that simple? Do I have the nerve to do that? What if he's still mad at me and rejects me? Then at least I'll have tried. Maybe if I wait until he's in bed and I—shit, I don't think I can do that! After the way I treated him when he tried to hold me. A few minutes later, I wanted to go to him and apologize, but he had such a hurt, angry look on his face that I didn't dare. A missed opportunity.

Her thoughts were spinning around and around. Should she make one last attempt to fix her marriage before she finally called it quits? Going over scenario after scenario in her head as to how she could get back in Nick arms, each idea that came to her seemed like it might work until she had to iron out the details, the part she'd have to play, and then she chickened out! Always, it came down to what if he rejected her. And her pride couldn't handle that. Part of her kept saying, "You won't know if you don't try," but another part said, "You'll never be able to hold your head up again if he doesn't want you."

She couldn't even call Jeanne and ask her opinion because the housekeeper was so blasted mad at her. *But I can guess what she'd say. "Go for it, girl, jump his bones when he least expects it!" That's a good idea.* Now when would he least expect her to make a play for him? When would he be the most vulnerable? Then it came to her—in the shower! All she had to do was listen for the shower to start running, Nick to get in, give him three to four minutes to lather up, and then she could drop her towel and step in next to him! *It would certainly have shock value! I don't think he'd tell me to get out, but if he does, then I'll know that it's all over between us. If a man rejects his naked wife, it's time for the divorce papers!*

She kept her door slightly open and, just after nine, heard Nick turn the shower on. She had already stripped and wrapped herself up in a towel, so now, she hurried down the hallway and through the living room, she put her head around the bedroom door, and was pleased to see her rings, her diamond lariat necklace, and earrings were still lying right where she'd left them. She put them all back on quickly and then turned down the bed. Next, she headed for the bathroom.

Nick was taking a regular shower, not a steam one. Kate, watching from the bathroom doorway, waited until his back was turned to her, took a deep breath, dropped her towel, opened the shower door, and stepped inside.

"Shall I wash your back?" she asked softly.

Nick froze, he was so startled and then, turning around, was now face-to-face with the woman he had fought so hard to keep and was now standing naked in front of him!

He stared at her. "What are you doing in here?" he asked.

"Conserving water," she answered, and he threw back his head and laughed as he hadn't in over two weeks.

"Is that your only reason?" he asked, suddenly serious, grabbing her by the shoulders and with a look that told her he would stand for no nonsense in her reply.

"Well, I heard that the guy who frequents this shower is really good in the sack and knows how to screw the hell out of his woman!"

With one hand, he grabbed her by the hair and then, talking in a low emotion-filled voice, said, "I thought I told you never again to use that terrible expression!" He pulled her to him and kissed her with his mouth open, searching for her tongue in her equally open mouth, which he found immediately as he ran his palms up and down her glistening body. They continued to kiss and embrace each other with a desperation that almost overpowered them. He turned off the water, and they rubbed each other's body down with oil they used when showering together. Stepping out of the glass-like stall, Nick picked up the love of his life and carried her to the already turned down bed.

They were longing for each other, as it had been nearly three weeks since they'd been together. He tried to wait as long as he could, but Nick was desperate to have her. "I need you so badly," he murmured.

"Go ahead," she told him.

Even after he was spent, he wouldn't let go of her. "I've waited so long for that. I was beginning to think I might never get to make love to you again."

"Nick, we can't ever let that happen to us again. To think, because of both our foolish actions, we nearly lost each other."

"Mmm," he murmured, still nuzzling her neck.

"Nick, did you hear what I just said?"

"Of course I did, and that was my answer. As long as you let me take you to bed, there will be no misunderstandings."

"That's your answer for everything?"

"It works, doesn't it?"

"Oh goodness, I just thought of something. Did your mother send in my letter of resignation?"

"No, she just told Dr. Greene you needed some personal time. You had the whole week off."

"Really?"

"Yes, and its only Thursday night, so you know how we're going to spend the rest of the time! After the last few days, I don't want to let you out of my sight."

"Don't you have to go into the office tomorrow?"

"I took care of everything in the past few days. I was planning on laying siege to you the rest of the week."

"Laying siege to me? What do you mean?"

"Staying in the flat, not giving you a moment's peace until you gave in and slept with me. I knew once you did that you'd never leave!"

"Nick Barkley, think you know me real well, don't you?"

"Well, we're in bed, and you're not going to leave, are you? So yes, I know you very well. I also know what I do to you that you like so much! We were made for each other, Kate. That's what you said a few weeks ago."

"Yes, I did. I'd forgotten about that. I said we were ordained to be together before the foundations of the earth were made."

"That's part of what kept me going through this rough spell—the hope you'd remember what you'd said."

"You know, Nick, no matter how mad I got at you—and I was sooo mad at you—I never, not for one second, stopped loving you."

"I know, babe. That was the hardest part of all—to know how much we were still in love with each other yet knowing I might have to let you go. Thank you for having the guts to do what you just did. I thought I was hearing things when you said, 'Shall I wash your back' and your smart-ass comment when I asked you what you were doing in my shower."

"I believe I said, 'conserving water,' and it's our shower, not yours!"

"You deserve to have your cute little ass paddled for what you put me through. I haven't drunk that much since I met you except for that one night in San Francisco!"

"Yeah, you were really hitting the bottle! But to think you actually put me across your knee! You weren't going to spank me were you? Not for real?"

"You're damn right I was. If your phone hadn't rung when it did, I intended to give you the whooping of your life! And you pull anything like that on me again, young lady, be sure I don't care if the trumpets are blown announcing the second coming, you'll feel the weight of my hand on your backside for real!"

"Nick Barkley, how can you make love to me the way you just did and then, a few minutes later, threaten to give me the whooping of my life? There are times I just don't understand you!"

"Think eighteen seventies, and it'll all make sense to you! That's when men were men and women were women. I know we've come a long way since then, but we've also lost a lot. I guess I want the best of both worlds all rolled into one. You're my woman, Kate, and you still don't fully understand what I mean when I say that. Maybe one day, you will."

Chapter 27

It has been over two months since the episode of the cat, the result being Nick and Kate more in love than they'd ever been. For the few people who were privy to the problem they had in their marriage, it seemed hard to realize that it had indeed happened. Outsiders would have never believed there could ever have been talk of her leaving. Nick and Kate both learned from those two difficult weeks that their love for each other had been tested, but they had overcome and moved on.

Nick came in from work about thirty minutes before Kate, and as it was Thursday, they would be joining the rest of their family for dinner. He showered, dressed in casual clothes, and sat down to wait for his wife. Only then did he notice the beautiful floral arrangement sitting on the dining room table. It was very similar to the ones he sent to Kate. Just then, his lady came rushing in the door, giving him a quick kiss. Having already picked out the dress she was going to wear, she hurriedly put it on, asking Nick to zip her up. She had just to touch up her makeup, and then they were ready to join the rest of the Barkley clan. It was only when they were on their way back upstairs at the end of the evening that Nick mentioned the flowers. Kate didn't know what he was talking about, so when they got inside the flat, she looked at them, and picking up the envelope, she took out the card; it was unsigned.

"Nick, come and see this. Someone has sent me these flowers anonymously! And look at the way the envelope is addressed."

Dr. Caroline Barkley,
AKA Kate

The Flat
Barkley Ranch
Stockton
CA. 55555

"Isn't that weird? The aka bit, and not many people put 'The Flat' on our address, although it is the right way to address mail to us. What do you think, Nick?"

"Has anyone been paying you an unusual amount of attention lately?"

"Not that I've noticed, but it makes me feel kinda uncomfortable that someone would spend that kind of money on me and then not let me know who they are."

Nick didn't pass any comment but made a mental note to call the florist in the morning and see what he could find out about who was sending flowers to his wife!

To take Kate's mind off the flowers, Nick made her a vanilla cappuccino, poured himself a brandy, taking them and Kate out onto the deck. When he went back in for his cigar, he brought out his guitar and, for a while, played and sang softly to his lady love, then going back inside, he put on the CD that Kate had made for him. Soon, the opening bars of the "Twelfth Of Never" could be heard.

They sat and enjoyed the coffee and brandy before Nick put out his hand and drew Kate to her feet to dance with him; they enjoyed dancing to "Islands In The Stream" but as the opening strains of Just Another Woman In Love" could be heard, Kate snuggled up tight in Nick's arms, with hers wrapped around his neck. By the time "Yours" was halfway through, they were headed for the bedroom, only stopping long enough for Nick to switch the speakers from the deck to the bedroom and turn the sound down slightly. The next morning, Nick didn't get to make his call to the florist until mid-morning because he and Kate had picked right up where they left off the night before!

It was going on ten by the time Nick got to his office that morning, not that he was complaining! After taking care of some business calls and other ranch-related matters, he called the florist that he used for all the flowers he sent, the same one the anonymous sender had also used.

He asked for the manager, and after exchanging pleasantries, Nick explained why he was calling. George, the manager went and looked up the order. He told Nick that they had found an envelope under their door when they opened. Inside was a typewritten note with instructions on what kind of flowers to be sent, who to send them to, that the card should be unsigned, and how to address the envelope the card went in. It was paid for in cash. *Stranger and stranger*, Nick thought. He thanked George for his help and hung up.

When he got home that night, Kate had tried out a new recipe for pork chops and seemed to have forgotten all about the flowers and the mysterious sender. Nick didn't, in the least, mind being her guinea pig and, in fact, thought the chops cooked in a cherry sauce were wonderful. She served them to him with rice pilaf and asparagus, definitely something he wanted her to make again. For someone who didn't get much of a chance to cook, she was really good at it. Kate had taken an apple pie out of the freezer, and they had that later with their coffee. She served the pie just the way Nick liked it—a la mode.

They sat out on the deck, just enjoying the evening, Nick smoking his cigar with his usual brandy. She went in to make herself a vanilla cappuccino, and as she was going back out, she stopped and thought, *why not?* What she did was put on the "Till" track from his CD.

"How many songs are we going to make it through tonight?" she asked Nick.

"Drink your coffee and we'll find out," he answered. He finished his brandy and waited patiently for her to finish her drink. Then he pulled her up and took her in his arms.

"Now we'll find out which of us can last the longest."

"Is that a challenge?"

"I guess it is."

"Okay, I'll take your challenge, Nick Barkley, but you'll have to excuse me, there's something I have to do first."

She was only gone a matter of minutes, but when she came back out, Nick's grey eyes opened wide. She had changed into a jade green full-length nightgown which was rather opaque and with the matching negligee.

"That's taking an unfair advantage," he told her.

"All's fair in love and war," she replied, grinning at him. "Now, let's see how long you last!"

"I can see exactly what you're not wearing underneath that nightgown. I'm not even going to try to resist you, it would be a waste of time. I know when I'm beaten."

And with that, he put his arm around Kate, and they walked inside, making sure the deck door was locked behind them. After they turned off the lights and switched the speakers over to the bedroom, he swept Kate up in his strong arms, fully intending to pick up where they had left off that morning!

Tuesday morning, while they were both at work, another floral arrangement arrived for Kate. Jeanne called Nick and told him about it. He phoned the florist and got the same story—another envelope with cash and typewritten instructions. His next call was to Sheriff Madden. He explained to Fred what was going on but was told, "No crime has been committed, just someone wanting to send Kate flowers, can't arrest a person for that!" Nick had told Jeanne to dispose of the arrangement before Kate got in from the hospital. He didn't want her worrying about another nut, she'd had enough of that once already in her life. He also called George over at the florists' shop and instructed him not to deliver any more anonymous bouquets to the flat, telling him that he would not have Kate concerning herself about who's doing this. Nick Barkley was way too good a customer to have upset, so George agreed to do as he asked and to call Nick and let him know if anymore of the "white envelopes" showed up. The envelopes continued to arrive at the rate of two a week, Monday and Thursdays. What Nick couldn't figure out was what this was all about. To date, six floral arrangements, making a total of eight, including the two which had actually been delivered, had been ordered for Kate. *What was the sender getting out of this?* thought Nick.

When a rather sexy short black nightgown from a well-known lingerie chain store arrived again anonymously, both Nick and Kate were shocked.

"What's going on?" Kate asked. "It's been weeks since those flowers arrived." At this point, Nick felt he had to tell his wife about the arrangements he'd made with George preventing the other flowers from being delivered.

"I appreciate your trying to shield me from my 'admirer,' but now he's not going to stop at just flowers!"

"There's nothing legally we can do about it," Nick told her. "I've already talked to Fred twice. He thinks you have a kind of benign stalker who's now upping the ante when he moved from the flowers to something much more intimate."

"The kind of flowers I like, anyone could find out about, but I don't talk about my preference in lingerie to just anyone. Obviously that's why he sent me a short nightgown. It would take someone who is really close to me to know I always wear long ones."

"Your friends from the hospital know that about you because that's what they bought you at the shower, wasn't it?"

"That was Ann's doing. Somehow we got into a conversation about night clothes. She said how much she liked long nightgowns and what did I think of them. I didn't realize she was fishing for information to tell the staff of my personal choice so they'd know what to get me for the shower, but you're right, it doesn't seem likely it's someone from the hospital. Finding out what I was given at the shower could be known without much difficulty. So who does that leave? Someone from town or the ranch?"

"I'd hate to think it's someone I employ. Are you close with anyone in town?"

"Not close, more like acquaintances than friends, and the people you employ, I'd say the same about them. The only people I'm really close on the ranch are the family and Jeanne. I take it you've told her what's been going on?"

"She knows about the flowers but obviously not about the latest 'gift.' I'll talk to her in the morning and ask her to put aside any packages that don't have a return address on them. That's about all we can do. I'm so sorry this is happening to you."

"It's just creepy knowing someone is out there with a kind of fixation on me."

"Well, how about letting the man who has the biggest fixation of all on you take your mind off what's been happening?"

"Oh, please! Yes, please!"

Kate didn't hear anything from her "admirer" for over a week, so she and Nick were hoping that meant he'd given up when the next package arrived. This time, it was a box of Godiva chocolates.

"He knows I like Godiva, but not specifically the truffles," she said to Nick. "But I don't get the point of all this. I mean, what could my stalker be getting out of it?"

"That's the question I've been asking myself for weeks," Nick told her. "But as long as sending gifts are all he does, I don't think we've got anything to be worried about."

It continued in the same vein for the next month; every week, flowers, lingerie, or chocolates were sent to Kate. The bouquets, according to Nick's orders, were not delivered, but the rest of the stuff, per the Sheriff's suggestion, Nick put in a box which was stored in the garage, just in case the unthinkable happened and the stalker moved from just plain annoying to something more sinister and they needed the gifts to prove what had been going on.

Friday night, Nick had to make a speech at a business association dinner in Stockton and of course Kate went along. When they came out, resting on the windshield of Nick's Land Rover Discovery was a white envelope addressed to Dr. Caroline Barkley.

She opened it and took out a single sheet of paper, on which was a typewritten note. Kate, after reading it, gave a little cry!

"What is it?" Nick wanted to know, taking the note from her hand. It was from her "admirer," who wondered how she liked the gifts he'd sent her and how he spent hours imagining how she looked in her new nighties!

"Oh lord," she said. "I feel like I need a long hot shower after reading that!"

"Oh, babe," said a now angry Nick. "I wish there was something I could do to shield you from this, but I know what Fred will tell me—that no law has been broken!"

When Nick got to the office on Monday, he put in a call to a private inquiry agent that Jarrod had recommended. He explained the situation and asked if the detective could be of any help.

"I could try tracking down the purchase of the lingerie and chocolates. But really, I don't hold much hope of getting a solid lead. In this day of the internet, it's easy to remain anonymous."

"Any help you can give me would be greatly appreciated. Spare no expense on this," Nick told him.

When the detective reported back, it was just as he'd feared—the orders were placed on an internet cafe computer, paid for with an over-the-counter debit card, and sent directly to Kate. No leads on the stalker at all. Nick was at a loss what to do next.

Fred had told him that thousands of women all over the country were dealing with the same problem, some for years, with no resolution. If the stalker didn't actually cause physical harm, nothing could be done.

Things only got worse when Kate receive in the mail some photographs of herself along with another note telling her that her admirer had copies of these in his room and wallet!

Nick immediately took all the items to the detective he had hired, only to find out there were no fingerprints on anything, and the photographs had been taken in Stockton whilst Kate was in a public place. Again, not against the law. Nick made sure she still had her Glock in the glove compartment of her car. "Oh yes, she told him, apart from wanting to protect myself from this nut, I still carry narcotics in my bag."

"Well, I hope you won't hesitate to use it if you feel threatened?"

"Don't worry about me. If my life is threatened, I know all about the double tap to center mass," she told him.

They tried to get on with their lives, but the stalker problem was always at the back of their minds. The next thing to arrive in the mail was a copy of a rather pornographic book, complete with pictures accompanied by a note saying that these are some of the things her admirer imagined them doing together. Nick hit the roof!

"After the kind of night clothes that were sent to Kate, this book isn't that much of a leap," Fred told him.

A week later, when Nick got home from work, he found Jeanne bound to a dining room chair with a gag in her mouth. He quickly untied her, and after making sure she wasn't hurt, asked, "What the hell happened?"

She told him that a man wearing a mask must have snuck in behind her car as she came through the gate that morning, because when she got out, he was right there with a gun pointed at her and was forcing her up the steps and made her open the deck door. Then he tied and later gagged her and started looking around the flat. He went into the bedroom, and she could hear him in the closets and opening and closing drawers. He stayed for about twenty minutes and then left the way he had come in, carrying a small holdall. She hadn't heard the gate open, so she assumed he'd just climbed over. She'd remained tied up for hours until Nick found her.

Steam was almost coming out of Nick's ears as he called the sheriff. Fred came straight over with a police technician who was going to dust the place for prints, but Jeanne told them, "It would be a waste of time, the intruder had worn gloves and the kind of a cap Kate wears when she's operating."

"That's probably to stop him leaving hairs, which could have given us a DNA sample. Damn," said Fred. "He thought of everything. Well, he's raised the ante now, going from stalking to a felony hostage charge, which could mean a life sentence! Have you checked if anything is missing, Nick?"

"Not yet, I didn't want to touch the place until you came out."

Just then, Kate arrived and wanted to know what was going on. Jeanne and Nick told her what had happened. She was full of concern for her housekeeper. "Are you okay? Did he hurt you?"

"I'm all right, my arms and wrists are sore from the way I had to sit with them tied behind my back for so long."

"Kate, would you look around and see if anything is missing?" the sheriff asked.

She took her time going around the kitchen, dining room, and living room before checking out the bedroom. When she came back, she was really perturbed. "My cream-colored nightgown with its matching negligee, along with a similar brown set and a couple of my bra and panty sets are gone. This is now more than creepy—it's very disturbing!"

Nick went over to Kate and put his arms around her; he could feel his wife trembling.

"I'm getting you a large brandy, and you're going to drink it. In fact, I'm getting one for you too, Jeanne. You've been through a terrible ordeal. I'm sorry, I should have given you one when I found you." There was a knock on the deck door. It was John looking for his wife. He had become concerned when a hand told him the sheriff and some deputies were over at Mr. Nick's flat. That and the fact Jeanne hadn't returned home made him come to find out what the problem was. Again, Jeanne told her story; this time, it was John who was steaming mad.

"I'll look and see what we have on the CCTV. I don't check it that often since we caught Jeff Scott, but maybe this creep took his mask off after he left the flat, not knowing there is a camera trained on the gate." But no luck, the mask had remained in place, at least until the intruder was out of camera range.

I'm not going to let this interfere with my life, thought Kate. She and Nick ordered Chinese delivery after everyone left. Later, when Nick was having his brandy and cigar, she went inside ostensibly to get herself a cappuccino but changed into her red lingerie set, which she knew were the ones her husband liked so much, and putting on his CD, starting at "My Own True Love," walked onto the deck. The result was what she had hoped for; Nick left his brandy to dance with her. They managed to get through to the "Power Of Love," when he felt his wife maneuvering him toward the door. That night, Kate made love with an urgency Nick had hardly ever known in her but responded in kind with great pleasure!

I'm not even going to think of what he wanted my stuff for or what he's doing with it! I'm going to put it right out of my mind, Kate thought, but when she wasn't busy at work, her thoughts kept returning to her stalker.

That night, when she got in from the hospital, there was a wonderful smell coming from the kitchen. Jeanne had fixed a pork loin which she knew was one of Kate's favorites, and for dessert, Nick's favorite—a cherry pie.

"Jeanne, you're an angel to make all this after the day you had yesterday."

"When I'm upset, I cook. I've made the same things for John. I've turned all my anger into food for everyone."

"Is Nick home?' Kate asked.

"Yes, he's in the shower."

Just then Nick joined them, his hair still wet, which Kate found very sexy! She gave him a big kiss, and then Nick poured them both a glass of wine, which, of course, came from their own vineyards. "I don't care if there's a code black at the ER tonight, you're not going back to work. They'll just have to get along without you!"

Jeanne told them dinner was ready and she was going home to have her dinner with John. Nick and Kate sat down and enjoyed the wonderful meal, Kate drinking two glasses of wine. After they cleared away the dishes, they sat down on the sofa to have their dessert and coffee. When they had finished, Nick excused himself, coming back into the room, carrying a box with a logo she recognized—Agent Provocateur!

"This is for you, darling," he told her. She took the box, and when she opened it, there, nestled in the tissue paper, was a beautiful red bra with matching panties and garter belt plus a black set, along with two pairs of stockings which matched the very sexy lingerie!

"I have no idea what color was taken, but I thought you'd like these." Nick had obviously shopped at the expensive lingerie store that she frequented. They had her size on file, so all Nick had to do was mention Kate's name, and the very helpful assistants could pull up her details on the computer. They not only kept track of her sizes but of everything she purchased; that way, Nick never bought anything she already had!

"Nick, you have a way of doing just the right thing. These are gorgeous. How did you get them here so fast?"

"I picked them out online, then those marvelous girls at Agent Provocateur had them sent special delivery."

"Do you want me to model them for you along with the stockings?" she asked, knowing how much he delighted in seeing her wear stockings!

"That sound like a great idea!" he said with a big grin on his face. She went in the bedroom and put on the black set. Going back to the living room, she paraded up and down.

"Aren't you pleased with your choice?" she asked him. He winked and continued to grin at her, his very cute dimples showing! Next came the red set. Red was the color Nick most enjoyed seeing her in. Needless to say, she wasn't the one who removed the stockings or the garter belt or the bra or the panties!

To ensure that no one sneaked in the gate behind Jeanne again, John arranged to have a ranch hand at the gate when his wife drove in.

There were no more incidents for two weeks after the break in. But then, one night, when Kate reached her car in the hospital parking lot, a man wearing a mask and pointing a gun at her appeared. He told her to get in on the passenger side and slide across to the driver's seat as he got in the back. Telling her to drive, he gave Kate instructions to a remote house on the very outskirts of town. They pulled into the garage, where she was told to turn the engine off and give him the keys. He got out, still pointing the gun at her, moving around to the driver's side and telling her to get out. They went through a door which lead into the kitchen, through that, into a sparsely furnished living room.

"Sit down on that chair," he told her, "and put your hands behind your back." He tied her up just the way he'd done with Jeanne.

"What do you want?" she asked him.

"I told you in the car—no talking or I'll be forced to gag you the way I did your gabby housekeeper. She just wouldn't shut up!" With that, he left the room, and she heard what she thought was the front door slam and the sound of a car engine starting up.

Oh lord, what is this maniac up to? she thought. *I'm in serious trouble, no one knows where I am, and Nick won't realize that I'm missing for hours—he'll just think I'm working late.*

The hours passed, and Kate was right. Nick just assumed she was in surgery and unable to call him. But when it got to eleven and her phone went to voicemail again, he called the ER's main number.

"Dr. Barkley left hours ago," a nurse told him. "When I came on shift a few minutes before seven, she was finishing up some paperwork and then was going to leave."

Where the hell could she be? thought Nick. *It couldn't be car trouble or she'd have called me. She's four hours late. I'm calling Fred.* He put in a call to the sheriff and told him Kate was missing. "She must have been taken by the stalker, there's no other explanation!"

"I'll send a deputy down to the hospital and see if anyone saw her in the parking lot. Do they have closed circuit cameras there? Do you know?"

"I'm not sure. Please, God, let someone have seen something. I'm going to drive down there myself."

Not only did the hospital have cameras in the parking lot, but the security guard had seen Kate drive out with what he thought was a passenger in the backseat! At the time of the abduction, the man whose job it was to watch the monitors had been on a break and missed seeing what had happened. Both the deputy and Nick watched as the tape was rewound and sat there horrified as they saw Kate being forced into her car at gunpoint and driving off the lot. Now Fred and Nick had evidence that man who had stalked her for so long had taken Kate, but for what reason?

"What does he want with her?" said Nick, his imagination running wild.

It was midnight when her kidnapper returned to the house, although Kate had lost all track of time. He brought with him a cheeseburger, fries, and a diet Coke.

"I'm sorry they didn't have diet Sprite," he told her. He held the burger up to Kate's mouth. At first, she didn't want to eat, but then she thought, *Be sensible, you don't know what he'll do if I don't go along with him.* So she ate the food and drank the Coke.

He started to tell her how long he'd admired her, that her English accent was wonderful, but she seemed so unattainable, so he just watched her from afar. Then he learned how much she loved wildflowers, and he couldn't resist sending some to her. He had found a place in the hills behind the Barkley mansion and, with binoculars, watched her and Nick as they danced and kissed when they were out on their deck and imagined it was he she was with instead of her husband, and that was why he sent her the nighties, because he thought she'd look better in short ones, but she'd never worn the ones he'd sent her.

He heard Nick mention once that she liked Godiva, so that was another gift to send her. As for the book, he wanted her to know that he could love her better than her husband ever could. He had made up his mind to take her away from Nick, but he wanted her to feel at home with him, so that was why he went into her the flat and took her own nighties and underwear. Maybe tomorrow she would wear them for him?

Oh lord, this guy is completely off his rocker. What am I going to do? I won't strip and put those things on for him, I just won't. I don't care what he threatens me with, I'm not going along with his plans for me, she thought.

The deputy who was in charge said they would try to track Kate's Land Rover with the closed-circuit cameras that had just been installed on the main streets of Stockton. The sheriff's department had been given a grant from the Federal Government and decided, in view of the current world crime climate, cameras in the city would be a good investment. Deputy Connor, along with Nick, reviewed the tape. They picked her up going along Main Street but lost her at the edge of town when she turned onto a minor road.

"At least we know the area she's in and he didn't hurt her," Nick said in a low voice.

"There aren't many houses out there," Deputy Connor said. "I'm going to check the records at city hall tomorrow morning and see who owns them. But in the meantime, I suggest you go home and get some rest, Mr. Barkley. There's nothing else we can do tonight."

"I don't know how much sleep I'll get knowing Kate's in the hands of some lunatic. By the way, call me Nick."

It was late afternoon by the time Deputy Connor had the list, and Nick came back down to the sheriff's office to look it over.

"I know him," he said, excitedly pointing to a name on the list. "He's worked for me on the ranch for at least three years. It wouldn't be hard for him to find out all those things about Kate. Also, it would be easy for him to know what time Jeanne goes over to the flat and follow her in. Can't we get into his house while he's at work on the ranch?"

"We couldn't get a search warrant with the little we know—the evidence is too flimsy."

Fred Madden stopped Nick before he left the station. "I know you. If you're planning to do something on your own, don't do it. To get a conviction, this has to be done by the book."

"To hell with the book, I just want Kate back." With that, Nick went storming out. He got to the ranch and talked it over with John.

"How do we get in that house legally and see if she's there?"

"Let me think about it for a while. I'll come up with something. Don't worry, Nick, we'll get her back soon."

About an hour later, John came knocking on the deck door. When Nick opened it, John burst out. "What about starting a fire and calling nine one one?"

"Huh, I don't want her to get hurt!"

"We'll wait until Henry is at work. I'll give him a job to do that will keep him busy for hours, then we'll go to the house, look in the windows, and see if she's there. If she is, we'll call nine, one, one and then start a small fire as far from Kate as possible. When the fire department shows, I'll tell them that I'm sure I heard someone calling for help. They'll have to break down the door and go in. They're the ones who'll find Kate. It will be perfectly legal and stand up in court. Henry Wilkerson goes to jail for kidnapping which, as I understand, is a federal offence. He could get as much as a life sentence."

"I hope they put him in a cell and throw away the key! Okay, it's too late today to do it. He'll be home now. We'll go first thing tomorrow. I hate to think of Kate spending another hour, far less another night, in the hands of this nutter, but she'll be home tomorrow. Tell Jeanne she can have the day off. I really want Kate to myself when I get her back."

"I understand, Nick. I'd feel the same way if it were Jeanne. What happened to her was bad enough. All I wanted to do after was hold her tight. I can't imagine what you're going through with Kate missing."

The next morning, John called Henry into the ranch office. "A large section of fence is down in the north pasture. I want you to fix it. Tom will go with you. I estimate it should take the two of you about six hours of steady work to properly put up a whole new section, including digging some new post holes."

"I was hoping to leave early today," Henry told him.

"Sorry, not today. It will take you close to half an hour to load up the lumber and equipment, and then you have to drive out there. You'll be putting in nearly an eight-hour day. If you wanted time off, you should have asked me in advance. Now get going before Mr. Nick gets here!"

After Henry left, Nick came into the office. "Let's leave now."

"I bought a disposable phone from a liquor store on the other side of town so the nine, one, one call can't be traced to either of us. While I was out, I scouted the area and found a lumber yard not far from the house. That will give us an excuse to be in the vicinity. We sort of got lost and saw the fire. No one can prove different!"

"I didn't think of any of that, John. Thank you so much for doing it all."

On the way to Nick's truck, John put on gloves, went to one of the sheds, and picked up a can of gas which he had bought in cash from a large hardware chain store the day before, being careful to leave no prints on it. They drove on side streets to Henry's house. There were no neighbors close enough to observe what they were doing. Parking a few yards from the front door, they crossed the street to the house, John carrying the gas can. They went around the single-story home, trying to look in the windows, but on most of them, the shades were drawn.

"What do we do now?" asked John.

411

"How are you at forcing a door open?" replied Nick.

"Never tried it."

"Let's look at the back door. That lock doesn't look so strong. I wonder if I put my shoulder to it, I could force it open." He did just that, and on the third attempt, the lock gave! Nick was through the doorway in a flash, calling his wife's name.

Kate had fallen asleep and thought she was dreaming when she heard her husband's voice calling her! "Nick, Nick!" she yelled. "I'm in here." In seconds, he was with her. "Untie and get me out of here," she told him as he hugged and kissed her.

"Are you all right? Did he hurt you?"

"No, he just kept me tied up all the time. Now please untie me."

"Listen, Kate, if I do that, we'll have no evidence against Henry."

"Henry?"

"Henry Wilkerson from the ranch, that's who's responsible for all this." Then he told her of their plan.

"What do you think? Are you up for it?"

"To put him in jail, I'll do anything."

"That's my girl. It'll only be a little longer, and then I'll take you home, and this nightmare will be over." He hugged and kissed her again and then left the way he had come in.

The back door had a bunch of tall grass growing next to it and was far enough from where Kate was being held prisoner to be the best spot to set a small fire. Nick used the disposable phone to call nine, one, one while John poured a little gasoline on the grass and threw a match on it. The grass blazed. He threw the can away in a nearby field along with the phone, and then both men hurried back to the truck and waited for the emergency vehicles to arrive. Within minutes, the fire department was on the scene, along with a paramedic truck. Nick and John didn't have to report hearing a voice from inside the house, Kate took care of that herself. Yelling at the top of her lungs, the firefighters were alerted to her presence. Some broke down the front door while others put out the flames. Those that made entry were shocked at what they found—Kate bound to a chair. When they got her outside, the paramedics checked her out and pronounced her in good shape considering the ordeal she had been through. The sheriff's department had been alerted, and Deputy Connor, hearing Kate had been found, responded to the call. If he was suspicious about the source of the fire and the presence of Nick and John, he didn't say so. He asked Kate if she was up to coming to the station to give her statement. Nick wanted to take her home and have her give the statement tomorrow, but she was adamant that she was going to do it now.

After hearing all she had to say, Fred went to Judge Andrew Peterson, who signed an arrest warrant for Henry Wilkerson. The charge: kidnapping in the first degree. Then deputies were sent to take him into custody. John had told them exactly where to find him. Completely surprised, Wilkerson was taken into custody without incident.

Kate, giving her statement, omitted the part of about seeing Nick and knowing about the fire in advance.

Nick and John stuck to their story about getting lost on their way to the lumber yard.

The firefighters told how they found Kate and the condition she was in.

When Wilkerson and his attorney heard all the evidence against him, they decided to take a plea deal, thus saving Kate and Jeanne the ordeal of having to testify in open court about the most terrifying events of their lives. Henry Wilkerson was sentenced to twenty years in a federal prison.

When Kate heard this, she gave a huge sigh of relief. "It's over, it's really over. Can we go out and celebrate?"

"Where do you want to go?"

"Let's go to Paul's and have *chateaubriand* for two."

"I'll call ahead and order it."

"Then we can dance to 'our' songs!"

"You've got it!"

Nick still marveled at the fact Kate liked small intimate restaurants, passing on the larger trendier ones in town, unlike many of the other women he had dated that he felt wanted to be seen with him at "in" places just to get their names linked with his in the society columns of the papers.

They had their special dinner and slow danced, Nick breathing in the heady perfume—Baccart Rouge—that he'd introduced her to recently. This time, for dessert, Kate asked for cherries flambé, another dessert that's so much fun to watch being made. Nick sat with his arm around her, occasionally leaning over and kissing her as only he could! She was wearing the red spaghetti strap dress that he liked so much. When they got home, they had difficulty getting up the steps to the deck, the problem being they were locked in each other arms.

"No time for dancing on the deck tonight," he whispered to her as he opened the door to the flat.

"What a way to celebrate," she murmured in his ear. "I'm free at last!"

Chapter 28

"Look, Nick, we've got an invitation to an engagement party over at the Ponderosa for Adam and a girl called Laura Dayton. He's a dark horse. He never mentioned her the last time he was here. It's three weeks on Saturday. Can we go, please? There's a note from Ben saying we should go the day before the party and make it weekend trip."

"Of course we'll go, it's nice to hear that Adam's found someone and is going to settle down. I hope they'll be as happy as we are."

Victoria told them that the whole family had been invited but the only ones able to make it were she and Audra. So the day before the engagement party, the four of them flew to Reno, Nevada, and then drove to Virginia City and onto the Ponderosa, home of the Cartwright clan. Everything was bustling when they got there; caterers were taking over the kitchen, and a huge marquee was in the process of being erected adjacent to the house to accommodate the band and dancing.

"Now, please don't worry about us," Victoria told Ben. "We'll take care of ourselves. We stopped on the way here and picked up sandwiches. We're going to take the food and spend some time looking around your beautiful ranch."

"Victoria, thank you so much. Just let me show you all to your rooms and then I'll leave you to amuse yourselves. You and Audra are sharing, if that's all right, and then this one's for you and Kate, Nick. They each have their own bathrooms, so you'll have plenty of privacy. You can see Adam's fine hand at work. We completely renovated the entire guest wing a couple of years ago!"

The Barkleys spent a leisurely afternoon looking around the Ponderosa, getting back to the house with plenty of time to shower and change for dinner. Laura Dayton had been invited, so along with her at the table were the four Barkleys and five Cartwrights, namely Ben, Adam, Hoss, Little Joe, and their cousin Will, who had been living at the ranch for nearly a year. The talk, of course, turned to ranching when the Barkleys found out that Laura had taken over her own ranch, the Running D, since the death of her husband about eighteen months prior. After dinner, Ben suggested the men take their brandies outside where they could smoke a cigar, leaving the ladies to enjoy their coffee and conversation.

Of course, the Barkley women were eager to find out all about Laura and Adam's romance. Laura explained that she had known the Cartwrights for about four years as neighbors, and then, after her husband was killed in an automobile accident, Adam was one of the people who stopped by to help her out with the running of the ranch. About a year ago, as she became more familiar with the workings of it and had hired a new foreman, Adam had continued to stop by, making sure things were indeed being taken care of. Then he'd take her and her seven-year-old daughter Peggy to church and out on Sunday picnics, stopping by occasionally for dinner and even giving Peggy a pony. It was only six weeks ago after she had mentioned that she was thinking of selling the ranch and moving to San Francisco to live with her aunt that he had proposed.

"When is the wedding?" Audra asked her.

"Oh, probably sometime this summer," was the reply.

Probably, that doesn't sound very romantic at all, thought Kate.

When the men joined them, Will asked Kate if it was true what he had heard that she'd actually been in the British army. Telling him it was indeed a fact, the two of them were soon deep in conversation about the Middle East, in which, it turned out, Will had traveled extensively. Nick, overhearing a little of their exchanges was quite happy to let them converse, knowing it wasn't very often that Kate got to talk to someone who had been to all the places she had been stationed, even down to Will knowing the countries in which she had taken vacations.

Nick sat, as usual, with his arm around Kate, always choosing to sit next to his wife and either holding her hand or having his arm around her shoulders. While she was talking to Will, Nick, his mother, and Ben talked about their respective ranches whilst Hoss and Little Joe were happy to entertain Audra, this leaving Adam and Laura to themselves. Although the supposedly happy couple were sitting next to each other on a loveseat, they weren't holding hands, far less him having an arm around her!

When they all retired to their rooms, Kate mentioned to Nick that she thought Adam and Laura didn't act much like a couple in love.

"We couldn't wait to get married. Our wedding was less than three weeks after we got engaged! And we'd only had a dozen dates before you announced to me we were getting married!"

"I wouldn't read too much into it," Nick replied. "You said when they first met she was married. It was only after she became a widow that he started going over to help her as a friend at first. Anyway, enough about them. Let's find out if the bed they have given us has squeaky springs or not!"

The next day, an informal lunch had been planned on the patio and then the house guests were left to their own devices for the afternoon. Victoria and Audra went for a ride whilst Nick and his wife found different ways to amuse themselves, which included a bubble bath, amongst other delights!

The party wasn't a black-tie event, so Nick had brought one of his immaculately tailored suits and Kate, the jade halter neck dress bought in San Francisco on their honeymoon. The other ladies in their party were attired in equally beautiful dresses. At seven fifteen Laura Dayton arrived, and then at seven thirty everything and everyone was ready as the first guests started to arrive. Nick and Kate thoroughly enjoyed themselves, he so proud of the way it seemed like every man in the room wanted to dance with his gorgeous wife until the lights slightly dimmed and the slower dance music started. That was when he asserted his rights and called a halt to any man trying to dance with her or cut in. He was the only one going to hold his Kate tight and slow dance with her cheek to cheek. He did modify the way he held her in public from the way they danced on their deck!

"It seems to me that's the way two people deeply in love dance," said Hoss, observing them and remarking to his father. "Now look at the way Adam and Laura are dancing!"

His big brother and fiancée were slow dancing, but not the way the two Barkleys were, and when one of the guests asked to cut in, Adam obliged and stepped away. Hoss wasn't the only one to have noticed the newly engaged couple's behavior; Kate had observed the same thing. What she'd also noticed throughout the evening were the glances that Laura and another guest, whom she found out later was the Running D's foreman, Ward Banister, were exchanging. *Whatever is going on there, doesn't bode well for Laura and Adam's relationship,* she thought!

Hoss, when he was returning from seeing some guests who had to leave early to their car, had even observed the Barkley couple in the garden with their arms entwined around each other and involved in a long and seemingly very passionate time of kissing while there was no sign of Adam and Laura. If anyone Hoss thought should be out here taking a break from the guests, you would think it would be them. After all, they are now officially engaged! Hoss wondered if he should talk to their father about what he'd noticed or if he should just mind own business. He decided, after mulling it over, that he would mention it to his father and then leave it up to the older and wiser man to do what he chose with the information. Hoss reasoned if he had seen something amiss with Adam's relationship, then surely their pa must have also noticed that things were not as they should be and was maybe just waiting for someone else to confirm his suspicions that what he was observing was not the behavior of a couple in love.

The party ended about midnight, the Barkleys thanked Ben for a wonderful evening and congratulated Adam again, and then went off upstairs. Nick and Kate picked up right where they had left off that afternoon! The next morning at breakfast, the talk was of, what else, the party, and how much everyone had enjoyed it. The one who had the least to say was Adam, but in the midst of the good-natured ribbing he was getting from his brothers, it was difficult to notice, unless you were paying close attention as Kate was. On the drive to the plane, Nick told his wife that Ben had invited them back for a three-day weekend the week after next.

"If you could get off work a little early, it would mean we could fly in on the Thursday night in time for dinner and come home late Sunday afternoon. That would give us plenty of time to discuss some new business plans we have. I'd really like to have you hear the discussions, and I know Ben and the boys would value your insights."

"I don't see a problem to my getting off shift a couple of hours early, and I'll pack the day before so as soon as I get home, we'd be good to go. Even though I don't think I'll have much to offer in the way of any suggestions, it will be interesting to hear all about this new joint venture that you have going with the Cartwrights."

The plans made, Kate left her shift just before five, and she and Nick were airborne by six thirty. They joined the Cartwrights for a late dinner and moved into the living room for coffee.

Ben, who'd had a long conversation with Hoss about Adam and Laura, was unsure what to do about his concerns for his oldest son and decided that, when the Barkley couple were over at his ranch, he'd bring the conversation round to what it took to make a successful marriage like theirs. You could tell by just looking at them that they were so very much in love, the type of relationship he wanted not just for Adam, but for all his sons and nephew.

So when they were all relaxed, drinking their coffee and having after-dinner drinks. *Here goes*, thought Ben, and he asked Nick and Kate, "How do you, as a two-career couple, both of which are demanding, have such a successful marriage? What is your secret?" Nick and Kate looked at each other, and then he replied for both.

"We treasure our time together. I ask Kate out on dates regularly. We have a small number of restaurants that we like to go to, mom-and pop-types, not trendy 'in' places. But most of all, we prefer to stay at home. Kate likes to cook on her days off or I barbecue, and then we dance on our deck. Occasionally, Mother asks us to help her host some function downstairs in the main house, and Thursday is family dinner night, but apart from that, we stay to ourselves."

"Hear that, Adam? That's some good advice to follow, especially the part about asking your wife out on dates and the dancing at home," said Hoss. Adam nodded but passed no comment.

"What advice do you have, Kate?" asked Little Joe, oblivious to the look his father was giving him!

"Just because you're married, don't forget to send your wife her favorite flowers and chocolates, and gifts of the more, shall we say, intimate nature from her favorite lingerie store are always well received," she responded with a grin. "Plus, a stroll in the moonlight never goes amiss and usually pays dividends, and there are nights when we just sit out on our deck and Nick plays his guitar and some-times serenades me."

"You two should write a how to book." Will laughed.

"Please don't think we haven't had our arguments and doozies at that. I don't have red hair and Irish ancestry for nothing," Kate told them.

"I can attest to her wild Irish temper," Nick said, laughing. "It's funny now, but facing it is no joke!"

They chatted for a few more minutes, and then Kate couldn't hide her yawns any longer. "I went on duty at seven this morning, so I'm pretty tired. If you gentleman will excuse me, I'll leave you, giving you all a chance to go out and smoke your cigars."

"That is one very special woman you married," Ben told Nick.

"Don't I know it? I knew the moment I saw her that she was the one for me."

"Did you really?" asked Little Joe. "How did that happen?"

So Nick told the Cartwrights about his and Kate's first meeting and how, later, Kate had admitted she had felt the same way about him.

"Love at first sight. I've heard about it but always thought it was a myth," Will put in.

Throughout the entire conversation, the only one who didn't join in was Adam. *I hope he's comparing what he's heard about Nick and Kate tonight to his own relationship with Laura,* thought his father.

The discussions of how both families were intending to expand their respective herds and then buy a small chain of factories together was very interesting to Kate as she sat and listened to all that was said. They, Ben, Adam, Will, Nick, and Kate talked and discussed plans all day Friday, taking a break in the evening to just relax. The meetings started again after breakfast Saturday morning and went on most of the day.

The food which the Cartwrights' cook, Hop Sing, supplied was wonderful, and for dinner on Saturday night, Ben had invited some of his neighbors and, of course, Laura. The meal was served buffet style, and tables were set up both indoors and out on the patio. Nick and Kate chose to eat outside. Adam and Laura also came to the patio, and Nick suggested the couple join him and his wife. They ate their meal, and then Adam excused himself, saying he needed to go and circulate among the other guests. This left Laura at the table with the Barkleys, who exchanged a look that said this was a most unusual situation, both knowing Nick would never have left Kate like that! Ben stopped by the table and asked if he could borrow Nick for a few minutes to meet some of the neighboring ranchers. Of course, Kate said, "Yes," rather gladly as the "threesome" was getting to be rather uncomfortable. After he had left the table, it seemed that the other woman wanted to talk with Kate.

"How long did you and Nick date before you got married?" asked Laura.

Boy, I don't think she's going to like the answer, thought Kate. "We only had a dozen dates, and then he announced to me we were getting married!"

"Twelve! That's all? And how long were you engaged?"

If she thought twelve dates was bad, she's really going hate the answer to this one! "Less than three weeks!"

"But how could you know he was the one after only knowing him for such a short a time?"

"If truth be known, we both knew it the moment we met."

"Are you serious? You mean it was a case of love at first sight? I thought that just happened in romance novels?"

"Nobody was more surprised than me. In fact, I wouldn't admit it to anyone, least of all myself for weeks."

"How long did you know Nick before you went on your first date?"

"Three, no, four days, but it's not as bad as it sounds. There was this terrible snowstorm, and I had been called into the ER because they had too many patients and not enough staff. I was at a dinner party given by his mother when I got the call, and Nick drove me to the hospital and then, very thoughtfully, he waited for me, and before taking me home, he took me out for coffee and a doughnut. But it was about eight weeks later that we had our second date, also over another coffee and doughnut."

"Why the gap in time?"

"Well, Nick was in and out of town for almost six weeks on business, and then I was still in what you call the reserves, and Her Majesty had called me up for two weeks to play war games. It was when we were both back in town after that that one of his men got shot, and that's when we went for our second coffee date, and he asked me out to dinner. And the rest, as they say, is history.

"And you're obviously very happy."

"I'm so in love with that man. That's not to say we haven't had our arguments. We've really only had two, but the second one was a doozy I don't have red hair and Irish blood for nothing! My temper sure took Nick by surprise. I think it'll be a long time before he does anything to get me that mad again! But oh was it ever fun making up!"

Laura pulled a disapproving face at Kate's last comment but went on to say, "Well, every couple argues. What I can't get over is how short a time you knew each other before you were married! But can I ask something?"

Without waiting for Kate to answer, Laura continued, "Doesn't it bother you the way he kisses you, and I don't just mean a quick peck, but the kind of kissing that most married couples reserve until they're alone but you two do in public?"

"The first time Nick kissed me the way you're talking about was two nights before we got engaged. And to answer your question—to have Nick kiss me like that sometimes in public doesn't bother me in the slightest. In fact, until you asked me just now, I'd never even given it any thought! Anything else you want to know, now's your chance to ask while we're sitting here without the guys."

"The way you two slow dance, it's rather provocative, don't you think?"

Why did I know that was coming next after her comments about the way Nick kisses me? thought the now somewhat bemused Kate?

"I'm not sure what is provocative about two people in love and him holding her very close and sometimes kissing her right hand—or indeed, her!—and she, wrapping her left arm around his neck and, maybe in our case, rubbing his neck, which Nick adores, all the time swaying to the music cheek to cheek! Nick is always very careful when we dance in public. In fact, most of the time when we dance in front of others, he holds onto my right hand, which he tucks into his chest, but rarely does he wrap both his arms around me. Of course, how we dance on our deck at home when we're alone is a different matter entirely and nobody's business but our own!"

"I guess we were just raised differently," Laura told Kate. "I could never let a man treat me like that in public, I'd be too embarrassed!"

"If you don't mind, let me give you a great piece of advice that I found in scripture right before I got married. It's that once you get married, your body no longer belongs to you, it belongs to your husband, and the same goes for his body—it now belongs to you. So anything and everything he or you want to do to the other is perfectly acceptable except, of course, for anything violent. You two will be one flesh. No more you and he, only we."

"You can't believe that," Laura said in a shocked voice.

"I do. What's wrong with it?"

"Well, a woman has be allowed to say no."

"Why?"

"Well, a man can't expect to do 'it' whenever he wants to!"

"Again, I ask you why not?"

"But he might want 'it' every night!"

"Well, that's fine. Don't you enjoy 'it?' And by the way, 'it' is called sex. I think it's the most fun and pleasure a man and woman can have together."

"You mean you never say no to your husband?"

"Not only do I not say no, I frequently start making love to Nick before he has a chance to start anything with me, and those have been some of our most precious and wonderful times together. And it doesn't always have to be in bed. There's always the shower, the bathtub, the sofa, or in front of the fire. Just go with your imagination and surprise him, and if Adam is anything like Nick, you're the one who'll reap the benefits from it!"

"I could never do that."

"What do you mean you never seduced your husband? Lady, you don't know what you've been missing! You must plan on seducing Adam, even if it's only in bed!"

"I just couldn't."

"Why not? What's wrong with making love to your husband like that, Laura? It's the most natural thing in the world, and one of the most beautiful! I could hardly wait to be married to Nick. Surely you must feel the same way about Adam? I couldn't wait to get my husband between the sheets and experiment a little on him. He loved it!"

"I just don't feel about sex the way you do."

"Try it my way for a while. You'll find out how really wonderful going to bed with the man you love and adore can truly be."

Before Laura could reply, Nick came back to rejoin the two ladies.

It wasn't long after that Laura told them that she could feel a migraine coming on and she'd better get home before it became full blown. She caught up to Adam and obviously explained to him her problem. He kissed her on the cheek and she left.

"Now do you understand what I was trying to tell you?" Kate said to her husband. "If you had left me like that when we were engaged, you would have seen my Irish temper a lot sooner that you actually did!"

"I can't believe Adam got up and left like that. I have never known him to be anything other than polite. Come to think of it, last night, after you'd gone to bed, Little Joe wanted to know how we met. Will was amazed at the 'love at first sight' part of our story. In fact, everyone showed a great deal of interest and asked questions, everyone, that is, except Adam."

"They don't show any of the signs of a couple so in love that they are ready to commit to spending the rest of their lives together," said Kate. "It's almost a marriage of convenience for them. She needing someone to be a father to her daughter and maybe afraid of being a widow for the rest of her life, and he has been a bachelor for so long that he figures that Laura being a former rancher's wife would understand the long hours and his absences, so he's settled for her. Not much of a foundation for a loving marriage," Kate said to Nick. Then she told him about the conversation she had with Laura whilst he was away from the table. Nick was insulted for Kate at the questions his wife had been asked and then was silent for a moment.

"It doesn't bother you when we're in public and I kiss you like I do, does it? You'd tell me if it did, wouldn't you?" he asked, his voice full of concern.

"Darling, if it bothered me, I'd have said something long before now. You know me better than that. And before you ask if I objected to the way we dance, and that includes when we're alone and your hands kinda slip down to my fanny, I would have spoken up months ago. In my honest opinion, Laura Dayton is a little, if not more than, a little on the frigid side!"

Nick looked appalled at the very idea! "Do you really think so?" he asked.

"It would explain why she doesn't approve of our affectionate behavior toward each other and why she and Adam never indulge in any. I'll bet it's because she won't allow it, not because he doesn't want to," Kate told him. And she went on to relay to him the rest of their conversation.

"You mean she never once seduced her husband?" he asked, horrified at the very idea!

"According to her, not only has she never made love to him, she doesn't seem to have allowed him to make love to her very often, and you thought I had a different approach to sex! How would you like to be married to someone who thinks the way she does?"

"After getting used to your wonderful and liberating ideas about lovemaking, I don't know how other men survive with a wife who thinks about it any differently from you! Well, if that's the case with

425

Laura, I'd say Adam will have a major problem to deal with. Imagine what their pillow talk conversations are going to be like if being frigid is her problem."

"Isn't that something Adam would have picked up on? After all, he's known her for quite a while, and it's not like he hasn't been around the block a few times!" Kate asked.

"Maybe he just thinks she's shy."

"She can't be that shy. She was married and has a daughter," was Kate's comment.

"But judging from what she said to you, her behavior could have come as a big surprise to her husband."

"That's true, as big surprise as it's going to be to Adam if what I suspect is true. How would you deal with that problem?"

"I honestly don't know how I'd deal with it. Like any other red-blooded male, I don't think I could handle being kept at a distance and having sexual favors handed out to me like they were something I had to earn for good behavior, especially by my wife. But thank good-ness having a frigid wife is not something I'll ever have to deal with," Nick said with a huge grin on his face.

Just then, Ben stopped by their table and asked how they had enjoyed the evening. They assured him they'd had a great time, and Ben told them that the rest of his guests were starting to leave, so if Nick and Kate wanted to take a walk or go in, they should feel free to do so. He'd see them in the morning at breakfast, and with that, he said, "Good night," and moved on to talk with some of his departing guests.

"Take a walk or go upstairs?" Nick asked his wife.

"I'd like to take a stroll round the garden before we go in, if you don't mind, darling."

"Of course not. Let's go now shall we?" They took a walk around the garden, but before they went in, they took advantage of the moonlight and did some kissing and other things that Laura Dayton would never have approved of in or out of the bedroom!

Going inside, they ran into Adam and Will, who had just poured brandies and were getting ready to go outside and have them with a cigar. They invited Nick to join them, and before he could refuse, Kate stepped in and said it was fine with her if he wanted to go with the guys and that she would see him when he came in.

"That sure is one understanding woman you've got there," Will said to Nick.

"You have no idea how incredibly well she understands me!" Nick told him.

Sure enough, over an hour later, when Nick opened the door of their room, one of the scented candles they always traveled with was already lit, casting a warm, inviting, and romantic glow in the room. Kate put down the book she'd been reading and gave him a smile, which left him in little doubt why she'd waited up for him!

"What did I ever do to deserve a woman like you, I'll never know. All I know is I'm forever grateful you said yes."

"I didn't say yes because you never asked me! I keep on reminding you, you told me we were getting married—there was no asking involved!"

"I keep forgetting about that. How about if I ask you if you want to make love? What's your answer going to be?"

"Yes, Nick. Yes, please, otherwise my being already nude would go to such waste!"

"You're nude already! In that case, it won't take me long to catch up with you," he said, swiftly shedding his clothes and joining his wife in bed as they started a session of extremely slow sweet lovemaking that lasted until the early hours of the morning!

They met with the Cartwrights for breakfast, after which, Ben, Adam, Will, Nick, and Kate sat down to go over more details of the proposed takeover of the factories. Kate didn't have much to contribute but listened intently to all that the others said. They took a break for lunch and then quickly wound up the planning so the couple could take time to view Ben's new stallion before it was time for them to leave to drive to the airport and fly back to Stockton.

When they got home, they found that Jeanne had been in and they had a hot meal to come home to. After dinner, Nick said he was going to take a quick shower and then have an early night as he was going to work with the ranch hands for the next two days, and that meant starting at six, so the alarm would be going off at five a.m.

Kate thought that sounded like a wonderful idea, so she gave Nick a couple of minutes and then joined him in the shower. They were conserving water was how she explained it to him as he grinned at her when she offered to soap his back. Thanks to Kate, Nick didn't get the early night he'd planned, but he didn't complain either!

Three weeks later, after Nick had been out to the Ponderosa on a mid-week overnight trip, he came back with the news that the engagement between Adam and Laura was off. Hoss had confided to him that Adam had stopped by the Running D unexpectedly and had overheard a conversation between Laura and her foreman, Ward Banister, leaving Adam in no doubt that she had feelings for this man. When confronted with the fact that he knew the situation, she dissolved in tears, saying she hadn't known how to tell him. Right then and there, they called off the engagement. Hoss hearing Adam telling their father that he had been dragging his feet and that he'd been unsure of the marriage; maybe he was more attracted to the idea of being married than anything else, but what really worried him was seeing and hearing Nick and Kate and the kind of relationship they had and how that's what he wanted but knew he didn't have with Laura.

"I'm glad they've called it off, even if Laura hadn't been attracted to someone else, Adam settling for the kind of relationship they had was wrong. He used to be unsure that I'd ever find the right girl, but I'd tell him I knew I'd find you. I just wish he had the same kind faith for himself. He'll never find another woman like you, but I'm sure a wonderful girl is out there somewhere waiting for him. I just wish he was more outgoing. He can be moody and withdrawn at times, not great traits to attract a wife."

"Maybe when those gypsy friends of yours are here next, you should invite him over and see if they can point him in the right direction," Kate suggested. "They sure were right about us."

"That's a good idea. I'll do just that. Now to another important thing."

"Which is what?'

"Which CD is going to play as we make love to tonight!?"

Chapter 29

Victoria was a little under the weather, although she was not going to admit it to her family, but Audra had been watching her mother closely and, when they went into town, insisted she see their physician, Dr. Merar.

"I can't. He's on vacation."

"So what about the new doctor? I'm sure he doesn't have many patients, so he could see you today."

"I really don't need to see him."

"Yes, you do."

"You've heard he's young and good looking and you want to see for yourself!"

"Mother! How could you think that?"

"Because I know you, but if you're going to keep on fussing, we can drop in and see how busy he is." When they stopped by the office, the receptionist told them the doctor could see them in just a few minutes, and then she whispered to Victoria that he had hardly any patients, being new in town. Just then, the door burst open. It was Fred Madden carrying Everett Gibbons in his arms.

"He needs the doctor now."

The receptionist hurriedly opened the door and showed them into an examining room, at the same time hollering for Dr. Beldon, who came running.

"What's happened to him?" the doctor asked.

"I found him hanging in his office. He was barely breathing. I cut him down and brought him in here 'cos you're just two doors down from his office. Thought it'd be faster than calling nine one one."

"Call an ambulance now, and I'll see what I can do. Shut the door on your way out."

In the examining room, Dr. Beldon finished what he'd started—with a pillow over Everett Gibbons's face!

The sheriff went back into the reception area, called the emergency services, and then sat down beside Victoria.

"I can't believe Everett would try to commit suicide. I've known the man for over thirty years, and I've never seen any sign of that in him."

"It wasn't suicide, Victoria. Someone tried to kill him. I could tell by the way he was strung up. Now I've got to call the station and get a team over there to check the place out for any evidence they can find. I want to find who the hell did this."

"I can't believe someone would try to kill him," said Victoria. "How is that you found him?"

"We had arranged to have lunch together, and I said I'd meet him at his office and then we could just walk over to Cindy's Cafe."

They could hear the sirens of the paramedics getting louder, but as they arrived, Dr. Beldon came into reception and announced Everett Gibbons had just died despite his attempts to save him. Victoria gave a little cry, and Audra put an arm around her mother.

"I can't believe that someone would do this to him. In all the years I've known him, I've never heard anyone say a bad word against him."

"Neither have I," chimed the sheriff. "And I've known him almost as long as you, Victoria. Now, I have to leave and join my men at Everett's office."

"We're leaving too," Victoria told her daughter.

"What did you want to see me about?" asked the doctor. "I've plenty of time to talk to you now."

"She's been having chills, has a slight temperature, and she doesn't seem to have her normal amount of energy," Audra told him.

"It's nothing, really," Victoria protested. "Just a touch of the flu, and if I don't feel up to par right now, it's because it's lunchtime and I'm hungry!"

"Well, if the symptoms continue, feel free to give me a call. As you can see, I've got plenty of time on my hands."

"It takes time for people to get to know you so you can build up your practice. Tell you what, I've invited a few people over for dinner tomorrow night, including Martin Erskin, the publisher and owner of one of our local papers. Why don't you join us? Who knows, maybe we can prevail upon him to write a piece about you in his paper. That would help introduce you to the community."

"Thank you very much, and I accept with pleasure."

"Let me tell you where our ranch is."

"Mrs. Barkley, I have heard more about you and your family than about Stockton itself since I got here! I know exactly where your ranch is!"

"In that case, we'll see you at seven-thirty tomorrow night."

After they had dinner, Nick and Kate excused themselves and went back to their flat. The men went to enjoy a game of pool. James Beldon proved to be the man to beat and won two games in a row. Martin told Victoria he had to leave and go back to the newspaper as they were putting it to bed that night, and he wanted to see that the piece he had written on Everett was correct, including the note the sheriff had found.

"What note?" asked Jarrod, who had overheard the conversation.

"I have a copy in my pocket. Here, read it for yourself."

Together, Victoria and Jarrod looked at the sheet of paper.

For what they did together, all will die as he did.

"It sounds like he's planning to kill again, this man, and I'm assuming it is a man, just because it would need strength to over-power and string up Martin. He's dangerous, this killer. The note doesn't say how many more he's got in his sights!"

As Martin was leaving, he told Dr. Beldon that he'd make sure to include the doctor's name in the "About Town" column in next week's paper. His leaving signaled the end of the evening to the rest of the guests. Audra told her mother to go straight to bed as, in her daughter's opinion, she was looking pale and had started coughing.

"It's nothing, really," Victoria insisted. "Just a touch of flu. It's going around, but I'll take you up on your offer to see the house is straightened up, and I'll go to bed."

"I'm going to look in on you later and make sure you're okay."

"If it'll make you happy, that will be fine, but if I'm asleep, please don't wake me."

When Audra looked in on her mother, she found that Victoria had put a couple of extra blankets on the bed. She appeared to be dozing, but when Audra touched her forehead, it felt hot! *I'm going to get Kate. I think mother needs to be checked by a doctor, no matter what she says.* And with that, she went upstairs and buzzed the flat's front door phone.

When Nick answered, his sister told him she had to speak to Kate urgently.

"Just give us a couple of minutes and then I'll let you in."

"Kate, Kate. Audra's at the door, and she says it's urgent."

They got out of bed, and pulling on some clothes, they hurried into the living room, Nick letting his sister in as they went. Audra explained about Victoria, and Kate said she'd come right down.

"Could you get my bag, Nick, and bring it to me?"

"Sure will."

Going into Victoria's room, the first thing Kate noticed was the cough.

Her mother-in-law looked up. "Kate, what are you doing here?"

"Audra is concerned about you and thought it was time the doctor in the family was called in."

There was a knock at the door, and Nick put his head around.

"Now what's he doing here?" Victoria said, irritation sounding in her voice.

"He's just bringing me my bag, and then he's leaving," Kate told her. "Now, let me check your temperature. It's one hundred one, not good. Now, tell me how you are really feeling, and the whole truth, please?"

"Well, I feel kind of run down, I don't seem to have my usual energy, I tire easily, and I've got a cough."

"Is it a dry one, or are you bringing up phlegm?" Kate asked her.

"No phlegm."

"What else?"

"Chills. I've put two extra blankets on my bed, but that hasn't helped, and I've got some body aches. That's what made me think it's flu."

"Do you have any chest pains?"

"Now that you mention it, yes, but I thought it was all part of the body aches."

"Let me listen to your lungs and heart. I don't like what I'm hearing in your lungs, and I think you should get a chest x-ray."

"Is that really necessary?"

"Yes, it will confirm what I think is wrong with you."

"Which is?"

"Pneumonia."

"What? You really think that's what I've got?"

"Pneumonia and bronchitis are very similar, and an x-ray will show us exactly which it is. But remember, I'm a trauma surgeon, not a GP, plus I'm a family member and shouldn't be treating you. Who is your regular doctor? You really should see him first thing in the morning."

"Dr. Merar is on vacation."

"Well, what about Dr. Beldon? He seems very nice and graduated from the St. Louis School of Medicine, which has an excellent reputation."

"Yes, Mother. You know he doesn't have many patients, so he'd definitely would be able to see you in the morning. I'll call him first thing," Audra told her mother.

"That's a great idea," put in Kate.

"I can see I'm outnumbered. Yes, I will go and see Dr. Beldon. You can set up the appointment, Audra. Now, will you two leave me alone and let me try and get some sleep!"

Audra kept checking on her mother during the night, who was getting more and more restless and starting to really shiver! It was about three a.m. when Audra ran into Jarrod, who was coming up the stairs.

"I fell asleep in the library," he said ruefully. Audra told him of her concerns about their mother and then went back to bed. Just after she did, Jarrod heard knocking at the front door.

Who the dickens could that be at this time? Jarrod thought as he went down the stairs to open the big oak door. It was Sheriff Madden, looking very perturbed, most unlike him.

"Come in, Fred. What's wrong?"

"I know this is a terrible time to come calling, but it's happened again. Martin Erskine is dead! One of my deputies on patrol saw his body hanging in his newspaper office and called me immediately. We found another note. That's why I'm here. I need to talk to your mother."

"Fred, she's really ill, and I don't want to disturb her. What's this all about?" Jarrod asked.

"Here, I'll show it to you."

This is number two. Sweet dreams, Victoria Barkley. You're number three.

"What's the connection between Everett Gibbons, Martin Erskine, and your mother?" Fred asked.

"Apart from being friends for over thirty years, there is no other connection that I know of," Jarrod told him.

"There has to be. You're sure they have never been in business together, sat on the same board or committee, anything like that?"

"Not that I've ever heard her talk about, but as soon as she's feeling better, I'll talk to her about it. Right now, I'm concerned for her safety, and I'll talk to Nick and Heath in the morning about setting up some extra security around the house. The one I won't tell is Audra. She's got enough on her plate taking care of mother. Let me make a copy of that note before you go."

Early next morning, before Audra was up and around, Jarrod told Nick and Heath what had happened the night before and showed them the copy of the note. Both brothers were shocked to find out someone was threatening their mother's life.

"I'll talk with John about which hands we should arm with rifles and station unobtrusively around the main property. I can work down in the library, and I'll keep a couple of handguns next to me," Nick told his brothers.

"The paperwork I have to do can be done in the living room, and like you, Nick, I'll make sure there are firearms handy, but not where Audra can see them," Heath said.

"I'll also work in the library if you don't mind, Nick. It has a fax and copy machine, so along with my laptop, it will be fine."

"Glad to have the company, big brother. Just bring your own sidearm, as Kate would say!"

When Audra called Dr. Beldon, his receptionist put her straight through. She told him what Kate suspected.

"I'll call the hospital and make arrangements for her to get a chest x-ray this morning and then take her straight home. They'll email me the results and we'll go from there, but make sure she doesn't take any cough medicine. With the dry cough and what Dr. Barkley thinks she's got, taking that kind of medicine would not be good."

The hospital called the Barkley home within a few minutes and said they had an opening at ten a.m. and if Mrs. Barkley could make it for then? Audra said of course and was a little surprised at how fast they had accommodated her mother. *But I suppose that's a perk of being chair of the board of directors*, she thought. The x-ray was done, and she had her mother back home in less than an hour.

Soon, James Beldon called. "Dr. Barkley was correct. It was indeed pneumonia."

"What do we do now? Mother is much worse than when Kate checked her last night. Going to the hospital really exhausted her."

"Tell you what, I have no patient appointments today, so I could make an old-fashioned house call."

"You'd do that? It would be so wonderful. I was wondering how I was going to get her back into town to see you."

"I'll there in about half an hour."

When he arrived, he examined Victoria. Her temperature was one hundred and three, she was shuddering with the chills, and toss-

435

ing around in the bed. "I'll call in a prescription for some Rexulti. The dosage will be on it, but I'll go over it with you when it gets here. In the meantime, I'm going to give her something to help her sleep. It is important she get that medication as soon as possible. I could stay with her if you want to get it."

"You will? That's wonderful. I'll go right now," Audra said and left the room.

Victoria, tossing and turning, was delirious. She began asking for Audra.

"I want Audra. Where's Audra? She's so precious to me, my only daughter. I couldn't live without her. Oh, where is she? I need to see her."

James Beldon was standing over her with two syringes, one containing a sedative, the other empty, intending to introduce an air bubble into her system, thereby killing her. But when he heard her talk about Audra, an idea came to him. Instead of killing Victoria Barkley, he'd take her daughter's life. What a way to punish his enemy than to let her live the rest of her life without the daughter she loved so much! He put the empty syringe back in his bag and gave his patient her shot. Within minutes, she fell into a restful sleep.

When Audra returned, her mother was sleeping peacefully. Dr. Beldon went over the dosage of the medication with her and warned her of danger signs in pneumonia—to watch out for bluish skin usually in the lips or fingertips or coughing up blood. "If that happens, no matter what she says, call an ambulance and get her to the hospital. I'd be happier if she was in one right now, but I understand she stubbornly refuses to go."

"For some unknown reason, my brothers agree with her."

On his way out, Victoria's sons met him at the bottom of the stairs and asked for an update on their mother. After he told them, he said he was curious to know why they were all against their mother going into hospital. The brothers looked at each other, and then Jarrod asked him to come into the library with them. They all went in, making sure the door was closed, and then told him about the second murder and the threat against their mother's life. Showing him a copy of the second note, James Beldon appeared to be shocked. Nick told him of the extra security around the house and that they were all working inside with handguns at the ready.

"We couldn't protect her like that if she were in the hospital. We'll do and pay anything to keep her at home. Whatever you want to charge us for this house call is fine. If you need to come back out a few more times, just add it to the bill. And if you think mother needs a night nurse, get one. Like I said, spare no expense. Give or send the bills directly to me and I'll see they get paid the same day," Nick said to the doctor.

"One thing," Jarrod told him. "Audra doesn't know what's going on, and we'd like to keep it that way."

"Of course, I won't say a word to her."

"We all want to thank you for coming out here today. We are in your debt. If there's anything we can ever do for you, you have only to ask," Nick said to him.

Victoria's recovery was slow but steady. A few days later, she told Audra that she didn't need to be play nurse all day.

"Jarrod said he was going into town this afternoon. Why don't you ride in with him and spend some time doing some shopping for yourself? Here, take this with you, and have fun."

"Mother, I can't take all this."

"Of course you can. You've earned it and more. Do you know what a private nurse costs? I do, because I called an agency. So you're paid on their rates. That plus a bonus. You just don't have to pay taxes!"

"Are you sure?"

"Absolutely. Now go, Jarrod is going into town. You can ride in with him."

"It's two p.m. now. I should be finished in the office by five. Is that okay with you?" Jarrod asked.

"That'll work out just fine."

As she was wandering around window shopping, she ran into Dr. Beldon.

"How's your mother doing?"

"She's much better. In fact, she insisted I come into town for the afternoon."

"I'm taking the afternoon off and planning to take a drive in the country. Would you like to come with me?"

"That sounds like fun. As long as I'm back before five, it will be fine."

"I just have to stop by my office, and then we can leave."

In the meantime Fred had called Jarrod and asked him to come over to the station.

"We've been looking at Martin's computer and found a very interesting email. He'd asked a friend of his in St. Louis if he knew the whereabouts of a Janet Davis. The answer he got was, 'She died in a mental institution, don't know where the son went.'

"That name, Davis, seemed vaguely familiar, so I did some research," Sheriff Madden told Jarrod. "There was an Emory Davis involved in a scandal at the Minor's Bank. He had overextended the bank's investing in some worthless mining ventures. He was forced to resign by the principal investors, Everett Gibbons, Martin Erskine, and Victoria Barkley. Davis later committed suicide by hanging himself. His nine-year-old son found the body. The mother and son moved to St. Louis. But here's the kicker. The old Davis ranch was up for sale for taxes for years, and then suddenly, an unknown buyer bought it but never moved in or did anything with it. The buyer was from St Louis—a John Smith! Isn't that where Dr. Beldon went to school?"

"You think he could be the Davis son?" asked Jarrod incredulously.

"All this started after he came to town, and he's about the right age."

"That's all supposition, Fred."

"Well, I'm going down to talk with him. Wanna come with me?"

"All right, I'll tag along with you just out of curiosity."

When they got to the doctor's office, they met his receptionist, who was just getting ready to leave.

"Dr. Beldon gave me the rest of the afternoon off. He's gone for a drive in the country with Miss Barkley."

"Audra! You don't happen to know in which direction they went?"

"I do know he likes to drive out to the old Davis place."

Jarrod and Fred looked at each and then raced for the car. As they drove, the sheriff called the station for backup deputies to meet him at the old ranch.

As Audra and the doctor were driving, he asked her to call him James. They chattered about the area, then, coming to an old sign for the Davis Ranch, he asked her if she'd ever been there. Saying she hadn't, he went on to tell her he had found the place on his last trip out and found it very interesting and he'd like to show it to her. She was agreeable, so they continued along the road. Getting to the main house, they parked got out and started to look around. "Let's go inside," he said to her.

There were a few moth-eaten curtains and some sad-looking furniture as they went into a room which Martin told her must have been the billiard room, judging by the fittings on some of the walls.

"Like to see the kitchen?" On the way to it, he told her that another room they were passing must have been the study. "Why don't you look in there?"

She went in and looked around. In the dim light, she saw a skeleton hanging by its neck, another empty noose hanging alongside it. She was so shocked she started to scream and turned around to find Martin standing right behind her, blocking her exit!

"That's how I found my father. It was Gibbons, Erskine, and your mother's fault. If it wasn't for them, he'd still be alive." Beldon was babbling how pleased his father would be when it was all over. Audra couldn't believe what she was hearing as he continued to talk about what he'd done to Gibbons and Erskine, but taking her daughter away from Victoria Barkley would be much more of a punishment than just plain killing her. As he talked, he moved away from the door. Audra, realizing the danger she was in from this completely deranged man, made a run for the now unblocked doorway. Getting to the front door, she yanked it open and raced outside. Beldon came chasing after. She continued to run down the road and almost collided with the sheriff's car as it came screaming around the bend in the road. Fred, a deputy, and Jarrod jumped out, and between sobs, she told them what had happened.

She stayed with Jarrod while the sheriff and the other squad car continued to the ranch house, but they were too late. Seeing that he couldn't carry out his plan, Dr. James Beldon hung himself using the noose he'd planned for Audra! The authorities found out the skeleton, which had frightened Audra so was, in fact, the one from Beldon's office. James was later buried next to his father.

It took a few weeks for Victoria to totally recover from her bout of pneumonia and even longer for Audra to forget her ordeal, but surrounded by her loving and supportive family, she was at last able to put it all behind her.

Chapter 30

John McIntire was spending some time down at the main corral, watching one of his men break a bronc. Heath came down to watch, and after he'd been there a few minutes, a friend of his, Ward Witcombe, drove up. Getting out of his truck, Ward walked over to join Heath and watched with him for a while. They were just chatting about the ranch which Witcombe rented when he asked Heath if he could borrow, seventeen hundred and fifty dollars, saying he wanted to "fix up some things at the ranch."

"That's the same excuse you used two weeks ago when you borrowed nine hundred dollars. Give my regards to Nora," Heath said and started to walk away.

"I really do need the money!"

Heath thought for a moment. "I'll give you a chance to earn it."

"Earn it how?"

"Break a bronc."

"Are you serious?"

"If you want the money, earn it!"

"Well, if that's the only way." Witcombe took off his jacket and climbed the fence.

"Mr. Witcombe will ride this one," Heath told the astonished John.

"Well, If you're sure he knows what he's doing," John said.

Witcombe climbed on the back of the bronc and called, "Let him go."

The horse went bucking and kicking round the corral a couple of times, then he threw his rider off his back right into the fence.

John and Heath and some of the hands ran to help while others caught the bronc and got it into an adjoining smaller coral.

"Call nine one one," shouted John. "Don't move him. We don't know what kind of injuries he might have, and any movement could make them worse. Just lie still, son. Help is on the way," he told Ward.

When Nick heard the sirens, he came running from his office to find out what was going on. He watched as the paramedics carefully placed Witcombe in a collar, thus immobilizing his neck, and very gently got him strapped to a backboard. They loaded Ward into the ambulance and, with blaring sirens and lights flashing, left.

"What the hell has been going on here?" asked a fuming Nick. "Did you let Witcombe on that bronc, John? Has he ever been on one before?"

"It wasn't John," Heath said. "It was me."

"Well," said Nick angrily. "I'll ask you. Has Witcombe ever been on a bronc before?"

"I'm not sure. But he's a rancher, so he probably has."

"You're not sure!" yelled Nick. "You put a man on a bronc, and you're not sure he's ever been on one before. Have you lost your mind? You blazing idiot!"

"Get your spurs out of me!" Heath yelled back,

"This is not helping Ward," John said, trying to get the brothers to calm down. "Somebody ought to go to the hospital."

"I'll go," said Heath and left.

"What actually happened here, John?" asked Nick.

John told him all he knew which wasn't much.

When Heath got back from the hospital the news he brought wasn't good.

"Ward has a spinal fracture impinging on a nerve in his spine. The result is his legs are paralyzed," Heath told his mother.

"You better let Nick know," Victoria said to her son.

"I know all about it. Kate told me," Nick told him and then hung up!

"He's still mad at me," Heath told his mother.

"What really happened?" she asked. "Why did you put Ward up on the bronc?"

There was silence for a minute then Heath said, "I got tired of him borrowing money from me so I thought I'd make him earn it."

"How much did he want to borrow?"

"Seventeen hundred and fifty dollars"

"And how much has he borrowed in the past?"

"Close to sixteen thousand dollars"

"Why have you loaned him so much money?"

"We've been friends since we were kids, and when he and Nora moved to Stockton and rented the old Palmer place, he asked for a little help, and I was happy to oblige. But then, it was almost every week he came to borrow more. He used the excuse that he was fixing up things at the ranch, but he never did."

"So what now?"

"Now I feel responsible for him being hurt. It was my idea for him to break that horse. If I hadn't told him to do it, he wouldn't be lying in a hospital paralyzed."

Heath went every day to visit Ward as the hospital continued to run tests, including MRI, bone scan, myelogram (a special CT scan taken after injecting dye into the spinal column), and EMG, an electrical test of muscle activity. The numbness in Ward's legs continued, and he couldn't stand on his own. His medical team consisted of a bone and a nerve specialists and physical therapist. All were a little confused at his condition in view of the test results. After five days in the hospital, he could go home with outpatient physical therapy appointments made and follow-ups with his doctors.

The only way he could move around in the living room of his house was in a wheelchair. The Barkley's arranged for the use of a hospital bed for as long as Ward needed it and had it set up also in the living room as he couldn't get through any doorways in his chair. Every other item the hospital recommended he have, they also saw to it he had the use of.

Heath started going over to the Witcombe ranch every day, doing the repairs which Ward had neglected to do and helping Nora

443

get him to all his medical appointments. After three weeks of this, Nick completely lost his patience.

"How much longer is this going to last?" he asked Heath at a family dinner. "You're neglecting work here!"

"As long as they need me. Now get off my back. I'll do my work for you in the evenings. Will that suit you?"

"I guess it will have to!"

The rest of the Barkleys talked together, covering up the silence from the two brothers.

When Nick and Kate got back to their apartment, he told her how angry he was at the whole situation.

"You can't do anything about it. You'll just have to let it go and accept it that Health is doing his work for you in the evenings."

"But…" fumed Nick as Kate cut him off.

"Nick, we've got better things to talk about than that."

"Oh yes, like what?"

"Like when you're going to take me to bed!"

"We don't have to talk about that for long, because my answer is now!"

"Are all family dinners going to be as contentious as that one?" Victoria asked Heath.

"I'm sorry, Mother, but Nick has a way of getting under my skin!"

"I think part of his problem is he's concerned, as am I, that Ward is taking unfair advantage of you."

"He didn't ask for my help. It's something that I just want to do."

"And how long is it going to go on?"

"I don't know."

"Is his condition still the same? What are his doctors saying about it?"

"Yeah, he's the same, and it's puzzling the doctors who thought there'd be some improvement by now. His legs now aren't numb, he can feel it if they stick a pin in his toe, it's just he can't stand up by himself. His legs just fold under him, and they're not sure why. Now

I'd better get to that work I told Nick I would do, or I'll have him on my back again."

After he left to go into the library, Victoria poured herself a glass of sherry and sat down in her living room and thought over all that Heath had told her. *I hope that Ward isn't making his injuries worse than they are, but from what I've heard, I wouldn't put it past him! Oh, Heath, I hope he's not pulling some kind of scam on you!*

Heath continued to help Ward and Nora, but as the weeks passed, he had reduced his visits to work around their ranch to twice a week. Witcombe continued to astonish the doctors by still being unable to stand. They ran all the tests again, but with the same results, they could find no medical reason why he shouldn't be able to walk. They even suggested he see a psychiatrist, but he balked at that suggestion!

One day, when Heath was over at their ranch, Ward invited him to have a drink when he had finished work. Accepting, Heath sat down, and Ward confided in him that he hadn't told Nora, but he feared that he'd be in the wheelchair for years—maybe even life!— that he couldn't go on accepting Heath's help, and running the ranch, even with a hand, was too much for him. What he wanted to do was to move into town in a house that could accommodate his wheelchair. But then, he'd need a steady source of income and showed Heath the paperwork of a business proposition a friend of his had offered him. The only drawback was he needed one hundred and fifty thousand dollars to buy into the deal.

"Where are you going to get that kind of money?" Heath ask him.

"I was hoping you'd help me out. What is the price of a pair of legs? It's mainly your fault I'm in this chair for who knows how long, maybe life."

"I don't have that kind of money," Heath told him.

"You may not have it, but your family does."

"I'll have to think this over. This won't be just my decision the family will have to okay it."

That night, Heath asked for a meeting of all his family members and told them what Ward had asked for.

"It's nothing short of blackmail," declared Nick. "There's nothing to prove he'll be in that chair for life."

"But there's nothing to prove he won't," said Jarrod. "Ward's injuries are kind of our fault. He got hurt on our ranch trying to break one of our horses with the permission of Heath and John. I think his case might stand up in court if were to sue us. But the bottom line is, what does Heath want to do? I say he can have the money." The rest of the family agreed. "What you do with it is your business, Heath," Victoria told him.

"First thing in the morning, I'll transfer one hundred and fifty thousand dollars to your personal account, Heath," Nick told him.

When Ward told Nora of his plan and that he was sure he was going to get the money from Heath to buy into it, she was appalled. "Why can't we stay here? We're making a decent living from the ranch."

"No, not when we can make the kind of money that would be ours in Doug's business offer."

"But we can't take advantage of Heath like that."

"It's his fault I'm in this chair. It's only fair I get some compensation."

"I can't face him when he gives you the money. I'm going on a long walk."

After she left, Ward got up out of his chair and stretch then walked to his desk to get the paperwork on the deal he was looking forward to getting involved in. Just then, Nora opened the door and stopped in her tracks. She stared at her husband.

"How long have you been able to walk?" she asked him.

"For weeks," he told her. "I was just looking for a way to make some money out of Heath for the accident. After all, it was his fault, and when Doug offered me this deal, it was the perfect way to get away from this ranch and live on easy street. It's not like the Barkleys can't afford it—they're loaded."

"You can't do that to Heath. It's like stealing. I came back to beg you not to take the money."

"Nonsense."

"If you won't tell him, I will."

"I won't have you ruining the best opportunity I've ever had in my life. You just can't do it, Nora. I won't let you."

"You can't stop me."

She tried to open the door to leave, but Ward was faster, got to it, and slammed it shut. He grabbed his wife. She struggled to break free, yelling at him to let her go. Trying to keep her quiet, he put his hands around her throat and squeezed. The more she struggled, the harder he kept squeezing her throat. Suddenly, she went limp. He picked her up and carried her into the bedroom. Checking her, he found she was no longer breathing. *I'll have to deal with this later*, he thought. *Heath could be here any time*. A few minutes later, Heath arrived. When he came in, the first thing Ward asked him was "Did you get the money?"

"Yes," Heath told him. "But before I give it to you, there's some paperwork that Jarrod wrote that will prevent you from ever trying to get more money from us."

"I'll sign anything if it means I get the money."

As Ward was signing the agreement, the door from the bedroom opened, and Nora staggered out.

"Don't give him the money, Heath. There's nothing wrong with his legs. He's been able to walk for weeks. When I told him I was going to tell you, he tried to strangle me."

"You lousy bastard!" And with that, Heath hauled Ward out of his chair and, hitting him with a right hook, knocked him back into the chair he had fooled everyone into believing he needed.

"Nora, let me call for help for you."

"No, Heath. I'll be fine, just let me sit down, and if you could get me a cold wet towel for my throat."

"I should call the sheriff and have him arrest Ward for attempted murder."

"Please don't do that. Not getting the money from you is a big enough punishment for him. I'm through with Ward. If you'll wait, Heath, I'll pack my things and I'm leaving. If you could give me a ride into town, I'll find a place to stay."

"You can stay with us until you work out what you're going to do next," Heath told her.

"Don't leave," Ward implored her.

"We're over," she said. "Don't make a fool of yourself by begging!"

Heath took her back to the Barkley ranch, where Victoria welcomed her and set about putting ice on her neck to help with the pain and bruising. When Kate came in, she heard what had happened and checked Nora out. As far as she could tell, Nora would make a full recovery but could expect to have a sore throat for a few days. When Kate told Nick what Ward had done to Nora, what Nick called him couldn't be repeated!

A few days later, Ward left town without telling anyone where he was going. Nora recovered from the attack and got a job, with a recommendation from Victoria, at the bank where the Barkleys had their accounts. A girl she met at work was looking for a roommate, so Nora was able to move in with her new friend. She thanked the Barkleys profusely for all they had done for her. A few months later, she got in touch with Jarrod's law firm and asked them to handle her divorce.

Heath bumped into her in town one Saturday and took her for coffee. She updated him with details about her job, how well she and her roommate got along, and the fact that, in the course of her divorce proceedings, Ward had been traced to Denver. He was not contesting the divorce. Lastly, she told Heath that she had started seeing a young man from the bank. Heath was very pleased to hear all her good news and told her to remember that, as his friend, he was always available to help her in any way she might need it. When they parted, Nora gave him a big hug and told him he was the best friend she'd ever had, and the reverse was also true; if there was ever anything she could do for him, he'd only to ask. They both left, certain that they each had a friend for life.

Chapter 31

It was Saturday afternoon, and the front door phone buzzed. Kate answered. It was Silas, asking for Mr. Nick.

"He's not here right now. He'll be back in about twenty minutes. Can I help?"

"Well, actually, there is someone here to see him."

"Well, send them up."

"I don't think that's a good idea, Mrs. Nick. I think he'd prefer to come down here and see her."

"You're sounding rather mysterious, Silas. Who is it?"

"A Miss Hester Converse."

"Is she a friend of Nick's?"

"In a manner of speaking."

"Well, like I said, send her up."

"If you're sure, Mrs. Nick?"

"I am, Silas."

A few minutes later, the buzzer at the front door sounded. Kate opened the door to find a young woman about her age standing there, accompanied by Silas.

"Come in, Miss Converse. Thank you for showing her up, Silas. Right in here. Please, sit down. Can I get you anything? Tea or coffee?"

"Coffee would be wonderful, and please call me Hester."

Just then, there was a knock at the deck door. "Hello, Jeanne. What are you doing here?"

"I was baking and brought you and Nick a couple of quiches for dinner and some muffins for breakfast tomorrow. Oh, you have a visitor. Let me put a pot of coffee on for you. I have a crumb cake just out of the oven. I'll run down and get it for you." And before Kate could say anything, she hurried out the door. Just then, the front door phone buzzed.

"Please excuse me. It's not normally this busy on a Saturday afternoon. Yes, oh, of course, please come in." She turned to Hester. "It's my mother-in-law."

"Kate, your mail was delivered to the main house, and I thought I'd bring it up to you. Oh hello, Hester. It's been quite a while since we saw you last."

At that moment, Jeanne came bustling in the deck door and exchanged a look with Victoria that Kate didn't understand. The housekeeper then went into the kitchen and busied herself pouring coffee for everyone and cutting slices of cake.

It was then that Nick could be heard whistling as he came up the steps. Coming in the door, he said, "Hi," to his mother, and Jeanne then noticed someone sitting with her back to him. When she turned around, he stopped dead in his tracks and his eyes opened wide.

What on earth is going on? thought Kate.

"Er...hello, Hester," he said. "It's been quite a while since you were in Stockton!"

That's more or less what his mother said. What on earth is going on, and more to the point, who is this woman? Kate wondered. There was an uncomfortable silence in the room broken only by Jeanne asking Nick if he wanted some coffee.

"Yes, please." And he went into the kitchen, leaving Victoria, Kate, and the visitor to make polite conversation!

"I understand you and Nick haven't been married very long."

"May second was our first year anniversary."

"Did you know him long before you got married?"

"No, not long. Where did you meet my husband?"

"In San Francisco, on one of his business trips."

"That was quite some time ago," put in Victoria.

"Please excuse me for a moment," said Kate, going into the kitchen where Nick was quietly conferring with Jeanne. "Would somebody please tell me what is going on?" she whispered to them.

450

"Nick, who is this Hester? Everybody seems to know, including you, Jeanne. Everyone, that is, but me!"

"I'll explain in a moment, but first, I want to find out what she wants," Nick told her. He walked into the living room and asked Hester what she was doing in Stockton.

"I have moved here for the foreseeable future," she told them, "and wanted to look up old friends and introduce myself to what I hope will be a new one." And she nodded in Kate's direction. "But I can see I've come at a bad time, so I'll say goodbye for now, but I'll see you all again soon." With that, she got up to leave.

"Let me show you out," said Kate and escorted Hester out the deck door and through the gate. "All right what gives? What do you all know that I don't?" asked Kate when she came back in.

"I think that's our signal to leave," said Victoria to Jeanne, and the two women duly got up and left, one by the front door, the other by the deck door.

"Okay, Nick, talk to me. Who is Hester Converse?"

"She's my former fiancée."

"Oh. Is that why Silas, your mother, and Jeanne didn't want me to be alone with her? Is that what they were afraid she'd tell me?"

"They were just trying to protect you."

"From what? Nick, I know that you were no saint before we met and there were plenty of women in your life. I have never asked you about them, and I never will, because it's none of my business."

"But I think you should know about Hester," Nick said to her. "I met her at Dave Wallis's party when I was going to San Francisco regularly on business. We continued to date each time I was out there. She was very popular. I knew that about her. At charity events and parties, there were always men lined up to dance with her. Unlike you, she relished going to trendy restaurants and nightclubs, enjoying having men cut in when we were dancing, and always having her name in the papers. Bottom line, I thought I was in love with her and asked her to marry me. She said yes, and when I brought her back here to meet the family, she wasn't too happy because Heath didn't give her the attention she was used to. So she went out of her way to try and attract him. Unfortunately, I was oblivious to it all.

451

Mother and Jarrod saw what was happening and tried to warn me, but I wouldn't listen. Without going into all the gory details, I ended up in a fight with Heath over what I perceived was an insult to her. I got pretty badly hurt and was laid up for a while. Anyway, when she saw all the trouble she had caused, she had the decency to call off our engagement and go back east!"

"Nick, I'm so sorry you had to go through that."

"I'm not. Less than six months later, I met you. To think I might have missed meeting, falling in love, and marrying you makes me go cold inside! I don't know why she has decided to move to Stockton. It doesn't seem like a large enough city for her. She normally likes the bright lights of cities like San Francisco or New York."

"Well, it's none of our business, but thanks to her, we've got quiche for dinner and homemade muffins for breakfast courtesy of Jeanne trying to find a reason to come up here and play nursemaid!"

The following Friday, Kate was running errands in town when she bumped into Hester at a local Starbucks. She insisted on buying Kate a vanilla cappuccino and cranberry scone. The two women found a table and sat down.

Kate inquired, "How are you settling down in Stockton?"

Hester replied, "It's a little different from San Francisco, but I'm adapting. Do you know San Francisco?" she asked Kate.

"As a matter of fact, that's where Nick took me on our honeymoon."

"Did he take you to his favorite restaurant, La Folie on Russian Hill?" Hester asked her.

"Yes, he did. We had a very romantic evening there. The food is delicious."

"Yes, it is. That's where Nick and I had dinner about two weeks ago."

"You...you did...er...that's nice. I'm sorry, I've just remembered an appointment. Sorry to run like this. Next time, my treat." With that, Kate hurried out and just about ran to her Land Rover and drove hurriedly home. Parking, she raced up the stairs.

"Did you remember to stop by Trader Joe's?" Jeanne asked.

"No, I forgot."

"How come? What's wrong? You look upset?"

"I ran into Hester Converse in town. She bought me coffee and made a point of telling me that Nick took her out to dinner about two weeks ago to a romantic restaurant on Russian Hill that he took me to on our honeymoon! How could he, Jeanne? How could he?"

"HE DID WHAT! Are you absolutely sure it was the same restaurant? I mean, there's more than one restaurant on Russian Hill?"

"No, no, it was the same one. She made sure I knew that, She even said its name, La Folie. Jeanne, I feel so betrayed by him. That was such an incredibly special evening for us. We had dinner, and it was what followed that changed things forever in our relationship, then he dares to take her there. It's just as well he's not here. I'm going to throw somethings in a bag and leave until I cool down. I'm afraid of what I might say to him if I saw him right now. I'll teach him to treat our special memories like this." And she stormed into the hallway to get a bag out of the closet.

What Kate hadn't realized was Jeanne had her cellphone in her pocket, and as soon as she went out of the room, their housekeeper put in a call to Nick. It went to his voicemail, so she left him a message.

"You are in so much trouble. You'd better get home really quick. Don't call back. Just get your ass here as fast as you can!"

Nick got the message a few moments later, not understanding what was going on but knowing Jeanne wouldn't have called him if something serious wasn't happening, left the stables where he was inspecting his new stallion, and raced over to the flat. Running upstairs, he opened the deck door to find his wife coming out of their bedroom with an overnight bag in her hand!

"What's going on?" he asked. "And where are you going with that bag, Kate?"

"Your girlfriend's been telling your wife how you wined and dined her a couple of weeks ago at your favorite romantic restaurant on Russian Hill, the one that you took Kate to on your honeymoon, that's what's going on," his housekeeper told him with a disgusted look on her face!

"Jeanne, would you leave us, please? I need to talk to my wife alone."

"Don't you dare hurt her any more than you've already done, or so help me, God, you'll answer to me, Mr. Nicholas Jonathan Barkley." And with that, Jeanne walked out the deck door, slamming it shut behind her.

"Get out of my way, Nick. I'm leaving for a couple of days until I cool down. It's the best way, I'm hurt, and I feel so betrayed by you. How could you share our special place with someone else? Obviously, that evening didn't mean nearly as much to you as it did to me. I'm afraid if I stay here I'll say something to you we'll both regret."

"Kate, please listen to me. That was a special evening for me too. You can't leave like this. You're not going to. You have to let me explain."

"I'm not interested in your explanations. Now let me past. I'm telling you, if you don't let me leave, I could say something that I won't be able to take back, so just please let me go," she said, fighting back the tears.

"Oh Lord, Kate, please don't cry. You've got to hear me out. You owe us that much!"

"Did you take Hester Converse out a couple of weeks ago, and was it to La Folie on Russian Hill that you took me to for dinner on our honeymoon. Yes or No?" she asked as the tears spilled from her eyes and ran down her cheeks.

"Kate, if you'll just give me a chance to explain, I—"

"Yes or No?"

"Yes, but—"

"That's all I need to hear. I have to get out of here until I calm down and think this through," she told him, wiping away the tears with the back of her hand.

"No, you're not leaving. If you'll just give me a chance to explain…"

"There's nothing to explain, Nick. That was such a betrayal of us. It wasn't just the romantic time we had at dinner but what happened after, or doesn't that mean anything to you anymore? Did you have too much to drink when you went to dinner with her? Does she enjoy your rough sexual behavior? This time, I really am leaving!"

By this time, the tears were coursing down her cheeks.

"I asked for that! Of course, I haven't forgotten our evening at the restaurant or what happened at the hotel. The way I behaved toward you and how you forgave me for it—that's why you can't leave. You can't believe I'd be unfaithful to you. I won't let you think that way, Kate. Now please stop crying and let me explain."

"I don't want to hear anymore from you. Let me past. You can't stop me going, Nick."

"Put the bag down and give a minute. Listen to me, please."

"Okay, you've got two minutes. Start talking."

"Hester called me when I was on my last trip to San Francisco about two weeks ago and said she needed my help. I hadn't heard from her since we broke up, and she was the one who suggested dinner, and at that particular restaurant. Well, I'd been there before with her, way before I met you, so it never occurred to me that I would be betraying you by going there.

"She had told me that she wanted to change her financial advisor and asked for my recommendations as to whom she should hire to replace him. We met, had dinner, and then I gave her a list of good replacement candidates. I can assure you that's all that happened. She said nothing about seeing me again or moving to Stockton. She was surprised when she saw my wedding band, wanted to know about you, how long we'd been married, etc. After dinner, I put her in a cab and said goodbye and honestly thought no more about it until I saw her sitting here a week or so later. I never mentioned seeing her because I didn't attach any importance to it. Please, Kate, listen to what I'm saying. I'm so sorry you're hurt, but you can't believe I'd cheat on you. You've got to know me better than that. Please, babe, stop crying."

"I want to believe you, Nick, but going to La Folie when we'd gone there on our honeymoon makes it feel like such a betrayal. You don't know what a fool I felt when she told me about the dinner. Why would she want me to know about it?"

"I don't know why she told you unless it was to cause a problem between us. But that wouldn't make sense, because she'd have nothing to gain by it. I love you, and I'd never do anything to hurt you or jeopardize our marriage. You've got to know that about me! I admit it was wrong of me to go back to that restaurant with her, but I didn't think anything of it. It had no meaning to me. Not like when we went there."

"If the dinner was so innocuous, why didn't you tell me about it? I'd have told you if I'd been out with an old boyfriend at a romantic French restaurant, to say nothing if it was an old fiancé!"

"Looking back, I can see I was wrong by not telling you, but like I said, it wasn't important to me."

"She must have known you wouldn't tell me!"

"I don't honestly know how she knew that."

"It goes like this, Nick. 'Gee, hun, you'll never guess who I took to a candlelight dinner at La Folie. My former fiancée! But don't read anything into it!"

"But it wasn't anything like that, Kate. It was purely a business meeting."

"A business meeting in an incredibly romantic French restaurant! Whatever you want to call it by not saying anything shows you didn't trust me Nick, but now you're asking me to trust you, hardly a two-way street is it? We haven't got much if we don't trust each other! I need a break away from you so I can get my head together."

"Are you crazy? Do you think I'll let you leave without putting up a fight? I love you way too much, and the marriage we've got is too important to let you go. Oh lord, why won't you listen to me? Please tell me we're not going back to you sleeping in the guest room and giving me the silent treatment. I can't—I won't—go through that again!"

And with that, he swept her up in his arms and kissed her and went on holding her as she fought against him, beating on his chest with her fists.

"Let go of me, let me go," she said as she struggled against him, never, up until that point, fully realizing just how strong he was!

"Please don't ask that, Kate, I've got to hold onto you some-how," he told her. "Don't fight to get away from me. I can't stand the idea of us being at odds again."

"Nick, let go of me! You're hurting—I said let go of me right now!"

Nick slowly let her go. "I'm sorry, I never meant to hurt you. Are you all right?"

"What's gotten into you? You've never done anything like that before. You've never put your hands on me and hurt me! Have you lost your mind?"

"I don't know what to say. I was just trying to stop you from leaving, but I never meant for you to think I was putting my hands on you to hurt you! Kate, you know me better than that! This started off as such a wonderful day, the way we made love this morning with the promise we'd pick it right back up at lunchtime! Tell me how it could all go so wrong so fast?"

"I met Hester Converse, and she blew the lid off your rendezvous!"

"How many more times—it was a business meeting, nothing more!"

"Okay, I believe you when you tell me that nothing happened, but that still leaves the fact that you took another woman, for what-ever your reason, to a special place that should have been ours alone!"

"You're right, I blew it. Now what?"

"What do you mean 'Now what?'"

"I'm admitting I shouldn't have taken anyone to 'our' restau-rant, and I shouldn't have put my hands on you, at least not like I did. Now what?"

"Are you making fun of me, Nick Barkley?"

"Not in the least. I'm just asking, as I've admitted to every-thing I've done wrong, what do we do now, and I'm waiting for your answer."

"I'm leaving. I need a place to think."

"And where is that?"

"I don't know. I'll find somewhere. I'm taking my overnight bag with me."

"Please don't. I understand you want to go off by yourself and think, but I'm asking you to please don't stay away overnight."

"Give me one good reason why not?"

"Because I worry about you, and please don't give me the speech about how you can take care of yourself. I've heard it all before! That doesn't stop me worrying and wanting to take care of you. And I still want to know where we go from here. I'm waiting for you to answer me."

"I told you I'm going away to think."

"You mean you had no idea what to do when I admitted my guilt? What did you want, a big fight so you could yell, slam some doors, and threaten to leave me? Well, I was wrong, I admit it, and like I asked you ten minutes ago now, what? You have a human being for a husband who screws up. Are you going to punish me for that? We had an appointment for lunch time. It's a bit late, but we weren't planning on eating, were we?"

"You can't be serious?"

"Of course I am," Nick told her.

"How dare you? Is this your new ploy? Admit to all and I'll forgive you everything? Well, it's bloody well not going to work! You can take your sweet-talking, Nick Barkley, and shove it! And wipe that stupid grin off your face or I'll do it for you!"

"You try that, little lady, and it'll be the last time you ever raise your hand to me! And take my 'sweet talking' and shove it? My, my, how fast you've picked up American slang! But it doesn't sound quite right said with an English accent. Better stick to your 'bloody hells' and 'damns.' Much more your style! What else was it you said? Oh yes, my new ploy. Well, what was so terrible with my admitting I was wrong? It's not a ploy. I'm just tired of arguing with you, and I've decided, if I screw up, I'll admit it and see where you want to go from there. And I'm still waiting for your answer. Are you going to move into the spare room for a week and give me the silent treatment? If you are, just let me know, and I'll move into the Cattleman's Hotel until my week of punishment is over, 'cos let me tell you, I'm not staying here and putting up with that kind of treatment any longer."

"You wouldn't dare! That will make us the talk of Stockton!"

"I don't give a damn!"

"What in hell's gotten into you, Nick Barkley?"

"I get a message to come straight home—that my ass was in big trouble. I get here to find that you are going to leave me because I really blew it, which I now freely admit to. But when I ask you to forgive me and where do we go from here, I can't get you to answer. In the past, it's taken a week of you sleeping apart from me and not speaking until you've decided that I've been punished sufficiently. Enough is enough, Kate. I'm not putting up with that any longer! Now spit it out. Where do we go from here? And I'm not moving until you answer me!!"

"The honest truth is I don't know where we go from here. What you did, whether you meant it or not, really hurt. You say nothing happened, and I'll give you that. If you want to move out, then just go ahead and do it. It's probably the best way, all things considered."

"What does that mean? 'All things considered?'"

"Well, obviously you're not happy. You've never talked about moving out before. So between the two of us, things don't look good for this marriage. I guess I should have paid more attention to what the gossip columns were saying about us and seen what was right under my nose. I'll go into a guest room to give you a chance to pack some of your things and leave. I take it you are moving downstairs? It'll only be for a few days, Nick, a week at the most, then I'll have my stuff out of here. I'll donate most of my clothes, the rest I'll put into storage, and Jeanne can send them on to me when I decide where I'm going to go. London probably, there are plenty of good hospitals in the city. I should get a job without any trouble."

"That's it?"

"What do you mean 'That's it?'"

"You're just going to give up on us like that? What we have isn't worth fighting for to you?"

"There doesn't seem to be much point. You already said you want to leave."

"Kate, were you really listening when I said I was going to leave? Because I don't think you heard anything other than my saying, 'I was leaving,' not the rest of the sentence. I didn't say I wanted out of our marriage, I said I wasn't staying here if you were going to sleep in the guestroom and give me the silent treatment for a week! That rather than put up with that kind of treatment again, I'd stay in the Cattleman's Hotel. And the next thing I know, you're telling me of your plans to go back to England! I feel like I'm at the Mad Hatter's tea party!"

"But you said you were going to leave me. I heard you, Nick, and if you're going, there's not much point in me staying here by myself, so of course I'm going back to England. Where the hell else do you expect me to go? What bloody Mad Hatter's tea party?"

"God give me strength!! Damn it, woman, do you ever listen? For someone with your IQ, you can be amazingly dense sometimes!"

"Don't you dare call me dense!"

"So now you're paying attention to what I'm saying!"

"Just pack your bloody bags and go. Who the hell is she?"

"Who is whom?"

"Whoever it is you're leaving me for?"

"What? How many more times...I'm not leaving you!"

"Are you sure?"

"Yes, I'm sure! Kate, are you paying attention?"

"Of course I am!"

"If you hear nothing else I say today, hear this. I am, and always will be, very much in love with you. I realize now how badly I screwed up with the Hester Converse situation. Will you please forgive me?"

"I'd almost forgotten what started all this."

"Does that mean I'm forgiven?" he asked her.

"I suppose so."

"And things are back to where they were before all this Hester Converse nightmare started?"

"Yes, I guess they are."

"Then can we start our late lunch?"

"Nick, are you still going on about that? You've got a one-track mind!"

"When it comes to you, babe, you better believe it! Well, Kate, do we start lunch?"

She looked at him for a few seconds, and then her response was to rip at the buttons of his shirt. In return, he pulled off her tee and unhooked her bra, relishing the feel of her breasts on his now bare chest. Within minutes, they were in bed, making love with an urgency that, when they were spent and she lay in the circle of his arms, it took them more than a few minutes to recover from.

"I told you months ago that we'd never have a problem if you'd just let me take you to bed and make love to you. See how right I was. How about we go to Paul's tomorrow night for some dinner and dancing?"

"Sounds wonderful, but what are we going to do tonight?"

"You mean after I barbecue some steaks and we dance to the CD you made me? Do you really have to ask me a question like that? I'm going to take you to bed and make very slow love to you!"

"Nick, I have one thing to ask you. Does Hester often wear dresses in that god awful style and in that putrid pumpkin color?!"

They went as planned next night to their favorite French restaurant and were surprised when, not long after they got there, Hester and a party of five others came in. Nick and Kate were going to ignore them, but then he realized they were all people he'd met in San Francisco and he was forced to acknowledge them. One of the men even came over and asked Kate to dance with him, which she politely refused. She and Nick danced the way they normally did at Paul's, him holding her oh so tight, occasionally kissing her right hand, her with her left arm around his neck, massaging it gently with her fingertips, the way he loved, all the time swaying to the music and staying cheek to cheek. But as they were going back to their booth, Hester stood up at her table and asked Nick when he was going to ask her to dance. Hester's date for the evening said to go right ahead, he didn't mind, which put Nick on the spot.

"It's okay," said Kate. As Nick led Hester and walked to the dance floor, she reached out and took his hand. Instead of dancing the way he'd expected her to, she put her arms around his neck the way she used to dance with him when they were a couple and snuggled up to him. He had no choice but to dance with her holding onto him like that.

He couldn't wait for the music to be over, but instead of letting go, she held onto him for a second dance. After that was over, he, as politely as he could, removed her arms from around his neck and escorted her back to her table. Going back to his wife, he held out his hand to her, and she gladly took it and went to the dance floor with him. Gus played "their" songs, and Nick kissed his Kate with soft gentle kisses whilst they were dancing, and he was holding on to her extra tightly.

"Do you want to leave?" he asked her when they sat down again.

"Absolutely not," she replied. "I'll not be driven from one of our favorite restaurants. Besides which, we haven't had dessert. I'd like cherries flambé please."

Nick ordered dessert, and they continued to dance, ignoring Hester and her party. He sat with his arm around the back of the booth, leaning over and kissing Kate on the mouth and caressing her neck until both knew it was time to leave! As they passed Hester's group, they said goodnight then left. Going home, they spent some time dancing on their deck then went inside to take up where they had left off the night before.

What they didn't know was their every word was being recorded from the wireless transmitters which had been placed in their home by the "cable" repairman who had been to the flat earlier in the week.

The next Friday, when Kate had told Jeanne where she was going on her errands she again ran into Hester, who was with a friend of Kate's from the hospital. There was no way she could get out of having coffee with the ladies. This time, the mention of Nick came when Hester told their mutual friend that she had known Nick so much longer than Kate and had, in fact, once been engaged to him! She said it loud enough for the ladies sitting at nearby tables to hear. Of course, this raised a few eyebrows. Kate felt very uncomfortable and couldn't wait to get out of there. That evening, when the couple went to Jose's, who should already be there with a group from the hospital but Hester?

"How does she know them, and how did she know we'd be here?" Kate asked her husband.

"Goodness knows how she met them, but there's no way she knew about us coming to this place except through your friends from the hospital."

"That must be it. I must have mentioned it to someone who suggested coming here tonight."

Two weeks later, when they went to Luciano's for Italian food and Hester was there with a mutual friend of Nick's from San Francisco, they couldn't believe it.

"It's like she knows our plans ahead of time."

But when Nick received some photographs sent to him at the flat of Kate taken in their living room, standing in the circle of his arms, topless, and wearing only the tiniest of panties, they knew they had a serious problem. Nick worked out that the shots were taken through the partially open deck door, which Kate was standing with her back to, with a telephoto lens. The photographs were taken at night with the lights in the living room on but without the shade on the deck door lowered.

"I'm so sorry, Kate. I never thought anyone could see you. I should have made sure the door was properly closed and the blinds were lowered before I put you in such a vulnerable position."

"Nonsense. It wasn't your fault, Nick. Who would have guessed someone was up in the hills with a camera taking pictures of us. I guess, from now on, we'll just have to make sure the door is closed and the shades are drawn before you seduce me like that again! But why would they want the photographs? And now that we know where they can take them, we'll make sure they can't take any more."

"Unless it was to cause problem between us, that you'd be angry with me for letting them be taken of you. But I can't think who would want to try and come between us. It doesn't make any sense."

Next came a business takeover that Nick was considering, which was done by someone else just days ahead of him putting in his final bid.

When the same thing happened a second time, Nick couldn't believe it!

"You didn't mention the name of the company I was thinking of buying to anyone, did you?" he asked his wife.

"Nick, I forgot the name thirty seconds after you told me. The leak must be coming from your office."

"I don't see how only Trudy and Heath knew about the second takeover. I made it a need-to-know basis after the first debacle! I just don't understand it, not even the family outside of Heath and mother knew I was looking at that company. I suppose the leak must have come from inside the corporation itself, which is a shame, because they lost themselves quite a lot of money by accepting the first bid! But that doesn't really explain the leak happening twice in a row."

A third merger went through without any problems, but this time, Nick hadn't mentioned the name of the company at home! *Kate can't have talked about my business deals to anyone. She knows better than that,* he thought but couldn't deny the fact that when she was unaware of it, the third deal went through without a problem.

I'm going to try something, he thought, and that night, he told Kate that he was going to buy a certain corporation in a surprise take-over. In the next few days, there was some heavy trading of shares of that company. *Someone was buying up stock low with, I'm sure,* thought Nick, *the intent of selling high when the takeover is announced. Well, they're in for a big shock when no takeover is announced.* Kate asked him a week or so later if the proposed deal had gone through, and when he told her he had changed his mind, she seemed unconcerned!

But Hester kept showing up at restaurants, particularly Paul's, when Nick and Kate did.

And each time, Nick was forced into asking her to dance, and each time, she danced with him in the same intimate way, not caring that Kate and the rest of the patrons of the restaurant were watching.

Joan did a piece in her gossip column about "how cozy Nick and his former fiancée looked dancing the night away at Paul's, and all Kate could do was watch jealously. That Nick was so dissatisfied with his marriage that he had arranged to have Hester move to Stockton so they could take up where they had left off less than two years prior and he regretted letting Hester go! That all she Joan had put in an earlier column about the Barkley couple had proved right, and if ever there was a marriage on the rocks, it was theirs. A separation and divorce were not far away, both parties regretting their hasty marriage."

Nick was furious, but there wasn't much he could do about it, and like before, felt the best way to handle it was to ignore it.

But the effect of the column was it didn't seem to matter where Kate went, at work or in town, even at the ranch, she could feel people staring and whispering about her. That, plus she kept running into Hester and didn't want to add fuel to the fire by ignoring her as she seemed to have gotten to know so many of the people that Kate worked with, which made it difficult to turn down offers to go to lunch or coffee. *I feel like a fly being drawn inexplicably into a spider's web no matter how I try to avoid it*, she thought. She didn't want to tell her problems to Nick as he seemed to be having business-type problems of his own.

So Victoria decided it was time for her to step in. She called her son's office and booked an appointment with him for the following morning. She wanted to talk to him when Kate wasn't around and thought going to his office was the best way to do it. To say her son was surprised to see his mother's name entered on his schedule would be an understatement.

When she came into his office at the appointed time, she turned down offers of coffee or tea and said she wanted to get right down to the reason she was there. She laid it all out for him what Kate had been going through with all the whispering and stares, the lunches and coffees she felt she had to go to with Hester and her friends from the hospital. Victoria had gotten much of her information from Jeanne and Ann, who were sure something nefarious was going on.

Nick was horrified at what had been happening to his wife and then told his mother the business problems he had been going through.

"If I hadn't been so wrapped up in my own concerns, I would have pressed Kate more on the reasons she has been so quiet. I just put it down to pressure at work and her being tired. I had no idea all this other stuff was going on!"

"You know, it seems to me, both sets of problems, yours and hers, can be summed up in two simple words—Hester Converse.

Ever since she moved here, it's been one thing after another. First, she shows up at the flat, then she announces to Kate that you took her to dinner at the same restaurant she knew you'd have taken Kate to when she heard you'd spent your honeymoon in San Francisco. Then she keeps showing up at Paul's and coercing you to dance with her in front of Kate in that completely inappropriate way, plus she seems to know when you'll be at all your other favorite restaurants. The photographs which could easily have caused a major problem between you and Kate, her blaming you, perhaps, for allowing them to be taken. Next, you have business deals go south, but only if you mention them at home, which throws suspicion on who else but Kate. And she seems to know just where Kate will be on her days off so they can 'accidentally' run into each other and how about she has gone out of her way to cultivate relationships with Kate's friends and colleagues, making it almost impossible for her to turn down a lunch or coffee invitation. But she knows, out of all the people in the hospital, who Kate's friends with. That's not just some lucky guess!"

"Everything has been designed to subtly drive a wedge between you and Kate. Each one looking at the other with suspicion. Her not trusting you, however unconsciously, about why Hester's in Stockton. Did you really invite her here to take up where you left off. And the seed being planted in you about Kate's lack of discretion concerning your business affairs. And who is waiting in the wings if you and Kate were to split up but Miss Hester Converse, who would be more than willing to help you get over a failed marriage! You said when you met her in San Francisco that she was surprised to see your wedding band. What if this whole thing has been a campaign to subtly destroy your marriage so you and Hester could get back together?"

"My lord, Mother. You're right, and don't forget Joan and the gossip column and all that it's led to and the pressure it's put Kate under. The "insider information" must have originated with someone, why not Hester herself! Saying that I brought her back to Stockton to renew our relationship and how Kate and I are headed for divorce because of it. It's insidious what has been going on, my poor Kate having to put up with all this. Now all we've got to do is work out how Hester is getting her information." He thought for a

466

moment. "I know this sounds crazy, but what about the flat being bugged?" he suggested to his mother.

"It doesn't sound crazy at all. In fact, it makes perfect sense. It would explain everything, even the problems you had with your business deals. Hester could have tipped off one of her friends with the information. They must have been plenty mad when you tricked them into buying what amounted to worthless stock," she said, laughing.

"First, I want to find out if any workman has been to the house lately, then I'll go from there. The private detective I used when Kate had that stalker should be able to sweep the flat for bugs."

Nick made sure he got home whilst Jeanne was still there but before his wife got in.

"Jeanne, could you look at these plants on the deck? I don't think you're giving them enough water." Before she could answer him, he showed her a piece of paper on which he'd written:

I think the flat's bugged. Come outside with me
so we can talk without being overheard.

She nodded and said, "I better go outside with you, Nick, and check those plants."

Once outside with the deck door closed, Nick quickly went over all that he and his mother had discussed.

"Oh, Nick, bugging the flat makes perfect sense, and there was a cable guy here a few weeks back. I didn't know he was coming, and he wasn't sure who made the appointment, you or Kate. He went back and forth between the DVRs in the bedroom and living room. I must be honest, I kept more of an eye on him when he was working on the DVRs in the bedroom just because of Kate's jewelry being in there than when he was working in the living room. I'm sorry, Nick, I should have paid more attention to what he was doing."

"Don't blame yourself, Jeanne. I would have done the same thing."

"What happens next? Are you going to tell Kate?"

"Not until I've had someone here to sweep the place and we know for certain what's going on. Not only do we have to find out about the bug, but ideally, we need to know definitely on whose orders it was planted. Suspicions are not enough if Hester is, as we think, really behind this. I want proof before I confront her."

The next day, after talking with him on the phone, the private detective arrived disguised as a repairman come to look at the oven which Jeanne had told Kate and Nick the night before was running hot and needed looking at before she started burning food. Nick told the housekeeper to call a repairman first thing the next morning and to get him out ASAP. Nick made sure that he was home when the "repairman" arrived, saying that he was going to go down to the stables after he did some work on his laptop and this way, he'd just write a check for the repairs himself.

The man kept up the pretense of taking the ovens apart whilst going around the kitchen, dining area, living room, and bedroom, sweeping for bugs. He found two bugs hidden inside the DVRs in the living room and bedroom. He had already asked Nick that, if he found anything should he remove it or leave it in place. Nick, after thinking it over, decided that, for now, the best thing to do would be to disable any bug found in their bedroom but leave any found in the living room alone until they worked out how to trap Hester, because he was convinced she was the one responsible for having them put in place.

Nick called Kate at work and arranged to take her to the King's Head after her shift and that he'd have her Range Rover picked up during the day, so they'd just go in his truck. Over fish and chips, he told her of his suspicions and finding the bugs that morning. She was shocked to say the least.

"Oh, Nick, the things we say and some of the sounds we make! To think Hester has been listening in is just awful. Our lovemaking is way too private to be shared with a third party. Thank you for disabling that bug. It's sick to think she has been listening in on us in our bedroom. The living room is one thing, but our bedroom! She must have heard the fight we had over her and, lord, the things we said and did when we made up!"

468

"What we have to decide now is how we're going to trap Hester in such a way that she'll leave town and never bother us again."

"Couldn't we just confront her and tell her that we'd found the bugs and that we don't care because nothing and no one is going to come between us? Something simple like that. What do you think?"

"I think that's a good idea. Let's talk about going to Paul's Friday night. She's sure to go, and we'll confront her then."

That night, when they got home, in between kissing Kate, Nick invited his best girl out on a date to Paul's Friday night for dinner and dancing.

"Hester won't be there. She thinks we only go on Saturdays," he told Kate, who was having a hard time not to laugh. Then he whispered a few things that he was planning on doing to Kate when he took her into bed that night, just loud enough to be heard by anyone listening in! Kate, who was blushing at the thought of Hester hearing all the things he was saying, shushed him by dragging him into the bedroom and shutting the door behind them.

Friday night, Kate, wearing Nick's favorite sexy red spaghetti strap dress and Nick in one of his hand-tailored suits, showed up at Paul's just a few minutes ahead of Hester and three friends.

After dinner, Nick, who was especially attentive to his wife, kissing her repeatedly with his special brand of deep passionate kisses and caressing her neck, danced with her to his special request that Gus not only play but sing "The Lady In Red." As he'd been in touch with the piano player a day ahead of time and told him of his request and tipping Gus handsomely, it was not a problem. Everyone in Paul's sat out the dance and watched as the Barkley couple alone swayed to the seductive music. Hester's face said it all—she was furious. On the way back to their booth, Nick and Kate stopped by and asked Hester to join them for a few minutes. She was happy to oblige. When they all sat down, Kate reached into her purse and took out the bugs, the second of which Nick had removed just before they'd left the flat.

"I believe these belong to you," Nick said, handing them to Hester and was delighted to see the expression on her face freeze.

"What are they?" she said, trying to bluff her way out of the situation, but Nick was way too good a poker player to be fooled.

"They're the bugs you had planted in our flat. It's all over, Hester, we've figured out your little game, and we're not playing. You might as well pack up your things and go back where you came from. You're not welcome in Stockton any longer, especially when word gets out what you did."

"You can't prove I had anything to do with planting those bugs!"

"I don't have to. Just a little hint here and there, which my mother is so good at doing. You're no match for Victoria Barkley when she's defending her family, then she's worse than a she-cat! You seriously don't want to tangle with her when she's angry, and let me tell you, she's plenty angry at you right now!"

Hester didn't say a word. She just got up and left the booth, going back to her table. She and her party left soon after.

"I think that's the last we'll see of her," Nick said to his wife.

"Was your mother really going to do that to Hester?" asked Kate.

"All that and more. You haven't seen her when she's mad. She doesn't have red hair, but she might as well have. All I can say is I never want the two of you mad at me at the same time!"

"Let's order dessert. The cherries flambé sounds good." They ate dessert and slow danced until well past eleven.

"Neither of us has work tomorrow, and I don't have anything planned, do you, Kate?"

"No, nothing. What did you have in mind?"

"That we could turn our phones off and spend all day and night in bed."

"Oh yes, Nick, yes please."

Kate heard from some of the ER staff that Hester had left Stockton to go back to New York, that a friend had an accident and she went back to help her.

"Is she planning on coming back here?" Kate asked.

"Don't think so," one the nurses told her. "She was going back in just a few weeks in any case, so she told me this just meant her going back a little earlier. Have no idea why she came here in the first place. Have you?"

"Not a clue!" Kate replied, keeping a straight face. She couldn't wait to get home and tell Nick the good news. For once, she was home before him. The emergency room being quiet, she slipped away a little before six and had a bottle of champagne waiting when he walked in the door.

"Do I have time to eat before my shirt comes off?" he asked her, laughing.

"If you eat the Chinese food I brought in with me fast, the buttons on your shirt will remain attached. If you eat slow, I'll not be held responsible for the state your shirt will be in!"

As they both sat down to dinner, he asked, "Tell me, what we are going to celebrate?"

"Hester's left Stockton," his wife told him.

"What? How did you find out?'

"One of the nurses at work told me. The excuse was a friend had an accident, and she's gone back to New York to help and that she was leaving Stockton in a few weeks anyway, so this just meant her departure was only moved up slightly! She has no plans to return here."

"Have you finished eating?" Nick asked her. "Because we've got some serious champagne celebrating to do. You put the leftover food away. Meanwhile, I'll take off my shirt!"

"Don't you dare, Nick Barkley. That's part of the fun—me removing it!"

"Well, never let it be said I spoil your fun. Just let me get comfortable on the bed and then have at it, Kate!"

She didn't need to hear his offer of fun twice!

The Barkleys were now producing cider on a large scale, the first year having been so successful. A new filtration plant had been installed, and orders were pouring in, each year more than the previous one. It was just another of Nick's ideas that had worked so well. He had hired the manager from the first-year full time to run it and had planted larger apple orchards.

Victoria was so glad that Nick didn't work such long hours, giving over more responsibility to Heath, John, and his vice presidents. He and Kate had already celebrated their first wedding anniversary and still behaved like newlyweds, occasionally going away for the weekend but mainly just holing up in their flat, enjoying cooking together and dancing on their deck. Neither of them liked to go to trendy restaurants or nightclubs, sticking instead to the mom-and-pop places they had always gone to.

One of the Sunday supplement magazines had asked for an interview with them after Kate had her third article published in the AMA journal—quite an achievement for such a young doctor. Kate, with her usual matter of a fact personality and distinct English accent, charmed the reporter, and the way Nick had grown the family holdings since he had taken over after his father's death was truly remarkable. So in the article, the writer referred to them as the newest "power couple of the west." Nick being such a successful businessman, she being one of best trauma surgeons on the west coast, that plus belonging to one of the richest and most powerful families in Northern California. When they saw the article, they were amused by it but wouldn't grant any more interviews. They rarely went to parties and refused to become members of the "in" set. All they wanted was to be alone as much as possible. When Victoria was entertaining, they would join her if she asked them to but made it clear it was a family affair not theirs.

Since Beth's death, Jarrod hadn't dated much, but Kate had set him up with one of her colleagues that he was showing some interest in. Maybe this would stop him from being so immersed in his work.

Heath was seeing one of the girls employed as a dancer at the Cattleman's Club; not what Victoria would pick for him, but she kept her opinion to herself and hoped it wouldn't last.

Eugene, when he finished medical school, intended to work at Stockton General, following in his sister-in-law's footsteps.

Audra still spent her time on various committees and boards following her mother's lead, developing her own insights into people. Her judgement of men had vastly improved, no longer dating those whose only interest in her was the fact she was a Barkley. Her mother no longer felt she had to keep an eye on her daughter, Audra was ready to fly on her own!

Victoria was very thankful that Nick was so happily married to Kate, who had turned out to be the perfect daughter-in-law. She often thought of the night Nick told her he'd met the woman he was going to marry and how crazy it sounded and yet how right he'd had been. If it hadn't been for Kate, Nick would have lost his life, but because of the depth of their love, she had been able to pull him back, and for that, Victoria would forever be in her debt.

Oh, Tom, she thought, *if you could just see your family now and how they have turned out, how proud you would be of them.* She knew that between Nick, Kate, and Jarrod, the family would always be taken care of and life in the big valley would go on for the Barkleys.

About the Author

Christine Toal was born and raised in the northeast of England. When she emigrated to the USA, it was to southern California before settling in South Carolina. Her two sons, daughter-in-law, and new grandson also live in that state. Her interests include collecting anything to do with the Big Valley and the actor, Peter Breck, who portrayed Nick Barkley, chatting online with other fans of the series, and also amassing a collection of classic movies. *The Big Valley Returned* is her first novel, but she's already hard at work on the sequel.

CPSIA information can be obtained
at www.ICGtesting.com
Printed in the USA
BVHW031034170921
616891BV00015B/22